Gem and Spider

Book 1

Eythreal

Christopher W. Selna

Rev. date: 04/18/2023

To order additional copies of this book, contact:
Xlibris
844-714-8691
www.Xlibris.com
Orders@Xlibris.com
849658

In My Own Words

Dear Reader,

You are about to embark on an extraordinary journey that nearly did not come into existence. I sat on this project for many years, not because I did not believe in it. Oh, no. If anything, I believed in it too much (and still do). In fact, I endeavored to write a half dozen other novels through these years but could not keep the fiery passion I first had when starting them; thus, I aborted them. Why? Because my heart was always and will always be with this series of books. I cannot and will not pursue another project until Timothy Huntsinger finishes the book he so magically procured.

But if there is one thing standing in my way, it is my mental capacity to stay stable.

Many of you readers know me from my high school days. I was a shadow of my true self during those years. You might have seen me walking through the locker corridors, going to class, trying out for baseball, attempting to play football, talking to this boy and that girl, laughing, and so much more. But none of you saw the real me. *I* never saw the real me. I kept on trying to live another's life. I was never meant for what little I accomplished in high school.

And it showed.

I was a delinquent in high school.

I still remember how I chalked up the school record for detentions, tying a buddy of mine. Let's call him Gio. We were both to be expelled for the number of detentions we received. He was a heck of a football player. I couldn't say the same. But I did have a last name that carried some weight and two brothers that graduated ahead of me. One of those brothers I infamously fought at a girls' softball game. Yes. Brother versus brother rolling around the dirt while spectators of the softball game watched. Our varsity head coach was the one to break up the fight.

To this day, I recall being on top of my much bigger older brother.

That same year, before the fight, I had to approach my father at a football practice with news of being kicked off the team. Why? Because I failed biology. I was disciplined right then and there, before my team and nearly all my classmates. Half an hour later, I was disciplined at my brother's football practice.

I don't blame being disciplined in front of everyone. And how could I when I didn't care?

The real me didn't exist.

I graduated high school with a 2.1 GPA. Not only that, but my academic peers voted me second most likely to become famous in our yearbook while voting me first in being a jailbird.

Yes, a jailbird.

Again, I don't blame them.

I wish I could say I improved or found myself right after high school. And what came after high school?

Marines.

But even in the Marines, I floated my way through; I did enough to get by.

Never enough to be seen.

After being honorably discharged from the Marines, I had options. One of these options was to become a firefighter.

I turned that down, which became a massive disappointment to my family.

What I wanted to do and aimed to do made the disappointment worse.

I wanted to move to LA and become an actor and screenwriter.

My time in Los Angeles was relatively brief and yet very constructive, especially the last year. I often saw a glimpse of who I was supposed to be. But still, alcohol, other drugs, the lifestyle of living near the beach, and making good money at a restaurant kept me from becoming the person I am now. And yet, it was my last year or so in Los Angeles that I finally sat down and executed what I always wanted to do.

I wrote.

And I continued to write.

While writing every day, I learned the real me. I also learned I needed to change my lifestyle drastically to be this real me.

It started with me leaving my two-bedroom, hardwood-floor apartment I shared with my brother, only a mile from the beach, for Oregon.

To be a novelist.

Two things happened in Oregon. I learned to live without the former lifestyle, while at the same time, I learned that I had been living with a crutch from way back to sixth and seventh grade when meeting with friends at Northsight Park, so we could smoke weed by using a Coca-Cola can. In high school, smoking weed on a near-daily basis blended with alcohol on Friday and Saturday nights. From there, I only drank heavier (much heavier) in the Marines. After the Marines, I received my first taste of cocaine from a few restaurant friends in Scottsdale, Arizona, only to continue it when meeting friends in Venice, California, while never slowing down on the alcohol and weed.

All of that kept me standing on my two feet.

And without self-medication?

After a bad decision to leave Oregon and return to Arizona, I discovered the truth the hard way.

I fell. And I fell badly. After nearly two years in Arizona, I tried to escape the mental anguish that kept eating away at me, which caused up to six months of sleep deprivation, averaging two to four hours at most on a nightly basis, by moving back to the Pacific Northwest, this time to Newcastle, Washington. I had hoped this move to the beautiful Pacific Northwest would mitigate my mental suffering.

But moving to a scuzzy apartment complex, and alone, to boot, only worsened matters.

I experienced my first manic episode that lasted over ninety hours, never receiving a wink of sleep.

Not even close to a wink of sleep.

To make this long story shorter, my mother came to Washington after an emergency psychiatrist said I was a danger to myself and others. We packed up and drove back to Arizona, where I moved in with my parents. I quickly saw my first psychiatrist outside the emergency one in Washington. I was diagnosed with bipolar disorder 1. I didn't want to believe him. I saw a second psychiatrist.

Same results.

I'm forty-four years old at the moment of writing this. Until six months ago, I had been off all pharmaceutical meds after years of being on Klonopin and other drugs. But with the birth of my son, I quickly found myself in a tailspin. I knew I couldn't afford to let it continue to a crashing end. I reached out for help again. I'm back on medication and see myself on them for another year or more. But I do plan on getting off them someday— someday when I reteach myself how to live with my anxieties and manic depression. Maybe when my child becomes a bit less unpredictable.

I don't know. Maybe never.

But I'll say this:

I've seen the bottom. I've strolled along the surface of the lowest level. I once even made plans.

I bargained with myself.

And it was then that God saved me.

This novel you're about to journey into has seen it all. It has witnessed each surface of my life. It has seen Christopher on crutches and without crutches. It has seen the happy Chris. The depressed Chris. The *angry* Chris. It has gone through all travels and changes in my very much altering life.

Its persona is me.

I'm the book. I may not be a character. I may not be a single word of writing. But there is no question that the story and the stories that follow this embody my suffering and happiness.

So enjoy. Enjoy and know what travels this story has gone through.

And thank you, for I know how wordy I can be.

Christopher W. Selna
3/16/23

P.S. Please accept my apologies when it comes to my self-editing. All great authors have an editor—seriously. Even Jane Austen had an editor. Some great authors even have ghostwriters. And all subpar authors *need* an editor. Regardless of where I fall, I only say this: I did not come close to having the funds to hire an editor. So I relied exclusively on my erudition when it came to reading books. I had been kicked out of a community college because I had failed Remedial English. Yes. I failed Remedial English. Thus, I could not rely on what I had learned from school all my life.

Part 1

Chapter 1

FOREST BEYOND

"Stop, Butch!" Timothy shouted, watching his golden retriever chase after the brownish rabbit scurrying along the lush forest floor.

The dog ignored his master and hurried farther into the forest, forcing the fifteen-year-old boy to choose to follow.

For now, Timothy chose to follow.

Although Timothy proved faster and more agile than any of his age, his speed and agility paled in comparison to that of the nimble and fleet-footed dog and rabbit. Thus, the boy struggled mightily to keep up with the two. Every passing second proved to be lost ground. His sister, Katelyn, six years his junior, struggled mightier. She struggled to the point of surrendering. Timothy sensed this about her, sensed her fatalism. And in doing so, he sensed his own failure to keep up with the two animals, especially when it meant leaving behind his vulnerable and frightened sister. He also understood the grave consequences of going too far into the forest, where he could end up at the barrier separating what his father liked to call Old Wicker's Forest and the *other* forest.

"Butch!" Timothy shouted again. "Don't go any farther! You have to stop!"

The dog did not stop, and the boy came to a halt.

Not turning around, he sensed his sister no more than twenty feet away, much deeper in the forest than he ever wanted her to be. He closed his eyes in despair. Butch had undoubtedly gone past the barrier and entered the forest never to be visited by a boy or girl of any age, and this forbidden forest those boys and girls liked to call the Forest Beyond. From time immemorial, the adults did everything in their power to keep the children from calling the forest by such a name, therefore referring to it as the *other* forest or just the *forbidden forest*, but never Forest Beyond, for it strengthened their will and curiosity in wanting to venture farther. Of course, the adults invariably failed at such a scheme to manipulate the boys and girls, seeing how they only made it worse by laying down harsh rules concerning the forest.

What made matters worse was that the adults had long since judged other adults if entering the forest.

Timothy opened his eyes to capture the last sight of Butch chasing the rabbit before the impending forest swallowed them up.

"Butch!" he again shouted. "Come back! Come back, I said!"

Butch could no longer be heard.

Katelyn approached from behind.

"Is he not coming back?" she asked, wiping tears away.

"He's coming back," Timothy answered with feigned, boastful confidence. He never wanted to betray such fear or negativity before his sister.

Unlike most times, Katelyn did not buy into her brother's answer.

More tears fell from her eyes.

Hearing her sob, Timothy turned around and stared tenderly at her.

"Don't cry," he said. "He'll be back." He said the latter words with the same pretended confidence. This time, it did not come out so confidently.

Katelyn wanted to fall to the ground because of her distraught emotions.

Timothy held her up, and they embraced. His eyes looked toward the sun. Timothy surmised one hour at most before sundown, from reading the sun's position.

An hour! he thought to himself. *Just an hour to get home before being too late? Butch won't make it.*

But what can I do?

Be strong—that's what you can do.

Timothy nodded in response to his inner debate and turned to his sister with bravado. Katelyn did not like this change in him.

The boldness spoke of danger.

"I'm going in," Timothy said, confirming Katelyn's worst fear.

"Go-go-going in . . . in . . . in there?"

"There's no better choice, Katelyn. I've got to get in there and bring him back."

"What about me?

"You? Home."

"Home?" she said incredulously.

"Yes. Home. Go home. But don't run into the house until one minute before it's too late. Run inside then and tell Ma and Pa I'm running a few minutes late."

"And Pa's warning?"

2

"I know the warnings. But what am I supposed to do? Leave Butch behind? No. I have to go after him."

"But Pa said never—"

"I know! Gosh, darn it, sis! I know his exact words and warning."

The boy's severe mannerisms did more harm than good to Katelyn, as she became overwrought with emotions.

Attempting to soothe her, he took her hand and said, "Pa warns us because he fears we'll get lost and never find our way home and something may happen to us like the Crowder kids. But what Pa doesn't know is that I've been to the fallen elm tree. I even ventured farther. And still, I found my way home. It's getting dark, sis, real fast too. I've got to go before the darkness falls upon us!"

"Pa's going to be mad—mad-mad!"

Understanding the truth, Timothy nodded.

"Also why you're not going to say a word to him. Your only words will be *Timothy is running a few minutes late.* Got it? Come on, sis. Don't look at me like that. We both know I must go into that forest and get him back. You do want Butch back, right? Isn't that what we *all* want? Meaning Ma and Pa too? He'll never come home without my help—that I promise you. I don't think Butch has ever gone this far before."

Katelyn became puzzled about what to think or do. She'd heard many terrible tales of what possibly went on in what they called the Forest Beyond—many tales. And to imagine her brother falling into one of those tales?

Devastating.

But they were tales. Even at the height of her current imagination, she saw most of them as fiction or fabrication.

What proved to be true to her was Butch being lost in the forest.

"Fine," she said, wiping away her tears. "But whatever you do, be careful, and come home. OK? Because I don't want to lose you too."

"You're not going to lose me, sis. Word of honor. You just get on home. Tarry around a bit. Then go on in and tell them—"

"You're running a few minutes late."

"That's right. Tell them Butch went chasing after a rabbit. But don't be telling them what direction. No Forest Beyond."

"But you're not *really* going into that forest, are you?"

Timothy looked away from his sister and stared into the forest.

"I may have to. Butch has gone far."

3

Katelyn felt a cold shudder run up her whole body.

"I'll be careful," Timothy said, returning his attention to his sister and placing a consoling hand on her shoulder. "Now go."

Katelyn didn't budge.

"Go now. We're losing light."

Inhaling a deep breath and exhaling slowly, Katelyn reluctantly turned around and started for home.

Timothy watched her leave with a frown fraught with disappointment. *She's scared*, he said to himself. *Way too scared. Her fears will betray me, and she'll be singing like a canary.*

Just too damn scared.

"The hell with it!" Timothy said defiantly. "What are a few whips on the butt compared to bringing Butch back home?"

The portion of the forest permissible for Katelyn and Timothy to run around and play in was as thick and feral as most other forests. As mentioned before, Pa named it Old Wicker's Forest, which had been passed down by his family since he was a child because the forest mostly belonged to his ancestry. But the forest ominously dubbed Forest Beyond showed much greater strength in density and wildness. The thickness of the forest suffocated all who entered. At the same time, its untamed wildness put a blanket over the canopy of trees, causing the sun to be hindered while also turning the forest into an inescapable gloomy labyrinth. This mysterious and frightful forest had been off-limits before the tragic saga regarding the Crowder kids. Again, from time immemorial, adults censured others for entering the forest grounds and did whatever they could to keep the kids from calling it the Forest Beyond, which only amplified their curiosity.

What happened to the Crowder kids, though, happened not long ago. Katelyn blamed the disappearance on evil dryads haunting the forest, or possibly, wicked forest fairies and sprites. Even evil elves came to mind. As for Timothy, a few years younger than his present age, he believed in the same, with a head full of imagination. Ask him now, and he'd profess how impossible that would be. Ask him now, and he'd tell you how foolish one must be to believe in such *things*. Ask him now what he thought about myths, fables, fairy tales, and so forth, and he'd tell you that it was all drawn up by one's mind, without a single shred of proof, mostly from unexplainable objects and events needing to be explained somehow.

But that would be a lie. Timothy had never given up his imagination as he pretended to do. He never once left behind any of his fantastical imaginations when supposedly stepping up and becoming a man, the same man his pa was renowned for being: Harold Huntsinger, the boldest, most vigorous, and most adamant and determined individual in town. To have a head and spirit full of imagination and be Harold's only son would be a travesty for all to see since many in town relied on the archaic Huntsinger family name, an emblem of strength and determination for all to be proud of. For that reason alone, Timothy had to be made of steel regarding the reality and sufferings of the cruel, harsh, and unforgivable world he lived in.

Thus, Timothy kept up the lie. He kept his imagination solely to himself and even learned to treat the imagination just as it was.

Imagination.

Timothy did not lie about his confession to his sister regarding his travel into the Forest Beyond, except he didn't mention how short a journey it ended up being. He had reached the fallen elm tree, the visible barrier his pa marked for any wanted or unwanted traveler to discern, thus giving the traveler or travelers a bit of breathing room before venturing where they should never venture to. When reaching that barrier not long ago, Timothy stepped beyond it and continued upon a vague path. Ten minutes on this path, he stopped at what looked to be another barrier, this time being two oak trees, each fallen long ago and now crossed over each other. He needed little insight to discern that this barrier spoke of the end and to go farther meant surrendering to the Forest Beyond. He remembered smelling the air. It seemed unpolluted, as if not one single creature stepped foot inside this forest.

The words of an illicit poem learned at school came to him.

Abandon all hope, all ye who enter here.

Well, Timothy did not want to abandon all hope. He wanted to turn around and run home. And that he did, but not before his eyes fell on two unique stones and an arrowhead resting on the forest floor.

The stones were identical. They each sparkled with a translucent radiance that gave the viewer a peek through them.

Timothy had never seen anything like this.

His eyes turned to the arrowhead, which fit the entire open palm of his hand. The arrowhead might have lacked the translucent glow, but the silver hue shone brightly. The more Timothy studied the arrowhead, the more he believed it to be just as mysterious and *impossible* as the two translucent stones.

He had to have them. He had to *possess* them. Not only that, but they also called to him. This calling came from somewhere far, far away. Somewhere—

Not from Earth.

Thus, before leaving the spot designated as the Forest Beyond, Timothy took the arrowhead and two stones with him. And when grabbing the stones, he noticed they each had a small hole. An idea popped into his mind. He could make a necklace out of them. He could go home and make a necklace out of each stone and give one to his sister at some meaningful time. As for the arrowhead, he decided then and there to give it to his best friend sooner than later since the latter person had a keen liking for bows and arrows, primarily due to his father choosing that weapon when hunting with his son.

All that was in the past, and now he stood in the present moment, staring intensely into the forest.

"I will find my way back," he said confidently, stepping farther into the forest.

~

It did not take long for Timothy to reach the fallen elm tree—once again, the barrier marked for one to go no farther. Another ten minutes and he'd find himself at the site of the two crossed oak trees. That thought alone stoked fear inside of him. He shook off the fear. He continued ahead as the path became difficult to track. The diminished sun made the following worse. The trees and their branches, along with various thick foliage, proved denser than before. The evening sun barely penetrated through the canopy of trees. Timothy relied on the weak, ethereal beams of sunlight ending on the forest floor.

As he stepped farther into the forest, a waft of breeze passed through this developing portion of the Forest Beyond. The branches and their leaves swayed, causing an eerie, whistling sound, which sent chills up his body, for everything seemed so calm and silent only a second ago. Thus, the breeze and the eerie whistling sound spoke to him as if the forest had come alive just as he stepped beyond the barrier. He now felt the woods to be animated, with eyes to see, ears to hear, and even more frightening: mouths to speak. The fear inside doubled. He dared himself by shouting Butch's name again, hoping that Butch would return before going farther, even if it meant betraying his presence in the conscious-minded forest.

On calling out the dog's name, Timothy received no answer, nor did the forest respond with anything but the breeze and sharp whistling sound.

Despair now took hold of Timothy's heart and squeezed. The boy turned in a circle, crying out Butch's name in every direction.

No response.

Despair squeezed tighter. Timothy's mind went wild. He impetuously hurried farther into the forest—farther into uncertain danger.

"Butch! Butch!" he kept shouting. "Butch!"

Finally, in his reckless abandoning of sanity, Timothy reached the two crossed oak trees.

And still, the boy betrayed himself by shouting.

"Butch! Butch!"

Those last shouts became more of a whisper, for Timothy lacked the strength to shout with conviction. This was because the fear and despair were too much for him. Plus, he felt more aware of the forest watching him than before, as if feeling for the first time the dire consequences of this forest he indubitably believed to be governed by spirits of evil and mischievous natures.

The boy wanted to give up. He wanted to fall to his knees and beg for Butch to come back.

Beg mercy from the forest.

But he didn't fall to his knees. He did continue to cry out for his dog.

"Butch! Please. Come back. Butch!"

And then …

Barking sounds!

Timothy jumped with joy when hearing Butch. This elation took a step back when seeing how much ground he had to cover. But the fleeting joy had already improved his spirits and invigorated him. At the same time, the dog's bark alleviated much of the fear and despair that strangled his heart—not all of it, of course, but enough to think less rashly and impetuously. What troubled him the most proved to be the unseen location of the dog's barking. Timothy stared at the crossed oak trees, fully aware that he must pass them. He looked farther—deeper into the Forest Beyond, trying desperately to receive any understanding of the forest.

What he could barely make out seemed to be a vague, inadequate, and excessively meandering pathway through the wickedly dense forest.

Not taking a step farther, Timothy called out the dog's name for confirmation.

"Butch!"

Bark

The joy returned as Timothy rushed headlong into the more significant part of the Forest Beyond.

"I'm coming!"

Timothy's rashness subsided as common sense prevailed. He slowed down to a manageable speed, finding it paramount to study the surroundings. He understood the path he took now must be the same when returning home. As he slowed down, he heard music—maybe not music, but bells chiming. His pace slowed down. He wondered where the chiming came from. Was it the wind playing tricks on him? *No,* he said to himself. *The breeze has lessened. Then what could it be?* After further thought, Timothy believed *someone* had caused the sound. Coming to that conclusion, he abruptly stopped. The reality of the situation came down upon him like a hammer.

He was not alone.

"No!" he said convincingly. "I have to be alone. Nobody else can be out here, nobody but Butch and I!"

Finding the courage to ignore vivid imaginations running amok in his mind, Timothy stepped farther into the forest, and as he did, the chiming grew louder. Not only that, but he also noticed a clearing in the woods ahead of him. In fact, not too far ahead, Timothy thought he caught sight of a capacious dell. Seeing this potential opening in the forest, his earlier fright returned. He also became confused. He had never heard anyone describing a dell. Not one murmur regarding a dell, even after the diligent search for the Crowder kids. What little he did know about the forest from too many mouths to count—each of them a secondhand witness—was that the forest seemed never to end when it came to its unruly thick denseness.

What added more mystery was that the sound of the chiming came not from bells. The chiming had now become more musical.

As if the sound came from a musical instrument.

Possibly a flute.

And if that weren't enough, whoever played this flute did so masterfully.

Timothy finally came to the foregone conclusion that he was not alone.

As if his nerves failed him, Timothy took a step back.

He captured positive thoughts in his mind.

"So what?"

I'm Timothy Huntsinger, son of Harold Huntsinger—the bravest and toughest man in town. Stop acting like a child.

Timothy adamantly nodded and stepped in the direction of the foreseeable dell.

Only a few steps in that direction and Butch made an appearance.

Timothy and Butch came together, and each fell joyfully to the floor. A wave of sheer relief passed through Timothy's entire body.

"OK, OK, OK," Timothy said, victim to Butch's slobbering. "I miss you too. Just don't be going and doing that again."

Butch responded to Timothy by barking toward the distant dell three times. Timothy stood up from the ground and stared in that direction. Fear slowly leaked back into his mind. But with Butch's companionship, Timothy found it less challenging to keep the fear from distorting his mind as he stood his ground and stared at the dell some fifty yards away. While staring closely at the dell, he noticed a vague silhouette of someone standing in the center of the dell. This puzzled Timothy's mind, for it moved and not only moved but danced. Timothy shook his head disconcertedly.

Not only is it impossible that someone is out there, but that someone is dancing!

That thought allowed curiosity to grow substantially in his mind. He could ignore neither the mysterious dell nor the appearance of someone dancing. He had to discover the mystery since, having come this far, Timothy found it impossible to turn around and ignore such a thing. Assenting to those arguments, Timothy looked above and studied the sun through the canopy of trees.

"I've got time," he said. *Not much. But it may be enough.*

He took his first steps toward the dell and the dancing silhouette of *someone.*

~

Timothy guessed correctly: the music came from a flute. His second guess came not so much correctly—and not so much incorrectly. The flute belonged to someone, but this someone was not what he thought. The playing of the flute came from what looked to be a boy or girl with a hunchback. And this boy or girl played the flute masterfully while dancing on top of the broadest tree stump Timothy had ever seen.

Timothy stepped closer.

Leaving behind the density of the forest and receiving his first clear view of the dell and the someone, Timothy stopped in his tracks. He couldn't possibly move. The boy or girl became something other than he imagined. Timothy stared at a gaunt, crooked figure (explaining the hunchback shape), and this figure no longer resembled a boy or girl, nor man or woman. Even upon Timothy's movement, this creature, thus no longer *someone*, continued to play the music in a lively fashion upon, again, the broadest tree stump Timothy had seen, so very smoothly and evenly cut from its main trunk.

The music produced by the flute stirred excitement in Timothy's mind. For a second, Timothy wanted to surrender to the music and dance till the following morning, or even longer. Sensing this spellbinding effect, Timothy looked down and noticed his feet stepping to the rhythm of the music. Astounded and slightly frightened, Timothy held his feet in check and studied the dell more. He discovered the dell to be oval-shaped, teeming with wide tree stumps close to the size of the one the creature danced upon, which resided in the center.

Allowing curiosity to surpass the fright, Timothy broke out of his trance and stepped toward the ill-shaped creature.

The closer he got, the more uncanny and preternatural the creature seemed. What Timothy thought to be clothes were substances of the forest. He spotted bark from the trees, leaves from the branches, and lush forest floor around the creature's body, acting not as clothes but as skin. Underneath this skin, Timothy could see *bones*—no real skin, no actual tissue between the forest and the skeletal frame of the creature.

No.

The creature's skin, flesh, and tissue were precisely what they looked to be: the Forest Beyond.

The creature's skeletal frame looked healthy to Timothy. No fossilization or decomposition showed on the bones. The bones were brilliantly white and bright gray. They looked to have never come close to the harm that comes when decomposition sets in. Therefore, Timothy deduced that he stared at a living, jubilant, nimble, flute-playing skeleton, with the Forest Beyond acting as its flesh and tissue.

A skullcap covered most of the skull, this cap the verdant lawn of the forest. Timothy noticed a cane set against the tree trunk. The cane proved to be a single bone, unlike any human one. Nor did it look like it belonged to the creature. At the crown of the cane was what looked to be a lion's skull, which Timothy marveled at. The lion's face was a look of raw strength and relentless determination.

The boy absorbed everything before him. He shuddered. He wanted to turn around and run like the wind.

He might have done that if it weren't for the creature speaking.

"And where oh where do you think you're stepping to, young Master Timothy Huntsinger?" the voice said in a crackling, hoary voice.

Hearing his full name spoken sans middle name, Timothy froze. Less scared and more astonished, he turned to face the creature.

"How do you know my name?"

"That is quite easy for the likes of me."

"But you're a skeleton."

"Not a skeleton, Timothy, not a skeleton."

"You're made of bones."

"Bones? These are no ordinary bones, Timothy. These bones are the infrastructure of what you and countless others live upon. And this skin you think I wear?" The creature shook its head. "It is not skin I wear," it said, tugging at a piece of bark. "It is the flesh of the forest and Earth combined. I am no skeleton. And you may simply call me Wood Dweller."

Timothy stared in disbelief. "This isn't happening. No. I'm dreaming. I'm unconscious and dreaming. I fell. I tripped and fell and hit my head on a rock."

"You never fell, Timothy—you never fell. And this is certainly no dream."

"But you're . . ."

"What?"

"Impossible. I'm imagining you."

"Imagining?" the Wood Dweller said, offended. "Me? Imagination? Who says?"

"Who says? Reality says," Timothy said. "You're a . . . fable. Like the stories Ma told me when young, you know . . . to put me to sleep."

"And the author of those fables? Where did they get their ideas?"

"From one's imagination."

"Uh-huh. And again, where did that imagination come from?"

"I, uh, well . . . They just . . . They made them up."

"Just like that? Poof! Out of nowhere—out of the nebulous cloud of ideas. Huh. Is that even possible? Truth is found in *every* perception of the mind, Timothy."

"I still don't believe."

"Still don't believe? Go ahead, then. Pinch yourself as they say to do."

Timothy stepped back. He again viewed his surroundings. Nothing showed to be a dream. He turned to Butch. The dog panted at his side. He turned to the Wood Dweller and its impossible existence.

No. This must *be a dream.*

Timothy pinched his arm.

Nothing changed, excluding a surge of pain.

"You're still here," the Wood Dweller said.

"So?" Timothy said, desperately trying to believe this to be a dream. "I could be dreaming that I pinched myself."

The Wood Dweller laughed.

"Stop laughing," Timothy said. "You're not real. This is all made up."

"So be it. Think what you want."

"I will. And I say you're make-believe. And I'm dreaming."

"Fine. Fine, oh fine. You're dreaming, Timothy Huntsinger. If that is the case, then I'm sure you're not interested in what lies under this tree stump," the Wood Dweller said, grabbing the cane and knocking it against the tree stump only *once.*

"Under the tree stump?"

"Under the tree stump."

"But that's impossible—unless you tell me that it's not impossible and that the tree stump is magical. If you say that, you'll be pushing it, as my pa would say."

"Don't you go pushing it, Timothy. You heard what I said the first time!" the unmistakable voice of Timothy's pa came from the Wood Dweller's mouth.

Timothy stood back, amazed.

"How did you do that?"

"Wanna find out?"

"How?"

"By following me," the Wood Dweller said, sprightly leaping off the tree trunk.

Landing on the ground, the Wood Dweller knocked his cane against the tree stump twice. On the second knock, the third in just a short time, the tree stump rattled. As it rattled, the top surface slid open and did not stop till a crescent-shaped hole appeared. More curious than frightened, Timothy stood taller and tried to see the hole better.

"Go on. Step closer. Look down the hole if you'd like," the Wood Dweller said.

"What's down there?"

"Oh. Don't you want to know? Or is it all too *made up* for you?"

Timothy knitted his eyebrows. He wanted badly to step forward, but in doing so, he'd give power to the creature.

Instead, Timothy insisted on not believing.

"Why? It's just a stupid dream."

"OK. Fine. But what's the problem with coming over here if it is a dream?"

Point to the Wood Dweller, thought Timothy.

Both he and Butch proceeded closer.

Reaching the tree stump, they each looked down the hole.

Everything about this being a dream dissipated; only wonders were emitted in his mind.

"Are those stars?"

Amazed by the sight of stars, Timothy tried to catch them and failed. The tiny particles of glistening dust resembling stars had their own mind.

"Beautiful, right?"

"Yes," Timothy said.

"Down there, Timothy, worlds are born, and never do they die."

Timothy continued to look down, seeing no bottom, only an infinite black space with scintillating prismatic-colored sparkling stars.

"Down there, Timothy, *it* awaits."

"What awaits?"

"What you must do."

"What must I do?"

"I don't know. But you do. Deep inside you, you do. They all do. And the only way to find out is by going down there."

The thought of going down the hole if this wasn't a dream proved too much for Timothy. He stepped back, and the wonder of the dilemma vanished.

"This is crazy. This is all so loony."

"Are those your words, or are they the words of all the adults that have insisted on you forgetting what you thought to be real and now only imagined?"

"No," Timothy fought hard to say. "It's me speaking."

"Is it?"

Timothy weakened. *OK. Maybe it's not me speaking. Maybe there was a time. But I'm older now. Soon to be a man, Pa says.*

So how could I believe in all this?

Timothy found no answer to that question. He did notice the descending sun and darkness creeping up.

"The time!" Timothy shouted alarmingly. "Look at the time. Pa is going to be terribly mad. Maybe another day, Mr. Wood Dweller."

With that said, Timothy turned around.

He took two steps in the direction of home when the Wood Dweller shouted, "There is no other day. And time, Timothy . . . Time as you know does not exist down there."

Timothy stopped.

He turned slowly around.

"Time doesn't exist? But how?"

"Don't imagine how. Believe."

"So if I go down there—"

"You'll come up without a second gone by."

"I don't believe it."

"Believe."

Timothy vaguely nodded his head.

Believe?

Years of being forced not to believe became bitter and loathsome to Timothy's mind as he answered vehemently, "Fine. OK. We go down."

Butch barked in consent as the Wood Dweller smiled.

Timothy returned to the tree stump and placed both hands upon it.

"How far is the drop?"

"Not far."

"But it looks—"

"Easy drop."

Timothy shook his head in frustration and watched the Wood Dweller proceed down the hole. Butch followed. Timothy responded by taking two hesitant steps down the hole, allowing the last of the sunlight to guide his way. A fourth step later, all light dissipated.

Everything went dark.

Timothy looked up. The stump had closed over the opening.

And that was when Timothy fell.

Chapter 2

PILLARS OF WORLDS

The Wood Dweller did not lie about the drop. Timothy slid down the hole and landed on level ground after a little over five feet. Once he was on the ground, light broke through the darkness. The light emanated from the lion's skull upon the cane belonging to the Wood Dweller. What the light revealed proved to be a hallway made of earth. Along the hallway were unlit torches. The torches were not alone. Scattered endlessly on the walls were clusters of exquisite rocks and stones, each glistening as the cane's light reflected off them. These stones protruded a few inches from the surface of the wall made of earth. Timothy tried to see more of the hallway but could not because the only torches being lit were the ones in their proximity, and the cluster of rocks and stones that prevailed farther upon the hallway walls waited for the light to bring life to them. The Wood Dweller watched Timothy stand up and dust himself off. The Wood Dweller then thumped the cane against the ground, and instantly after, the torches in the distance burned with fire.

But the exquisite rocks and stones stayed dark, for they waited not for the torches' light but, instead, for the light emitted from the lion's cane.

Timothy now looked ahead and saw no end to the hallway. He followed the Wood Dweller, and they came to an end after a few minutes.

At first, Timothy did not believe this to be a door. It seemed as if the hallway made of earth had ended abruptly. But at second glance, Timothy could see something far beyond just a wall of earth, something beyond his imagination, something resembling a magical barrier—one that could only be opened or passed through with the right magic incantation. He studied the door. He noticed a style of writing written upon it that could not be deciphered. The writing seemed fresh, as if one had etched it onto the door seconds ago. Curious, he extended his hand toward the writing but quickly drew his hand back because the rest of the door's embellishment became clear for him to see.

Clouds.

Clouds of many shapes and forms hovered upon the door as if alive. Moving his eye from one cloud to the next, he swore he saw the clouds move.

He then noticed stars. Countless stars decorated the door. Very much like the clouds, the stars seemed alive.

Surrounding the stars were seven moons, each one as brilliant as the other. Below the celestial firmament flowed a calm and soothing blue ocean, while rough and agitated water flowed alongside. Ancient sea vessels struggled to keep afloat along the disturbed water while sea creatures of fierce strength and horrid looks lurked below; as for the calm water, a single ship calmly stayed afloat, manned by a party of warriors, along with innocent sea creatures lurking below. Each of the vessels and sea creatures, except for a few familiar ones—turtles and dolphins—reminded Timothy of fabled stories he heard from his ma. And like the stars and clouds, the vessels, the men and women that crewed the ships, along with the sea creatures swimming about, seemed very much alive, as if the water flowed before Timothy's eyes.

"Fancy door?" the Wood Dweller said.

"Yes."

"But there's more."

"On the door?"

"Yes. A darkness lies behind the drawing."

"There is?"

"Do you not feel it?"

"I . . ."

"Clear your mind. Absorb your mind with what's before you."

Timothy nodded. He stood calmly and cleared his thoughts.

"Now close your eyes."

Timothy closed his eyes, and everything he saw on the door came alive. No longer did he see the writing on the door. Instead, he watched the writing be etched upon the stone by a hand holding a quill and this hand covered by a cloak. The writing turned alive. The clouds were no longer imprinted on the door. The clouds hovered above him in the sky that seconds ago had been the ceiling of the underground hallway. Timothy lived in the picture. He lived with the stars and the seven moons. He also found himself on calm waters. The water grew turbulent. He then heard the warriors shouting at each other to hurry up, dodging dangerous sea creatures at each turn and sharp, catastrophic sea stacks that would rent the most powerful of sea vessels.

Darkness appeared.

What remained of calm water exploded because of this darkness. The already tumultuous waters became immeasurable tidal waves, destroying everything in their path. Seeing this tidal wave coming their way, the warriors cried out their imminent death throes. And as the wave closed in on them, the malevolent creatures—nowise daunted by the darkness—added insult to injury by breaking the surface of the water and attacking the vessels. No aid came from the benevolent sea creatures. They vanished when the darkness appeared as if they had never existed before. The firmament above also altered for the worse. Stars disintegrated into dust. Worst of all, the seven moons became lifeless. Impotent. Not a single shine to their once all-powerful luster.

Timothy's mind turned dark. And when dark and without light to cling onto, Timothy heard a voice—the voice of no man or woman.

A monster!

"Enter and destruction will be the path you tread upon. Everywhere and everything will succumb to this destruction. Turn around. Turn around, boy, and let no destruction follow your every step."

Timothy opened his eyes on hearing that. For the smallest of seconds, he *saw* the voice.

The vision of the voice vanished, and Timothy stepped back in fright.

The Wood Dweller stood calmly, reflecting on what transpired.

"Your eyes are now yours again, and they are opened," the Wood Dweller said. "You have seen what haunts eternity."

"What was that *thing*?"

The Wood Dweller's eyes dilated.

"Was it gargantuan?"

"Yes!"

"Mean and dangerous-looking?"

"Very."

"With an unruly dark and straggly mane for hair?"

"Like a lion. Except . . . not tawny. And the hair was . . . snakes—I believe."

"Then it was no lion?"

"No," Timothy said.

"Hmm . . ." The Wood Dweller pondered.

After a second, the Wood Dweller continued, "No, Timothy. I'm not exactly sure what you saw. But then again . . ."

"Then again, what?"

"There is nothing I can tell you about what you saw that you don't already know."

Timothy's face contorted in confusion.

The Wood Dweller stepped aside from the barrier, raised the cane, and used the lion's skull to bang against the barrier three times.

The barrier trembled.

"We're going through there?"

"Of course we are."

Timothy stood motionlessly as the door trembled. He could hear air seep through the cracks. The air had a freshness that the boy could not describe, for it seemed far too clean and free of any particles to be real. He felt the air to be of his Earth and others' Earthlike world. He allowed this air to permeate through his body, and his skin tingled from both under and outside. No longer did he feel the fear of the monster that represented the darkness from before. The mystic, pristine air gently lifted him and placed him upon a soft, fluffy cloud, drifting gently along a clear blue sky.

The trembling barrier door opened, and the Wood Dweller gave room for Timothy to examine. Timothy spied another hallway.

"Where does it lead to?"

"Only by passing through this barrier will you find out."

Timothy hesitated.

"You can't give me a hint?"

"You already know where. How's that for a hint?"

Timothy shook his head.

"Nothing to fear, Timothy. Not *yet*."

"What does that mean?"

"Follow me and find out."

The Wood Dweller stepped past Timothy and through the barrier. Timothy watched.

"Come. Or forever regret and *forget* what you're meant to do."

Unsure what the Wood Dweller meant, Timothy took a step forward and passed through the barrier.

The Wood Dweller smiled.

"Yes. This way."

The Wood Dweller led Timothy through the hallway as the barrier behind them closed. Not long into this hallway, they ended up inside a circular chamber. In the center of this chamber resided—

"Stairs?" Timothy exclaimed incredulously, staring at a spiral staircase.

"But that's impossible. Those stairs lead up, and by the look of it, very high up, when I only fell a few feet—and I know for sure that we haven't been stepping downward."

"We haven't descended," the Wood Dweller said. "But we're also not exactly in the same place as before. Did you not feel the change in the air?"

"I did sense something different. Where are we, then?"

"*Nowhere,*" the Wood Dweller said and stepped toward the spiral staircase, "while also being everywhere."

Shaking his head in confusion, Timothy looked down at Butch. The dog barked.

"OK, boy. Here we go."

Timothy followed the Wood Dweller.

"I was right," the boy said, seeing how high the stairs went.

"And it goes even higher for some."

The stairs proved lengthier than Timothy imagined. But not once did he feel exhausted—not a bit. And never did he contemplate that strange fact.

He was still too in awe of the situation and the surroundings.

"Now watch your step," the Wood Dweller said as it vanished from above. Timothy grew apprehensive. But the fear vanished as he found himself at the end of the stairs.

One step over, he alighted upon another ground level of the underground.

Receiving his first look, Timothy spoke in a long, drawn-out word.

"W-o-w . . ."

The wow came from him staring into another chamber. Unlike the room before, this one proved far more spacious and not only that, but filled with many bookcases, as if being inside an underground library; this underground library seemingly had no end in sight. The bookcases were packed tightly with books, each different from the rest. Artistically decorated candles hung securely upon each bookcase, emitting much light for one to utilize. Not far in his view, a candle far more extravagant than the rest could be seen. Beside the candle lived the only table found in the chamber.

As far as he could tell.

Timothy stood riveted. He loved books. *Cherished* books. Books were his life and more. He now believed he had to be dreaming.

Timothy gazed upon the other side of the library.

His heart fluttered when he turned to his left and realized that the three of them stood upon a precipice. Timothy looked beyond the ridge and found only space—a dark, endless realm of freedom. He couldn't believe it. He had to be seeing things. He walked toward the cliff, and as he did, he continued to see only dark space. But once he stepped to the near edge, the dark area opened up to him.

"What is this place?" he said, staring into what had been an empty space a second ago, now filled with countless shining stars. Some of these stars were on the move and smashed into one another, forming even more stars. These stars were far more formidable than the ones before the bang. Alongside the stars resided magnificently towering stairs, each hovering on space alone. The most prominent sight was the countless pillars, each standing—or floating—alone. Each of the pillars ended with a door at the very top. And not one pillar was annexed to a set of the hovering stairs, although a link did exist between the two, except existing beyond the scope of any mortal or immortal creature.

"Impossible," Timothy muttered.

He turned to the Wood Dweller.

"There's no end. How can this be?"

"It is only a question to you because you still think you're on your Earth. Stop thinking that. Start to realize that you left behind *much* when crossing the barrier."

"OK. Then where is here?"

"I like to call it the Pillars of Worlds," the Wood Dweller said, waving his cane slowly in the air, showcasing the entire surrounding. "This dwelling is where worlds collide, coincide, and propagate. There is no beginning and end to any world here, for there is no beginning or ending to any world that exists. There is only Oblivion to some. Outside Oblivion, one might think a world is eradicated, destroyed by a boom and bang, or any other catastrophic phenomenon. But one does not realize another world will feed off that world, and in a sense, this new world will become two, for it keeps the eternal spirit of the former world alive, festering inside that newer world. And forever and ever will this continue."

"No stop?"

"No stop. Out there," the Wood Dweller said, pointing the lion skull at the Pillars of Worlds. "Out there, nothing has an end. While nothing has a beginning. Everything there exists on an infinite plane of Creation. It is Creation you see out there. Creation exists in all aspects of the infinite and endless space and time you see and feel now. It is Creation that makes up every particle of your body and mind. Creation is the true beginning and end of all things."

Seeing the boy staring into the space, the Wood Dweller turned around and faced the library side of the chamber.

"Take this chamber of books," the Wood Dweller said.

Timothy turned around.

"Each one of these books is of its own world. Not one book tells the story of the same world found elsewhere in this chamber. But in a very significant way, they *share* a world—each book found here shares the same spirit even if they are of different worlds. That's why they share the same domain. This single chamber is the root of your world and the rest of the worlds that coincide with this same space. This single pillar you stand upon is the seed of those worlds that fill every book you see."

"We're standing on a pillar, like the ones out there?"

The Wood Dweller nodded.

"And these worlds you speak of are the endless books I see?"

"In *your* perception? Yes. Others? Not so. It is your perception that only counts. Someone else may see something other than books. And most importantly, do not imagine the Pillars of Worlds look the same to anyone else, especially one that does not belong to this pillar you stand on. Oh no. Those pillars out there belong to worlds vastly different and separate from those surrounding you. What best describes your world and the worlds found in those books are these pillars. I must say many see them as a book as you do. But the books may not look exactly how you see them now. They will fit that person's time and place and their world."

"And the stairs and doors on the pillars?"

"Do not ever worry about their use. The only entrance into the pillar you need to worry about is the one we used—through your world."

"This is all so..." Timothy stared confusedly at the books and then at the Pillars of Worlds. "Confusing."

"Timothy," the Wood Dweller said, turning the boy's attention to the library. "You're smart. I know you are. Another reason why you were chosen! Look. All those books you see mark specific moments in different worlds. Each one! Not one book represents the same world. Thus, each book you open will tell a story about a different world. But since they are together in this chamber, and this chamber is confined to this singular pillar, they are each joined together, connected in a subtle but unmistakable way. Some creatures have even found a way to get lost in multiple worlds. It is where fantasy comes from. How do you think one world created an elf when many other worlds see them as only myth and fiction? Because they're neither. It is because the spirit of the entity leaked from one world to the other and, consequently, was drawn up by another's perception.

"Now take this space full of other pillars," the Wood Dweller said, turning to the Pillars of Worlds. "Out there is where worlds are vastly different. The world you came from, one you call Earth and so forth, and the other worlds in these books that share this same pillar and domain are in no way bound to the other Pillars of Worlds. I cannot, and I mean *cannot*, overemphasize how different their perception may be. They will not see what you see as the Pillars of Worlds. Forget seeing a book. They wouldn't even fathom what a book may be. They may not even have the comprehension of what a pillar may be."

"So you're saying each of these books in this chamber is of a different world and yet compatible with another?"

"*Exactly.*"

"But out there . . ." Timothy said, with eyes staring into the Pillars of Worlds.

"Out there, one cannot imagine what one sees."

Timothy stood contemplating.

"I'm not dreaming, am I?"

The Wood Dweller carefully shook his head.

"And I certainly did not hit my head on a rock?"

"No."

"Why? Why me? Why bring *me* down here?"

"Does it matter? Does the why matter? You are here. That is what is important . . . for now."

"Not even a hint on why me?"

"Why? To comfort your mind?"

"I guess."

"This isn't about being comfortable."

"Then what is this all about?"

"An adventure, Timothy."

"An adventure?"

"Yes. A real-life adventure."

"Let me guess. Not of my world?"

"Not of your world."

"Sounds dangerous."

"It is. Very dangerous. You may even die."

Timothy stepped back.

"Now, why would I want to do that?"

The Wood Dweller abandoned all frivolity and stepped toward Timothy somberly.

"Because only you can save them."

"Save? Save who?"

The Wood Dweller smiled.

"Choose," the unworldly creature said. "Choose the book that speaks to you the most. Choose wisely, for every book will speak to you. But you are destined for only one."

"And if I choose the wrong book?"

"Not the wrong book. The one you're bound to."

"OK. If I choose the book I'm not *bound* to."

"Complete chaos to the destined world, while you'll be stuck in a world unlike yours for eternity—never to have a purpose or end."

"So you want me to pick a book and *hope against hope* it's the one I'm bound to?"

"Precisely."

"And you're not going to tell me which one?"

"No."

"Forget this. I want to go home."

Timothy turned to leave.

"Timothy!" the Wood Dweller shouted.

Timothy stopped.

"Look around you. This is everything you ever wanted: a chance to dive into a world that you call magic."

"Yes. But not to be destroyed or stranded on a world unfamiliar to me for all eternity."

"And your Earth won't destroy you or leave you stranded—abandoned by all peers?"

"Yes. But . . ."

"But what? No one is immune to death or loneliness, Timothy. No matter what world you tread upon."

"But how am I supposed to know which book if you don't tell me?"

"Much of this world has already spoken to you."

"It has?"

"Don't think of it as words. Think of it as . . ." The Wood Dweller trailed off, allowing Timothy to connect the dots.

Timothy thought of everything that had happened so far. He thought of the door—the barrier.

"The barrier," Timothy softly muttered.

Seeing no acknowledgment from the Wood Dweller, Timothy took a step toward the start of the vast library.

"So I just . . . choose a book? Just like that?"

"Something like that. But know that it is your book—nobody else's. Never think to give to anyone else."

"What happens?"

"All in good time."

Timothy shook his head in frustration.

"Let me ease your mind by saying he'll come if you choose wisely. Others will follow too."

"Who's he?"

The Wood Dweller shook his head.

"Decisions, Timothy. Only you can decide, and it's the choices you make that will impact what needs to be done."

"I'll have the power?"

"Near omnipotent. But don't go thinking you're a god. You're the furthest from one."

Timothy continued to stare at the books. He felt troubled. The idea of these books being another world fascinated him. But the idea—the very thought of uncertain danger lurking inside each of them greatly troubled this fascination. Ultimately, the fascination, the wonder, the excitement became too much. He must at least investigate the books.

I have to. And what's wrong with just checking them out?

As if the Wood Dweller had read his mind, the creature smiled.

Timothy stepped closer to the books.

"So many of them. And each of them so beautiful and *different*."

"Beautiful. Different. Yes."

Timothy's hands felt along a shelf of books and stopped his hand on one of them. "This book. If I pull it out, does that mean I choose it?"

"No. You must cross through the barrier for it to be yours. And don't think to open it here."

"No?"

"No."

"Then how do I know?"

"Let the book speak to you."

Timothy studied the adorned cover and closed his eyes.

A surge of fire blazed through his mind, followed by a dragon climbing upon the steep edges of a giant cliff.

Timothy opened his eyes.

"No," he said.

"You don't like dragons?"

"It's not that. It's just . . ."

"Not the right one?"

Timothy nodded and proceeded to examine more.

And more.

And much more after that.

Each book Timothy pulled out and studied fascinated him. Their magic stimulated him, along with each book's loss, gain, excitement, and terror. He wanted them all. He wanted to fall into each world and never return. He could not decide.

But he did not choose any of them, for not one of those books spoke to him as the door to this domain spoke to him.

He kept searching.

Finally, Timothy pulled out a book, and when doing so, he sensed the book's cry for help.

His help.

He also sensed the book to be more alive than the rest. This life was imbued within him. *Timothy* felt more alive. He felt like he had become another Timothy—a strong, formidable, battle-scarred warrior. And older—but how much older he could not sense. He could sense growth. It scared him while also intoxicating him with pure adrenaline. He wanted this change, regardless of what must be done. He did not believe the difference—the transformation—would easily be given to him.

With this change, he sensed a trial of danger and calamity unlike anything he could fathom.

This is the book, Timothy told himself.

He could now feel the true touch of the book.

The binding of the book consisted of a silky fabric. The forest-green hue seemed natural—as if no green in the world could match its authenticity. A perfectly shaped, translucent, bright green gemstone adorned the book's center and captivated his attention. Inside the gem lay restfully a young woman of golden, reddish braided hair, with streaks of silver running alongside the two colors. Timothy had never seen such flawless beauty and believed her incapable of being real.

To Timothy's eyes, she wasn't a drawing. But she was real, and not only that, too real. To him, she was an actual living being lying dormant in a gem.

The gown she wore shimmered in various colors. Upon her head sat a jeweled tiara. The jewels of the tiara were seven spherical orbs. Timothy then noticed a change in her. Everything changed about her. The color of her hair, skin complexion, and so forth changed, yet she never became less than a matchless beauty, one Timothy believed to be a goddess.

The awe of her naturally lessened. Timothy now realized she might not be *restfully* lying inside the gem. She was imprisoned—her eyes forced open because of a curse.

Timothy believed that wholeheartedly. He believed this goddess or queen came from a magical kingdom and had been cursed or bewitched.

What guarded this gem confirmed his suppositions.

Clutching the gem in a hostile and guarded fashion appeared to be a most hideous and terrifying spider. The spider's eight legs grasped the outside of the gem, threatening Timothy with its venomous dripping fangs. Above these fangs, Timothy discovered the head of the spider, with three eyes staring at him; each of these eyes was of a different color: a sharp yellow, ruby red, and a soft sky blue. Not only that, but the eyes also mirrored the exact contour of the gem the spider guarded.

To Timothy, this abominable spider was the keeper of the gem and cursed goddess.

This conjecture of his wanted nothing but to discover the truth. It wanted to discover why this goddess was locked inside a gem.

More importantly, Timothy wanted to know *how* he could save her.

His excitement reached a boiling point. He looked at the book's title.

"Gem and Spider."

The Wood Dweller nodded.

"This is the one, isn't it?"

"Only you know."

Timothy stared more at the book—enthralled by its beauty and, more importantly, the mystery surrounding the cursed goddess and how to save her.

"I want this book," Timothy said as he went to open the book.

"No!" the Wood Dweller vehemently shouted, smacking Timothy with the cane. "You will not open that here. Never here!"

"OK, OK," Timothy said, rubbing his bruised hand. "Not here. Outside."

"Yes. Outside."

"Well, then, I guess I choose this book."

"Wise choice."

"So I did make the right choice?"

"Time will tell."

"You're no help."

The Wood Dweller smiled.

"Can you tell me anything?"

"Trust your decisions. Know the choices that face you."

"Anything else?"

"Trust your decisions. Know the choices that—"

"Yes, yes. I get it. Know your choices. But there has to be something more you can tell me."

"Don't give up, even when giving up makes much more sense than pushing on. And again, never let the book out of your possession, for your world and the other world's sake."

"My world? What does my world have to do with the book?"

"Everything."

"Everything?"

The Wood Dweller nodded.

"What will happen to my world?"

"Suspended."

"Suspended? What do you mean by that?"

"Placed away in what you call the heavens."

"But it will return, right?"

"Finish the book, Timothy. Finish the book and—"

"My world will return to me?"

The Wood Dweller smiled. Behind that smile resided mischief. "Of course."

"You promise?" Timothy asked, sensing a possible connivery.

"Cross my heart and hope to die," the Wood Dweller said, mimicking the saying with his bony hand.

"That's what the church says when swearing on something," Timothy said.

"And the church is always honest, right? For how could the church ever lie or be wicked to another?"

"Uh," Timothy said, unsure what to think. "I guess. That's what everyone tells me—especially my pa."

"Then finish the book."

"Right. The book. How hard can it be? I've read countless books. Countless!"

"Good. Now, run along. It is time. Time for your adventure to begin."

Feeling overly confident, Timothy turned around and took his first steps the way they came in.

The Wood Dweller stopped him.

"Wait! One last piece of advice, and that's it."

Timothy listened keenly to these words:

"You may feel that the book is leading you into these choices and decisions you must make, but that does not mean you need to follow them. You're the writer—you're the one that fills in the book. You choose to follow or not follow what the book leads you to. But remember this: the book wants one thing and one thing only. It wants to be finished. So altering the course of the book may risk hindering your progress to finish the book. But then again, you may feel it wise to choose another direction on your advice or another's. Just know there'll invariably be consequences. Good or bad, it matters not. They are consequences nonetheless. Consequences that will greatly affect *everyone*."

Stepping back from the boy, the Wood Dweller ended with "Now go. Go and start your adventure. And good luck, for I will never be seeing you again.

"Or let us hope not!"

Timothy held the book tighter than ever while soaking in those words.

Seeing the boy's hesitation, the Wood Dweller slammed the cane upon the ground.

Timothy jumped.

"Scram!"

Timothy's eyes grew big as he fled from the scene. He departed from the chamber within seconds and continued marching toward and down the stairs. At the bottom of the stairs, he reached the hallway and stopped before the barrier door. A second later, the barrier opened. Timothy stepped through. The barrier closed. Hearing the door close startled him. The sound and perception of the door closing on him meant a closure inside his mind he did not like. He felt as if there was no going back now. No matter what, the dice had been cast, regardless of not having opened the book yet.

Disquieted in his mind, he turned around to face the door and failed to push it open.

Deducing that only the Wood Dweller's cane, explicitly the lion skull upon it, could open the door, he faced reality.

There was no returning the book.

With that settled in his mind, Timothy hurried along the hallway, only to find each burning torchlight flickering off as he passed by, along with each glistening stone upon the walls, thus leaving him with the slightest light ahead of him. Therefore, he groped his way through pitch blackness when reaching the end without a torchlight or stone to rely upon. Coming to what Butch hinted to be the end, he looked up and continued to stare at the darkness. The darkness dissolved because of the tree stump sliding open, giving light from the outside.

Timothy and Butch climbed five feet up.

Chapter 3

BLASPHEMY!

When Timothy had stepped out of the hole and landed on the forest floor, the tree stump closed behind him.

Timothy looked at the closed stump.

"Magic."

He looked at the sun. No change.

Magic.

Timothy sat upon the stump with a minute to spare and opened the book. To his shock and dismay, he found only blank pages.

"What the?" he cried out incredulously.

He investigated the book again.

Blank.

"Where's the story?"

Timothy followed that up by slamming the book shut. He stared wrathfully at the stump and kicked it.

"Where's my *Gem and Spider*?"

The kicking did not stop. He did feel the sun dropping by the second.

"I don't get it," Timothy said sullenly.

The sun grew darker.

"Damn. I've got to go."

Wasting no more time, Timothy hastened through the dell and reached the two crossed oak trees. He stopped. Something seemed different—very different. He looked around. Nothing *looked* different. He scented the area. No change had come to the air. He looked to Butch. The dog showed the same confusion as it started to probe the area as if everything had become unfamiliar.

Butch barked not long into the investigation.

Timothy turned to the dog and saw him shoveling his nose into a thicket at the side of the oak trees.

Timothy hurried over there.

"Can't be," Timothy said while looking down.

A trail had appeared.

"Impossible," Timothy said.

The boy looked ahead in the distance. The suffocating, poorly lit woods blinded him from a clear view. He took a step forward. As he did, a gust of wind suddenly came through that portion of the forest and knocked the book out of his hand. Timothy stepped back. He felt like the wind spoke to him, leaving him scared and confounded. Recovering his senses, he noticed the book was missing. He spied around the ground and found it two feet away. He went to grab it, and as he did, he noticed writing. Excited and terrified by what it could mean, Timothy grabbed the book and turned to the first page.

What had been blank minutes ago turned out to be anything but that.

"Magic," Timothy said as he stood back reverently.

Taking up most of the page, Timothy found this:

GEM AND SPIDER

Eyes bigger, Timothy turned the page.

Chapter 1
The Treasure and Danger
That Lurks Inside
a Scary Black House

Timothy read over the title four times. After each time, excitement grew. Feeling as if this excitement could not withstand such growth, he turned the page mindfully, trying his best to savor every moment. When the page turned completely, Timothy discovered a drawing. The drawing was artistically drawn up using black, white, and ashen-gray colors. The artist looked to have used chalk, not ink—thus unlike the writing. And yet, the chalk upon the page showed zero chance of being impermanent. No eraser in any world could alter the drawing or even cause the tiniest of smudges.

And Timothy believed that also.

Timothy first noticed the drawing of the two crossed oak trees. Beside them resided the never-before-seen trail. The trail ended at a black house.

The ebony-black house looked diabolical to Timothy. Derelict and dilapidated it showed to be. He studied how alive the house looked. Not dormant. Not oblivious to the presence of any eyes on it. He studied the surroundings, being a feral and unruly lawn, mostly filled with mischievous weeds vying desperately for another spot to take over and truculent ivy strangling the entire property and the house itself. The scary sight of the black house invoked a fear Timothy had never felt. Ever. Feeling this fear, Timothy cringed. He cringed as if somebody had grabbed him by the shoulder and thrown him into a dark pit filled with the dead. In this pit, he would die by rotting away slowly, seeing the pit too high to climb out of.

What daunted him more was how the scary black house summoned him.

"It's only a drawing," Timothy was forced to tell himself. Multiple times.

A bit relieved, Timothy compared the trails.

Identical.

"Magic," Timothy sighed fearfully.

Turning the page, he found the rest of the book blank.

He closed the book.

Go home?

"No. The book. The book leads me . . ."

The scary black house.

"I have to go. I have to see what it wants me to see."

He looked up. Night approached. He closed his eyes. He felt the gravity of the book weigh heavy on his mind. He became determined.

Timothy abandoned his anxieties about the scary house and the inevitable punishment from Pa and hurried along the path.

The strange empty feeling he felt when at the two crossed oak trees grew stronger. He looked around. Again, nothing seemed different. This portion of the Forest Beyond consisted of thicker and stronger trees than Old Wicker's Forest and even the Forest Beyond he traveled through to reach the dell. But nothing else coerced him to think he abandoned his world for another. He sure felt it, though. Yes. He felt and sensed a disassociation of worlds. The more he traveled along the trail, the more he noticed how healthy the forest had become. The forest he now traversed through felt newer than where the two crossed oak trees resided. This forest felt not a day old, as if God came down and raised the forest from the ground up the day before at first sunlight. By many accounts, Old Wicker's Forest had been considered the healthiest patches of forests that surrounded the more significant part of the town he belonged to. But seeing this forest, Timothy concluded that no other forest could be more alive and pristine than this one, as if he seemed to have reached Eden, a garden his town's church spoke about.

Nothing in his life had smelled or felt as fresh as this forest, excluding the underground he had visited not long ago.

Thus, onward he went, believing he traveled through a magical forest.

~

The night left the last amber light for Timothy to see. He panicked and hurried even faster along the trail.

Not long after, he came to a break in the forest and slowed down.

"Another dell?" *Or is it . . .*

A scary black house?

The thought sent a shiver up his spine. He steeled himself and stepped forward.

A minute later, the forest cleared and revealed a lot, overwhelmed by shrubs, thickets, and thick bushes.

"Somebody's property?"

He looked farther ahead.

The scary black house.

No horror could come close to what he felt just then. The drawing of the house seemed like child's play compared to the real thing. The house looked not only alive but exhaled this life. This breath smacked Timothy in the face and tasted sinister. The evilness of the house, being the wicked feeling Timothy felt, along with the crumbling walls, shattered and boarded-up windows, broken doors, a shabby veranda, and so much more, stared at Timothy with its diabolical intentions running through its mind since, indeed, the house had its own consciousness, a powerful and morbid one.

Timothy could hear the house speak. Its words weren't articulate but discernible. The house yearned for Timothy to enter.

While also warning him not to enter under any such circumstance.

Timothy looked to Butch.

"What do you think?"

The dog answered with a trembling bark, turning his eyes away from the house.

Timothy nodded.

"You're right. We can't do this. It's too . . ."

He wanted to say "scary," but to do so would only break him even more.

"We have to go home."

Timothy turned to the sky. The last of the amber light disappeared. Sheer darkness took over.

"Now we're really in trouble."

~

The scary black house's grip on Timothy did not go away so easily, even when returning to the two crossed oak trees. Fortunately, the night sky couldn't be any more beautiful. The crescent-shaped moon shone undisturbed, along with countless stars. The few existing clouds turned dark to pellucid gray when passing before a bright cluster of stars. A smooth breeze also passed through this night. This breeze spoke to Timothy of autumn slowly closing in, ending a hot and dry summer. Everything about this night soon helped diminish the house's grip on Timothy.

Now, as far as him being late, well . . .

The book held in his hands conquered any anxieties over him being late.

"I'll be late. But who gives a damn? Once they get a load of this," Timothy said, gripping the book tightly.

A magical book!

Another thought came to mind—a prudent thought.

"They won't believe me. They'll take the book away, and that I cannot let happen."

I've got to tell somebody. Can't keep this a secret for myself only.

Zachary?

"Too risky. Too many eyes around him."

Katelyn?

"No. She'll tell. Or . . . maybe she won't."

Maybe tonight will be the moment I give her what I gave Zachary? The moment I've been waiting for . . .

Timothy smiled.

A few minutes later, Timothy exited Old Wicker's Forest and stealthily crept along his family's immediate grounds toward the house. Noticing the gas lamps burning brightly by the kitchen window, Timothy believed his family to be sitting down for evening supper. He snuck around the house until he reached his bedroom window to hide the book inside. On reaching the window, he had a change of mind. He could be wrong about his family being in the kitchen. They could be anywhere. And he couldn't risk it. Instead, he turned around and pondered over his next move.

His eyes fell on the nearby pile of firewood and bricks resting against the house.

"Of course."

He walked the ten steps toward the pile, carefully lifted a few bricks and firewood, and buried the book.

"Good enough for now."

Come morning, though . . .

Under the bed.

On the way to the front door, Timothy ensured he was not seen.

"Now steel yourself," Timothy said, readying himself for the anger and disappointment to follow.

Timothy humbly entered the house and found his family sitting around the kitchen table with steepled hands in prayer. Wisely, Timothy stood motionlessly until the prayer's end. His pa surprised him. Harold Huntsinger, a daily devotee of the only church in town, the same church Timothy, his sister, and their ma attended weekly, broke concentration and leveled his gaze upon Timothy.

The prayer ended, and everyone but Timothy sighed, "Amen."

Pa's eyes turned to his food while Katelyn and Ma stared at Timothy.

"Sit down," Pa said gravely.

Timothy sat down.

"Say your grace."

Timothy closed his eyes, lowered his face, and made a steeple with his hands. The rest of the family turned to their meal. Katelyn ate halfheartedly. She could not take her pitiful eyes off her brother. Timothy's ma, Beth, also found eating difficult. She felt her husband's silent anger and disappointment for their son. As for Harold, he ate casually. Not a trace of disappointment or anger could be found in his demeanor.

Deep within prayer, Timothy felt this silence sharp as a knife.

Finished with his prayer, Timothy muttered, "Amen."

"How far you go?" Harold asked, staring only at his food.

"Far," Timothy said.

"I asked how far, not whether you went far."

"Beyond the oak trees."

Harold's implacable head budged an inch.

"You broke the rules."

"But I had to. Butch went after—"

"The dog is not my son. And that dog would have easily found a way home. Don't underestimate a canine's tracking ability, especially his breed. You got lucky this time. That forest you traversed through is not kind to trespassers. And trespassing is exactly what you did. Although, it seems you didn't come away completely unscathed. You look like you lost your way and had to crawl home."

"I wasn't lost, Pa. I . . . I found something."

Harold faced his son. Timothy found himself facing a new challenge: how to tell Pa a trail miraculously appeared.

"There's a trail."

"Where?"

"Where the oak trees cross each other."

"Impossible," Harold said. "If you're going to break the rules and be caught, don't be lying about it. Face your mistakes. Never cower in the face of the consequences of your actions."

"But I'm not lying, Pa."

"Damn it, boy!" Harold said, finally showing the anger they each expected. "You will not continue to lie before me."

"But, Pa—"

Beth stopped him from saying more by taking him by the shoulder.

"Timothy," the relatively young and pretty mother said. "Stop. Stop this now. You're only making matters worse."

"But I'm not lying. The trail is there, and it leads to a house."

"Blasphemy!" Pa shouted, hitting his clenched fist on the wooden table. "You lie when you know you're lying. Blasphemy."

"It's not blasphemy. I swear it on—"

"No!" Pa shouted louder than before. "No, you won't. You will not take the Lord's name in vain."

Surrendering to his emotions, Timothy stared at Pa with watery eyes. A teardrop fell.

"But," Timothy said, wiping away the teardrop, "I'm not lying."

Harold wanted to scream louder. But the sincerity of his son's emotions softened him, for he rarely saw his son cry. He now saw Timothy's outlandish story in another light. *Maybe*, Harold thought, *being alone and scared in that forest allowed his imagination to grow rampant, unbridled.* The boy would have been vulnerable to anything the forest wanted him to imagine. And who could blame him? He was still a boy and once an overly imaginative boy, vulnerable to losing touch with reality.

Harold's thoughts softened his anger even more.

"Timothy," Harold said compassionately, "I know these woods like the palm of my hand. Only a handful of days in the year do I not work my way to the crossed oak trees. Sometimes, since it is more so my land than anyone else's, I go *beyond*, especially when rumors swirl about the forest taking another victim—the Forest Beyond, as you children call it. I have even been at that spot earlier today. Timothy. My son. There is no trail. Only the forest. So how can you sit here and tell me there is a trail? And not only that, but you say a house. No such human lives in the Forest Beyond. Most folks, if not all of them who have traversed that suffocating and unforgiving forest, believe it to be uninhabitable.

"Now stop this and tell me the truth."

Showing no signs of his tearful emotions, Timothy answered back assertively. "I'm not lying. You must believe me."

"I will not!" Harold snapped. "And I will not allow you to sit at this table with these lies." Harold pulled away Timothy's plate of food. "Now go to your room. If you want to start telling the truth, you may find some breakfast in the morning. But tonight, you're going to bed on an empty stomach."

Timothy did not move.

"Did you not hear me, boy? I said leave us."

Timothy stood up and stared at his pa, keeping his emotions in check, thus staying strong and not weak.

He turned to his sister and ma.

They each cried.

"Now!" Harold said.

Timothy turned away and hurried to his room.

Butch followed.

Once in the room, he kept the door open until Butch entered and closed it. He placed his ear to the door.

Nobody had spoken for a long minute. The minute passed, and Timothy heard Pa's voice pleading to the others.

"Please eat. Don't let it disturb your meal. The boy needs to learn a lesson."

"But what if he's not lying?" Beth said.

"Are you saying that a trail has emerged in less than a day? One leading to a house?"

"He just seemed so sure."

"Yes. I know. That's what troubles me."

A second of silence passed.

"Sweet pea," Pa said, "do us a favor and give comfort to your troubled brother."

Hearing this, Timothy stepped behind the door and waited. The door opened, blocking Timothy from being seen, and Katelyn entered. Finding no Timothy on either of the beds, she panicked. Before the panic could be heard, Timothy placed a hand over her mouth and signaled her to be quiet. She obeyed. He motioned her to sit down on her bed. She again obeyed. Timothy returned to the closed door and placed his ear upon it again.

"What are you doing?" Katelyn whispered.

"Just keep quiet."

Pa spoke.

"It just can't be. What he said about the house and trail is impossible. There is a path. Yes. There is a path. But it leads to a lonely dell full of old tree stumps. And yes, that is strange, for it seems to me nobody in town has ever seen it but me. It's been a recollection I've desperately tried to forget for years since how extraordinary it is that nobody has ever said they've seen it. But again . . . no other trail. No trail that leads to a house."

"He was just so sure—so very sure."

"Maybe he dreamed it?" Pa said. "You know, fell asleep out there. We all know how imaginative that boy is—more imaginative than we can imagine. Remember what his teacher Mrs. Keary said a few years back? How she has never crossed paths with a boy so powerfully imaginative. She even said his imagination surpassed mine when I was a boy his age. And you know how much I lived in fantasy. I nearly allowed it to rule my life.

"Yes," Pa continued, "alone and scared. He fell asleep. He dreamed. And this dream . . . I tell you, Beth, those woods could muddle any man or woman's mind—no matter how strong you think you are, and I know Timothy . . . He's strong—but not strong enough. Trust me. As kids, we also didn't call it the Forest Beyond for no reason. It goes beyond what one mind could ever go."

"But I still think we behaved too rashly. Let's be honest. The boy has never lied before."

"Yes. And that's what terrifies me."

"Why?"

"For if he didn't lie and maintained he did not dream this up . . ."

Timothy sensed hesitation in Pa. He removed his ear from the door—something troubled Harold. Timothy could hear it in his voice.

Hoping his pa would pick up where he left, he placed his ear back on the door.

"When I was a kid," Harold said discreetly, "I, uh, well, I uh . . . imagined I met someone out there. It is all but a vague dream now. But what pieces of the broken memory I do remember is this something—a creature of some kind—showing me another world. Pillars, I think. Anyways, I remember not believing in it enough. I chose not to believe. Thus, I ran. I ran back home. When returning home, I realized how much I've allowed imagination to rule my every step in life, imagination so strong that I was making things up. I swore to myself then and there never to allow imagination to control me. Since then, I've lost my capacity to conjure imagination. A good thing! My mind has and will always be clear and open to the thoughts and ideas of Christ and family."

"Why have you never told me this?"

"How could I? For it must have been a dream."

Shocked to hear what his pa had just divulged, Timothy stepped back and turned to his sister squeezing one of her stuffed dolls.

What does this mean? Has he—

His thoughts would have gone further if it weren't for the doll being thrown at him.

"What was that for?" Timothy said.

"You were supposed to be only a few minutes late. Not an hour!"

"I was delayed."

"Why?"

"By something."

"And this something?"

Timothy moved over to the bed and sat across from her.

"If I tell you, you must keep it a secret."

"OK."

"No. I'm serious, sis."

"So am I," Katelyn said, straightening herself into a more serious posture.

"This isn't playtime. This is real serious."

"And I am serious."

"I need something more from you to prove that."

"Pinky swear?" Katelyn said, extending her pinky.

"No," Timothy said and moved off the bed. "More."

The boy dug under his bed. A second later, he pulled out a small shoebox and placed it on the bed.

"This."

"What is it?"

Timothy opened the box and pulled out two necklaces, each consisting of a bright, translucent stone.

"W-o-w," Katelyn said, captivated by the stones. "Where did you find these?"

"The stones I found in the Forest Beyond."

"What? Today? Is that why you were so late?"

"No. I found them months ago."

"You went to the Forest Beyond months—"

"Yes. But not far. I reached a spot where two crossed oak trees blocked my way. I couldn't go anymore—too scared. When I turned around, I saw these resting on the ground over by—" Timothy stopped. He became aware of the trail precisely where he had found the stones and arrow tip.

"What's wrong?" Katelyn said.

Timothy snapped out of his trance, wondering if the coincidence had any meaning. He shrugged his body.

"I found those stones with an arrow tip. I knew they were each special, like they didn't belong to our world. Foolish to think that, but I'm wondering if I'm not wrong—seriously. Anyways, I noticed a hole in the stones and made a rope out of the tough fibers of a strange root I found in that area and made a necklace out of each of them. The two necklaces belong to you and me. As for the arrow tip, I gave it to Zachary, being my best bud and all. I didn't tell you this because I was waiting for the right moment. And now is the right moment."

"Why?"

"Because I need you to keep the greatest of all secrets. By accepting this necklace, you're sealing an oath you must swear upon it."

"An oath?"

"Yes."

"I can do that."

"You have to if you're willing to accept the necklace."

"I'm willing."

"Then promise me. Give me your word that what I tell you, you won't tell another soul?"

"I give you my word."

"Good."

"Will you give me your word on something too?" Katelyn asked. "While giving me this necklace."

"Of course. What is it? You look distraught."

"Ma said something the other day, about you getting older and you'll soon be leaving us."

"You're afraid I'm going to leave you?"

"Yes."

"By saying leaving, you mean forever?"

"Yes."

"Never. I'll never leave you. And I don't know why Ma mentioned that to you. It is not for another two years before I become McDuff's apprentice. And he lives in town. It's not like I'm going abroad. Why would she mention that?"

"I hurt myself the other day," Katelyn said. "Not bad. Ma told me to take it easy next time. Don't go running too fast. I told her it was OK. 'Timothy will always be there to help me. He'll never let anything bad happen to me.' She sat me down and then told me that you won't always be there. I told her she was lying. She shook her head and said no. 'He's turning into a man as we speak. He'll be leaving not long from now, and you won't see him as you do now.' I cried. I got scared and cried. I asked God why Timothy would do this. Why would Timothy leave me and let bad things happen to me?"

Timothy gently placed a hand on her shoulder.

"Katelyn. What Ma said was only to prepare you for the worst. Truth is, I'll never leave you. I'll never go too far from home and let anything bad happen to you."

"Promise?"

"By wearing this other necklace, I promise I'll never leave you or let anything horrible happen to you. So I guess we're both taking oaths."

Katelyn smiled. "Then it's a deal."

The two came together and embraced in a hug. After the hug, they each put the necklaces on. They hugged a second time.

Timothy turned serious. "Now stay here and be quiet as a mouse."

Timothy stepped off the bed and reached the window. He then opened the window and climbed out. Less than two minutes later, Timothy returned.

"What is that?" Katelyn asked, seeing Timothy hold on to something reverently.

"All in good time," Timothy said, copying the Wood Dweller's words.

Sitting across from his sister again, Timothy recapitulated the events leading to the possession of the book before showing it to her. Not once did Katelyn show a sign of disbelief. To her (and many others), Timothy was incapable of lying. She believed him to the point of growing awfully scared when listening to the details, especially about the monster he felt that lurked beyond the magnificent embroidery of the barrier door. But the fright lasted only so long. She became elated and even envious when Timothy described the library chamber and how he stood upon a precipice that belonged to the Pillars of Worlds.

"But the book was empty," Timothy said, reaching the part when outside the tree stump.

"Empty?"

"Yes. So I hurried on. I found myself at the two crossed oak trees. And that's when it happened."

"What happened?"

"The blank book was no longer blank," Timothy said, pulling the book from behind him.

Katelyn's eyes grew big when seeing the front binding of the book.

"And you think the spider is guarding the gem and princess?"

"Goddess. It has to be a goddess, I would think. But yes."

Timothy opened the book to the chapter title and the sketch that followed.

Katelyn stared at the written title and its drawing in wonder. But seeing the scary black house at the trail's end, she became scared.

"You saw that house?"

"I did. And let me tell you: this drawing does no justice to how scary it really is. It studied me. The house . . . It wanted me to enter while also warning me not to. Do you remember what Preacher Thomas told us about demons possessing kids? That's how I felt about this house. I couldn't even move because I was so scared. But I finally did and ran home."

"This is what you were trying to tell Pa?"

"Yes."

"And he doesn't believe you?"

"Either that or doesn't want to believe me."

"What does that mean?"

"I think Pa knows. I heard him speaking to Ma just now. He said something—something very significant to me. He was a boy, just like me. I don't know. For him, maybe it was a dream—the last of a nightmare that still lingers in his mind. But I don't think so. I want to believe that Pa experienced something similar except, well . . . he chose *not* to believe, whereas I chose to believe. And because of that, I obtained this book—this magical book."

"Magical book?"

"It has to be. For how else—"

Timothy stopped.

"Footsteps. Pa's coming!"

Timothy jumped off the bed and shoved the book under the bed.

The door opened as Timothy returned to the bed.

"It's getting late," Pa said, standing at the opening with a plate of food in his hand. "I want you both to finish your supper."

Both kids nodded.

"I also need to apologize," Harold said. "I never meant the word *blasphemy*. That's an unjust word. I'm ashamed. I'm ashamed I said such a word to my beautiful and strong son. What you saw out there, I'm not sure of. I say that because, deep down, I do believe you. I do. I believe because it comes from you—not anyone else."

"What about me, Pa?"

"Sure, sweet pea. I believe you too. But, Timothy! Don't be getting any ideas that I believe what you said to be possible, because I don't. I still believe you must have dozed off and dreamed this. Your mother has told you that dreams seem to last forever, except they are only a second or two of your time. You could easily have dreamed this. But I'll do this. After our morning and afternoon chores tomorrow, you and I will travel to the two crossed oak trees. We will discover the truth. How's that sound?"

"Best plan ever," Timothy said.

Both father and son smiled while Katelyn grew apprehensive. She felt something ominous about discovering this *truth*.

Chapter 4

THE SCARY BLACK HOUSE

Timothy received a good night of sleep but endured a bitter end. A malevolent black spider, three or four times his size, infringed upon the last minutes of sleep. It hung from the ceiling of a dark cellar, spinning an endless web over three bodies in its clutches. Timothy identified these bodies as his pa, sister, and ma by their naked faces. Timothy then saw himself in this dream, sitting on the ground floor, paralyzed, unable to stop his family from being fodder to this monster. He noticed the spider and its eyes, neither of them being gems. He also noticed streaks of a violet color running across the spider's side, along with blue dotted spots plastered on its underbelly.

Inside the dream, Timothy screamed.

But no answer came, not even from the spider.

The next scream from Timothy broke through the barriers of the dream.

He woke up.

He woke up in a sweat and had to convince himself for a long minute that it had been only a dream.

It sure didn't feel like one. It felt more like . . .

On impulse, Timothy reached under his bed and unearthed the book. He opened it up and, to his relief, found no changes. He placed the book back and noticed the first streaks of morning breaking through the closed drapes. Recalling what his pa said, he leaped off the bed and hurried to start the day.

Most of the chores were to be done in the earliest part of the morning. Timothy and Harold would be the first to wake up and indulge in a small snack consisting of bread, berries, and a half cup of milk. They would go outside and work without relenting for three or four hours. By then, Beth would signal them inside for a more extensive breakfast consisting of oatmeal, eggs, and bacon. The two would return outside for another three or four hours till lunch break. The day's laborious—not time-consuming—chores fell after lunch. This meant the fieldwork surrounding Harold's land. The two would finish before evening and tend to the firewood until sundown. But on this day, they finished the fieldwork around four, and Pa turned to his son.

He spoke gravely. "There won't be any firewood today."

Understanding the implication, Timothy nodded.

"Stay right here." Pa turned away, and Timothy watched him head into the house.

A minute later, Pa returned, holding a rifle.

Timothy's eyes widened.

"For the unexpected," Harold said. "You know . . . A wolf or bear."

Timothy did not believe him but still nodded.

The two turned away and stepped toward the forest.

~

"It's so quiet," Timothy remarked as the two traversed Old Wicker's Forest.

"Yes. Too quiet," Harold said.

Timothy did not like the tone of Pa's voice. It only strengthened the conviction he had in mind that his pa has misgivings.

The book! Timothy shouted in his thoughts. *Why didn't I bring the book? How did I forget it? Damn it, Timothy. Not wise.*

Timothy remained silent, angry with himself, seeing that the book could be of great use. This silence remained when reaching the fallen elm tree.

The silence between the two continued as they traveled to the two crossed oak trees.

Finally, they received their first glimpse of the barrier.

Harold sped up.

Timothy followed.

Harold reached the spot first and stopped. He looked around. Quickly after, and to his astonishment, Pa's eyes fell on the new trail.

"Goddamn," Harold said softly. "God . . . *damn.*"

As the revelation became even more real, Harold's insides softened. His knees buckled. His entire body became lame. The strong and vigorous man felt like someone had stolen his inner strength. Timothy noticed this. He did not like it. He started to scrutinize the judiciousness of divulging the trail to Pa on seeing him so weak. His pa! Harold Huntsinger, the bravest and strongest man in town.

And now?

Weak and flimsy.

Timothy heard the Wood Dweller speaking somewhere unimaginably inside him.

"*Choices.*"

Timothy closed his eyes and silently muttered, "Yes. My decision. My decision to tell Pa and now forgetting the book."

Too debilitated by discovering the trail to hear his son, Harold crept closer.

"It cannot be. But I was—" He stopped.

"What?" Timothy asked. "You were what?"

Pa shuddered and kept his eyes on the trail.

"I was only a boy."

Timothy grew excited. "And what? What did you see?"

Pa looked away and stared in the direction of what might or might not lead one to a dell.

"Out there, I ran into something. My memory is oblivious to it now."

Before Timothy could say anything, Pa turned to him.

"You were right, son. You were right."

"I wish I weren't," Timothy said.

"It is too late for that."

They each looked at the trail.

"What are we to do now?" Timothy asked.

"The only thing."

"You're going down that trail, aren't you?" Timothy rhetorically questioned.

"Yes."

"You can't. You just can't."

"Go home, son."

"No, Pa. You can't. You see—"

"Home. Now. Tell Ma very little. And if I don't return by sundown, I want you to get on Abigail and hurry over to the sheriff's ranch and grab him. Don't tell him much, either. In fact, tell him nothing about this trail and what you found out there. He won't believe you. Tell him I went missing in this direction, and he'll be concerned. He'll want to investigate. Do that, Timothy, and don't be hasty about it. Give me time—until full sundown, no earlier. This is our business—you and me. Only you and I are to know about it, and I've got a feeling we're not alone. You hear me, son?" Pa said, smiling at his son while placing a loving hand on the boy's shoulder.

"But, Pa—"

"No arguing."

"Wouldn't you want Sheriff Riggins with you now?"

"No. This, again, is our woods—our secret. Only we have been chosen."

"Chosen?" Timothy said. "You know all about it, don't you?"

Harold rubbed the temple of his head.

"It's . . . like a fragmented dream. It doesn't matter now. What matters—"

"Don't go," Timothy pleaded. "Please don't go out there. I've got a bad feeling about this."

"So do I, son. But it's time. It's time for me to face what I've been hiding from for so very long. Home, Timothy."

Harold leaned in and gave his son a rare kiss.

"So proud of you," Harold said. "So very proud of you. I love you."

Harold then turned away, and when doing so, he regained much of his strength and determination. He unslung his rifle and took his first steps on the trail.

As Timothy watched his pa leave, the image of the morning's dream appeared vividly. He could feel the black spider creeping closer to his family.

"No!" Timothy screamed.

"Go home, Timothy," Harold shouted in the distance.

"But you can't go. You see, there's this spider. It's big, real big. And it's scary."

"Home!"

"Even you fear it."

"One must overcome fear to know what it's truly like to be free. Never forget that!"

"But, Pa—"

Still visible, Harold never answered back.

Timothy tried one last time. "A book!" he cried out. "I've got this book. It's a magical book. I can show you. Come back home, and I'll show you. Please. If you just see this book, you'll change your mind. You'll know the dangers that await. Please, Pa. Please."

But the distance between the two proved too much. Harold had vanished into the forest.

Timothy's head fell. "What have I done? I just stood there—just watched him leave. What kind of fearless son am I?"

A son that obeyed his pa.

"No. I'm a cowardly son."

A son who chose.

"And what choice did I make? I forgot the damn book!"

With Butch nudging Timothy, the boy looked at his dog and thought about the rest of his family.

"I have to take care of Ma and Katelyn. That's what Pa wants me to do."

Timothy nodded. He looked Pa's way one last time.

"OK, Butch, ready to go home."

Butch barked.

~

Timothy arrived home to his sister building sand castles in the sandpit his pa and he made for her, which resided near Ma's garden. Seeing her brother approach, she stood up and hurried toward him with a greatly relieved smile, for she questioned whether she'd ever see him again, alive or dead. Seeing no Pa, her smile dimmed like a burning candle losing its oxygen.

"Where's Pa?"

"Out."

"Out where?"

"Never mind where. He'll be back soon enough."

"I don't believe you."

"You're going to have to," Timothy said sternly.

He brushed past her and headed toward the front door.

Katelyn stood motionlessly distraught.

Inside the house, Beth had just finished the prep for a roasted chicken dinner when hearing Timothy enter. She called out, "Tell your pa I need those potatoes I placed in the bin for supper."

"Um," Timothy said. "Pa's not home yet."

"What do you mean?"

"He's um . . ."

"Spill it out!"

"He's busy."

"Busy where?"

"Investigating?"

"You're not making sense. What's he investigating?"

"I . . . uh, I'm not supposed to say."

"Timothy, say it."

"He's, uh . . . well, he's investigating the trail."

"What trail?"

"The one I found yesterday."

"Please don't start that again. Didn't you learn anything?"

"It's there, Ma. And Pa discovered it too."

"Timothy, this is no time to fool around. Where is he?"

"Hopefully, on his way home."

"From where?"

"From the trail."

"Stop that! I stood behind you yesterday. I won't do it today. Now go and get those potatoes washed up. When you come inside, I want the truth."

Timothy didn't budge.

"Now, I said."

"You don't believe me?"

"No. I don't."

An infuriated Timothy turned away.

Not wanting to aggravate the situation by ignoring her command, Timothy grabbed the potatoes, washed them, and stealthily returned to the kitchen. Putting the potatoes down, he snuck into his bedroom, where his sister waited.

Ignoring her, he went to the window and stared at the sunny late afternoon sky. "Still got time."

"For what?" Katelyn asked.

"Nothing."

The bedroom door opened.

"You thought you could sneak in here and not be seen?" Ma asked furiously. "Enough. I want you to start talking. Where's Pa?"

"On the trail."

"There is no trail!" Beth stammered angrily. She quickly settled down by sitting on the bed. "Just tell me, Timothy. Tell me where your pa is. Please."

Timothy didn't answer. He sat down on the bed across from Katelyn and sulked over Ma not believing him. His sister, feeling the tension in the room, cried. Timothy turned to her and then to his ma. Beth also cried. *She cries because deep down, she believes me and is scared—scared to believe me and scared for the man she loves.*

Scared like I am for Pa.

"He's in the woods," Timothy said remorsefully.

"Doing what?"

"I don't know. He didn't tell me. He only told me that come sundown and he's not home, I am to ride over to Jack Riggins's place."

"Sheriff Riggins?"

"Yes."

"But why?"

You won't believe the why—that's why.

"I don't know."

"He's in the woods?"

"Yes."

"And you're to grab the sheriff come sundown and no Pa?"

Timothy nodded. He watched Ma's face betray the immense worry she tried to hide.

"It's going to be OK, Ma."

Not caring for her son to see her so distraught, she nodded.

"Shouldn't you go and stretch Abigail? She's been penned up in there all—"

"Ma, he'll be back. Pa will make it home."

Timothy said that to soothe his ma's worry. He was nowhere near to be sure. But he knew now more than ever his duty fell to taking care of her and Katelyn. He had to bear the burden—the cross for his family. By doing that, he needed to keep their anxiety low, even if it meant lying to them, for it was downright dishonest of him to insist that Pa would surely be coming home.

It worked. Beth recovered and stood up. "I'll have supper ready soon."

A second later, Katelyn and Timothy were alone.

"Ma's going to be fine, right?" Katelyn asked.

"Sure. Ma's strong. And she knows how strong Pa is. Knows it more than we do. He'll be home, and everything will be fine."

"But you don't believe that."

"I do too."

"You're lying."

"And so what if I am?" an irritated Timothy said.

Startled and upset at her brother, Katelyn moved farther away from the bed.

"And I bet you're not going to tell me what really happened with Pa."

"No, I'm not. Because not even I know what happened."

But the book might!

"Yes. Of course. The book."

Timothy fervently leaped off the bed and pulled out the book from underneath. When he jumped back on the bed, Katelyn moved closer to his side. The anticipation of opening the book was tangible. They could taste it. It was sharp and poignant, bitter and sweet like the strongest of kids' medicines. It was a belligerent storm at sea, waiting to wreak havoc on a floundering ship, or a peaceful storm appearing to push them away from the impending destructive storm. There was nowhere to go, nowhere to turn. They must swallow this medicine for the good and the bad. They must face the chance of seeing either a peaceful or destructive storm. They must collide head-on with what resided next in the book.

"What's the matter?" Katelyn asked.

Timothy surrendered to his emotions before his sister.

"I'm scared. I'm really scared."

A teardrop rolled down Katelyn's face.

"What are you scared of?" she asked.

"The book. Whatever appears next may not be favorable to us. But I know I must be strong. Must be positive. Like Pa."

"You are strong. You're the strongest boy in town. I know this. Everyone knows this. You're my big brother, and everyone is jealous of your strength."

Timothy smiled.

Holding on to the corner of the page with the chapter title's sketch, Timothy inhaled deeply.

He exhaled and turned the page.

The chapter continued.

No sketch, not for the first two pages. The two stared only at the writing. The writing was impossible to understand.

But familiar.

"The writing," Timothy said. "I've seen it before."

"Where?"

Timothy did not have to think long and hard to answer that. "The door."

"What door?"

"The barrier."

Without further ado, Timothy brought the book closer to his face and smelled the writing.

"Fresh, like fresh ink. Just like what I smelled on the door, except . . . I don't think it's the ink you and I know of."

Katelyn smelled the same. She looked around the room questioningly, as if the writer stood in their presence, for how could they not be, with writing that fresh?

"Only if we knew what it says," Timothy said.

Timothy turned the page.

More writing. But the page to his right contained a small drawing. Again, this drawing was sketched not with ink but with some chalk or mineral. The sketch revealed Pa following the path leading to the scary black house. Timothy turned the page. More writing. The upper-right corner, taking up most of the page, revealed three sketches, the first showing Pa entering the house. Below this sketch, another drawing showed Pa falling through a pit on the house's first floor. Both Katelyn and Timothy cringed. A second later, the two suffered even more fright, for the third sketch showed a sizable portion inside the house, and studying this sketch, they noticed a thick funnel of spider web running down the gable end of the house, down a set of stairs, through a hallway, again down a set of stairs, and finally stopping at an open trap door leading to what they imagined to be a cellar or basement.

"Turn the page! Turn the page!" Katelyn cried, allowing the fear to break through.

Timothy turned the page and found only writing on the left page. The page to the right had no writing.

One giant drawing instead.

Pa had fallen through the hole and landed in a cobweb-infested basement littered with variously shaped and variously formed cargo boxes. Some of these boxes had writing on them. The writing on the boxes was of their language, except they could not understand them, for they were primarily written in abbreviation. DVD and CD were among the few boxes, along with "Made in China," "Sony," and "Microsoft".

"China?" Timothy said. "What's a box doing out here saying China? And what are the other words or letters mean?"

The question lingered until the concern for their pa quickly evaporated all curiosity about the boxes.

Seeing Pa on his hands and knees, Timothy noticed in the background a faint silhouette of what looked to be—

"Spider." Timothy shuddered.

Katelyn's eyes turned to that spot.

"In the webs," she said, seeing the silhouette of a black spider looming in the backdrop.

Timothy turned the page after seeing nothing else could be learned. The next page's sketch depicted Pa struggling through a mighty wall of spider webs. The thick wall of spider webs looked more like a snare than anything else. But Harold persevered and cut through with his knife. Not far ahead of him, a hint of a bluish glow could be seen on the drawing, somewhere within a small chest resting upon a bench at one of the farthest ends of the basement.

This chest attracted not only the eyes of Timothy and Katelyn but also the eyes belonging to Harold.

More writing followed.

Timothy turned the page.

The following page brought relief to Timothy and Katelyn. The sketches were aligned with one another. They looked more like comic strips. The first drawing showed Pa having reached the bench. Another showed Pa's hands on each side of the chest. A faint blue glow seeped out of the chest. The sketch following this one showed the chest opening and Harold's hands cupping a translucent blue-colored gem. Unfortunately, Harold's hands covered most of it, hindering one from seeing its clearness. But Timothy knew. He knew what resided in the gem, regardless of it being a different color from the green gem upon the front binding of the book.

"Is it the same?" Katelyn asked.

"I would think so. But that would mean—"

Timothy took a more extended study at this sketch, and yes, behind Pa, still in the distance, but having come closer, a giant black spider loomed in the darkness.

This spider revealed blue smudges on its underbelly and violet-colored streaks on the sides.

"Look behind you!" Timothy shouted as if his pa could hear.

"He doesn't see it! He doesn't see it!" Katelyn cried out. "Turn the page. Turn the page, Timothy!"

Timothy turned the page.

The page on the left showed only writing, while the page to the right exhibited a single sketch. Found in this sketch was Pa battling a spider three times his size. Not only that, Pa battled thick, sticky walls of spider webs entangling him. The drawing also presented Harold aiming his rifle at the spider, with smoke discharge emitting from the muzzle.

"Did he kill it?" Katelyn asked, understanding what the smoke from the muzzle meant. "Please tell me he killed it."

Timothy turned the page.

Writing on both sides.

Timothy turned the page again.

A drawing.

The sketch proved ambiguous and yet dreadful to look at. At first, the drawing showed promise. Harold escaped the spider with his life. But he didn't escape the basement completely unscathed. He had stacked cargo boxes upon one another and used them to climb through the pit he fell through. His upper body made it through, while only a portion of his waist did, along with one leg, leaving the second leg to dangle. Another square drawing beside this drawing showed a close-up of Harold's face. Tear marks outside his eyes could be seen as if he grimaced and screamed in agony.

"Did it bite him? The spider. Did it bite him?"

"I don't know," Timothy said.

The two held on to the page a bit longer, too scared to turn it.

"But we have to," Timothy said.

He turned the page.

The following page emitted much writing, with a small portion for a single drawing. The drawing depicted Harold, alive, back on the trail, heading away from the scary black house. Both kids sighed in relief. The relief did not last long. They noticed Harold's feeble condition. Not only that, but the drawing denoted a limp in Harold's walk as if he had to drag his left leg along the trail.

They also noticed a blue glow coming from his pocket.

"The gem," Timothy said.

He turned the page, believing the chapter had ended.

He believed right.

Chapter 2
Spiders! Spiders! Spiders!

The title of the new chapter did nothing to pacify the anxieties the two had over their pa. It made them worse.

"Spiders?" Katelyn asked. "Where?"

"It's just the title," Timothy said.

"What does it mean?"

Timothy shook his head and turned the page.

The following page opened up the chapter title's drawing. Both grew confused and frightened on seeing the drawing. The drawing showed their ma and pa's bedroom. The walls and furniture of the room were dominated by itty-bitty spiders, too many to even think to count.

One person restfully lay on the bed, free of a single spider.

"Is that Pa?"

"Has to be," Timothy said.

"He's alive. That's good, isn't it?"

"Yes. He's alive. But . . ."

"The spiders. You're afraid—"

"Why aren't they on him?" Timothy asked.

"Do you think they're in his room now?"

"No."

"Then what does this all mean?"

"I don't know. All I know is—"

Timothy stopped because of the sound of thumping from the front veranda.

"Pa!"

Chapter 5

MAN OF THE HOUSE

Timothy and Katelyn rushed out of the room and hastened to the front door. Beth had done the same. Faster than the two, Timothy beat them to the door and opened it, revealing Harold Huntsinger barely standing on his two feet. His precarious stance did not dismay Timothy. His foul looks did. He looked unrecognizable. His tan complexion had turned pale, and it was riddled with patches of sallowness. He looked disturbed and confused. Unsure of everything around him. Numb to the world. His emaciated and yet swollen hands struggled to reach out for help.

Aghast by his looks, Pa's family took a step back. And they continued to step back while Harold reached out for help and nearly fell to the ground. He tried to voice this help, but it sounded more like mumbling due to a severe numbness in his mouth and tongue. Besides his deathly pale skin, morbid sallow patches, and swollen, puffy skin, Harold greatly perspired.

And the rancid stench!

One could sense a growing stench coming from the sallow patches of skin.

Beth finally broke free from her paralysis and risked an uncertain infection by taking Harold by the arm.

"Quick," she said. "To the bedroom."

Timothy envisioned myriads of spiders crawling in the room.

"No!" he shouted.

"What do you mean *no*?"

"Not the bedroom," Timothy pleaded. "Why not the living room?"

"That makes no sense," Ma said. "He needs the bedroom for comfort and isolation. We don't know what's wrong with him. He very well could be contagious."

Timothy wanted to protest more but recognized the futility of continuing to do so, even though she had already risked herself and the others.

But she was right. The obvious place was the bedroom.

Spiders sneaking through the window appeared in Timothy's mind.

I will not let that happen.

"Timothy!" his ma shouted.

Snapping out of his deep thought, Timothy nodded. "We need sheets on him," Timothy said. "He's shivering. I think he's got the fever."

"Yes," Beth said. "And water. The doctor too."

"Dr. Tennenbaum?"

"Yes."

"What about the sheriff?"

"No. The doctor, Timothy."

Timothy hesitated.

"Pa needs medicine," Beth said. "Not the law."

~

Not an hour later, Timothy returned home with the short, rotund, irritable old man named Ervin Tennenbaum, otherwise known as Dr. Tennenbaum.

Keeping to his casual ways even after Timothy zealously described how sick his pa was on multiple occasions, Dr. Tennenbaum took his time to enter the house and then the bedroom, where he found Katelyn and Beth huddled by Harold's bedside.

Neither of them moved.

"Move aside," Dr. Tennenbaum said.

Startled, Ma looked at the doctor and gave him room.

"My god!" the doctor exclaimed.

"What's wrong with my husband?"

Dr. Tennenbaum ignored her and leaned closer.

"He's getting worse," Ma said. "His skin is mostly yellow."

"Sallow," the doctor said. "As if . . ."

"As if what?"

"As if his skin has become infected. And that smell? It does have an air of infection. But no abscesses so far. It isn't pox. It could be . . . hmm. Wait."

Dr. Tennenbaum turned to Timothy. "Didn't you tell me Harold was exploring the woods that . . . You know what I'm getting at."

Timothy nodded.

"Well, there you may have it. It could easily be a strange and potent allergic reaction to some weed or plant. We don't know anything about what lives in those woods."

Timothy thought over that and found it reasonable.

"What about a spider? A big spider. Could he have an allergic reaction to that?"

"You shush," the doctor said.

Timothy wanted to say more. He wanted to bring the book and show them.

The crabby, mean old man would burn it.

"So maybe just some allergic reaction?" Beth asked.

"Yes. Perhaps."

"He will live?"

"I've seen much worse," the doctor fibbed. He turned away and grabbed the apothecary bag from Timothy. "I'll need to examine him more. First, precautions. Here," he said, giving them each a handkerchief to wear over their mouth and nose. "I want these on at all times when inside this room," he said while not putting one on himself. "And I mean it. Don't be foolish."

"You think he's contagious?"

"Don't know yet. These aren't poxes, from what I can see. And I've seen a lot. But we can't be too sure. Now leave me."

Katelyn and Beth sidled out of the room, leaving a hesitant Timothy. But not wanting to be alone with the doctor, he turned away.

"Hold on there, boy," Dr. Tennenbaum said. "Harold is sick. That's obvious. And real good sick. But I know Harold. This here sickness won't keep him down for too long. Still, he's gravely ill, and it'll take time. That leaves you in charge. Do you know what that means? You're the man of the house now. Best be strong. Calling that trail your father went on by the name of Forest Beyond is childish, just silly-childish. And now, just a minute ago, spider? Some big spider? That's even more childish. There ain't none of those black widows out in any of these forests. No spider alive can do this. Allergic reaction is what I'm thinking. Or worse, some pox I've never come across. I don't know. He's breathing, though. Strenuous, but he's alive.

"I'll be leaving soon, seeing there isn't much for me to do. I'll be giving you and your ma instructions on how best to care for him. I brought medicine and remedies to get you started. You'll oversee this. You'll oversee the whole damn house while I'm gone. Do you understand me?"

"Yes," Timothy said.

The doctor turned to the invalid. "Now leave me, boy."

Timothy obeyed and left the bedroom.

~

The doctor stayed ten minutes longer. After the doctor's leave and instructions on how to care for Harold, which included multiple refills of water, after forcing water down him, soaking the sweat from his body with a cold rag, and short routine checkups, Timothy helped his ma turn the sofa into a bed, while also soothing her agitated mind. He got her to lie down, along with Katelyn. The two snuggled on the couch together and calmed their worried minds. As for Timothy, he sat beside them on the chair Pa invariably sat on when reading the scriptures from his Bible.

Timothy now waited—waited for his family to fall asleep.

When Ma and Katelyn fell asleep, Timothy took with him the chair and crept into Pa's room. Sitting near the invalid, Timothy pondered over various thoughts leading to this moment, along with many views of the future.

No matter how much he tried, his thoughts centered only on the choices he had made so far.

If I had just shown him the book! He would have believed me. He would not have gone into that house alone.

He nodded his head.

"Yes. I'm the cause of this."

And now Pa won't wake up.

"Wake up, Pa," Timothy said, leaning closer to Harold, nowise afraid of him being contagious.

Seeing no change, Timothy shook his head.

"What have I done?"

That stupid book. And that stupid Wood Dweller.

"And that stupid—

"The gem!"

Not caring whether he woke up his ma or sister, Timothy rushed out of the room and headed to the front door with Butch at his heels. Timothy opened the door and entered the night. He hurried around the house and toward his bedroom window. Before reaching the window, he stopped at a large basket containing clothes Ma meant to wash and dry the following day. He opened the basket and searched inside—searched for Pa's overalls. Finding them, he pulled them out and noticed a heaviness to them. He nodded. He assumed Beth's plight made her ignorant of the heaviness of the overalls when putting them away.

Appreciating the good fortune, Timothy cracked the smallest of smiles and dug into the pockets. He grew a bit more elated when feeling the contour of the gem.

His elation died when grasping the whole perception of the gem, meaning the horrible events that led to this moment, as he grudgingly pulled the gem out of the pocket.

But no grudge could compete with the true beauty of the gem and what resided inside.

Timothy forgot all worries and tragedy and stared breathlessly at the beauty.

"It's so," he said, unsure how to describe it. "It's the same girl. No. It's not the same girl."

The beautiful girl he spoke of rested inside the gem with both eyes open, each a soft blue, and hands folded neatly over her bosom. Besides that, many other differences appeared, including this girl younger than the mysterious one on the front cover, possibly younger than Timothy. She wore a tiara like the one on the cover, except this one held three stars, not seven brilliantly white orbs. The girl's hair, eyes, and skin did not change. Her hair stayed reddish, with blue streaks matching her soft blue eyes. She also wore a darker, more midnight-blue dress, a dress that fitted the gem's translucent sky-blue color.

Her lips were ruddy red, and everything about her seemed alive—an actual breathing creature.

Her magnificence was startling for Timothy to behold, although still not as magnificent as the woman inside the green gem on the front cover.

But that one did not rest in his hands.

"*Gem and Spider,*" he said, thinking over the book's title.

But what does this all mean?

Not knowing the answer to that, Timothy returned to the present plight.

"I must hide it."

But where?

His eyes landed on the bundle of firewood and bricks.

"Why not?"

Timothy hurried over to the bundle, and as he hid the book earlier, he did the same with the gem. Afterward, he tiptoed back into Pa's room.

Butch did the same. Sitting on the chair, Timothy found a book from Ma's bookshelf and tried to read—tried, because it was challenging to concentrate. His eyes then grew heavy. He forced them to open a few times. After a few nods and a few pushbacks, sleep became too much. He lacked sleep. It had been a long day. He gave in.

He fell soundly to sleep.

Chapter 6

WORSE TO WORST

"Timothy."

Timothy climbed out of sleep when hearing his name. Ma stood before him. Her hand was on his shoulder.

"You're not supposed to be here," Beth said.

"You think the doctor could keep me away from Pa?"

Beth smiled. "You should sleep on your bed. I'll take the watch."

"You sure?"

"Positive," Ma said. "Morning will be here soon. The entirety of the chores falls on you. You'll need the rest."

Timothy saw the logic in that and nodded.

A minute later, he found himself in his room. Katelyn followed. They sat across from each other on their bed.

"Will Pa be OK?" Katelyn asked.

"Sure," Timothy said.

Too tired to resist a lie, Katelyn smiled and rested on the bed. Timothy found comfort in the girl's forgetfulness of the book and the eerie chapter title.

He too rested and prayed for this to be a nightmare.

One horrific nightmare.

But a few hours later, another shout of his name reminded him that this was no nightmare.

The shout of his name came from Ma and from the bedroom. Therefore, Timothy slipped out of bed and noticed Katelyn was still asleep.

"Good for her," he said as he left the bedroom.

Seconds later, he took two steps inside Ma and Pa's bedroom and reached a standstill.

"I fell asleep," Ma said. "I woke up and . . . this."

Timothy mustered what courage he had and stepped fully into the room. One glance told him all.

Pa looked more alive than before. The fever had departed, for he exhibited no signs of the chill, and the paleness dissolved away. But no good could come out of the sallowness from before. Instead, the sallowness took on a whole new level of destruction. It prevailed on every inch of the body and brought with it even more swelling, combined with the previous inflammation that showed no letdown. Instead, the swelling increased. And the putrid stench from yesterday also grew in strength, although never pungent enough to force one to shrink away or gag for an extended period.

"Is he dying?" Beth asked. "Look. Look at my Harold."

Timothy chose silence. His thoughts rested only on the drawing of the new chapter.

But where are the spiders? And Pa still does not resemble the other Pa. What's this mean?

"What do we do?" Beth asked.

"We fetch Dr.—"

The interruption came by means of that same doctor shouting, "By god!"

Both Timothy and Beth turned around and stared at a ghastly-looking Dr. Tennenbaum. Behind the latter stood a disturbed Sheriff Jack Riggins. So disturbed, the sheriff unholstered his handgun.

"What's wrong with my husband?" Beth asked.

"I thought you said a bad fever—possible allergic reaction?" the sheriff stammered. "This is . . . What is this?"

"I know what I said," Dr. Tennenbaum said. He turned his focus sharply on Timothy. "What happened here?"

Timothy shook his head.

"Hmm. This isn't good. It confirms my suspicion, an allergic reaction of some kind. And now it has turned into an infection. But of what? What could do such a thing in those woods?"

"A spider bite," Timothy said. "Like I told you last night."

"Spider?" a confounded sheriff said. "What's the kid talking about?"

"Don't listen to him," the doctor said. "And what did I tell you about that nonsense? No spider in the world could do this."

"But even you said there's no telling what's in the Forest Beyond."

"Didn't I say not to use that term? And I wasn't talking about some spider. I was talking about botany. And maybe, just maybe . . . an insect. No spider!"

"But isn't a spider—"

"Shut up," the sheriff said. "This ain't no spider bite, kid."

Timothy could no longer stand idle. Pa's looks had grown far more terrible than he imagined. He had to do something. He must give proof. But how to do that without risking the book or gem?

There's no other way.

Then we have to do it.

But the risks involved?

To save Pa's life?

He received his answer. He stepped before the doctor.

"What is it?"

"There's something I need to tell you," Timothy said.

"Save it. You've already wasted valuable time. Right now, it's all about getting to the root of Harold's suffering."

"That's what I want to talk to you about."

"Make it quick, boy."

"There's this book," Timothy said. He stopped because of anxieties overwhelming his mind. His breathing became erratic. His fortitude diminished. But he had to go on. He had to push through. "Remember the trail I spoke about?" Timothy said that toward his ma. "Well, it was made by—" The word or words couldn't come out. Thus, he expelled them rashly. "By a book I found. It's not what any of us think a book is. And I didn't find it. It was given to me. Or I should say, I chose it. You won't believe how and by whom I was given this chance. But it was given to me, and this trail appeared when I opened the book. Not only that, I learned that this trail leads to a very scary-looking black house. Something horrible hides in it. I swear. And I'm also very sure it is a spider. Monster size. That's where Pa went. And this spider, you see, this spider came down from the—"

"Stop!" Dr. Tennenbaum shouted in the quietest of voices. "Stop."

Timothy looked around. Sheriff Riggins stared at him maliciously.

"Screwing around, kid?" the sheriff said. "At a time like this? With your pa possibly on his deathbed?"

"No!" Timothy shouted. "I'm not screwing around. I can show you. I can show you the trail and—"

The sheriff interrupted him by grabbing him by the shoulder with much hostility. "Now you listen to me, kid," the sheriff said, squeezing Timothy's arm. Timothy held back a wince of pain. He dared not give the sheriff the pleasure of seeing him in pain. "Your pa and I have been best of buds for some time. So I don't want to hear this damn crap, especially seeing how much he suffers. You hear me?"

The sheriff squeezed tighter. "Answer me."

"Ye-yes . . . yes, sir."

"Good. Now get on out of here and let us adults—not children—worry about Harold.

Timothy slowly stepped away when released by the sheriff. He stopped at the doorway and turned around.

Did I do enough? Maybe I didn't. I didn't show them anything. But they'll never believe me, even if the truth smacks them in the face.

"What are you waiting for?" the sheriff said. "Out with you!"

Timothy crept back into this room with a single conviction in mind. Only he could save Harold.

~

Timothy did not have the luxury to ponder his options for long inside his room. The day's chores awaited. Therefore, he left the room and his sister behind. His sister seemed OK with that. She fell into her fantasy world while playing with her dolls and toys. Not once did Timothy attempt to steal her away from her make-believe world. He knew better not to. This was her defense mechanism. Her escape. She found no sorrow, no pain when inside her imagination. Timothy did not mind this. His ma felt it to be harmful. She felt her level of fantasy needed to be curbed. Beth also felt the same about Timothy when he was Katelyn's age. Timothy shook his head at that thought. Ma could not have been any more wrong.

Outside the house, Timothy commenced on the morning chores.

His entire plan centered on finishing early and hoping both doctor and sheriff had departed. This did not work in his favor. The two decided to keep watches. The sheriff took the first watch while the doctor left for other visitations. Timothy tasted bitter defeat when seeing the handshake between the two. He felt trapped. Powerless. This feeling grew worse as the day lengthened and came to an end. The doctor returned to relieve the sheriff. But the doctor did not return alone.

A nurse stood at his side.

Seeing this nurse, Timothy became demoralized.

He returned to the last of the chores, crestfallen. He now contemplated going to the extreme by revealing the gem.

"Worst idea yet," he uttered to himself.

Shaking his head, he regained strength, overcame despair, and finished the chores.

Returning home, he stepped inside the house and quickly spotted a second makeshift bed in the already crowded living room.

Who could that be for?

An image of the nurse manifested itself in his mind.

"No," he muttered.

Timothy discerned the nurse and doctor both in Pa's room. Maybe even Ma inside the room too.

He didn't want to be near them.

Timothy snuck back outside.

~

An hour passed by. Timothy did not enter the house during that hour to check up on his pa. To do that meant confronting the doctor and nurse. He still didn't have it in him to do such a thing. He wanted to be alone, away from everyone. He *needed* to be alone—alone with his thoughts. He kept himself busy outside the house. He ventured farther to the creek, where he grabbed rocks and skipped them along the water. He even thought about going farther. But he decided it might not be prudent to distance himself that far from the house. He even felt the creek to be too far, thus the reason he did not stay at the creek for that long. He had spent only so little time there before returning home. Luckily, when he reached home, his ma called for him to attend supper.

At the kitchen table, he found everyone there—nurse and doctor. An empty chair waited for him between Katelyn and Beth. Many fruits and other assorted provisions were found on the table, each picked by Timothy and his ma.

Timothy reluctantly sat down.

"Timothy Huntsinger," Dr. Tennenbaum said formally, "meet Nurse Teeter. She's going to be taking good care of Harold."

Timothy nodded.

"A polite greeting besides a nod of your head is the least you can do," the doctor said.

"It's OK," the nurse said. "I'm quite used to what is obviously an ungrateful, spoiled child."

"I'm not a child."

"And he's not spoiled or ungrateful," Ma said.

The nurse emitted a humph.

Everyone fell to eating but Timothy. He sulked instead.

"Best you eat," Dr. Tennenbaum said. "You're going to need your strength. The daily chores are yours for an unforeseeable future."

Timothy picked up his fork. But a single glance toward the doctor and nurse forced him to place the fork down.

They disgusted him. Just staring at them eating the food his ma and he labored all day to bring to the table, and not a single sign of gratitude disgusted him. He saw it in their faces. They didn't care. What did it matter to them that they stole from the fruits of another's hard labor? Hell, they enjoyed this. They enjoyed this free room and board and food to boot.

He wanted them out—out of the house before they became glued to the walls and contaminated everything inside.

Out of the house before it was too late for a priest to exorcise their remnants.

"Don't want to eat, eh?" the doctor said, snapping Timothy out of his hateful trance.

Timothy stayed silent.

"Nor speak? How about work? You finished everything?"

Timothy nodded.

"How long ago?"

Timothy shrugged his shoulders.

"I'm assuming far over an hour," the doctor said. "That said, you've been done all this time and not yet have you checked up on your pa?"

Timothy grinned the doctor's way.

"Sounds like an ungrateful child to me," the doctor said. "Even if your ma says different. No time to visit your pa? What a shame."

Timothy's angry grin turned wicked. The doctor did not see the change; he stuffed his fat face with a giant chicken bone.

"Very sad," Nurse Teeter said. "Not only are you breaking your pa's heart, but you're doing the same to your ma. If I were her, I'd give you a hard lesson in manners. Give you a cold slap over that head of yours. And this I promise you! You'd not be sitting around this table, eating this hard-earned food. Oh no. You'd be locked in that room, repenting."

"Except," Timothy continued, "you're not my ma. You're a stranger—an old hag! Just like him," he said with a finger pointing at the doctor.

"Timothy!" Beth shouted. "Apologize right now."

"For what?"

"Timothy!"

"Don't you see what's happening? They're trying to take control. And I won't let them. This is our house."

Beth felt the truth of what he said. Her anger lessened. But what could she do? Pa's plight had decimated her greatly.

"Timothy," she said feebly. "Please. Apologize and stop this bickering."

Before Timothy could respond, the doctor responded first. "Timothy," he said pitifully, feigning condolence. "We're not here to take control. We just think your parents deserve better, more love from you."

"More love? You're questioning my love for them?"

"That's not what we're saying," the nurse said. "We're saying—"

"I know what you're saying. And I don't want to hear it," Timothy said.

He turned to his ma. "I don't want them here. They're horrible people. They're maggots, seeing how they're feeding off our weakness."

Feeling he had gone too far, Timothy stood up. "Please excuse me from the table."

Beth shook her head. "I'm sorry. But I want you right here with your sister and me. We're family."

"If I may interject," Nurse Teeter said. "I don't think it's a bad idea to excuse him. Give this ungrateful child a time-out."

"Ungrateful?" Beth turned to the nurse wrathfully. "Never has my son been ungrateful—and again, he's not a child! Now," she said, calming down, "I'm his mother, and I tell him when he is to be excused from the table. Not you. And certainly not you," she said, with eyes on Dr. Tennenbaum.

Timothy felt a surge of pride for his mother and smiled.

"Thank you," he said, placing his hand on Ma's shoulder. "But I'd still like to be excused."

Beth gave in with a weak nod. "But don't be saying you're not hungry. I know you are. I'll stop by your room with some food."

"Thanks, Ma."

"What about me?" Katelyn asked. "May I be excused?"

Seeing the melancholy written on his ma's face, Timothy answered. "You stay. Stay with Ma and ensure she has somebody who loves her and Pa by her side. OK?"

Katelyn nodded while the doctor and nurse glanced scathingly at Timothy. Timothy returned with his own scathing look.

He turned away and left the kitchen, but not before giving his ma and sister a kiss on their forehead.

~

On his way to his room, Timothy stopped at Pa's room. The door stood cracked open. He placed his hands upon the handle, and when doing so, he felt a wave of apprehension. He could not find the strength to open the door. He feared that by going inside, he'd find no Pa. Instead, he'd find a horrible-looking monster waiting for him, a great, giant black spider wanting to devour his entire family. But then, it wouldn't be a spider. It would be something else. A creation from the venom Pa received from the spider. A monster of defiled looks, yet resembling Pa in every other way.

"No," Timothy said, shaking off that image.

Pa will be fine. Just open the door and see to it.

Timothy pushed the door open.

When he saw his pa and not some grotesque monster, much relief came to Timothy. He looked closer. No changes could be found. But that did not mean bad news. The swelling and sallowness continued to prevail. As Timothy crept closer, he noticed rasping breathing, seeing Pa's chest expand and decrease more than ever before. Timothy didn't think much of that. He attributed this change to Pa's breathing from his last two days of suffering.

"Please be an allergic reaction," Timothy said. "Not a spider bite. Not a spider bite. And if it is, not from such a big spider. Tell me it's a lie. The book made it up. It's just a book, right? But if it's not just a book, I don't want it. I don't want any of this. Why did I agree to this? Why did I open that stupid, stupid book? This is all my fault. I did this. I did this to everyone. I should never have opened the book. I should never have believed. And I never should have allowed you to go on the trail alone. Why? Why didn't I stand up to you? How did I allow myself to be so weak? You ordered me to go home, but I should have defied you. I'm a coward. I ran away. I never gave you a chance to believe."

Shaking his head, Timothy clenched his fists.

"Stupid Wood Dweller!"

His venting softened. "I'll fix this. You watch. I just need more time. Then I'll save you and the rest of the family from my stupid decisions."

A minute later, Timothy arrived inside his room. Not more than two minutes later, Katelyn and Ma joined him.

They each came together and embraced.

"We'll always be together," Timothy said.

"You promised," Katelyn said, clutching her necklace.

"Yes," Timothy said. "And I mean it now more than ever."

"And I mean it too," Ma said.

They hugged one another tighter.

"Enough of this," Beth said, releasing herself from the embrace and wiping the tears off her face. "No one is going to lose anyone. Understand me?"

The kids both nodded. They hugged again.

"How much longer?" Timothy asked as the embrace softened.

"Until?"

"They leave."

"I guess until Pa is better."

"And if they can't help him?"

Ma blinked. "I don't know. Timothy?"

"Yes."

"Where did Pa go?"

Timothy cringed and looked down. "You know where," he said.

"The trail?"

Timothy looked up and stared into his ma's eyes as if he could force her to believe. "Yes. And you must believe me."

Timothy saw a credulous look upon Ma's face for the first time since speaking of the trail.

"I know how it sounds," Timothy said, taking advantage of this moment. "I do. Sounds impossible. Fantasy. But it's there, Ma. It really is. And it leads to—" He stopped. He couldn't say it. He didn't want to ruin what he had just gained by sharing too much. "I can show you something that will help you believe me. Yes. I can show you this," he said as he reached under the bed. Just as he pulled the book out, Dr. Tennenbaum's vehement shout interrupted Ma's concentration.

Timothy lost all momentum he built inside of Beth.

"Come quick, Beth! Come quick! Great news! Great news! Come quickly now!"

Timothy endeavored to hold back his ma. He had just seen Pa. He perceived the doctor as acting dramatically for deliberate reasons.

What could have changed in such a short matter of time?

Nothing. He made it up to steal Ma away from me, as if I'm poison to her vulnerable mind.

His hold on his ma broke down completely when hearing the doctor's voice again.

"Come now, Mrs. Huntsinger. Now!"

Ma stood up from the bed.

"No, Ma," Timothy said. "Let me show you this first. And then a second thing—"

"Hurry, Mrs. Huntsinger!" came the nurse's voice. "No time to lose. Your husband needs you."

"He needs me," Beth said plaintively.

Timothy felt the pain in her eyes.

He let go in defeat.

Beth hurried out of the room as Timothy watched. He then walked to the closed door and put his ear against it.

What he heard confirmed his suspicion—nothing but malarkey.

Timothy snarled while hearing the meaningless talk. He turned back to his bed.

"Good news?" Katelyn asked.

"The worst."

Chapter 7

UNDER LOCK AND KEY

"*He's coming,*" the voice of Wood Dweller said inside Timothy's sleeping mind.

"*He? Who's he?*" Timothy answered.

"*Never mind who he is, only that your choices have led him to come sooner than even I thought. Choices, Timothy. They've been . . .*"

"*Been what?*"

Timothy's sleeping mind discerned a smile on the creature's face.

"*Look around,*" the creature said. "*This is all because of your choices.*"

"*So, it is true. I am to blame. I caused all this. And it's exactly what I fear: a spider bite. Am I not right?*"

"*Why do you humans seek answers to questions you've already answered? Do not for a second underestimate the opening of the book. You have unleashed an unimaginable power. One cannot fathom the power invested inside the book. The importance of it has no rival. The importance you must know for now is that your world will no longer be your world. Your world will cease to exist. It will become a world suspended in Void,* hoping *to return. And if not returned, it will be forever lost—doomed to Oblivion. You must not quit, Timothy. You must never quit. You must see the book to its end. And I, Timothy, I cannot do what I am doing now. I should not be helping you. And I shall not help after this. I have no part in all of this, no part of anything. Don't forget that. Don't forget that I am not an entity of any kind. I will suffer no consequences whether you fail or succeed. It doesn't matter to me. The sooner you grasp that, the better it will be for* all *the worlds you touch upon.*

"*Wake up, Timothy! Wake up. A storm comes your way.*"

Timothy woke up with the belief of having dreamed, except not a glimmer of the dream lingered.

"But I'm sure I dreamed," he muttered. *A dream I've never experienced before.*

With this dream came the belief of conversing with someone unknown to him. And yet, not a single word or purport of the conversation could be extracted by his mind. Nor would it be for a very long time. His dream ventured far too deep for him or anyone else to recall, even with assistance of some kind. His dream traveled beyond all realms of consciousness, the subconscious and the unconscious mind. His dream stepped into a forbidden territory where one's mind should never cross: a land of desolation and many consequences, a place where many lose their mind, never to have it return.

Nor would they want their mind to return from such a consequential place—afraid of what the mind may have turned to in order to survive such a place.

But he survived with his mind intact.

Timothy slowly stepped off his bed without waking his sister. He turned to the drapes and noticed no morning sunlight.

Only darkness.

He couldn't believe it. He swore he slept past his usual time.

Shouldn't it be dawn?

Leaning toward the drapes, he opened them and saw a distant storm brewing, blocking what should have been the sun.

Oblivious of the last words the Wood Dweller spoke and yet strangely familiar with this impending storm as if expecting it, Timothy greeted the storm with a nod of his head. He then left his room to visit Pa.

Before entering Pa's room, Timothy glanced into the living room. Nurse Teeter slept soundly on the floor in her makeshift bed. Ma was nowhere to be seen. He turned his attention to Pa's room. Again, the door stood cracked open. He spied inside and noticed his ma sitting on a chair beside Pa. Timothy silently stepped into the room and kissed his sleeping mother on the forehead. He directed his eyes on Pa. The sheets covered most of his body, and the gloomy outside hindered Timothy from any view. He stepped closer. He leaned over Pa's face.

He looked down.

What he saw made him step back.

"It can't be," he uttered.

He wanted to see more, though. He had to see more. He took one step forward and grabbed the corners of the sheets.

One. Two. Three!

On three, he pulled the sheets off. What came next from his mouth was a scream capable of waking the dead.

"What is it?" Beth shouted, awake. She stood up and joined her son. First, she looked at her frightened son. She looked down at her husband.

She, too, could not hold back a monstrous cry.

The nurse came bustling in a second later. "What's the commotion?" She stopped at Beth's side and looked down. "Good Lord."

As for Katelyn, she didn't come close to the door before turning away and finding escape in her fantasy world.

The cause of this horror came by means of poxes.

A plague of poxes prevailed upon Harold's entire body, including his entire face. These abscesses proved far too swollen and thick to be any sort Nurse Teeter had ever seen, with the oddity of them mimicking each one perfectly while leaving the very tiniest of space between them. The pus inside them seemed to be ten times more than usual.

Along with the appearance of abscesses, the swallow color that diminished a bit the night before returned with a vengeance.

The putrid stench also returned.

The three stood paralyzed for a long moment. The moment ended, and Nurse Teeter shook her head.

"I've never seen anything like this. Look at them. There are so many of them. And how fat they are! We should not be here. We must leave the room."

"And leave my pa alone?" Timothy objected.

"Yes. We're already at risk where we stand," the nurse said as she dragged Ma away by her shoulder. Ma proved too weak to resist.

Timothy did not want to leave. No. Not as long as Pa could breathe. But this was different. These poxes were different.

He needed to learn about them.

How to learn about them?

"The book!" he said.

Timothy ignored the nurse when asked where he was going. He entered his room.

Inside, he found Katelyn absorbed in her toys and dolls. He stood and watched her for a good second or two. He hoped to god that she'd never leave this fantasy world of hers, at least not until Pa could walk again. Timothy also became envious of her. He, too, wanted to fall into oblivion and feel no more pain and anguish. He also wanted to escape the guilt he kept feeling for causing all this. The longer he stood watching her so immune to what felt like a vise squeezing his heart, the more depressed he became.

But he could not let this rule his mind.

"The book," he said.

Katelyn popped out of her fantasy world when hearing Timothy.

"Is Pa dead?"

Timothy shook his head when reaching the bed.

"But the screaming?"

Timothy ignored her and pulled out the book.

"Not that," Katelyn said. "Please, not that! It's the devil."

Ignoring her again, Timothy opened the book to the current chapter title and turned the page. To his dismay, blank pages followed.

"Damn," he said.

He returned to the chapter title.

"Spiders. OK? What else?"

He turned the page to study the drawing.

"Yes. Millions of them. But what does this mean? Where are these—"

He stopped. He closed the book.

"What is it?" Katelyn asked.

He turned to the closed door as if he could see through Pa's room and the countless poxes.

"They've been here the whole time."

"What has?"

"Incubating."

"What are you talking about?"

"The spiders. They're *inside* Pa."

~

A clear vision of countless spiders popping out of the sacs riddled over Pa appeared in Timothy's mind. Impetuously, he jumped off the bed with the book and left the room. He didn't stop his impulsive rush till he barged into Harold's room, never taking notice of both doctor and sheriff conversing with each other by the front door. Nurse Teeter and Ma sat on the sofa, trying to salve the wounds they received when discovering Pa's new condition.

"Timothy!" Beth screamed, seeing Timothy rush through the living room hall. "Don't go in there!"

Timothy ignored her and didn't stop until reaching Pa. He looked at the countless sacs. He then placed a timid finger upon one. He pushed down. He felt a liquid goo inside. He went to examine more, but a shout from Dr. Tennenbaum stopped him.

"Get your hand off those poxes!"

"They're not poxes," Timothy said. "Nor are they reactions to allergies. They're sacs. Egg sacs, filled with spiders."

The doctor wasted no time in grabbing Timothy by the collar and shoving his face before his. By this time, everyone but Katelyn had joined them in the room.

"You listen to me—"

"I'm telling the truth!"

"The hell with your truth. They're not goddamn spiders. There's no such thing. It's a disease, one that I'm unfamiliar with."

"No. And I can prove it."

Timothy pulled the book out before the doctor's face.

He opened it.

"You see this?" Timothy said, showing him the contents of the book. "That's Pa. Those are spiders. They're going to burst out of those sacs."

Not one adult came close to glancing at the book. They were too stunned by hearing Timothy's theory to think of doing such a thing.

"Timothy," the doctor said after a few seconds passed. His tone was filled with sorrow for the boy, as if he did pity him this time. "Oh, Timothy, you have to forget this fantasy, this delusion of yours, for that is what you are suffering—delusion."

"But this book—"

The interruption came from Sheriff Riggins stealing the book away.

"No!" Timothy shouted. "You can't take it."

"Too late, kid," the sheriff said. Timothy tried to take the book back. The two fell into a struggle. Surprisingly, Timothy showed great strength.

In the end though, the sheriff's older strength proved victorious.

"You can't have the book," Timothy pleaded. "Only I can possess it. The Wood Dweller said there'd be consequences, grave consequences—not only for our world but also for the world to come. I must finish the book. It's a magical book. There lies another world inside it."

Everyone looked unimaginably dumbfounded at Timothy, even Timothy, for he realized precisely what he said.

"I can explain," he said.

"Wood Dweller?" Beth questioned. "Some magical book you must finish? Another world? Is this what you wanted to share with me?"

Timothy looked down at the ground.

"Answer me!" Beth exclaimed.

"Yes," Timothy said. He lifted his head and stared into her eyes. "It is magical. I can prove it. I can show you the gem. It's unlike anything in our world. One look at it and—"

"Enough!" Beth screamed.

"But, Ma—"

"No."

"You have to listen to me. You have to—"

"Your room."

Timothy wanted to cry. He wanted to break down and open the floodgate to his emotions. He wanted to show them how afflicted he had become from not being believed, especially his ma. But this he could not do. He would not allow the breakdown. He would not let them defeat him. He would stay strong and not give in to anger and grief, which both gnawed away at him. Steeling himself, he faced his adversaries with much scorn and anger on his face, excluding his ma. These were his enemies. He despised them as anyone would despise their closest foes. He had no feelings for them. They could rot in hell, and he wouldn't give a damn about it. And he would use this anger and hatred to fuel the fires burning inside him.

"Fine," Timothy said. "Have it your way."

~

"Are you all right?" Katelyn asked as Timothy entered the bedroom.

"Never been better."

"Something is wrong."

"Leave it alone, sis—for your own good."

"But—"

The door of the room opened. Beth stood at the opening.

"Grab your stuff," she said to Katelyn. "You're leaving the room for the day."

"What about Timothy?" Katelyn asked.

"He's staying in here . . . alone."

"For how long?" Katelyn asked.

"For as long as I say so."

"But—"

"Katelyn. Out."

Katelyn hurried and gathered her toys and dolls. She kept looking over at Timothy sadly.

Timothy had eyes only for Ma.

"You're making a big mistake," Timothy said.

"It's for your best."

Timothy stood up. As he did, Ma could not help but see the replica of her husband in Timothy. An exact copy. She saw the strength, determination, and powerful stature found in Harold. This frightened her. The fear did not come from him harming her. The fear came from the unmatched resolve that could break anybody's stubborn will. If he wanted his way that very second, there would be very few people in the world to stop him from doing so.

But like Harold, Timothy carried a sincere and caring heart, making it near impossible to take advantage of one's inferiority.

"Ma," Timothy said in a severe tone, "what's best for me is best for all of us. You must start believing me now. You must get rid of these outsiders and give Pa to our caring, and soon! We don't have much time. There is a storm coming our way. I don't know why I know this, but this storm is unlike anything we've witnessed. It will come like a metallic darkness.

"It comes for us and for the world that will follow."

Timothy had gone too far. His immature age defeated him, for he had his ma lured in but lost her once speaking of the storm and the other world.

"No," Beth said. "Listen to yourself. What you say is . . ."

She couldn't find the words. She turned to Katelyn.

"Out, I said!"

Katelyn stood up defiantly. "No. I'm staying with Timothy."

"No, you're not. Resist me, and I'll drag you out of this room *without* your toys and dolls."

The prospect of being without them proved fatal to Katelyn. She'd find it much more difficult to slip into her fantasy world. She thus dropped her head and gathered the last of her belongings.

"I'm sorry," Katelyn said as she sadly left the room.

Timothy nodded back.

"And I'm sorry too," Beth said.

"Not as much as I'm sorry for you and the mistake you're making," Timothy said adamantly, scaring Beth again, for his tone was fierce and razor-sharp.

"It has to be done," Beth said, more for herself.

"No. What has to be done is you start believing me over those strangers."

"But," Beth said and shook her head, "I can't."

"And again, I'm sorry for you," Timothy said that and looked away.

Beth eventually nodded and left the room.

Never did they say goodbye to each other.

~

A minute following Ma's leave, Timothy's bedroom door opened.

Thinking his ma had a change of mind and heart, Timothy's eyes grew zealous. But instead of Ma, Nurse Teeter stood at the opening.

In her hand, she flaunted a house key.

"In case you have ideas of escaping," she said.

Timothy smiled. The smile wiped away the one Nurse Teeter carried. What Timothy said next unnerved her even more.

"See you in hell, you old witch!"

Nurse Teeter's heart trembled. Nobody had ever spoken to her like that. She even lost grip of the key as it fell to the ground, and she scrambled to regain it. Her trembling hands made it difficult to possess the key. Timothy laughed at this. She recovered enough composure to still her hands. She picked up the key, stood back, and went to leave the room.

Timothy had one last word to say to her.

"Bitch!"

Nurse Teeter felt another flutter in her heart. She stood stunned. She then shook it off and slammed the door closed.

Timothy heard the lock of the door.

His mind shifted to something far more critical.

The book.

"Now, how to get the book back?"

Before he could contemplate how to solve such a problem, tapping at the window stole his attention. He turned to the window and stared back at the face belonging to Sheriff Riggins. The sheriff had used the book to rap against the window. His look of mockery beckoned Timothy over. Seeing the boy hesitant, the sheriff's derisive smile widened.

"Rap, rap. I'm rapping at your window," the sheriff teased. He chuckled. "That's fine. Bold spirit. I like it. I also know you can hear me. Don't be worried about the fieldwork. I've got my sons over here soon. As for the book, well, you'll have it again. But not now, not until you cease this childish fantasy of yours. Soon as that happens and your pa is on the mend, I'll hand it over to *him*. Let him decide its fate. Until then, this here is my book."

Timothy wanted to lash out in anger but felt it wise to stay calm and collected.

But the sheriff wasn't finished. "By the way, if you're thinking of climbing out of this window, bet again," the sheriff said as he revealed a heavy brass bar. He prevented the window from opening by placing the bar on the windowsill. "For your own well-being."

Timothy's state of calmness nearly snapped. He had to use all his willpower not to turn wrathful.

As for the sheriff, he rapped on the window one last time and left Timothy's presence.

Chapter 8

THE RECKONING

Timothy watched the sheriff depart. When the sheriff was out of sight, Timothy focused on the closed bedroom door. He now decided that he must kick open the door. The door seemed strong to him. But he believed a powerful charge and a few hard kicks would do the trick. He settled his mind on that. He only had to wait. And as he waited, his mind drifted to the storm. He believed the storm outside was only a prelude of something greater—a harbinger of a much more consequential storm as if the storm's sole purpose of existence was to lay the groundwork for a cataclysmic storm to appear not long after.

He did not know how he knew this, including the thought of this second storm being no ordinary storm but one full of blackness and metallic lightning.

He attributed the mystery to the already mysterious dream he believed he had.

He also thought about his pa's condition. No longer did Timothy doubt. *There are like a thousand or more spiders inside him, waiting to burst out.*

But what on earth could he do?

"Show her the gem," Timothy said.

Yes. But how to get it?

He looked to the window. Ignoring the impediment, being the brass bar, he focused on the soon arrival of Sheriff Riggins's sons. To escape his room now would only land him in their custody. They were bigger, older, and stronger. If it were one or two of them, he'd have a chance. But three of them? No. The boys would also crave an opportunity to be his demise. They never liked Timothy. Of course, this stemmed from jealousy. They were jealous of how the town heaped praise on Timothy, whether he deserved it or not. They were also jealous of Timothy's brute strength and advanced intelligence.

Being the son of the most revered person in town also did not help the jealous complexity.

But the boys would have to leave at some point.

"And then I'll make my move."

~

Three o'clock came, along with the first drops of rain. The heart of the storm was still hours before touching down. For most of the day, Timothy watched this storm. Watching helped ease his mind while also organizing his endless thoughts. Besides this storm being a precursor for another, he viewed this coming storm as a direct link to Pa's suffering. Again, he had no reason why he came up with this theory. But the theory proved strong in his discombobulated mind. He thought this first storm would trigger a response in Pa, or maybe the other way around: something must happen to Pa before the storm could show its true face.

No, Timothy thought. *The storm is the trigger. Pa is the gun.*
The bullet is the following storm.
What uncertainty comes after the second storm is the impact and consequence.

~

Five o'clock came, and Timothy watched Sheriff Riggins arrive.
He came for his sons.
Before his final departure, the boys closed in on Timothy's window and snickered in his direction while the sheriff told them to stop teasing that foolish child with a derisive smile.
Timothy ignored both.
Thus, the sheriff and his boys left, leaving only the nurse and doctor. Not an hour later, the doctor said goodbye.
Nurse Teeter now remained.
Timothy would execute his plan regardless of whether the nurse left or not. If she tried to stop him, he was ready to do anything necessary to hinder her from him procuring the gem. Once possessing the gem, he believed Ma and even Nurse Teeter could no longer repudiate his story. Because how could they when seeing a real-life person locked inside a hand-sized gem? How could they not believe this to be magic? They would then believe in the book. They would believe in everything.
He'd be exonerated.
He'd be free to order everyone out of the house, explaining the imminent danger.
He'd stay, though. He'd see this through.

He owed that to his pa.

But as far as saving his pa's life?

Timothy took a deep breath in and a deeper one out.

I can't save him.

"And that's why I must finish the book," Timothy adamantly said, thinking that this all would return to normalcy by ending the book.

"Because that's what the Wood Dweller said, right?"

He tried to recall the exact words the Wood Dweller said. In doing so, he heard something very favorable to him.

The nurse geared up to leave for the night.

~

Beth led the nurse into the rainy outside, with a gas lamp in her hand. The nurse reached her horse and turned to Beth.

"Ugly storm or not, I'll be here first thing in the morning."

"Thank you," Beth said.

"Don't thank just me. Thank us all. Thank yourself. You've been strong, Beth Huntsinger, very strong. Now, stay strong. Don't let that childish boy put a spell on you. The good Lord knows he can."

Beth nodded her head perfunctorily.

Nurse Teeter nodded back and climbed up on the horse. Beth helped. A second later, the nurse rode away.

"He's not a childish boy," Beth muttered.

She turned away and stepped toward the house. She caught sight of Timothy's window. She felt pity swelling up in her. The closer she came to the house, the more she wanted to free him. She shook her head at that feeling. *He needs to learn. He needs to know that he's been acting foolishly and it needs to stop.*

Taking one step into the house, Katelyn confronted her.

"She's gone?" Katelyn asked.

"Yes."

"Good. We can free Timothy."

"No."

Before Katelyn could argue back, Timothy could be heard softly speaking from the bedroom.

"Ma?"

"I'm not talking to you. You're to be punished."

"I just want to know if everyone is gone for the night."

"They're all gone."

"Then it's time," Timothy said gravely. The gravity of his words captivated her. "It is time for you to see her."

"See her? Who's *her*?" Beth said as she took a few steps toward the closed bedroom door.

"Wait!" she said and stopped. "This is another game you're trying to play. I'm not falling for this."

"It's no game."

"Maybe not to you. But I bet the second I open the door, you'll fly right out."

"I give you my word that I will not do that. I want you to believe on your own. Outside my window, I buried an object under the bricks and firewood. You'll find it there, and then you'll believe."

"You want me to go out in the rain—again?"

"To save our lives? Yes."

Beth gulped down some air. She believed he meant the truth. She believed that in his mind, *everything* was true.

She had to give him this chance.

"Fine. But if—"

"Don't worry. You will."

The drizzling rain came down harder when Beth stepped outside again. One must be extraordinarily dumb not to realize how hard the rain would soon be. Flashes of lightning could be seen—vaguely—followed by rolling thunder, still some miles away. Ignoring the rain as best as she could, she hurried over to the pile of firewood and brick and put her lamp down. She looked toward Timothy's window. He had planted his face on the window. She stared into his eyes. He stared back and nodded. He pointed toward the firewood and bricks. She looked at them again and shook her head.

"Fine," she said. "But it ends now."

She removed the first piece of dry firewood, seeing how a shelter above protected this area from rain.

A bluish glow quickly sparkled in her eyes after lifting the firewood. The darkness of the night made it much easier for the light to be seen. This light fixed her attention. Deep below this bundle of firewood, something she could not fathom resided, and the more the light sparkled in her eyes, the more enthralled she became. The light became everything to her. She must have this light. She must possess what object this must be that gave off such a mesmerizing glow. And when she came to the last of the firewood and lifted it, she nearly fainted backward, only to regain strength to stare more deeply at the object.

"It . . . it can't be," she muttered.

"Now, do you believe?" Timothy said, audible enough for her to hear through the window.

Beth nodded her head.

"Free me."

Beth procured the gem from the bottom of the firewood and stood up. She walked the rest of the way to Timothy's bedroom window.

A look of anger crossed her mesmerized face upon seeing the brass bar.

"That mean man," she said.

She tried to pry the bar loose.

She failed.

"Forget the brass bar," Timothy said. "Just come back inside and grab the house key."

"Of course," Beth said.

Inside the house, Beth stepped into the kitchen and didn't stop till reaching one of the cupboards.

Instead of finding the house key, she found a note.

The note read:

> *If you're reading this, then you have fallen for his tricks. It's OK. You're in a weak state, making you all the more vulnerable. He has taken full advantage of that vulnerability.*
>
> *But I promised I would not quit on you. And I have proven my tenacity by stealing the key to the ungrateful child's room. You'll have it back first thing sunup.*
>
> *The boy has already had his supper and plenty of water. So he has nothing to complain about when it comes to that. As for his toilet routine, the bucket inside the room will suffice for the night. You will find a healthy child in the morning, let us pray, a more grateful one. This should teach him a grave lesson in allowing one's imagination to rule one's mind. Soon, you both will thank me. As will your husband once fully recovered. Although I do think it's best we keep your failure between us. We don't need a convalescent Harold Huntsinger to learn about the weakest moment of your life.*

Good night and best wishes,
Nurse Teeter

"You bitch!" Beth shouted.

"What is it?" Katelyn asked, running into the kitchen.

Beth ignored her and crumpled the note. Letting the note slip from her hand, she hurried toward Timothy's room.

Stopping at the door, she tried the handle.

Locked.

She pushed the door.

No chance.

"She took the key?" a deflated Timothy asked.

"Yes. I'm sorry. I'm so sorry that I doubted you."

"It's OK. I'd not believe myself either. But I must get out of this room. I must get us all out of the house. Stand back."

Beth stood back.

On the other side, Timothy took four steps back from the door and readied himself for a charge and a solid kick against the door.

The second before charging, a scream of agony echoed throughout the house.

The painful cry came from Pa's room.

"Pa!" Timothy shouted.

As for Beth, she turned away and focused on Pa's room.

Timothy envisioned horror.

"No!" Timothy shouted, sensing Ma's leave for Pa's room. "Don't go in there. Ma! Ma! Stay out of the room."

Oblivious to Timothy's words, Beth continued her way.

"He's in pain," she screamed back.

"Ma! Ma! Stay out of the room. Spiders!"

Timothy abandoned the screaming and launched a desperate assault on the door.

The first assault failed. The wood proved stronger than he thought. He geared back for a more powerful charge and kick. Again, he bounced off the door without making a dent. Staggered, Timothy charged a third time, putting both shoulders and back into the collision. And yet, he bounced right off and crashed to the ground. He looked to the door and wondered, *Where in the* world *did Harold find such a tree?*

~

Ignoring her son's warnings, Beth entered the dark bedroom and turned on the gas lamp on Harold's bedside counter. The screaming by now had stopped. She lifted the lamp and looked over his body. He looked terribly emaciated, as if his body shrank, leaving only the healthy, countless, much fuller abscesses from before. The abscesses looked as if they had drunk the insides of Harold and left only fleshless skin and bones. Beth could not take her eyes off these monstrous-sized abscesses. *How could they have grown this much bigger?* She had to cover her mouth and eyes after staring at them. And with her eyes closed, the vivid thought of Harold's inside being eaten and drunk by whatever lived inside those abscesses appeared in her mind.

But what lived inside them?

She opened her eyes and noticed the transparency of the abscesses. She could see through them.

Beth wanted a better view. She leaned down closer, with gas lamp in hand and—

~

Forced to take a break from charging at the door, Timothy returned to his futile shouting, for Beth could not concentrate on any of his words.

~

While staring through them, Beth nearly grazed one of the abscesses with the gas lamp. She noticed a squirminess inside.

The squirminess took shape.

"Worms?" she said.

But in a louder tone, she said, "Are they—"

"Spiders!" The shout from Timothy came at the perfect moment, for it finished her question. Thus, the word finally broke through to her.

"Spiders," she said softly. She visualized myriads of spiders popping out, her next scream being "Spiders!"

Believing the freedom of the spiders to happen soon, she turned away. As she did, Harold grunted with life. This caused her to hesitate.

She looked down at him.

Spiders!

"No! I must save them. I must save my family."

She turned to escape again. Harold shot out his left arm and seized her by the wrist.

The vice-like grip hindered Ma from escaping.

"Let me go!" Beth screamed vainly.

"Agh," Harold screamed back.

"Let me go!"

By this time, Katelyn had broken through her catatonic state and rushed into the bedroom. In came Butch too. Katelyn joined the struggle by grabbing Ma. With their strengths combined, the two still badly failed in freeing Ma. Butch chipped in by biting Harold's arm. Because of Harold's absence of pain, the dog's bite proved futile unless the dog could rip the arm off, which the dog tried to do.

But Butch never had the time.

Pa's grip tightened as he raised his upper body and screamed one last time. He dropped back down and showed no sign of life.

Beth stopped struggling for one second to see her husband die. She closed her eyes. Opening them again, the reality of her plight returned. She tried to pull free again. Then she stopped. A vague sound had come from Harold's body. Was it life? She listened for another second. The sound seemed squishy and squirmy. She looked away from Harold's open and dead eyes and stared at the abscesses. They looked ready to burst open.

"Get out," Ma said softly yet fiercely, leaving no room for rebuttal.

Ma had given up. But she wouldn't allow Katelyn to give up her life for hers.

Katelyn, though, shook her head.

"Leave!" Ma said. "Leave me and get out of here!"

Katelyn again shook her head.

"Katelyn," Ma said softly again, but without the fierceness. "Please. Dear God, please. Leave and save yourself."

"No," a distraught Katelyn said. Tears came pouring out of her eyes. "I'm not leaving you."

"Do it for Timothy. He now needs you."

Hearing that stopped Katelyn. She looked in the direction of Timothy's room and—

Pop.

The popping sound drew both of their attention. They looked at Harold and watched a single sac burst open.

A thick, syrupy yellow liquid oozed out.

More abscesses burst open, followed by the rest.

"What is that stuff?" Katelyn said, seeing only the ooze.

The answer came a second or so later when itty-bitty spiders trudged through the thick ooze.

The first shout from Ma and Katelyn came out muffled. Hopelessness strangled their voice. When free, Beth's entire body screamed. She trembled violently, and in doing so, she knocked over the gas lamp. The lamp fell onto the bed, spilling highly flammable oil onto the sheets and wooden floor, while the burning flame of the lamp ignited the spilled oil.

Quickly after, the bed sheets and bedroom floor caught on fire.

Soon after, the entire room became an inferno.

Most of the spiders proved too crafty and quick for the fire; they found a way to flee the scene. Only a small number perished.

As for Katelyn and Ma…

They weren't so crafty or quick.

~

Timothy heard Ma and Katelyn's cries and made one last charge at the door. Again, he bounced off and found himself too weak to try again.

He cursed the wood Harold used to build this door.

But he would not give up.

He scanned the room.

"Now, why the hell didn't I think of that earlier?" he said, staring at the brass bars holding his bed up.

Pulling off a bar from the bedframe, Timothy used it to shatter the window just enough to reach his arm through. Not wanting to shred his body with sharp glass, Timothy pulled off the sheriff's bar and opened the window using what little strength he had left. Timothy cleaned most of the glass from the shattered window and climbed through. Many shards of glass still cut up his body.

Blood soaked his clothes.

Outside, he hurried toward the front door.

Arriving at the front door, he stopped. His entire body grew limp. His insides turned to gel. He could see nothing but flames and smoke. Most of the house by now had been engulfed by the fire. No survivors looked to remain. But that undeniable fact did not stop Timothy from repeatedly screaming his sister and ma's name as if they would miraculously step out of the burning house unscathed. His screaming did invoke one miracle.

Out of the house came Butch.

Butch charged out of the fiery house and embraced Timothy. Timothy, shoving him away, continued to face the house.

"They're all gone."

He fell to his knees. Tears intermingled with the blood on his face. Ashamed of himself for letting his family perish, Timothy stood up and ran headlong toward the house. Butch hurried over and barred Timothy from passing. The dog even barked angrily, flashing his sharp, canine teeth.

"Get out of my way!" Timothy shouted.

Butch barked louder.

"Move!"

Butch did not budge.

Timothy saw no way past him except by battle. That he did not want. "Butch," Timothy said gently, "please."

Butch still did not waver.

Finally, reality came striking down upon Timothy again.

They were dead.

"All of them. All because of me. My choices. My choices alone."

His head sank.

The slightest glimmer of hope flickered in his mind.

The book had not been in the house.

"If I can just get it back and finish it. Right? Right, Wood Dweller? Tell me I'm right!"

No answer. But he must believe.

He nodded, believing everything would return to normalcy after finishing the book.

He recalled the book's whereabouts.

The sheriff.

"I guess I'll just have to steal it back."

But I'll need help.

Chapter 9

GAWUL'S RISING

Zachary Youngblood found sleep very difficult on the night of the storm. When he did fall asleep, he found himself dreaming, a dream similar to the ones he had suffered as of late. But this one proved far more potent than before, whereas the ones before already felt real enough that it sometimes took him a half hour or so to grasp reality. It wasn't necessarily about how real this dream seemed to be that made it much more potent than the ones before. It was because of the macabre and wickedness found in this dream. He didn't remember much when waking early in the middle of the night. But he certainly felt the lingering terror of the dream. He recalled being chased by a horde of grotesque, ill-defined creatures he believed to be goblins. He guessed that from his experience reading fairy tales and so forth. These goblins chased him along what Zachary considered a battlefield, but one recently torched by a blaze of fire.

These goblins were not alone. Flying creatures with the faces of fairies or nymphs—for he didn't know the difference between them—passed over him, wanting nothing more in their wicked life than rend his body into shreds. Their faces were beautiful and, at angles, innocent. But seen through their eyes, one would recognize a malevolent sparkle—diabolical, to say the least. Their hands were sharp claws, ready to rip open the strongest abdominals and devour the insides. Of course, they had wings, but these wings were not of fairies or sprites. These wings were of bats, along with their clawed feet. And their claws were not the worst of their features, for their mouths lavishly dribbled with poisonous saliva stemming from their sharp batlike fangs.

Zachary wished those creatures to be the last he recalled from the dream.

His wish had not been granted.

Wolves pounced after him. These wolves were not the size of wolves from his forest. These wolves were the size of horses and then some. They were black as night and deadly as sin. They had an extra thick coat of fur running down their spine, making them even more intimidating to behold. Their charge at Zachary could not be denied; no other creature could stop them.

And even they weren't alone.

Female warriors charged after the boy. These tainted warriors attired themselves in the finest of weapons and armor. But like them, their array of weapons and armor was cursed and decayed. Rotten to their inner core. Their faces, once so beautiful, powerful, and formidable, now ugly and grotesque, weak and yet powerfully threatening. They were the decayed images of their majestic yesterdays.

Following these warriors came what Zachary believed to be elves. Barely recalling this image, he did remember something strange about them.

The elves hid unseen in the shadows of the battlefield.

Upon this battlefield, Zachary felt the lingering memory of allies.

But he could not come close to recalling a single ally—only the feeling of not being alone.

Again, this dream shook Zachary's inner core. He saw no return to sleep. Thus, he rested his back on his bed and stared up. The aggressive nature of the dream did not lessen. Having experienced this before, from these same dreams, except not at this magnitude, Zachary climbed off the bed and searched after the one object that helped ease his mind.

From under a layer of clothes inside his dresser, Zachary pulled out the arrowhead Timothy gave to him. Simply handling the object soothed his mind and body.

He smiled. The disturbing effects of the dream washed away. Instead of putting the arrowhead away, he took it to bed, which he had done on the previous nights when experiencing such malevolent dreams. Never had he questioned why this enigmatic object soothed the fear and anxieties that came from those dreams. If he did investigate the reason, he'd probably realize that these dreams did not start until he first possessed the arrow tip.

He would have known the arrow tip was his bane and fortune.

Feeling the advance of sleep upon him, Zachary closed his eyes, only to be interrupted by a tapping at his window.

Climbing off his bed, Zachary moved to the window and opened the drapes.

"What are you doing here?" Zachary asked, seeing his best friend on the other side. "And in this storm?"

"Just open the window," Timothy said.

Zachary opened the window. A rain-soaked Timothy climbed through.

"You're a bloody mess," Zachary said. "Wait! That really is blood on your clothes."

Timothy did not stop inside the room until he reached the farthest corner from Zachary. Zachary looked even more startled at him.

"Something bad?"

Timothy nodded.

"And of all nights," Zachary said, thinking of the ominous storm and his dream.

After a short pause, Zachary continued.

"I must say . . . that arrowhead you gave me? I don't know why, but I believe it has some kind of mystique to it. I think there's much more to it than we think."

Timothy nodded, believing in that assumption more than ever.

"Keep it in your possession at all times," Timothy said, "wherever you go, no matter what."

"It's with me right now," Zachary said. "But I don't think it's just me that will be needing it."

After a short pause, he surmised, *We'll* be needing it."

Timothy nodded again.

"Now tell me what happened and get out of those clothes. You may be taller than me, and I may be wider than you, but I'm sure you can fit in my clothes for the time being."

Timothy shook his head. "I'm fine in these clothes."

"They're soaked with blood and all torn up. I can see pieces of glass in them."

Timothy shook his head again.

"Be stubborn. But you'll tell me what happened, or I'll never talk to you again."

Timothy clenched his jaw. He let go.

"They're gone. They're all gone."

"Who?"

"My family."

"What do you mean *gone*?"

"Gone."

"But where?"

"I said *gone!*" Timothy cried out. "I'm the only one left. And Butch— he's with Abigail in your stable. I brought them with me. I couldn't save the rest. I only ask for shelter this night. I've got a lot of thinking to do. The path ahead of me. I . . . I don't know where to start."

"Can I help?"

Choices.

"I shouldn't ask for your help—it wouldn't be fair. But then . . . I may need it."

"Whatever you need."

"I need to take something back that belongs to me."

"Where is it?"

"It's not about where. It's about who. Sheriff Riggins—the bastard stole something from me."

"Why?"

"Never mind the why. Help me steal back the item, and I'll explain everything."

"Sure," Zachary said.

"And promise me you'll keep this between us—like the arrow tip I gave you."

"Not a soul. Not even my sisters."

Timothy nodded his head. "I should get some sleep."

"How about food?"

The thought of food did not sound appetizing. But the likelihood of a journey upon an uncertain road made him think twice.

"Sure," he said. "And maybe I should take you up on the offer for some clothes."

Zachary nodded and grabbed some clothes that would best fit Timothy. Not sticking around to see Timothy change, he snuck out of the room and returned shortly after with a plate of food.

The smell of food made Timothy's stomach growl.

He had no trouble finishing every bite.

And surprisingly, sleep came to him immediately after.

~

Timothy's eyes opened. He no longer resided in Zachary's room. Instead, his eyes opened to him standing outside what formerly had been his family's home. Only the smallest structure remained, most of the former house now being ash and cinder. The structure that remained looked to be a skeletal frame. As for the ash and cinder, embers everywhere continued to glow throughout the dark and rainy night.

Timothy stepped closer. He wanted to see what resided underneath, as if there could be a survivor, and that he did not abandon his family to the cruelest of fates. But the closer he came to the house, the more he realized the improbable chance of one surviving such a calamity.

"I killed them," Timothy said, standing close enough to the house to feel his skin burn from the embers.

Why? he asked himself. *Why am I here?*

"They're all dead."

Is it not painful enough for me to see this once?

Why have I been brought back here? And by whom?

A sliver of his thoughts came to a revelation.

"The gem! How could I have forgotten? Why didn't I grab—"

Timothy recalled his ma taking the gem with her.

He now saw how difficult it would be to procure the gem.

But I must try.

Not exactly thinking this to be a dream, Timothy stepped closer to the front door, feeling the searing of his skin as he searched for a way through the burning debris.

Impossible. It would mean his death to try to enter—a very harsh and cruel death.

Taking a step back, Timothy noticed a movement under the cinder and ash in the area of his ma and pa's room, at the heart of the tragedy.

He stared at the area with the slightest optimism and moved to the side to receive a better view. Could someone be alive?

Impossible, he thought to himself.

And yet, a second later, a hand rose from the ash and cinder. But this hand could not have belonged to a human.

It had fingers. Yes, five of them. It had the shape and form of any human hand. But still, it could not be human. The hand showed more than just burning. It revealed tissue and flesh that had become rotten, along with the markings of something vile and disgusting imploding from under the flesh and tissue. The bones could be seen on a portion of the hand, rotten to the marrow. Timothy watched a second morbid hand push free from the burning rubble. This second hand fared no better, no worse. Timothy took another step back, afraid of what these hands and arms meant. His fear expanded when the rest of the cadaverous body rose from the tragedy's destruction.

Monster.

Timothy thought that at first, but then . . .

"Pa?" *Can that really be you?*

The thought alone proved more disturbing than the physical manifestation of what rose from under the house.

"No," Timothy said. "It's a monster."

It has to be a monster.

This monster mimicked Harold's exact frame. Of course, the entire body also mimicked the vileness of the hands and arms. Thus, most of the tissue and flesh hung off rotten bones. The spoiled insides of the monster could also be seen because the clothing covering Harold had been burned off. As for the eyes, Timothy became even more frightened. Yes, they were Pa's eyes, except they were dark and hollow, and soon, they would only become darker and hollower.

Timothy wanted to run away when the monster flashed its baleful eyes at him. But he could not find a way to move. The monster had paralyzed him. Fortunately, the monster did not care for him, for the monster knew that Timothy did not exist before him as a corporeal body. No. Only the monster stood as the rain became heavier. Alone did this monster raise its arm to the sky. The monster then opened its sickening mouth and emitted a scream that sent shivers up Timothy's spine. The scream would have done the same for any man or woman, regardless of their fortitude, for this cry was not human. It was a repressed cry from a monster finally free to scream after time immemorial.

The monster's scream came out in one word, and this word, as if gorged inside the monster's throat, could not be deciphered by Timothy.

This scream ended, and Timothy watched the monster settle down and peruse its surroundings. By perusing, it felt its surroundings.

And then it felt *it.*

The monster, not having to move, bent down and scoured among the remains of the house. Timothy watched as it excavated the body of what he believed to be his ma. Of course, the cadaverous body was burned to the very bone. But some of the clothing had not been burned completely. Thus, the monster searched the pocket that gave off a bluish glow.

The monster then pulled out the gem.

Timothy's eyes widened.

How did it know about it?

Luckily for Timothy and the future of his world and other worlds, this monster was ignorant of something else hiding in the debris of the charred house, something nearly as essential as the gem.

With the gem in hand, the monster stood up. It then took its first steps out of the carnage.

It headed toward the forest, Old Wicker's Forest.

It would venture farther. It would make its way into the Forest Beyond. Then, it would seek shelter from the impending *second* storm.

Timothy discerned this. He now learned why he had been brought here. He was to learn. He was to sense.

To sense much.

For Timothy sensed this monster's return home. Sensed this monster's return to where its master slept.

To its queen.

And this queen had a name, her name being—

Chapter 10

A FAVORABLE BETRAYAL

"Wake up, boy!"

Timothy woke up to a shout and the shaking of his body. He looked up, expecting the monster. Instead, his eyes opened to Sheriff Riggins standing over him, breathing his foul breath, and using both hands to shake Timothy out of his sleep.

The eyes of the sheriff were dilated and intense.

"That's right, kid. Wake up!"

Pushing the sheriff's hands away, Timothy leaped out of bed and stood adamant before the sheriff. He stared back with anger and defeat.

Snickering from two deputies behind the sheriff could be heard.

Farther in the distance stood Zachary's parents, each of them restraining their son from charging over to help.

"I'm sorry!" Zachary screamed. "I didn't know it was going to be like this. I only wanted to help."

Timothy's eyes went from Zachary back to the sheriff. His anger surpassed the feeling of being defeated.

"Now, now," the sheriff said, seeing the change in the boy. "Don't be thinking foolishly. You're coming with me, kid. And that's that. So be on your best behavior and make this easy for all of us. I've seen the house. I know what you did."

"I didn't do anything," Timothy said. "You did! You and that accursed doctor and nurse."

The backhanded slap came as no surprise to Timothy. Timothy didn't budge an inch against the hard impact of the stronger Sheriff Riggins. The boy looked formidable. The sheriff cringed because of this. For a second, the sheriff thought he stood before Harold Huntsinger, someone he feared to ever anger. But the sheriff could not afford to reveal this. He stepped closer and grinned.

"You watch your mouth," the sheriff said.

"I didn't do anything," Timothy repeated.

"So you say. But you're still coming with me."

The sheriff signaled the two deputies. They each approached Timothy. Timothy wanted to fight back and escape through the window.

But a thought came to him.

This is what I wanted, right? He's got the book.

Timothy surrendered.

By then, Zachary had freed himself and tried to stop the deputies. Sheriff Riggins stood before him and pushed Zachary away.

"Hey!" Zachary's father shouted. "You don't ever touch my son again! If I knew this was how you would treat Timothy, I'd never have sent for you, *Jack!*"

"You saw the house," Sheriff Riggins pleaded. "You saw what the boy did."

"You're out of your damn mind if you think Timothy could ever do something like that."

"Agh! It doesn't matter. The kid is coming with me. We're in need of a serious talk."

The sheriff led Timothy and the deputies out of the room. They continued their way through the house and ended up outside. The storm had passed through and left destruction in its wake, including a sunny, sultry late-morning sky, with the slightest breeze to alleviate some of the unusual (for these parts) sticky humidity. Puddles of rain looking more like ponds could be seen strewn about the Youngblood ranch, while the livestock mostly took refuge in the multiple barns.

Few animals braved the unusual conditions, including Butch.

On seeing Timothy, the dog broke free.

The two came together.

Satisfied that Timothy was alive and well, the dog snarled at the deputies and sheriff.

"Best put a muzzle on that dog, or I will," the sheriff said.

Timothy settled the dog down.

"Who's going to take care of Butch while I'm gone?" Timothy asked.

"I will!" Zachary clamored. "And I promise I'll take far better care of him than I did with you. I failed. I'll *never* fail you again."

"OK," Timothy said, nowise indignant over his best friend betraying him.

He might have done the same if the roles were reversed.

Timothy looked to the stables.

"I've got Abigail," Zachary's father said. "You'll find her happier and healthier when you return."

Timothy nodded.

"Now can we go?" the sheriff said, vexed. "Time's wasting."

~

Timothy thought over every detail that came into existence since his action in opening the book while sitting in the backseat of the sheriff's automobile—one of the handful of automobiles found in town. It never dawned on him that one of his wishes had come true: he was riding inside the so-called vehicle of the future. No. He didn't care. He was utterly oblivious. And he would have remained oblivious and lost in his thoughts if it weren't for arriving in town and seeing all the townspeople staring incredulously at him.

Why on earth was Timothy Huntsinger, the only son of Harold Huntsinger, riding in the back seat of the sheriff's vehicle?

Timothy frowned and quickly returned to his thoughts.

His thoughts landed on this scenario being exactly what he wanted.

He was close to the book.

Yes. The prospect of being locked up did not sound encouraging. But like his pa had incessantly said, "Son! Life turns on a dime. Prepare to be not prepared."

And that could be no less than the truth regarding Timothy's power in choosing and deciding what to do.

Timothy only hoped fortune would smile a bit more at him.

His thoughts then settled on his parents dying because of those exact choices and decisions.

And soon, he believed, the town would fall to the same fate. This time, it would fall to the spiders as the culprit.

Not liking those thoughts one bit, he tried pushing them away—especially his decisions leading to his family's death, for he knew it could spell his doom.

His mental state must be sane, and for it to be sane, he must steel himself; he must not ruminate over the sufferings from his actions.

As for the town?

The town is doomed.

Again, he did not like this thought, but it didn't prove easy to challenge, especially as he looked out the window and stared at the many townspeople.

They had no idea what wickedness came their way.

And here he was, stuck in the back seat of the sheriff's vehicle, unable to do a thing.

Sheriff Riggins couldn't stop looking back and forth at Timothy in the front seat behind the steering wheel. He saw the troubled look on his face. The sheriff attributed that look to Timothy noticing all the happy townspeople staring perplexedly at the boy in the backseat. The sheriff pitied him—a true sentiment of pity. This pity drove him to park the vehicle around the back of the station instead of the front, where the whole town would have been able to see Timothy being ushered out, even though it wouldn't be long until the harsh news of the Huntsinger family spread its way to everyone in town.

"You're doing all right, kid," the sheriff said.

The vehicle came to a stop, and the sheriff allowed Timothy out on his own. The deputies did step ahead and behind him when entering the station.

Two more deputies were found inside, each lollygagging around. One dared to sit behind the sheriff's desk. The other sat far too relaxed to be considered casual while reading the morning's newspaper. They each jumped out of their spots and attempted to look busy at the sheriff's entrance.

"Monkeying around, are you?" the sheriff said scathingly.

"Um, no, boss," one of the deputies said.

"No? Then what do you call it?"

"Uh, well—"

"Just shut up. You're screwing around. Ain't that right, McKinney?" the sheriff asked one of the deputies that accompanied him and Timothy.

"Looks like two monkeys screwing around to me."

"You hear that? But what the hell? It's not like anything *important* has happened. Or has there? I want to know one thing from both of you. You find him?"

"Uh, no," the deputy behind the desk said.

"Is that so, Redding?"

The sheriff turned his eyes on the other deputy, sitting straight and firm.

"What about you, Mitchum? Are you telling me the same?"

"No, sir."

"You mean you found him?"

"No. I mean. Yes—no."

"Which one is it?"

"We didn't find him."

"Didn't find him? So you two are telling me a man who had been on his deathbed—and I mean his deathbed—as recently as yesterday, climbed out of his bed on his own two feet and simply strolled out of his burning house, only to disappear? That I cannot believe. What I do believe is that you two shooting the bull cost me precious time. You get that search party out there, and you get going now. You hear? He couldn't have gone far."

"And the boy?"

"The boy stays with me—for now. The rest of you, out. And do I have to tell you 'closed lips'?"

"No, boss."

"Then keep them shut."

~

"I'm not arresting you," the sheriff said to Timothy as he led him down a flight of stairs, which led to the jail-cell floor.

Not one cell had been occupied. There were four altogether, two on each side of the hallway.

"Not yet, that is," the sheriff said, stopping at the first cell on the left. The sheriff took out a bunch of keys and unlocked the cell door. He opened the door and turned back to Timothy. "I don't want to arrest you. But I also can't afford you running around. I need answers. I need to get to the bottom of this mystery. This is a catastrophe already, and it will only grow worse. We need answers and the truth before that worse comes. So go on in that cell, and the truth better spill out of your mouth."

Reluctantly, Timothy stepped inside. He turned to face the sheriff. The sheriff closed the door. Timothy put both hands on the bars.

"So the truth," the sheriff said. "Out with it! What happened last night? And where on god's green earth is your pa?"

Timothy closed his eyes after hearing that past question. He recalled the dream.

It was a dream, right?

"My pa?" Timothy asked with eyes open.

"Yes. He's missing."

"He's not in . . . in the . . ."

"No."

"Can't be," Timothy said.

"What can't be?"

"The others?" Timothy asked. "My . . . my ma and sister?"

The sheriff saw no guile in the disturbingly sad look on the boy's face. "You don't know?"

"I mean," Timothy said. "I've got a feeling. But no, not positive. Are they . . ."

"They're gone," the sheriff said in a soft tone. "If you have anything to do with it, then damn it, Timothy, tell me the goddamn truth! Tell me exactly what happened last night. Give me the honest version, and I'll be at your side before Judge Hawkins, no matter what you did. Just give me the truth. You know, everyone in town respects you more than any young adult around. They do. They see Harold in you. The news of his illness spread like wildfire. They've heard nothing but sick and disturbing gossip centering on his health. Who would blame you for going a bit . . . uh, well, bonkers?"

"Give me the facts, kid, and you'll be taken care of."

"You wouldn't believe me before, so why would you believe me now?"

"You're talking about that book, aren't you?"

Timothy stayed silent.

"That stupid book! Why? What's so magical about it? It's goddamn empty. Not a single trace of writing, just the drawing on the front binding and its title, *Gem and Spider*. What the hell does that mean?"

Timothy's eyes betrayed him.

Empty? How?

"Yes," the sheriff said, seeing Timothy's confounded eyes. "Blank."

"No writing?"

The sheriff turned away and left the jail-cell floor. Less than a minute later, he returned with the book. He stopped at Timothy's cell and opened the book. Timothy leaned and stared at the open pages.

He saw writing and sketches.

"You don't see it?" Timothy said.

"See what?"

Timothy grew even more confounded.

Katelyn saw it. How come not him?

Timothy had no answer. But he did take full advantage of the sheriff's ignorance of the book's contents.

"You're right," Timothy said, changing his tune. "There's nothing there. I don't know what to say."

"You can start by telling me the truth. What happened last night? Did your morbid fantasies become too much for you?"

"I . . . I guess so."

"What did you do because of them?"

Timothy wanted to lie but found it too difficult. He'd be smearing the lives of his family.

"I didn't do anything."

"Not that shit again. What happened last night?"

"I don't know!" Timothy shouted. "The only thing I know is that this town is in grave danger."

"The only danger I see is you."

"Wrong."

"OK. What is this grave danger?"

Timothy shook his head.

"Not going to tell me? Too ridiculous to say? Let me guess. Spiders, right?"

Timothy's choice to stay silent answered the question.

"Those damn spiders," the sheriff said with a hysterical look. "You really did lose it. You lost your goddamn marbles. And, Timothy, they may never return. We'll have to lock you up in one of those big-city loony bins they call asylums. Spiders!"

"They're coming," Timothy said. "And they're going to destroy everything in their path."

The sheriff wiped the hysterical smile off his face and nodded in disgust. "What a shame."

He made his first step to leave.

"Wait!" Timothy said.

"What?"

"The book."

"No."

"Give me the book, and I might be able to recall a bit of what happened last night."

"That almost sounds like blackmailing. Are you blackmailing *me*?"

"Call it negotiation."

The sheriff snarled. He leaned in closer. The bars stood only a few inches from their faces.

"This is what I'm going to do. I'm going to leave this book here while I check up on the investigation. When I come back, I want answers. And when I say 'answers,' I mean the goddamn holy Christ of truths. That's how this *negotiation* will work. Understand me?"

Timothy nodded.

The sheriff handed over the book.

Seconds later, Timothy stood alone. He didn't waste time. He opened the book to the last chapter. Nothing changed about the title or drawing.

With a heavy heart, he turned the page.

Writing.

Again, the writing proved incomprehensible, while a few sketches could be seen here and there. As before, the drawings aided him in what he could not understand from the writing. Many times did Timothy want to slam the book closed. The drawings were macabre, sad, painful. They detailed events leading to the agonizing deaths of his family. One sketch showed the exact moment of their death. The drawings showed more than that. They showed him standing before the house alone, watching it burn and crumble to ashes. They showed him reaching Zachary's home, only for Zachary to sneak out of the room to wake up his father. The sketches showed Zachary's father, the sheriff, and a few deputies searching the smoldering house once belonging to the Huntsingers. Lastly, and far more potent than any other sketch, a drawing showed Timothy what he thought was a dream.

"It can't be," he said, seeing the monster standing out of the rubble of his home, flashing his malevolent yellow eyes at him.

Its hand held the gem.

"No," Timothy said with a shake of his head, seeing the perfect contour of the monster mimicking his pa.

"But if it is true," Timothy said and stopped.

Pa?

Eyes closed, Timothy turned the page.

He opened his eyes to a new chapter title.

Chapter 3
Rajur's Awakening

The chapter title did little to entice him. He wanted the drawing. He wanted what would give him more information. Thus, he turned the page and discovered the title's sketch, again taking up the entire page. The sketch depicted an individual kneeling beside a tree. This tree resided near a healthy-flowing creek. The creek puzzled Timothy. It looked familiar to him. In fact, the entire surroundings looked familiar to him, including the tree; again, everything was drawn black, white, and ashen gray, along with the smallest of vibrant colors. As for the figure, Timothy perceived it as a male because his frame was too solidly built for any female he had ever met. The figure's shoulders were also broader than any man in town, including his broad and muscular pa. All of that he discerned even though the person wore a green hooded cloak.

The hood could not cover the entire individual's meticulously braided dark and golden-colored hair.

A dual-bladed baldric hung across the cloak. Only one of these sheaths was home to a blade, while the other remained empty. This blade consisted of a uniquely embroidered hilt. Timothy discovered a girdle around the waist with the cloak pulled back at one side. Various little objects were attached to the girdle. The most prominent of objects were two half-moon, crescent-shaped boomerangs—or what he thought to be boomerangs. Besides the embroidery of the hilt, the brilliant shine of the two half-moon crescent objects attracted most of his attention.

Timothy looked over the outfit more and could not help but find it outlandish and strange. And yet, he found it familiar—familiar because it reminded him of heroic tales of fantasy: heroes destined to vanquish dragons, heroes that bested ogres and goblins. And always did this hero find a way to save the princess at the end with an explicit *And they lived happily ever after.*

"Like a fairy tale," Timothy said.

The sky above this scene confused Timothy. He noticed his moon. But besides his moon, a second vague moon appeared—without a single wrinkle, too smooth and brilliantly white to be real.

"Magical moon?"

He studied the moons more, and the more he studied his moon, the more he realized a change.

Is our moon fading away?

"If it is, what does that mean? What does any of this mean?"

That very question led him to inspect the once-boring title of this chapter.

No longer did it seem boring and of no relevance.

"'Rajur's Awakening,'" he said.

After a long pause, Timothy added, "OK. Now, who's Rajur?"

Chapter 11

THE STRANGER THAT CAME IN FROM THE WOODS

Rajur opened his eyes. The blackness that came for him vanished within a blink of an eye. The irrevocable damage caused by the blackness accomplished its goal. He found himself transported. He did find himself kneeling, as he did the moment the blackness came and stole him away. But he no longer knelt in the lowest-level dungeon of a long-ago abandoned castle, cursed by the waters surrounding it. Instead, he knelt by a tree. The tree resided a few steps away from a creek, both belonging to a deep forest and this forest unfamiliar to him—at first. But as he absorbed the forestry more, he sensed a common ground, too long forgotten by him to recall the likeness.

More importantly, everything he worked for—everything he strove to achieve—was lost to him.

And now, *where is here?*

Never panicking, Rajur studied his surroundings more. One of his worse fears had come true.

Eythreal no longer belonged to Her. It had been taken from Her and was now possessed by an object only one could possess.

But who?

Dismayed at this fact and yet staying calm and collected, Rajur moved into a crouched position. He pulled his cloak over his entire body, revealing his boots only. He looked at the forest floor and pulled out a tuft of weeds and grass. He put both under his nose and gave them a good whiff. His dismayed look turned acrid and bitter. He sifted deeper through the forest floor until his eyes spotted a patch of sparkling green roots. The stems of these roots were also green, but no sparkle to them. The stems did have a shiny green glaze upon them. An incipient bud could be found at the end of each stem.

Rajur ripped the stems and roots from their soil and placed them before his face. No sniffing this time. He only eyed them.

"Waldo root," he said.

The bitterness diminished. He felt more at home. He placed the roots back into the ground. The roots reattached themselves to the soil and animated with life.

"Eythreal," Rajur muttered.

He leaned back in his crouched position and closed his eyes.

A logical explanation for the turn of events came to mind.

He opened his eyes and stammered out angrily, "Wood Dweller!"

Rajur then grabbed a locket that hung from his neck and under his attire. He held on to it meaningfully.

"Iria," he said. "So close. Misha. I was even closer to you. In these hands of mine," he said when dropping his hands from the locket.

"And him—elf, sorcerer, half god, *old friend*. So close to your immortal death."

Rajur shook his head madly. He put an end to his pining over the unfortunate events and searched for optimism.

He remembered something of old.

"Maybe," he said. He pondered in the furthest portions of his memory. His pondering landed on an almost forgotten suspicion of his.

"Maybe I'm right. This is meant to be. The one chosen comes for . . ."

Too much to think of for now.

"Let us hope this one has been chosen more wisely than the others."

He nodded.

"And now it is all about who has the knowledge."

And what to do next?

Before standing up and unbuttoning the hooded cloak, which would have revealed him, Rajur took one last study of his surroundings. This time his examination went further. And with a vision unmatched by anyone on this current world, he could see much and thus sensed only the harmless critters and animals inhabiting this forest.

Satisfied, he stood up.

He unbuttoned the cloak at the near top. The cloak fell to his sides.

He became exposed.

~

Rajur stood over six feet tall, formidable, and stout on the muscular side. The attire he wore was close-fitting, along with being rare and unique. Wilda, the Enchantress Maiden of Gerhaert Forest, used her needles and thread to design his attire, including the hooded cloak. She accomplished that as a reward, a reward he received for successfully undertaking the Trials of Deception. The attributes of this attire were many, including being impervious to fire for a long duration and thermal heating for frigid temperatures.

Feathery light, elf-made boots protected his feet. The fabric and build of the boots came from Nererrenda, bequeathed to him by King Arà Rázrwayn of Nererrenda. The elves of Nererrenda also gave him his girdle, specifically made to hold two enigmatic objects, besides various other objects. The two important objects were no other than Rajur's Moon Beams: two half-crescent-shaped objects fitted to his hands' grip. The Moon Beams emitted a glow that could cut through most of Iria's Dark while at the same time never betraying Rajur if hiding in shadows.

The origin of the Moon Beams was unknown to every scholar and historian of Eythreal. And this included Rajur.

What little Rajur knew about them, he never breathed a word to another.

Rajur wore a particular set of gloves to handle the scorching touch of the Moon Beams. The gloves withstanding the contact of the Moon Beams was possible because they were wrought from Godstone, otherwise known as Gailala: an extraordinarily scarce and undefinable nonmetallic rock found inside Eythreal's core and the exterior surface. Many historians and scholars believed the stone to be not of Eythreal's natural substance— instead, left behind by *others* and slowly integrated with the geological minerals of Eythreal's core structure. When discovered, Gailala became the most sought-after stone or metal on Eythreal, although barely a fraction of Eythreal inhabitants found the smallest bit. Over time, others found a way to create a synthetic alloy of the stone.

A tiny fragment of Godstone could cost one a filled soul ruby.

Not long after the creation of the gloves, those same gloves were fortified.

Dragon Might.

The now gauntlets with the designation of Dragon Might were forged by the blacksmiths, enchanters, and enchantresses of the Iron Dwarf Kingdom. Of course, none of that could have been possible without the help of the Nameless Wizard: a stranger among the dwarves, yet asked by the strictly secluded kingdom to be their guardian for the unforeseeable future. The thin and tight-fitting gauntlets, very much the same as the before gloves, were made from the scales of various dragons. Each of these dragons' names was enchanted upon the scales, giving the gauntlets a portion of their attributes. It was that feat alone that the dwarves could not do, nor any other race on Eythreal. The Nameless Wizard had been the one to achieve what no other could do.

Rajur also received a chestplate from the dwarves. This chestplate was forged with the scales of the greatest of the Dragons Under Eythreal, one that Rajur defeated.

Enchanted upon these scales was also the dragon's very name, Satay-Ri, along with the sketch of the dragon herself.

A heaping amount of Gailala forged in with the dragon's scale improved the chestplate even more.

The last item that must be mentioned is the blade that filled one of the two sheaths upon his dual baldric: Storm Breaker.

The origin of this blade proved more unknown and mysterious than the already obscure and secretive Moon Beams. Historians, scholars, and others who master Eythreal's lore had their conjectures. Most of it falls on this blade being incipient of something greater. Like the Moon Beams, Rajur was just as much in the dark as everyone else: unsure of the truth, why it received its name, and why he was given it when ordained by ones that pray upon his prophecy.

As for the reason why the second scabbard remained empty, he hoped that in time, the *necessary* blade would fill the void.

~

With the cloak not being buttoned and enshrouding him as it did before, excluding the boots, it lost one of its main attributes, the chameleon effect.

When standing, he decided to button his cloak, pulling it over his body just as he stepped closer to the creek. Reaching the creek, he bent down and cupped a handful of water. He shook his head when tasting the water.

"As I thought."

He emptied the water from his hands and mused.

Little to no mana. A world of very little consequence. Maybe . . . maybe it was given a chance, but not anymore. Now dry, desolate.

Rajur procured his spyglass while thinking of mana. He viewed the sky above.

Two moons.

One of the moons, the one fading away, looked unfamiliar to him, while the second moon, also vague and yet fading in, looked familiar.

"Eythreal," Rajur said.

Soon.

Nodding, Rajur and his keen hearing picked up distant sounds.

Footsteps.

"Two sets of them," he muttered.

Fearlessly, Rajur stayed by the creek and waited. Many seconds passed, and he could see two men. The men were too distant to capture Rajur's silhouette; therefore, Rajur watched these men approach him undetected and studied their outfits. They both wore uniforms of strange sovereignty. He noticed both had a star-shaped brass medallion pinned to their breast pockets. He also noticed a vaguely familiar weapon sheathed in a small scabbard.

The two stepped closer.

"I am here," Rajur said impassively, seeing that the two were about to travel past him without being detected.

The second he spoke, the cape lost its attributes, even if they didn't catch sight of him with their eyes.

Deputy Mitchum and Deputy Redding stood fifteen feet from Rajur.

"Jesus H. Christ!" Mitchum said. "I knew it. I goddamn knew I saw something. It looked—"

"But he just appeared out of thin air!" Deputy Redding said, continuing to look dumbfounded.

"I knew it! I gosh-darn-it knew it!"

"There was the creek. Here is the forest, the leaves, trees, and shrubs around us. And he just . . ."

Rajur stood patiently while one bragged and the other tried to solve the mystery.

"I understand your confusion," Rajur said, seeing time being wasted. "It is right for you to be confused, for I know how well I can blend in with my surroundings."

"The hell you do!"

The deputies settled down. They studied the stranger's outfit.

"What are you wearing? I mean, look at you! And who the heck are you?"

"He ain't no Harold—that's for sure."

"Well, no shit, he ain't no Harold."

"He sure ain't from around here either."

"Tell me something I don't know."

"Again, you are both right," Rajur said. "I'm not from around here."

"And where is not from around here?"

"Far," Rajur said.

"Far? I think he's a bit off. Drink too much moonshine last night?"

"Moonshine?" Rajur asked, bewildered.

"Oh Jesus, he doesn't even know what that is. He's definitely lost it."

"He could be dangerous," Redding muttered to Deputy Mitchum. "What are you doing here?" he asked Rajur. "Do you not know this area is near off-limits? It borders a forest not to be trespassed, especially by damn weirdo strangers like you. You cross that creek, and you're breaking town law."

"I'm looking for a boy," Rajur said. "Or maybe a girl. I don't know which. And it really doesn't matter since either one will do."

"Oh god! Did he just say what I think he said?"

"That's not good, mister."

"Not good at all."

"I don't mean what you are thinking," Rajur said. "Things are happening and happening very fast."

"You betcha! I think we need to introduce him to the sheriff. What do you think?"

"Oh, he'll love him."

"You got any weapons on you?"

"My sword," Rajur said. "A few other trinkets."

"He's got a sword! Well, ain't that something? He has a sword over his back."

"Should we take it from him?"

"Mitchum! What in hell is he going to do with a sword against these?" Redding said, unholstering his firearm.

Rajur smiled.

"I think I know where I'm at," Rajur said, staring at the gun. "It makes sense. Moonshine. Do you mean some sort of *intoxication*? Yes. You do. And now those."

"What do you mean?"

"Guns. Of course. They fire—what do you call them—bullets? I see them at the trade center in Ghalia. And other trading ports and centers."

"Oh god. Oh god. He really is mad."

"You say 'god' a lot," Rajur said perplexedly. "But you essentially have no mana here. Why? Why do you invoke a god that you forced never to exist again? How can one believe in what can only be believed by faith when faith is without merit where one is incapable of believing?"

"What did he just say?" Mitchum asked, confounded.

"I don't know. But Sheriff Riggins is going to love this guy."

"Oh yeah. Love him *and* hate him."

"He'll be the talk of the town."

"Town?" Rajur said. "Will you take me to this town? It would be wise."

Rajur extended his weaponless hands to the men and opened both palms face up. "I come in peace. Take me to your leader."

The deputies' eyes almost exploded. They looked astonished at each other.

"Do you think what I'm thinking?"

"That he's some alien? A Martian? Come down from some distant planet?"

The deputies smiled as they turned back to Rajur.

"We're going to be famous!"

"Then you will take me to town?" Rajur asked.

Seeing him step toward them, the deputies each placed a hand on the holster of his weapon.

"You just slow down there," Redding said.

Rajur stopped.

"Now, listen to me. You're going to step ahead of us. And we're going to steer you in the direction we want you to go. Understand me?"

"I understand you," Rajur said.

"Good. Make an awkward movement, and it's bang-bang. You know what that means?"

"It means you're going to fire those *bullets* at me."

"Exactly," Redding said. "Now move on."

"What about Harold?" Mitchum asked.

"I think this will take precedence over Harold Huntsinger's whereabouts."

"*Huntsinger*," an intrigued Rajur said. "Who's this Harold? And his last name is Huntsinger?"

"You just hush."

~

Timothy took advantage of the time given to him. He took a nap. The previous night's sleep had not been much, and this catnap did wonders, for when we woke up, he felt more relaxed and less worried than the days before. Was it because of this *Rajur*? He didn't know. He did sense this Rajur to be more than likely friend and not foe. What really soothed his anxieties was the book being restored to him. Of course, neither this book nor any other book could soothe the pain he felt for his family. But with this book returned to him, he clung to the hope again, the same hope that dissipated when he felt the book out of his possession.

If I could only finish this book . . .

Deep in his thoughts, he tried to recall the Wood Dweller's exact words regarding his world and the finishing of the book.

But the pungent smell of tobacco interrupted his thoughts.

"Miss me yet?" the sheriff said sarcastically. He brought with him a chair from the nearby guard desk. "Had to round up Bernie. You know Bernie? He's the hound keeper. We're going to find Harold. Make no mistake about that."

"You won't have the time," Timothy said.

"What do you mean by that?" the sheriff said with a twitch to his face.

"Forget I said it."

The sheriff deliberately blew smoke Timothy's way. "You're talking about those spiders again? I should whip you, boy. Whip you good. Whip the goddamn nonsense out of you."

The sheriff leaned back in his chair.

"But I won't. I won't because of the very close friendship I have with your pa."

"Funny," Timothy said. "He never liked you or your sons."

"Keep digging yourself a grave, kid. Now, about that negotiation of ours."

Before another word could be said, Deputy McKinney joined them.

"What you got for me?" the sheriff asked his deputy.

"Footprints. Recent."

"And?"

"I've got Deputy Redding and Mitchum following the trace now. They broke toward Neville Creek's Bridge. They're heading near—"

"Forest Beyond," Timothy said.

"You shut up," the sheriff said. "Go on," he said toward Deputy McKinney.

"I told them boys to find a good place to leave a marker, come back here so we can return with the hounds. That's if somebody has been, uh, successful in waking up ole Bernie from his stupor. Just another crazy night of debauchery for that old drunk last night."

"It's done," the sheriff said. "We'll be seeing him shortly—him and the hounds. But for now," the sheriff said, with his eyes on Timothy, "this boy owes me some answers. Now out with it!"

"But you won't believe me."

"You're goddamn right I won't believe you if it has anything to do with that cow dung of earlier. I told you I want the truth! No fantasy, no spider and magic book, and so forth."

Timothy remained silent. "Give me that damn book back! I should have known you'd squirm your way out of a man's deal."

The sheriff stepped toward the cell and extended his hands through the bars.

Timothy stepped back.

"I found the book in the Forest Beyond—and yes! I said Forest Beyond," Timothy stammered out.

To his shock, the sheriff kept quiet.

"I got lost. Butch went off chasing a rabbit, and I tried to follow them. I then found myself lost and heard some music—"

"Be careful," the sheriff said.

"I followed the sound and encountered a—I don't even know what it is."

"The truth," the sheriff said.

"The truth is that we're all doomed if I'm not given a chance to do something about it."

"Do what? And give me that damn book," the sheriff said, reaching out again for the book.

Before the sheriff could retrieve the book, they both heard footsteps.

Deputy Redding and Mitchum arrived, along with a stranger lurking behind them.

The sheriff pulled away from the cell and turned to his deputies.

"Back already?" the sheriff asked.

Seeing past the deputies, the sheriff's question became moot as his mouth gaped open at the sight of the stranger.

Unfortunately for Timothy, he had no view of the end of the corridor where the three men approached. He did witness the sheriff's astonishment. Thus, he stepped to the front of the cell and leaned out as much as possible to receive a better view. What he saw excited him. But sensing the stranger's stare directed his way as if the stranger anticipated not only Timothy's stare but also the very fact that he remained inside the cell (which Rajur did, even without a view inside the cell), Timothy immediately shoved the book behind him and scurried to the back of the cell room, only to sit upon the bench. It did not sit well with Timothy that this character from the book had already sensed his presence even before revealing himself to him. His trust in this enigmatic figure now teetered from being friend or foe because of this clairvoyance.

This person became *dangerous* to Timothy.

"We hurried back here for a reason," Redding said. "Thought you might want to meet this stranger we here encountered."

The sheriff sought calmness. He examined the stranger from head to toe. His eyes returned to the sword sheathed over his back.

"Is that a goddamn sword?"

Rajur nodded as the deputies stared at Rajur and again at the sheriff.

"You let this hooligan come into my station with a weapon?" the sheriff asked.

"I told you so," Mitchum said to Redding. "I told Redding to disarm him. But he wouldn't!"

"You lie."

"Shut up, the both of you!" The sheriff turned to the stranger. "You've got a lot of explaining to do."

"He said he's looking for a boy or girl, and it does not matter which one."

"He said what?"

"He then asked us to take him to our leader."

"He did?"

"Those were his exact words."

"He also said he comes in peace," Mitchum added, seeing a smile develop on the sheriff's face.

"Did he now? He comes in peace? Take me to your leader? Well, I'll be damned. We've got ourselves a loony here, boys. And this loony here is equipped with a sword."

The sheriff stepped toward the stranger. "Do you know what these here are?" he said, gripping the hilt of his handgun.

"That he does," Redding said.

"Said he sees them in Ghalia. A trading port, isn't that right?" Mitchum asked the stranger.

Rajur nodded. "They're mostly owned and traded by Runners."

"By what?"

"Runners?"

"Men and women exiled from each of the Four Kingdoms and now harrow bound for hire."

"Men and women exiled from each of the Four Kingdoms and now harrow bound for hire," the sheriff repeated. "What the hell are you talking about?"

"What's harrow?" an intrigued Mitchum asked.

"Short for the Harrowing."

"What's the Harrowing?" Mitchum asked, again, intrigued.

"A realm of infinite boundaries, governed by Iria's Dark—home to an endless amount of pain and suffering."

"Oh," Mitchum said, "kind of like our hell? Except for all that *Ir-i-a* stuff."

"Aye," Rajur said. "Hell. You can almost say that."

"And those Runners are like mercenaries?" Mitchum continued.

"Will you shut up!" the sheriff said. "Stop patronizing him. He's crazy—a loony. And I want that sword of his. And the belt too. Looks like there are all kinds of *toys* on it."

Rajur smiled. "You're asking me to surrender my weapons?"

"You bet I am."

"I've never surrendered my blade to any one person or *thing* . . . ever."

"Well, there's a first time for everything. McKinney! Take his sword."

McKinney smiled back roguishly. He enjoyed this. He walked up to Rajur fearlessly, ready to bully the stranger into submission. But this undaunted intimidation came to a screeching halt, for he examined the stranger closer and noticed a look of wear and tear one could not fathom to have endured. Not only that, but he also noticed scars that could only be made by god knows what, and yet, the stranger proved victorious.

And for the briefest of seconds, McKinney thought he saw the hilt of the stranger's sword coming to life.

"What are you waiting for?" the sheriff said. "Take the sword away!"

McKinney tried to muster the little courage he had. But it failed him. He took a step back and remained motionless.

"I can't."

"What do you mean you can't?"

"I just can't," McKinney said and broke away.

"What the hell do you mean you can't, and where the hell do you think you're going?"

McKinney said not a word as he cowardly left the building.

Feeling enraged, the sheriff rushed toward Rajur and stopped dead in his tracks. He, too, felt diminutive and highly insignificant before this warrior.

"What are you?" the sheriff asked.

"I am not from around here."

"I see that. But why are you here?"

"Things are changing."

"What kind of things?"

Rajur stayed mum.

"I can't have you here with your weapons at your disposal," the sheriff submissively said. "But I also can't take them from you. I'm asking—"

"I'll do it," Rajur said, finding it pointless to argue, for the weapons would always be at his disposal, and time could not be spared. He needed to talk to the boy attempting to hide from his eyes. "But I'm not surrendering my weapons. I'm only putting them down on the desk over there and leaving them there for the time being. Let it be known that I never surrendered my weapons to you or anyone else who walks on this world or the next. Do you hear me?"

The sheriff nodded his head graciously.

Rajur proceeded to unstrap the baldric that sheathed Storm Breaker. The crowd around him noticed a faint glow from the sheathed sword. Rajur looked toward Mitchum. He trusted him the most. He also sensed no desire in Mitchum to possess Storm Breaker. Thus, he handed the dual baldric to Mitchum, and the latter grasped it reverently. Mitchum then gently placed the baldric upon the desk where the sheriff sat earlier, smoking his pipe. Rajur loosened his girdle and extended it to Mitchum. Mitchum again grabbed the equipment reverently. But this time, he grew nosey. His left hand neared one of the Moon Beams, and he'd have touched it if it weren't for Rajur.

"I wouldn't do that," Rajur said.

Mitchum feared the stranger and compliantly agreed. He placed the girdle on the same desk as the baldric. But his eyes never left the brilliant white sheen of the Moon Beams.

"What are they?" Mitchum asked.

"What they are, no one understands. Even I don't understand. I have my guesses. But they have zero evidence to back them up."

"They're so . . ."

This time Deputy Redding walked up to the girdle. "Shiny."

"Aye," Rajur said. "Shiny and yet . . . terribly dangerous."

"Dangerous?" Redding said. "How can they be dangerous? They're just—" Redding went to grab them.

"I'm warning you!" Rajur admonished.

Redding smiled. He smiled, ignored Rajur's warning, and touched the edge of one of the Moon Beams with his right hand. On touching it, he cried out, "Son of a bitch!"

He followed that up with an excruciating whimper while shedding tears like a scared, lost child and doing everything he could to put pressure on the wound.

"Let us see! Let us see!" a jovial Mitchum said.

Redding continued to cry out in pain.

"Come on! Let us see!"

The sheriff demanded Redding reveal the wound. Redding removed his left hand and the material of his uniform used to put pressure on the wound.

A portion of the top half of his finger fell to the ground while what had touched the Moon Beam had been dissolved by the burning essence of the weapon.

"My God," the sheriff said, staring at a bloodless, severed right-hand index finger on the ground.

"It burned his finger right off!" Mitchum said.

"Cauterized it," the sheriff said.

"I warned him," Rajur said.

The sheriff responded by unsheathing his handgun. But he lacked the nerve to point the gun at the stranger.

He could only wave the handgun around.

"Now you listen to me," the sheriff said, no longer calm and lucid. "You're going into that cell with the boy. Something is going on here. I don't know what it is, but—"

"I do," Rajur said. "There's a storm coming. And it's not like any storm you know of."

"Well! Whatever the hell it is, I can't take it anymore. Get in that cell. Get in there and let me . . . let me . . ."

"Boss?" Mitchum asked. "You all right?"

The sheriff whipped around and faced Mitchum with his gun pointed at the deputy. Mitchum jumped back with hands in the air.

"Of course, I'm all right. I mean . . . No. No! I'm not all right. Something . . . something is afoot here. Get in that cell!"

While holding the gun in one hand, the sheriff unlocked Timothy's cell door, and Rajur leisurely stepped inside.

He didn't stop till he sat close to Timothy as if they'd been best buds for their entire lives.

Timothy did not budge. He had been captivated by the whole scene and was now even more confounded on what to think of the stranger.

"You're going to stay inside until this all clears away."

"That will never happen," Rajur said.

"Shut up!" the sheriff exclaimed. Afraid of what the stranger could do to him, he softened his tone. "Just . . . please be quiet."

Unsure of his next move, the sheriff took a few steps back. He noticed Rajur's eyes steer in the direction of the cell floor's entrance.

Seconds later, the sheriff heard footsteps landing on their ground floor.

"Finally," the sheriff said, relieved to see his fourth deputy alongside Bernie.

Seeing no hounds with them, the sheriff's face returned to anger.

"The hounds?"

"Forget the hounds!" Deputy Dexter Bennings shouted.

"Forget the hounds?"

"Yes. Forget the damn hounds. Forget the whole town!"

"What? What are you talking about?"

"Everyone has lost their minds—that's what *I'm* talking about!" Bernie, the ole hound keeper, interjected.

"What's he talking about?"

"Spiders!" Dexter said. "Thousands and thousands of them, millions maybe. They're devouring everything that comes in sight. From the Chester residence to the Youngblood ranch, they've all fallen—fallen to these itty-bitty spiders!"

"Fallen as in?" a slightly recovered Redding asked.

"Poisoned. Spun up. Being decomposed as we speak and their insides sucked out. Or whatever spiders goddamn do!"

"It's nothing but crazy talk," Bernie said. "Everyone has lost their minds."

"And you've seen this?" Sheriff Riggins asked Deputy Bennings.

"Firsthand? No. But that's what they're saying. And I mean everyone!"

"As I said," Bernie said, "the whole town has lost their minds."

"Then explain the goddamn moons?" Dexter said scathingly.

"What's he talking about?" the sheriff asked. "Moons?"

"In the sky," Dexter Bennings said. "Well, how can I put it? There's uh, well, there's our moon. But it's . . . it's no longer alone. A second moon, growing brighter. And so . . . not like our moon. Not a wrinkle on it."

"Impossible," the sheriff said. "Bernie is right. You've all lost your goddamn minds."

"Then why don't you go outside and look for yourself!" Deputy Dexter Bennings said loudly.

"Are you shouting at me?"

"You bet I am!" Bennings shouted again.

The sheriff looked sternly at the deputy.

"Boss?" Mitchum said. "What if the boy is right?"

"You're all crazy," the sheriff faintly said. "But I'll go out there. I'll go out there and see for myself that you're all crazy."

The sheriff holstered his weapon and went to leave. Timothy pitied them, especially after learning about the death of Zachary and his family, for how could anyone survive the mass of spiders if they came in their way? He didn't want anyone else to die. He readied himself to stand up and reveal the book to the sheriff again. This time, he believed the sheriff would see the contents, namely, the depiction of Rajur.

It would make sense to them.

Rajur perceived this action of Timothy's and held the boy down.

He whispered in his ear, "Let them go. It's too late for them, for all of them."

Painfully, Timothy understood the truth of what he said and settled down.

"What about them?" Mitchum said. "We can't just leave them locked up."

"Not with all those spiders," Bennings said. "They'll be here in no time."

"Are you telling me what to do?" the sheriff asked.

Nobody responded.

"They stay locked up."

Chapter 12

FLEE!

Timothy didn't hesitate to ask Rajur what could easily be considered the most critical question in his adventure thus far—possibly the most crucial question of his entire life.

"Friend or foe?"

"It depends," Rajur answered. "What are your intentions?"

"My intentions?" Timothy repeated. "Well, let's see. I've killed my family. I've murdered my best friend and his family. I'm not long from killing everyone else in this town too. Hell. I've possibly killed off this whole world of mine because of my stupidity. My intentions? My *intention* is to finish this book," Timothy said, pulling the book from behind him. "And by god—and there better be a god!—everything will then return to normal, to the very moment I set foot in the Forest Beyond."

"If you stand by those words, then I am your friend," Rajur said.

Relieved, Timothy relaxed his shoulders.

"This is you?" Timothy said on opening the book to Rajur's chapter.

Rajur nodded and extended his hand out. "Here. Give me the book so that I can see better."

Timothy squeezed his eyebrows. He recalled the warnings. The Wood Dweller gave no exception to the rule. But this man was to be his ally, and possibly his most trusted ally. How could he not trust him? Timothy nodded his head and offered the book.

Rajur shook his head, closed his hand, and pushed back the book.

"First and foremost!" Rajur said sternly, his eyes drilling a hole into Timothy's brain. "Never give the book to anyone. Never. I don't care if it is just for that person to have a better view. It never matters. You are its possessor, reader, and scribe. You and this book are more aligned with each other than any two things in this world or the one to come. And the book can only have one of you.

"What is your name?" Rajur asked.

"Timothy."

"Last name."

"Huntsinger."

Rajur betrayed himself by cracking a smile and nodding.

"What is it?" Timothy asked, noticing Rajur's change of look.

"It is nothing. But yes, you have a strong and unique name."

"Strong?" Timothy said.

"It has to be because you alone have the power to finish this book."

Timothy nodded.

"Good," Rajur said. "First lesson over."

"So you understand the book?" Timothy asked.

"I have come across a few things in my life. I know the lore of it, one could say. But none of it can be proven."

"What can you tell me now?"

"Not now. And not here. There are far too many uncertainties to prioritize for now. For now, I need you to let me read this book."

"How?"

"Place it on your lap. I'll have you turn the page. Don't get me wrong. It's not like touching the book is a death sentence. Nor would it deliver me or anyone else pain. I just don't want you in the habit of giving the book to anyone to read—even me. Later in your adventures, friends and foes will come to you deceptively. You may think you're handing the book to your closest ally, only for them to be your greatest nemesis. Never forget that. This book is about you and you only. Nobody else could ever understand."

Timothy nodded and opened the book to page 1.

"Turn the page."

Timothy turned the page, and Rajur scanned the contents with his finger, brazing the writing. He did so quickly. He asked Timothy to turn the page. With the page turned, Rajur studied the writing and sketch with ease and told Timothy to turn the page again.

Throughout this entire diligent summarization, Rajur never betrayed a single emotion. His stoic look cemented itself upon his face.

"You can close it now," Rajur said upon reaching the end, which was "Rajur's Awakening."

Timothy closed the book.

"You read it all?"

"Aye."

"You can understand the language," Timothy said joyfully.

"No," Rajur said. "The writing comes from before the ancient text of Thrandor—thus, before the first language ever spoken on Eythreal. It is from an age far beyond us."

"Thrandor? *Eythreal?*"

"Soon," Rajur said, putting a hand on the boy's shoulder. "Very soon."

"Sounds like you don't understand anything," a bitter and disappointed Timothy said.

"Oh, I understand. I understand a lot."

"OK," Timothy said. "Good. Why don't you start by answering this question? Is that my pa?"

"You speak of the monster with the gem?"

"Yes."

"Your pa is no longer, for the monster is no longer a living creature. It is of a cursed spirit now possessing your pa's body—Gawul."

"Gawul?"

"Aye."

"What is this Gawul?"

"A servant that serves only one master, a queen. This queen of the most hideous of natures. Abbigatha."

Rajur said the last word absentmindedly, drifting off in his thoughts while grasping a chain over his neck. His hand slid down the chain and stopped at a locket.

He closed his eyes upon feeling the locket.

Timothy watched. He saw pain manifesting on his face.

"Three eyes," Rajur muttered.

"Huh?"

"Three sockets."

"What are you—"

"Three gems."

"Yes. Gems like what the monster has?"

Rajur opened his eyes.

"The Daughters of Iria cursed and imprisoned."

"The girl inside the gem," Timothy said.

"Aye. Yvonne is her name—the one that Gawul possesses. She is the oldest of the three. Not long before this moment, I was in possession of Misha, the youngest. Coming here, I lost her. I fear what hands possess her now. Hildadore, the middle child, well, her whereabouts have long been unknown to us. We must pray that no one but us finds her—more importantly, not found by the one that knows the way back to where the gems belong."

"Where is that?"

"Inside of three eye sockets."

"And the sockets they belong to?"

"The same queen that monster is servant to."

"That Abbigatha?"

"Aye. Queen Abbigatha."

"She's an actual queen?"

"Queen of spiders." Rajur turned to Timothy with a gloomy and concerned look on his face. "I do not envy you, Timothy Huntsinger. There's not a single living creature that would want to be in your shoes. They'd be fools to think otherwise. No one else but you must face the unspeakable dangers that come for us all, and yet, just like the rest of us, including me, you are oblivious to what those dangers could turn out to be."

"Can you tell me something? Teach me something?"

"There is no time at present. There is only the storm. We must ready ourselves."

Rajur stood up and stepped toward the bars.

"This storm that comes," Timothy said.

"A transformation, you might say. It comes as a Void. It will empty your world and replace it with the world existing in the book. The same can be said to have already been done to Eythreal, except it never crossed paths with the Void. Eythreal became nonexistent to itself but stayed existent in the book. Thus, its effects on Eythreal were minute, and nearly all inhabitants and lands were oblivious to them. As for your world, the Void takes it with It, now to be a suspension over Oblivion, for that is where the Void leads to, everything and everyone except," Rajur stopped and turned back to Timothy.

"Turn to the page with me kneeling."

Timothy turned the page to "Rajur's Awakening."

"There," Rajur said, pointing at the sketch.

"I believe I know that place. Most people think it's still part of Old Wicker's Forest, which mostly belongs to my family. But I'm not so sure about that. Remembering now, I've been there a few times. And each time, I feel like I'm hovering on the border of the Forest Beyond. Thinking about it now, how could anyone be so sure of the borders of that forest? I think that spot may as well be the Forest Beyond. Maybe not the full essence of it, but more like a window into the heart of the Forest Beyond."

Rajur listened to him as if he knew exactly what Timothy meant. He even nodded his head.

"I believe you to be right, for I appeared there. I would not have been left in a place of only your world. We'll be safe there. Some of this town may survive, for if the book wants it to, it will. However, I doubt if anything would be left over. But this we cannot be sure of. What I am sure of is that location. Let us not tarry. Let us further ourselves from this town as much as possible and make this tree and creek our intended destination. And let us hope you know the navigation to this location. I may be one of the most skilled trackers, but this is new territory for me. The smell and taste and feel of your wilderness confuse me."

"And how are we supposed to do that, seeing that we're locked up?"

"Do you imagine I'd let us be locked up if I didn't know a way out? But not to worry! Another way comes to us right now."

"What are you talking about?"

"Listen."

A few seconds later, Timothy heard footsteps coming down the stairs.

"Zachary!" Timothy shouted when the former made his appearance before them. "You're alive!"

"Alive? Yeah! And you won't believe what's going on. Everyone is going berserk!"

"We've heard."

"Everyone!"

"We know."

"The sheriff . . . he's running amok and—"

"Zachary! We know."

Zachary settled into a calm demeanor, even though his body trembled from head to toe because of excitement.

"I need you to calm down," Timothy said, "need you to focus."

"Yes. OK. Focus. Right. I'm focused. I came here because I felt terrible for what I did. I never meant to rat you out. I was sulking all morning long when Tom Sickle came all drunk to the ranch. He talked crazy talk. I didn't hear everything he said, but I heard something about spiders. I don't know, just that there are tiny spiders devouring the whole land. My eyes grew big. Timothy could be right. I saw this as a distraction too. With my father busy, I slipped away and headed here as fast as possible. On the way, I saw only madness. No spiders, but madness. And now," Zachary said and stopped, eyeing Rajur for the first time. "Who's that?"

"This is Rajur," Timothy said. "Right? I'm only guessing that from the page."

Rajur nodded.

Timothy turned back to Zachary. "We don't have much time. Know that he's a friend, and we must get out of here."

"Oh. Yes. Sure. Let me go find the keys."

"You'll be wasting time," Rajur said. "See that girdle beside the baldric?"

"Girdle? Baldric?"

"Belt."

"Oh."

"Bring it to me. But whatever you do, do not touch those shiny *things*," Rajur admonished.

Zachary turned to the desk, and the lust from the Moon Beams captivated him.

"They're so beautiful!"

"Zachary!" Timothy shouted. "Don't touch them. And hurry up!"

"OK, OK," Zachary said.

Zachary's eyes landed on the sword's hilt when he reached for the girdle. "Is that a sword?"

"Yes," Timothy said. "But grab the belt!"

Zachary's eyes focused more on the hilt of Storm Breaker. The embroidery showed ocean waves crashing against mountains. The more he studied the hilt, the more it came alive. The waves of the sea crashed harder against the mountains. Thus, the mountains soon toppled over and fell into the raging sea. Subsequently, the sea swallowed them up and eventually came to a calmness, allowing ancient vessels to cross the waters with impunity. Land neared these voyagers. The sea vessels made their way to the land and anchored. Hundreds of warriors climbed down from the ships and rushed onto land. The sea disappeared, and only the land could be seen on the hilt. The warriors found peace on this land. They built villages and dwellings. They prospered greatly. But the peace and prosperity proved short-lived. Comets came crashing down from the sky and exploded on the land. Fires from the explosions burned down everything. The men and women were forced to leave land for the sea again. After they departed from the sea, the sea was enraged even more and spit out the drowned mountains, and the hilt once again became a panorama of mountains and sea.

Zachary wanted more. He wanted to live inside this hilt. He wanted to be the sword. He thus reached out for the hilt, and before he grasped it, the embroidery came alive again. The sea became enraged again and did not crash against the mountains this time. This time the sea became a single tidal wave and crashed *over* the mountains. When it receded, it left behind a flat land, which was no other than a jungle of thorns and vines seeking the Trespasser. And from out of these thorns and vines came three snakes, each of them with two heads. The snakes greeted Zachary with poison-dripping fangs. Zachary froze in terror. The snakes would have pounced on the boy if it weren't for Rajur playing a soft tune. The tune emitted from his mouth calmed the vines' and thorns' aggression while also pacifying the threatening snakes.

But the snakes weren't wholly pacified. They were still ready to end the life of the trespasser.

"Don't move," Rajur said calmly. "And don't think you're quicker than the snakes."

"But they're like a foot away from me," Zachary said.

"That's because the blade knows your thought. Clear your mind."

"What are you talking about?"

"The blade knows that you not only want to possess it but also *desire* it. No man, woman, or other creature can possess this blade but me. And to desire it as much as you have has triggered an alarm. You must empty your thoughts of desiring this sword. And do so now, for these snakes will strike. Clear your thoughts, and when clear, think of something far different from this blade. Do it. Do it now."

"I'm trying!" Zachary said as a two-headed snake hissed an inch from his face.

"Close your eyes."

"I'm closing them."

"Take hold of all your thoughts and place them into a barrel."

"A barrel?"

"Do it!"

"A barrel!"

"Put a lock on the barrel. Dig the deepest of holes. Drop that barrel in there. Cover it with dirt. Imagine it gone forever."

"I did."

"Now, think. Think of something so influential to your mind that it will distract your memory of the barrel."

"My family."

"Imagine yourself with your family. Imagine all the possibilities you share with them. Imagine . . ."

As Rajur fed Zachary scenarios of Zachary and his family, the snakes slowly returned to the jungle, while the jungle also returned to the sword's hilt.

Timothy watched as the embroidery of the hilt showed another catastrophic turn of events: a flood prevailing over the jungle, which led to the coming of the next age.

"Now, open your eyes," Rajur said calmly.

Zachary opened his eyes and stared at the sea and mountains.

"The girdle," Rajur said.

Exhausted to the point of nearly swooning, Zachary grabbed the girdle and brought it over to Rajur. Rajur fastened the girdle to his waist. He unsheathed a Moon Beam and cut through the bars evenly with the slightest of touches, leaving behind a gaping hole for Timothy and him to pass through. Timothy, amazed, hesitated a second. But sensing time being wasted too, he passed through the hole.

"What are they again?" he asked Rajur.

"They are called Moon Beams."

"OK. But what are they?"

Rajur shook his head. "Given to me by the strangest of means."

"And the sword?" Zachary asked.

"Not so. Although more of a mystery than the Moon Beams, the sword was given to me when I was ordained."

"Ordained for what?"

"This prattling must not be. We are in grave danger if we stick around here longer. We must go."

Rajur sheathed his Moon Beam and placed the baldric over his body. He went to leave with Timothy.

"Wait!" Zachary shouted. "Where? And what's going on here?"

"Shelter," Rajur said. "We need to find shelter."

"From what? These spiders everyone is talking about?"

"Yes and no. It wouldn't be wise for us to encounter them. But something far greater comes, and we need to be prepared."

"Prepared for what?" Zachary asked.

Rajur looked at Timothy.

"He may not be here when the storm passes," Rajur said.

"You mean," Timothy said, realizing what Rajur meant.

"What's he talking about?" Zachary said. "What are you both talking about? Not here for what?"

"But he's in the book," Timothy said.

"Aye. That he is. But many other things about your world are in the book, and I guarantee that most of them will not be around. Only what relates to what you call the Forest Beyond will for sure remain."

"But I don't relate to the Forest Beyond," Timothy said.

"You relate more with the Forest Beyond than anything else, for you are the Forest Beyond since it is the book that now consummates it all. And you and the book are one. Come."

Rajur hurried away.

Timothy and Zachary stayed behind.

"What's this all about?" Zachary asked.

"I'll explain later. What I can say is that our world is no longer relevant. And we must do what he says," Timothy said and hurried off.

Zachary hesitated. He pondered over his options. The hesitation did not last long. "Wait up!" he shouted as he chased after the two.

~

The three exited the station and stopped. Before the three stood an empty town. Not a single person could be seen.

The silence and eeriness unnerved the boys and warned Rajur of coming danger.

"Where did everyone go?" Zachary asked. "Just a few minutes ago, this place was mad with people."

"Spiders?" Timothy asked Rajur.

Rajur could only stare.

"Spiders?" Zachary also asked.

"We've wasted too much time," Rajur said. He stepped into town. The boys followed.

"I hid Abigail and Breeze up the hill into town," Zachary said.

"Abigail and Breeze?" Rajur asked.

"Our horses," Timothy said.

Zachary pointed the way to the distant hill, and Rajur led them in that direction. Shortly into their travel, the boys stopped when they noticed two townspeople sitting upon the front entrance bench of a usually populated saloon. The vision of the boys was hazy. Zachary stepped in the direction of the two men, far too curious to know what happened to ignore them. Timothy followed. Rajur could only shake his head. He decided to hang back. He knew what they would find. But he also didn't want to stop them. He felt it wise for them to see it for themselves. He wanted to show them how real everything had become and the danger they faced. Thus, he watched the boys slow down, for they perceived a strange glossiness about the two men. The boys also noticed more people behind the broken-down entrance. Ignoring the two glossy men on the bench, the boys crept closer to the saloon and stared through the entrance.

They never made another step after that.

Inside the saloon, the boys discovered a horde of unconscious townspeople, including the sheriff and his deputies, with eyes and mouths gaped open.

The boys saw them being spun by silky, impenetrable spider web.

Most of the personages in the saloon were already spun, while some were fully cocooned, waiting to die, and ready for the next stage: supper for the spiders.

The very thought of so many personages, which included women and children, being fodder for the spiders, numbed the boys to a catatonic state.

Their eyes then noticed the specks of dust swarming the fresh victims.

"Are those . . ." Zachary said and stopped.

"Spiders," Timothy said.

The two quietly stepped back.

"You think they hear us?"

"I don't think so," Timothy said as they continued to step back.

"Wrong," Rajur said. "Do you not feel that?"

The boys stopped and listened. Instead of hearing a sound, they felt a slight reverberation from under their feet.

"It's like a tapping," Zachary said.

Rajur nodded. "And now do you hear them?"

Both Timothy and Zachary heard the smallest of noises.

"It is tapping," Zachary said.

"Coming our way," Timothy said.

"Are they under us?"

Rajur nodded and pointed toward the other end of the saloon. The eyes of the boys followed his direction and noticed a wave of dust coming for them.

"Spiders!" Timothy let slip.

"To the hill," Rajur said imperatively.

The boys did not hesitate. They ran like never before toward the hill.

Rajur followed calmly and mindfully. He soon found himself on a narrow path between two buildings leading to the hill. He pulled out a small flask from his girdle. Undoing the lid, he squirted a green liquid at one of the buildings. As soon as the liquid hit the surface, it caught on fire. Rajur continued to squirt liquid out by making an arch, thus forging a wall of fire from one building to the next, cutting off the spiders from using their path to the hill. As much as Rajur wanted to burn a larger blaze, he knew it would be futile. The spiders were not dumb. And they were legion. They'd find another way.

Rajur turned away from the fire barricade and caught up with the boys.

Upon the crest of the hill, the three found Abigail and Breeze.

"Strong steeds," Rajur said, examining the horses. "They will do good for us."

"I better hope so," Zachary said, climbing upon Breeze while Timothy climbed upon Abigail. "This is all we have."

Rajur nodded and climbed upon Abigail.

"To the creek and tree?" Timothy said.

"Aye."

"Wait!" Zachary cried out.

"We don't have time to wait," Rajur said.

"I can't go," Zachary said.

"What do you mean you can't go?" Timothy said.

"I've got to go warn my family that Tom Sickle—"

"Zachary," Timothy said, "it's too late."

"What do you mean?"

"I heard the sheriff and deputy talk. Your family—"

"Don't say it!"

"Please, Zachary, we don't have time. Come with us. I promise I'll explain everything."

"No."

"Zachary, listen. I know how to return everything to the way it was. This book," Timothy said, pulling out the book. "This book will bring everything back to normal. Isn't that right?" Timothy said toward Rajur.

Rajur leaned back questioningly.

"But the Wood Dweller," Timothy said. "It said something like that. I don't recall the exact words."

"The Wood Dweller will tell you what you want to hear for its own pleasure. It wanted you to choose and walk away with that book."

"You're saying it lied?"

"I'm not saying it did. I'm only saying that you must believe."

"What's he talking about?" Zachary said. "What about my family?"

"Zachary," Timothy said, "we must believe. I mean, I believe. Give me time to explain. Come with us. It's not just your family. And it's not even about my family. It's about all of us. You must trust me and come with us, and I'll explain everything."

"You better make a decision now," Rajur said. "They've found another way. I hear them coming."

"Zachary? Will you come with us?"

"But—"

"We've been best friends since our birth. Please. Trust me."

Wiping away tears from his eyes, Zachary nodded.

"Then we ride!" Rajur shouted.

Chapter 13

ABBIGATHA'S REIGN OF TERROR

"We're edging closer," Rajur said, sitting behind Timothy on Abigail. Timothy nodded. "I know."

A few minutes later, Rajur called out. "I see the tree, and I can hear the creek."

"You do?" Zachary said.

"Never mind my hearing and vision. It is not like yours or most others."

Five seconds later and Timothy shouted, "I see it too!"

The boys slowed the horses.

Closing in on the tree, Rajur climbed down. The boys followed. Rajur stopped at the exact spot he knelt. He pulled out a tuft of grass and weeds.

"Yes," he said, pulling out Waldo root from the ground. "Eythreal is here."

"Eythreal?" Zachary said.

"Has that plant been there the whole time?" Timothy asked.

"The plant has not. But this land it grows on sustains it, thus why a little of Eythreal shows here on my arrival. Eythreal is the world where I belonged before the blackness came for me. And it will be Eythreal that will appear after the next storm passes us by."

"Next storm? I see not a cloud in the sky," Zachary said.

"Look to your east," Rajur said.

Skilled in navigation, the boys looked to the east. A mass of ominous dark clouds gathered in the far distance. "Geez. Is that lightning inside them?" Zachary said, on account of the dark clouds being faintly translucent, allowing them to spy the faintest streaks of lightning scorching *inside* the clouds.

Not one streak of lightning crossed outside the clouds.

"The storm is unlike anything you've faced," Rajur said. "There'll be no rain, no thunder. Lightning? Yes. An endless stream of lightning, but this lightning is not what you think it is. Even I don't know the cause of the lightning. Inside those dark and yet transparent black clouds, worlds are altered and transformed."

"Like a . . ." Zachary said and stopped. He tried to recall a fancy word he had learned in school. "Like a metamorphosis?"

"Aye."

"And you're sure we're safe here?" Timothy asked.

"Strictly speaking, we're safe from the storm anywhere. It is our position when the storm eventually leaves that could endanger us. Eythreal breathes here already. Our surroundings will not alter much since we stay close to Eythreal grounds. Outside of this position, I am unsure. It is an entirely different story. We could wake up from this storm and find ourselves in a very unfavorable location on Eythreal—a world that neither of you could fathom."

"Again!" Zachary said. "Eythreal. Storms. Metamorphosis. Spiders. Will one of you start explaining to me what this all means?"

"It's a lot to swallow," Timothy said.

"It looks to me that we have the time."

"We don't," Rajur said. "The storm moves fast. We need to ready ourselves."

"No," Zachary said. "You have to give me something, or I'm out of here!"

Rajur and Timothy turned to each other. The former nodded. "Tell him what you can while I grab some wood for the fire. We will need to eat soon."

A second later, Rajur left the site, and Timothy pulled the book out to share with Zachary.

"OK," Timothy said. "You see . . ." Timothy showed Zachary the book's cover and turned to the first page.

"Do you see the writing?"

Zachary nodded.

Timothy smiled. *He believes.*

With the smile turning serious, Timothy divulged as much as he could to Zachary. He did his best to omit not a single detail. During this time, Zachary listened intently and, surprisingly, credulously. Not once did Zachary choose to disbelieve Timothy. He often asked Timothy to repeat himself so he could understand it better.

In the end, Timothy finished with "And that's why I must believe everything will return to us as it was when finishing this book."

Zachary sat back in deep thought.

"But what if you're wrong? What if nothing about our world reverts to its earlier self?"

"I don't know," Timothy said. "I guess I just have to believe."

"Believe? Hah! Look around you. What's there to make you believe that? There are these tiny spiders that just devoured our whole town, murdered our families, and are probably coming straight for us now!"

"They won't find us," Rajur said.

The boys became startled when Rajur approached them with a faggot of wood in both hands and a freshly killed doe over his shoulder.

"Hey!" Zachary exclaimed. "How did you do that? You didn't even make a noise, and I didn't see you. Are you going to tell us you're invisible?"

"Invisible?" Rajur said. "No. It is this cape. It is not like other capes. First off, it has been stitched and enchanted by one of the most powerful enchantresses of all Eythreal—an enchantress that lives in a forest none wish to enter. Its attributes are many. One of them is that it gives me the ability to mimic my surroundings as long as I'm not detected, when each of these three buttons is buttoned. And by *detected*, I mean making a sound or my silhouette seen by anyone."

"Like a chameleon," Zachary said.

"Yes. A chameleon, for there are chameleons on Eythreal also. And with these elvish boots of mine, I emit the smallest of sounds when stepping on the noisiest of paths. So you neither saw nor heard me."

"You got another one of those?" Zachary said.

Rajur sensed no joke in that and shook his head.

"About the spiders," Timothy said. "They won't find us here?"

Rajur placed the wood and female deer down.

"I am sure. They'll be dead come morning. These spiders' life span is very short."

"How short?"

"Dawn. No matter what, they die upon the following dawn, whether that be your sun or the Star of Nod."

"Star of Nod?" Zachary asked.

"What about the giant spider that attacked my pa?" Timothy asked, too eager for this answer to wait on Zachary's question.

"Princess Celia?"

"She has a name?"

"Bluish underbelly?"

"Yes."

"That is Princess Celia. Her other two sisters are very much alike—except they each have a contrasting hue on their underbelly."

"Wait!" Timothy said. "Did you say *sisters*? And they're princesses?"

"Aye. They are the daughters of—"

"That queen of spiders you mentioned earlier," Timothy said. "Abbigatha."

"Aye."

"Who? What?" Zachary said.

Rajur and Timothy ignored Zachary's question.

"All three are giant ugly spiders?"

Rajur nodded

"Great!" Zachary said, looking over at Timothy. "You still think you can finish this book?"

"With the right help," Rajur said.

"I assume you speak of yourself?" Zachary said.

"I speak of many."

"And this Queen Abbigatha," Timothy said. "We must fear her greatly?"

"For now, she sleeps . . ."

"And if she awakens?" Zachary asked.

Rajur's look intensified.

"How would she awaken?" Timothy asked.

"The three gems."

"Three eye sockets!" Timothy said. "That's what you meant. You mean those three gems—"

"Are her eyes. Without those gems, she is powerless and dormant—more like being catatonic, for those gems hold her power. How I don't know, but she transferred all her power into those gems. I imagine when she cursed the Daughters of Iria and imprisoned them—again, this is just an assumption. She may not have done it. Maybe she was tricked—tricked into doing that action unwillingly. Who knows? What we do know is those gems harness not only the powers of Iria's daughters but also the power of Abbigatha. And her power is not to be trifled with. Her power matches that of Goddess Iria."

"But she won't awaken until the gems are returned to her?"

"Aye."

"And the Gawul has one of the gems."

"Aye."

"Gawul? What are you talking about?" Zachary asked.

"What I showed you in the book. The monster that is now my pa—it has a gem. Rajur said it is a servant to one master—to Queen Abbigatha."

Rajur nodded.

"Should we not be out there hunting it down?" Timothy asked. "We must stop it, right?"

"The Gawul would prove too crafty for us. And time is not on our side. But what is on our side is the Gawul's pace. For obvious reasons, it cannot simply travel the land wherever it wants, for it must be hidden from all eyes, never to be revealed. And because of its want of any magic that deals with transportation or transformation, this travel isn't easy."

"OK, OK," Zachary said, shaking his head. "Let me get this straight. OK? There are three gems."

"Aye."

"Each gem has a daughter of Iria inside."

"Aye."

"And their powers—are they as great as Iria?" Timothy asked.

"Of course not. But far greater than you and me! Far greater. They are the Daughters of Iria, goddesses in their own right."

"And who is this Iria?" Zachary said.

"She possesses the seven moons that give life to Eythreal."

"And Eythreal is the world we're turning into?"

"Aye."

"So then this Queen Abbigatha . . ." Zachary said.

"Once a goddess."

"Wait. Let me finish. *Wait!* Did you say 'once a goddess'?"

"I'll let you finish before I expound on that."

"This Abbigatha—she's the one that locked the Daughters of Iria into these gems that are her eyes?"

"Aye. Where she got the gems from, none of us know. How she removed her own eyes and swapped them for the gems we are also ignorant of."

"And with these gems, which hold the power of each of the daughters, she added her own powers into them?"

"Yes, for it seems that is what happened. Again, did Abbigatha mean to do this or not?"

"So these gems are like, really powerful?"

"Yes and no. Yes, to those who can harness their powers (which we only know of two people). No to the rest of Eythreal."

"Abbigatha, I presume, is one of them?"

Rajur nodded. "There is little we know about her. Long ago, Iria's daughters left Eythreal for the Realm of Cosmos, following the ominous absence of their mother to investigate the origin of Abbigatha. By then, we came to a conclusion that she was no mortal being and presumably some goddess, maybe disguised, as she wreaked havoc on Eythreal like no other. The Daughters of Iria gathered what they could, for they did not stay long while also warning the Council of Nod of Iria's longtime disappearance during a time of turmoil. They returned to Eythreal. But they returned to an ambush, hence their imprisonment in the gems—because of that, they could divulge only so much. What we were able to gather was that Abbigatha *is* a goddess—a very narcissistic and envious goddess. Supposedly, she consorted with an exiled god. Because this god was banished from the Realm of Cosmos, her actions were criminal. She stood trial, and her punishment equaled the god she conspired with, although with a horrific twist.

"Her being so narcissist and vain, the Council of Nod turned her looks into the most hideous of monsters, one resembling an aarachè, which, on Earth, I believe you call an arachnid."

"So she too is a spider?" Timothy asked.

"If it helps your mind to perceive her that way, then yes, a spider. But far beastlier is she in one's eyes than a spider could ever be."

"Is she still a goddess?"

"Not even the Council of Nod could unmake her true creation or existence."

"So she's like, hard to kill?" Zachary asked.

"She's not only immortal. She is a goddess. She is not fated to die."

"Then how do we kill her?"

"Who says you have to kill her?"

"Isn't that what this book is about?" Timothy said. "*Gem and Spider.*"

"*Gem and Spider,*" Rajur said. "Aye. If I had to guess, the book wants to tell the story of how the Daughters of Iria are to be freed. And to do that, I imagine no other scenario but vanquishing Abbigatha and releasing her hold on them. But that doesn't mean you, for you cannot. You are no god, Timothy, even though one could say you have as much power as they do, or I should say, consequence. It is your decisions, and your decisions alone, that will allow the book to reach its end. And there is no end but one. Although you can easily manipulate how the book reads, it will not end until it reaches the one end it has *already* destined. Therefore, know this, and always—*always*—remember this: the book wants to be finished just as much as you want to finish it. It will give you a path. It will lead you. It will allow your decisions to reach the end. If the end is exactly what we said, it will not allow you to reach it blindly."

"But what if it doesn't give us a path?"

"Timothy! With the right decisions and choices, it will lead you. But with the wrong choices and decisions, the harder it will be."

"And if this Gawul reaches Abbigatha with the gem?" Zachary asked.

"Woe to us all. But!" he said, with one finger. "It will be only one gem. She will awaken, but only with a trifle of her power. What we must not let happen again is for her to receive all three gems. Never. Never can we allow that to happen. Long before she invested her powers into the gems, and while the Daughters of Iria roamed freely on Eythreal, she came out of her hiding and proclaimed herself Queen Abbigatha of Eythreal. She amassed a great army, a much bigger army than the one that we discovered after the rumors of her doings in Migra—wicked rumors at best. But Eythreal was at a time of relative peace. There was no chaos. We got along. There was structure and rule. We came together as one, that is, Thrandor, the Four Kingdoms, the leaders of each of the Noble Elven clans, the Iron Dwarves, the Empress of Qharthlyions, and many others, and pushed her back to her hiding spot, although we failed to learn of her hidden lair.

"She failed because Eythreal was at peace and unity. But this unity and peace slowly faded from Eythreal. Disturbances were ubiquitous. Disturbances among the Harrowing spread throughout Eythreal's surface. Worshippers of the Harrowing came to the callings of rebellious Dark Ones that not only inhabited the Harrowing but were also the wardens to that endless domain. By doing so, a few Dark Ones had even penetrated the surface of Eythreal—something that is not allowed and against a very compact and strict binding between the Light and Dark of Iria.

"The Witches of Ravenscroft woke up something they could not fathom, and it spread like a diseased wildfire. So much more against the good of Iria had come to existence. So much more . . .

"It was then, at this very time, seeing how all this came to be at Abbigatha's arrival and the long disappearance of Iria, the Daughters of Iria left Eythreal for the Realm of Cosmos to learn something.

"The fall of Thrandor followed not long after. The Four Kingdoms started to crumble. I can only guess that the Daughters of Iria must have heard about the fall of Thrandor and cut their investigation short. As mentioned before, they were ambushed, cursed, and imprisoned inside the gems soon on arrival, which led to Abbigatha investing in their power and her investing her power into them. With her allies intact, Eythreal under heavy distress, and the gems' additional power, Abbigatha would have come out of her hiding and easily have conquered any force upon Eythreal. She would have ruled all Eythreal, and not even Iria's return could have saved us."

Stirring the fire, Rajur hesitated. His hesitation ended with "But she didn't."

Rajur again stirred the fire.

"And know that if fully awake now, it would be an even worse fate for all of us. The noble elf clans are down to one. One! The remaining elves have either exiled themselves from all communication with other clans or have found a way to work against Eythreal by betraying Iria. The Iron Dwarves are the last steadfast clan of dwarves. The remaining dwarves do not care and live by debauchery alone. The Qharthlyions, maybe the greatest power besides men and women on Eythreal, are in a state of riot, wholly disbanded. Their ruler, Empress Tabithlyeen, was slain not too long ago, and the rightful heir to the throne barters exquisite wine and goods for a living instead of fulfilling her duty and bringing union to Zal-Rasha and peace upon Telammonial.

"If Abbigatha woke up now, she wouldn't even have to leave her lair to rule over Eythreal. You have opened a chapter of Eythreal during one of its darkest times."

Silence passed them by. Timothy and Zachary tried to digest everything they heard without going mad. He mentioned elves, dwarves, even witches—and something about Qharthlyions. They could not believe all this—or could they? Everything Rajur divulged to them was told to the boys through fairy tales and other books filled with imagination.

Fictional.

Not anymore.

It was always real, the boys each thought.

Concluding that this must be, both boys became calmer in mind.

Timothy recalled something Rajur had said.

"Why didn't she come out of her hiding when invested with the three gems if it was going to be that simple to conquer Eythreal?"

Rajur stayed mum and stoked the fire again.

"What happened?"

"She was going to," Rajur said. "But before she initiated her war with the additional power given to her from the gems, her eyes—the gems—were stolen from their sockets."

"How? Someone just ripped them out of her eye sockets?" Zachary asked.

"I guess you can say that because nobody knows. What we do know is who did it."

"And?"

Again, Rajur tried to stay mum.

"And?" Zachary repeated.

Rajur continued to stay strong and did not answer.

The boys looked at each other as Rajur lifted off the ground and pulled a knife from his pocket.

"It will be time to eat soon," Rajur said, readying to skin the doe. "Let us rest our weary and overwrought minds."

Reluctantly, the boys stayed quiet. In their minds, nothing could be any more different. Thought after thought raced around unbridled. Rajur sensed this and chose not to mitigate their perturbation. He wanted them to absorb everything. He knew the importance of them coming to grips with the reality of the situation. They must face these stark facts and fight through them. He even left their sight by filling water pouches from the creek, washing down the skinned doe, and stepping into the forest, where he found fruits, seeds, nuts, and mushrooms. He brought back these provisions and placed them in their pot over the fire.

He sat down.

On sitting down, Zachary climbed out of his mind with a perturbed memory of his.

"You said earlier that I may not be around after the storm. What did you mean by that?"

Seldom did Rajur betray his inner emotions, but now twice in less than a day he had. He did so this time by squeezing his facial muscles.

Zachary read it perfectly well.

"It's that bad?"

Rajur relaxed the muscles of his face.

"Tell me. You must."

Rajur felt the pressure to speak from both Zachary and Timothy. He must tell.

"It means exactly what I said. You may not be around here after the storm. You may not belong to Eythreal."

Trying to console the boy, he added, "But try not to dwell on it."

"Try not to dwell on it?" Zachary said in derision. "Did you hear that? He said I should try not to dwell on being dead come morning."

"Not dead. Placed in a Void. Nonexistent for a time. A suspension above Oblivion."

"Oblivion? Void? Great. I thought death couldn't be any worse."

Seeing Rajur not understanding the sarcasm, Zachary grew angry.

"I was kidding! I'd rather be dead! Nonexistent? Are you kidding me? How am I supposed to not dwell on that?"

"Why should you?" Rajur said. "What is the point of dwelling on something entirely out of your control? What is the point in riling yourself up to anger when anger does not solve a single thing? Anger cannot alter this fate. *You* cannot alter this fate. Nor can we. You will either exist or not exist. You will either stand with us when the storm passes and aid Timothy in finishing the book, or you will disintegrate into tiny particles, where a vast vacuum will suck you up into a realm of nothingness, where, again, you wait for your possible final destination, being Oblivion.

"Why worry about that?" Rajur continued. "You'll have no emotions, no feelings—no sense for anything. You'll not have the capacity to think."

"And this shouldn't trouble me?"

"No," Rajur simply said. "Again, why fume over something out of your control? Why worry about something you'll be ignorant of?"

Zachary nodded his head. "Thank you. I feel much better now."

Rajur nodded.

"I was being sarcastic!" Zachary said. "Sarcastic! Do you even know what that means?"

"I do. A very wasteful set of false emotions. I choose to ignore one being sarcastic."

Zachary shook his head in frustration. He picked up a nearby rock and threw it into the creek. He picked up another and did the same.

"There's nothing we can do to ensure Zachary stays with us?" a grief-stricken Timothy asked.

"No. It is the book's will."

"But did you not say I'm the possessor?"

"Aye. But that does not mean you have power over it. No one has power over it—no one. You are its reader—and its scribe, as I've mentioned. You are the one to fill in this book and see it to its end. But again, do not for one second think you can alter its predestined fate. This book—no matter what its contents may turn out to be—has only one front cover and one back cover. It has only one beginning and one end. You've already allowed the beginning to open. You must now allow the end to reach its course."

"Predestined? You're saying," Timothy raised his arm, "by me raising my hand, the book already knew I was going to do it?"

"No. You're not listening. The book doesn't know any of its contents on how it is to be finished. It only knows what *finish* it wants, and you're the one to finish it. Any action or decision you make this second, the book and you did not know about."

"So there's no chance to help Zachary?"

"No."

Timothy leaned in closer to Rajur. "You know, you can at least say something encouraging. Maybe raise his spirits."

"Lie to him?" Rajur said out loud.

"No," Timothy said subtly. "Just—"

"Timothy," Rajur said sternly. "You are soon to wake up to an unimaginable danger. You won't know where you are. You won't know anything about your surroundings. You'll soon encounter creatures you have only dreamed of until this moment. You cannot imagine the perilous road you'll be traveling on. I cannot even describe it to you. And you're worried about Zachary? Don't. You must be *impossibly* strong, formidable like a Great Lion. You must be. I advise you now and forever: steel yourself for what comes next and forever do so until you finish that book. Tomorrow comes a chapter in your life that no person or thing or whatever that lives and breathes in any world can prepare for.

"Now, both of you, eat."

Surprisingly, Zachary returned to the log and sat by Timothy.

"I just want you to know I'm not happy about this," Zachary said. "But I guess you're right. I don't have a choice. Why aggravate the situation?"

Rajur found much reverence for Zachary in seeing the boy bravely resigned to his fate. He gave them both a plate of food.

The boys found it difficult to eat.

"Please," Rajur said softly. "Try. You'll both need your strength."

"Not me," Zachary said.

"Don't think like that. Believe."

Zachary looked down at his food. He took a few bites. Timothy watched him and felt more at ease.

Rajur also watched Zachary while turning his eyes to Timothy.

He, too, found rest in seeing the boys eat.

Not long after, Rajur joined them on the log and ate.

Chapter 14

CAMUS

The imminent storm finally encroached upon the boys' somewhat peaceful minds while eating. Both Timothy and Zachary turned to it.

"How much time before it comes?" Timothy asked.

Hearing that question, even though he too wanted to ask it, Zachary's mind reawakened to the thought of him being nonexistent. His mood turned sullen. Negative thoughts roamed inside his mind and prevailed over his positive thoughts.

Rajur saw the change in Zachary and hoped he could find his courage again.

"No longer than an hour," Rajur said.

Both boys looked fretful.

"I'm scared," Zachary said.

"So am I," Timothy said.

"Why?" Zachary asked irritably, as if Timothy had no right to be scared. "You know where you stand."

"Doesn't mean I don't care. Doesn't mean I don't want to lose you."

"It shouldn't matter to you. I'm of no consequence here. Nonexistent."

"You're wrong."

"I'm right. I am of no importance pertaining to the book. Why would the book want me around?"

"Because I want you around."

"That's stupid."

"No, it's not. Why are you acting like this?"

"Because it isn't fair," Zachary said. His eyes swelled with sadness and anger. "It's not fair that I have to sit here and wait to be dissolved."

"I know it's not fair. But try to at least—"

"No!" Zachary shouted.

The shout silenced Timothy and brought attention to Rajur.

Rajur examined both of their faces.

He nodded his head.

"Camus," Rajur said.

"What?" both boys said perplexedly.

"Sorcerer. Elf. Half god."

Both boys looked profoundly at Rajur.

"The one that ripped out the gems from Abbigatha's eye sockets."

"Camus?" both boys said.

"Aye. We don't know how, but somehow, he snuck into her hidden lair and stole the gems from her eye sockets. The timing could not have been more perfect. We were too distracted with other problems to track his movement. If we weren't, we'd have learned of Abbigatha's whereabouts from watching Camus. And how Camus learned of her whereabouts is just as much a mystery as to how he snuck inside undetected. How? To this day, nothing boggles my mind more than how he could have simply snuck into her lair and ripped the eyes out of the second most powerful enemy Eythreal had ever faced. Second to Iria's Dark. Just not possible . . .

"Anyway, he did, and he succeeded. She fell into a catatonic stupor—again, something very mysterious too, for how did he know that would happen to her?

"Learning about this not much after, we became terribly unnerved. So much mystery and so many unanswered questions.

"One of the greatest worries became our worst fear. Camus had somehow managed to do what nobody could do on Eythreal. He managed to harvest the powers of the gems, which included Abbigatha; thus, why I said only two could do that on Eythreal. Now, though, we have an idea of how he did it . . .

"Regardless, we had to act—fast. We couldn't possibly give him time to learn the possibilities of the gems' powers.

"And we acted. An extremely secretive conclave ensued between me, the Elves of Nererrenda, and the Iron Dwarves. Very, very secret. No man or woman of any of the Four Kingdoms could be trusted. And as for a Qharthlyion, well, the death of their sovereign and most of her family still proved too sore. Thus, we three made a union, and this union will forever bind us.

"Our intention?

"To sneak up on the impregnable land called Deghrad, invade Camus's castle, also called Deghrad, and come away with the three gems.

"An impossible mission. But an impossible mission that more or less succeeded.

The Iron Dwarves and a host of the Elves of Nererrenda served as decoys, while an elite force of those selfsame elves and I snuck into the castle.

"It wasn't easy. Many of us died. And we came away with only one of the gems. Fortunately, the other two were stripped from Camus's possession too. Where the other two went, nobody knew. Of course, one of those gems ended up in a place meant to be found by you. But it was your pa you chose. Don't look sad. I did not bring that up to pain you. I only wanted to remind you how consequential your choices are. And don't think you erred. I don't think the book wished you to be the one to enter that house. Because if you did, I could almost guarantee you'd not come out alive. The book would cease to exist, along with us and your world.

"More good came out of that battle than we initially thought. We came away with another very essential item. We came away with one of the two Spider Keys. Only those two keys can open the hidden door leading to Abbigatha's lair. How Camus received the key is as much a mystery to us as everything else regarding his way into the lair. No scholar or historian could come close to explaining the mysteries. And I believe it is a mystery that will never be solved. Unless . . ."

Rajur stopped. He nodded his head.

"Why?" Zachary said after a long moment of silence.

"Why what?" Rajur asked.

"Why did you fear Camus when it sounds like he did Eythreal a big favor?"

"Because Camus is a symptom of Chaos and a harbinger for Destruction on Eythreal that we're so very ignorant of."

"He's that powerful?"

"He is. Is he as powerful as a fully awakened Queen Abbigatha? No. He is only a half god, whereas Abbigatha is a goddess, regardless of her present nature. But could he prove to be as powerful? Absolutely—hence why we invaded Deghrad. We invaded because we could not afford to give Camus time to harness the powers of the three gems after hearing that he had already done so by a minute amount. If they were harnessed any further, he'd have Abbigatha's capabilities at will, along with the Daughters of Iria. After that, he'd learn how to utilize those powers. He would use them to sow chaos upon Eythreal, only for a mysterious other to reap the total destruction of Eythreal. I believe, along with few others, that that was his purpose in being born."

"So he's evil?" Zachary asked.

"Evil? Sure. But remember this: nothing is ever born evil. You'd have to travel *before* his birth to know how Camus became evil."

The boys looked eagerly at Rajur.

Rajur turned to the storm and felt slightly at ease regarding time. He turned back to the boys.

"What I speak of, I speak of only minor details that surround something far greater."

The boys nodded.

"Eythreal is mainly made up of water. I believe your Earth is the same. There are seven designated realms upon Eythreal, each of these realms home to towns, villages, cities, and so forth, along with kingdoms and even an empire. Of course, because Eythreal is much water, there are many islands, some of which are the size of this campsite, while others are almost as big as the smallest realm. Not only are there islands among Eythreal, but there are also a few (for we think it is but a few) unknown lands scattered about Eythreal. These lands are never to be traveled upon by any Eythreal inhabitant for reasons many know and many do not know. Much of it has to do with a treaty between Iria's Dark and Light, and the unheard-of danger of attempting to reach those uninhabitable lands that are found in the oldest of scrolls. But there are always a few rule-breakers.

"About those realms, I said seven when there are only six now since Thrandor, the greatest of the realms and what some call the capital of Eythreal, has fallen. The other six remain very divided. One of these realms is named Daardannea. It is a land mostly made up of forestry, surrounded by a sylvan setting. Its beauty is exquisite; unmatched by any beauty found on Eythreal. Different, though, it is now—very, very different. Dark. Swallowed up by shadows of a curse given to the whole land. Before this change, it was home to the most prominent elves' clan, the Elves of Daardannea. For thousands and thousands of moons did this clan prosper in such a warm and inviting setting. Lady Gwynn, queen of the Elves of Daardannea, was its most recent ruler, very fair and wise and gentle—all the hallmarks of a prestigious elf of Daardannea, compared to other elf clans on Eythreal, including the more stern and unforgiving Elves of Nererrenda. Lady Gwynn ensured peace continued to reign on her land and succeeded.

"But a dark cloud loomed over her every step. Prophecies spoken by the oracles of their clan prohibited Lady Gwynn from giving birth. These prophecies were around long before her arrival on Eythreal; long before a single Daardannea elf stepped foot on Eythreal. For some, it would not be such a damaging blow to their people. Another would become the successor. But elven blood is far more sacred than that. Only the direct blood of her lineage could rule over Daardannea. Unfortunately, she was the last of this direct bloodline. Thus, without a child, she would end up being the last ruler of Daardannea. Consequently, there would be no more Elves of Daardannea. They would no longer exist. They would dissolve into other clans until their time came to cross the Passage of Twilight. All this was what the oracles *believed* the prophecy meant to happen.

"I say *believed*, for they could not be sure. Anyway, Lady Gwynn still had much time before her final passing through the Passage of Twilight. But regardless of this much time, it mattered not. Ultimately, she would still have to pass through the Passage of Twilight and leave the Elves of Daardannea to their ominous fate. The uncertainty of her clan's fate gnawed and festered in her endlessly. To her, the Elves of Daardannea deserved more: they deserved a chance to continue to live and prosper as the Elves of Daardannea and not some other clan, or worse, exiled or forced to leave Eythreal by means of the Passage of Twilight. She would find herself on many lonesome walks, musing over ways the prophecy could be wrong. Maybe the prophecy meant something else? Maybe the text, so scrutinized and yet never completely understood, meant something other than being unable to give birth to a child?"

"Not able? Or not allowed?" Zachary asked.

Rajur looked proudly at the boy.

"A wise observation, Zachary. The truth is that the prophecy could not answer that question. And it had been a fervid debate among the most intelligent beings on Eythreal. Outsiders of all parts of Eythreal came to the oracles of Daardannea, and not a single person of such extreme knowledge could decipher the true meaning of the prophecy. What they did agree on was that they should not tempt the fates and not follow the prophecy by any means.

"And she never did. Moon after moon, she mused alone on her walks and pined over the unfortunate fate of her people. Until one moon she came back . . ."

"And?"

"What can I say?" Rajur said. "She came back in disarray, without memory of what occurred. She quickly fell ill. Not long after, Daardannea clerics came away with her being one with child."

Rajur breathed in deeply and exhaled quietly.

"I was in Daardannea at this time. My first training on Eythreal had not come to an end. I remember how quickly the news snuck out of Vallyihaal, the capital of Daardannea. Her being pregnant reverberated around the circumference of Eythreal in the shortest of time. As for her people, the news came to them and brought mixed thoughts. Some saw this as a miracle Eythreal needed. Others, yes, her own people, with the most gentle and softest temperaments of elves on all Eythreal, wanted to rip open her insides right then and there and steal away the seed that was causing the rift against the prophecy.

"And I dare say they were not alone, especially of *other* elvish clans. But the former thought prevailed. This was a time of slow-seething chaos. Abbigatha had arrived, but she was driven back. Although the Daughters of Iria had not left for the Realm of Cosmos, they kept their distance from this conundrum, mostly because their mother, Goddess Iria, always instructed them to leave most affairs to the inhabitants of Eythreal, only to intervene when extremely necessary. I must say, the Daughters of Iria erred greatly in thinking they did not need to intervene in this plight. But one cannot blame them. They had their own turmoil since their mother's absence had been far too long, especially since she never came to Eythreal even when Abbigatha made her first appearance.

"Therefore, the Elves of Daardannea fell to the belief that Lady Gwynn's conception was connected to Iria's long disappearance and ignorance of Eythreal's turmoil. In other words, they chose to believe the child in her was a gift to them from Iria.

"Of course, Lady Gwynn did not argue this. How could she renounce her only child? In the end, Camus was born."

"And?" Zachary asked, sensing the end of Rajur's story.

"Very little else could be said. Camus was born. And because Lady Gwynn's blood was a direct line to the Elves of Orrow's Starlight, Camus was also born to that ancient bloodline. Thus, we all knew how powerful he would be at birth. But never in our dreams could we have imagined how powerful he turned out to be. He assimilated mana at his birth, unlike any one creature born upon Eythreal. And that included sorcerers and sorceresses born with the Mark, along with enchanters, enchantresses, and mages. As for wizards upon Eythreal, they are not of Eythreal. They are of their own dimension, like many others that inhabited Eythreal in its nascent age.

"The question of him being allowed to be born surfaced once again.

And as always, they came away befuddled. By default, they again settled on him being a gift from Iria.

"At first, Camus dispelled any thought of him being an ominous creation. He was the best of child elves. Everyone loved him. And he loved everyone. And this included all visitors to Daardannea. These visitors came for him—scholars and historians. Even a few El-Dahn from the Four Kingdoms came to visit him, along with personages from Thrandor, since Thrandor had not fallen yet. The only opposition Camus and the Elves of Daardannea faced came from the Elves of Nererrenda, who were to be my next guardians. They had done due diligence on Lady Gwynn's consummation and swore never to interact with Daardannea again. What I learned later was that they had other measures set up. One of these measures was to be acted upon before Lady Gwynn gave birth. Oh, what life would have been if they had followed through.

"Anyways, know that Camus was looked upon as hope instead of doom, for I looked at him as a friend. We became inseparable. He learned to trust me more than anyone else.

"But like his mother, a shadow loomed over his every step. This shadow could not be seen. I can only guess that Camus sensed this shadow and fought tooth and nail against it.

"And yet, he succumbed to it at the end. Camus grew disconnected from everyone but me. He sulked wherever he went. His temper became quick. He found life in Daardannea tedious. Even when archmages of various mage guilds visited him did he scoff at them and the lessons they tried to impart to him, seeing that he could do great wonders for all Eythreal if he just learned. He shouted at them and called them hurtful names. He told them he'd learn independently so he wouldn't be fooled like them.

"Everyone shared this abhorrence but me. He still held me as a friend—his only friend in a very lonely childhood.

"As for me, I understood him. We . . . we weren't so different. I too had much looming over my every step.

"During our walks, which became a morning ritual, he trusted me to share some of his dark, brooding thoughts. I'd help as best I could. He'd come back to Vallyihaal and would be somewhat in better spirits. But I couldn't be there all the time.

"My time in Daardannea was coming to an end. And I remember, on one of our last walks, Camus implored me to leave behind my prophecy.

His words: 'Forget what the prophecies say about us. It is nonsense. You don't need a bunch of ancient texts to lead you where you must go. Let us both be free. The rest can save themselves.'

"He said more, much more—most of it dark and ominous. I didn't speak of it when we returned to Vallyihaal. I . . . I hoped he'd grow out of it.

"He didn't. He drifted away from me after that walk. From then on, I walked alone, as he also walked alone. And then came my leave.

"I was to live with the Elves of Nererrenda for the second stage of my training. There, I'd learn to face the first of many destined trials.

"I was not to see Daardannea for a very long time. Camus was to be truly alone.

"On the morning of my leave, before the Star of Nod showed life, I went in search of Camus. I would demand a last walk with him. Sadly, he could not be found.

"Soon after, I learned from trusted elves that he had not been seen for some time. I did not like this news. He had never gone more than one moon from Vallyihaal. With very little time left before my departure, I left the capital in search of Camus. The forestry of Daardannea is vast since, as I've said before, the whole land is one sylvan setting. But the skilled tracker I was then should have found his tracks. I couldn't. And I couldn't use up more time. Reluctantly, I turned away and returned to my abode. There I found his mother waiting for me. She looked distraught. Her whole demeanor seemed crushed by a malady none could see. I tried to get it out of her, but could not. She kept telling me she came only to say her goodbye, a very heartfelt goodbye, for she had been like a mother to me. But I knew it was more than that. The affliction on her face. No. It was about Camus. And before I could get it out of her, we were interrupted by another elf.

"'A guest has arrived and said he must see the both of you.'

"I told the elf the guest must wait, seeing that Lady Gwynn had started to cry, with her hands over her face. I was close to prying the secret from her.

"Until the elf revealed the guest's name. It was a name and individual I could not refuse—*we* could not refuse.

"Zorlof, one of the last wizards of the Circle of Ester living on Eythreal—he could not be trifled with. And the timing so . . . My last day on Daardannea.

"Anyway, the wizard had suffered a bad streak at that time. Many believed him to have gone mad.

"Gossip, though. He must be heard.

"And the truth is, it is very hard not to hear about a wizard when that wizard wants to be heard, just as it is impossible to hear about a wizard when that wizard does not want to be heard.

"Mad or not, he must be heard. Lady Gwynn must not refuse because of gossip.

"And she didn't. Wiping away her tears and acting as if nothing had happened between us, she went to Zorlof with me at her side.

"What I can say occurred between us three I can only say . . ."

Here, Rajur leaned back.

"I shouldn't say. But I guess . . . I must.

"Zorlof came to us with what he thought of Lady Gwynn's true conception of Camus. He believed her to have been raped."

Both boys leaned back also.

Rajur continued, "Aye. And not only raped but raped by a god. Zorlof then divulged to us that this god is the one behind Eythreal's calamity."

"He said much more. But what evidence he followed up on came out to be *zero*. It was only the mind of *Ester*, he said.

"What became Lady Gwynn's breaking point, since she believed not a word he said, for which I didn't blame her, for I also had trouble believing him, was when he divulged to us what we should do: 'We need to find the way—and I think I have—to kill Camus, for his other blood is not of a mortal being.'

"That put an end to Lady Gwynn's listening ears. What followed was Zorlof pleading to me to listen; thus, he begged me to do what he said, for Eythreal's sake, which was joining him in Camus's destruction."

"I could do no such thing. Again, zero evidence to back up his claim. Lady Gwynn being raped and not knowing about it? A god on Eythreal? At this point, the Daughters of Iria had just left for the Realm of Cosmos to convene at the Council of Nod. Thus, we knew nothing of Abbigatha's true identity.

"I could only shake my head while Lady Gwynn commanded Zorlof's head to be ripped off.

"Of course, no such action could be done to the wizard. We simply watched Zorlof laugh to our faces and vanish as easily as he appeared.

"I left for Daardannea that very moon. I left with not an ounce of belief in the mad wizard, but I couldn't eliminate the question of what if he was right.

"Could Lady Gwynn have lied? No. She couldn't have.

"I arrived in Nererrenda sometime after, and the harsh environment of that land, so very contrasting to Daardannea, slowly eradicated my worries about Lady Gwynn and even of Camus. And Nererrenda being immensely secluded, thus prohibiting any outsider from encroaching upon their realm, what news I heard from abroad was given to me by my guardians. It was they who chose what I needed to know. The Elves of Nererrenda chose well. They didn't want to distract me from my training, but they also felt it to be prudent and beneficial for me to hear of something very particular—personal to me.

"News of a very powerful young elf, not even past the age of a child elf, traveling upon Eythreal and leaving secrecy and corruption behind. The elf we knew to be Camus.

"Rumors of him continued to come our way. Camus continued to grow, as did his followers.

"Soon, we learned of the disappearance and theft of ancient artifacts, including the oldest of Rune Stones and Sorcerer Tablets.

"Rumors became even worse. Supposedly, Camus journeyed into the Caverns of the Whispering Dead. What we could only guess but to become skilled in necromancy."

"As in bringing the dead to life?" Zachary asked.

"Aye. But only the dead that belonged to the Caverns of the Whispering Dead."

"What are the Caverns of the Whispering Dead?"

Rajur nodded his head. "The importance of that will come when the time is right. For now, we must educate you on Camus. Camus will be . . ."

Rajur shook his head. "Ill and omen news kept coming to us. Disturbances of all kinds came to the Four Kingdoms: Ontairo, Kavalox, Rhinehart, and Kalahania. Discord was ripe between them. Many believed Camus and his followers were the instigators and not Abbigatha, pining away and trying to find a way to strengthen her position. The inner turmoil grew worse.

"The worst of the news then fell. Thrandor, the most important realm upon Eythreal, home to the shrines of Iria and her daughters, faced a calamity no one could ever have seen. Consequently, the gates and walls of Thrandor closed upon anyone trying to enter and leave that holy land.

"The restriction of Thrandor's ingress and egress proved short-lived.

Thrandor came to an end, the last beacon to the Four Kingdoms now obliterated.

"By this time, I was afforded suspension from my duty, and I sought Lady Gwynn. I wanted the truth. I no longer believed Camus's birth was anything but a curse upon Eythreal. I came to her and demanded the truth. I came to her as the Rajur you see now. My exploits among Eythreal had become legendary. I had long been ordained with Storm Breaker. My Moon Beams became a topic of myth. *I* had become a topic of myth. And I do not boast. I only wanted you to know how difficult it was for Lady Gwynn to stare into my eyes and continue to plead with a lie.

"But that she did not do. She revealed the truth. And what sickness I felt when hearing it."

Rajur spent a long moment of silence.

"And?" Zachary asked.

"What can I say?" Rajur said, pushing his hair back from his sides, clearly pained to rethink that moment. "I can only say that she had lied. The wizard spoke the truth. Lady Gwynn was raped—raped by what we presume to be a god, for how else could someone take the appearance of an elf of the Elves of Orrow's Starlight, since what she claimed was that she had met one of them in the forest, had been seduced by him, then became smitten, which led to a romance between the two? The Elves of Orrow's Starlight were the very first clan of elves to inhabit Eythreal and have long departed Eythreal for the Passage of Twilight. Some say those elves brought Twilight and its sequences to Eythreal. The idea of one roaming on Eythreal is impossible. She was simply desperate and deceived."

"What happened? Did you go and find Zorlof?"

"It was too late. He had . . . He had *certainly* gone mad by that time. I had to leave. I had to return to my prophecy. Thus, I left Lady Gwynn and her people, and never did I see them again."

"Why?" both boys asked.

Rajur contemplated what to say next.

"They are no longer. Her people are now only shadows of a curse."

"And Lady Gwynn? The same?" Timothy asked.

Rajur shook his head.   "Worse."

"What about Camus? What more happened?"

"Bane Singer."

"Bane Singer?"

"A scepter—no one yet has discovered how he received it and from whom, for it is a scepter not made in Eythreal. More importantly, it is the weapon—the device—that allows him to do the impossible: to harness the powers of the gems."

"And where is he now?"

"Now?" Rajur said, feeling even more pain and disturbance affect him. "Maybe on his way back to Deghrad. But I know where he was the moment I was stolen away by the blackness."

"Where was that?"

"In these hands of mine!"

"What?" both boys said.

"I still heeded Zorlof's advice, even though I was too late. I made it an ambition of mine to follow the wizard's path when it came to Camus's destruction, even if I couldn't persuade him of the madness that took over him. Again, his madness led him too far astray for any of us to recover his senses. But my allies and I learned of what he had devised and strove to do it ourselves, even without the Daughters of Iria's aid, for they had left for the Realm of Cosmos by then. And we were close. Much, much later, following the return of the Daughters of Iria, their abduction, imprisonment, Camus retrieving the three gems, and our secretive ambush of Deghrad, we took advantage of a debilitated Camus and were able to draw him away from Deghrad by subterfuge. This deception led him to a desolate and morbid castle and down its dungeons below, where I waited, where I was to execute my plan."

"The plan?" Zachary asked.

Rajur shook his head. "Just know this: it came to a screeching halt."

The boys deduced that Rajur spoke of the blackness that stole him home away—a blackness created by Timothy's decisions.

"I'm sorry," Timothy said.

"You don't have to be sorry. To me, it must be fate. It must be."

After a moment of calmness, Rajur looked toward the storm.

"The storm is closing in on us."

Rajur stood up and put the provisions away. The boys stared intensely at the storm. The various colored lightning streaks captivated them. They felt wonder and awe while also sensing fear. A great excitement seethed inside them, colliding with the storm's terror—a terror fraught with unimaginable consequences. Their perceptions of all things became precarious. Their hands shook. Their feet trembled. And their mouths chattered. Excitement or fear, excitement or fear, excitement or fear. They could not grab onto one alone.

"How long will the storm last?" Timothy asked.

"The storm will encompass *everything* and drift away, back to its Void. When that happens, Eythreal will be revealed."

"And this Eythreal," Timothy said. "Will everything return to what it was before the storm?"

"Not necessarily. For the most part, yes. And no one will be the wiser on what has just happened."

"No one will have felt the storm?" Zachary asked.

"All of Eythreal will be oblivious to the storm. But yes, there will be a few personages of Eythreal who have the discernment to feel a shift in their world. Only a handful, mind you."

"And this Gawul?" Zachary asked.

"The Gawul knows of the approaching storm. I'm sure it has found a safe spot right now, for it knows the land just as well as I do."

"Then it will make its return to Abbigatha?"

"Aye."

"Will it be a long travel for it?"

"As I've said, the Gawul must move at a very intricate and slow pace. Not to mention, Abbigatha's lair is hidden somewhere in Migra."

"Migra," Timothy said. "You mentioned that before."

"Migra is one of the seven realms of Eythreal. A sizable chunk of land—a land very few want to travel on."

"Why?"

"It is there on Migra that the cracks of Harrowing came about. It is there on Migra that Iria's Dark besets Iria's Light."

"What does that mean?"

"Unfortunately, you will see firsthand the meaning of that at some point in your journey, unless I'm mistaken."

"So after this storm, we're off to Migra?"

"Good Iria, I hope not," Rajur said.

"But you just—"

"I said 'at some point.' That is because of what we discussed. I believe the book's fate wants you to free the Daughters of Iria. And again, to do that, I see no other way than to end Abbigatha's reign on Eythreal, meaning her death or nonexistence. That means you may be making a trip to Migra and accomplishing what to me is already impossible—the slaying of a goddess. But that doesn't mean the book wants you to step on Migra's land, somehow find the lair on your own, and defeat this immortal goddess all by yourself—which would be even more impossible. No. Remember the importance of what I said earlier. The book wants nothing else but to be finished. To be finished means you must survive long enough to finish it. It will lead you to its fate. And for that, I imagine much, and I mean much, must be done before even thinking about heading to Migra.

"To start with, we need you to make a few friends. If I'm correct, our starting point will be a few moons from a town called Cyrcle."

"Cyrcle?" Zachary said.

"Sarah's Town to most. But not to Sarah. She dislikes it when one calls it Sarah's Town. She named it Cyrcle for a reason, and a reason that I don't even know. There, we'll be secluded and protected. Everyone minds their own business. It's a town we'd be wise to visit, especially since it could turn into an advantage for us. The travel toward the town is also one of the more peaceful paths in Eythreal. Not one creature of malevolence can travel near this town or even come close to entering its forest and surroundings. I'll explain why later. In this town, we'll find rest and the advantage I spoke of, being you boys clothed properly while equipping you both with weapon and armor."

"And this Sarah is a friend of yours?"

"One of my dearest friends. She's an immensely loyal and highly talented mage of the white."

"Mage what?"

"White mage," Rajur said. "Or what some like to call a witch."

"A witch?" both boys said in awe.

"Aye. But not a witch as in one that practices in the Dark. Those are the witches that one must worry about, for they are destructive and know only evil. But the truth is, she's *not* a witch. She's a mage. But many people on Eythreal discredit magic and believe that if one practices magic, thus assimilating the mana that gives life to Eythreal, they each fall under the disreputable designation of a *witch*. How wrong they are when actually facing a witch—a practitioner of the Dark! And such ignorance and bigotry that drive some people to that belief! But aye, she's a white mage. Thus, she practices the magical arts that deal with healing, protection, and neutral spells.

"She's also an anomaly. Sarah is of a man-folk descent, and unless a man or woman descends from Thrandor, he or she rarely, and I mean rarely, is born with capabilities to assimilate the mana from the Seven Moons of Iria as much as she can—for she has proven to be a mighty white mage—one that is known and feared by many. Yes, feared. One should fear a white mage as much as one should fear a black mage. But then, some say Sarah's descendants are not what most believe them to be, even to her knowledge. Nobody, including her, has been able to discover the truth of her heritage, for her entire ancestry was murdered when she and her sister were very young, leaving absolutely nothing behind.

"There is much behind Sarah most people scoff at. Not I. I don't know the truth. But I know it's not what she's been told."

"And she will help us?"

"She will help us while in her town. She will help with the supplies and provisions and, of course, a peaceful and restful visit."

"But she won't join us?"

"Not on your life!" Rajur said.

The ground below them rumbled for the first time. The trees and foliage shook as if a gale of wind made its way to them.

"It is nothing to worry about," Rajur said, seeing the concern on the boys' faces. "Get used to it. The rumbling and wind will only grow stronger. Let us crouch near one another. Standing would be hazardous. The static! The static will be felt much more when standing."

"What about the horses?" Timothy asked.

"A more stable creature than us. They'll be fine."

"That's if they make it through," Zachary said, downcast.

Rajur turned to Zachary and placed a conciliatory hand on his shoulder. He smiled. "I no longer doubt your existence beyond this storm. I see great potential in you, Zachary. The book would be foolish to omit you from Timothy's adventure, for there is no better companion he'll ever find but you. And that includes me. So fret not."

Zachary perceived pure honesty from Rajur's eyes and face. His confidence in surviving could not have been greater.

Thus, the boys followed Rajur's orders and secured themselves near him. They waited.

The wait did not last long.

The storm finally came for them, and everything around them became swallowed up. Darkness followed, along with the various colored lightning strikes.

Harsh static of electricity prevailed upon their entire body.

"It's happening!" Timothy shouted.

"The earth is moving."

"My eyes! The lightning—"

"Close your eyes!" Rajur said.

The three closed their eyes and kept them shut.

Part 2

Chapter 1

EYTHREAL

Timothy opened his eyes to discover a thick coat of mist blinding him, leaving him ignorant of anyone's presence near him. Timothy wanted to scream. He wanted to be sure he was not alone. The thick coat of mist weakened before he could scream. And as the mist faded, so did his troubles. A sense of calmness settled inside him. He closed and reopened his eyes and stared through the fading mist, and the sight before him captivated him. The mist glowed. The former thickness of the mist became translucent. This transparency of the mist finally came to an end, and when it did, no longer did the mist exist; what the mist left behind captivated him even more, for it left behind a shiny morning—a morning not unlike a morning on his former Earth, except a sky and surroundings he knew not to be Earth.

At first glance, much seemed similar. The sun shone brightly with an orange, fiery glow. But this sun seemed friendly, to stare at it.

Timothy also discovered two moons. One moon was very much like yesterday, vague and without wrinkles and craters. The second moon also did not reveal a single crease or crevasse while not being vague, for it glowed with full might.

No trace of his Earth's moon could be found.

And possibly, never again.

Looking away from the sky and studying the surroundings, he saw little change while also noticing that he still remained by the creek, and the horses were safely tethered to the same tree. He spotted Butch asleep at the exact spot he decided to hunker down when the storm came.

He looked at Rajur, seemingly asleep.

He looked at—

"Zachary," Timothy muttered gleefully when he saw his best friend sound asleep.

The book—it chose you. I knew it would.

Smiling, he took in more of the forest surrounding him.

He noticed first how the forest resembled the portion of the Forest

Beyond he ventured into upon reaching the black house. Very similar. But this forest seemed even more salubrious and grand. This he couldn't believe. He already had trouble believing how pristine and salubrious the Forest Beyond proved to be.

And now this forest? To him, it seemed that no creatures had ever plodded a course through this forest.

And how wrong he was to think that!

The forest floor felt damp to Timothy, but not damp to the point of leaving a puddle of water or an uncomfortable sogginess. Surprisingly, the forest floor received more light than one would have imagined. And because of that, much life and vegetation blossomed on the forest floor, including what Timothy saw to be strange-looking foliage and mushrooms. The weeds on the forest floor seemed much different than Timothy's while proving stronger and more alive. But there were also weeds similar to those on his Earth, prospering just as well.

Timothy turned his attention to the many flowers. Again, some flowers were familiar to him, while others were different; both were beautiful. Variously shaped and variously colored bees droned about, traveling from one flower petal to the next, never showing an ounce of aggression to Timothy or his companions. Birds could be heard chirping in the trees, along with half a dozen flying from one tree to another.

Timothy felt a sense of enjoyment in listening to the birds' warbling; the music from the birds eased him into his awakening.

He then turned to the creek and found the water crystal clear and flowing perfectly upon the river rocks. The fish were abundant and easily seen, for not one of them camouflaged with the creek's surroundings. Some loitered about. Some traveled upstream. Others traveled downstream. Timothy studied these fish and found their scales different from any fish he knew. But their shape and form were much the same as on his Earth. But most of these fish had more color to them—artistic patterns.

And again, not one fish blended in with the creek's surface, nowise afraid of predators from above.

Some fish even had wings, allowing for swifter travel while taking flight in the air for a good twenty yards.

The wonder and excitement inside Timothy came bursting through his seams. He watched the fish enviously.

"If only I could be a fish for one day," he said, seeing how marvelous it looked to swim so freely, so sure of its safety.

Timothy held on to this excitement for far too long without sharing it.

"Wake up. Wake up, both of you. Wake up!"

Rajur stirred awake. He looked astonished to see Timothy awake before him. He bolted upright and took in his surroundings with a single glance.

Eythreal.

Zachary took a minute longer to awaken. When awake, he first examined his existence.

"I'm alive!" he cried out. "You hear that? I'm alive. I'm here. I'm not nonexistent. I'm actually here."

"Yes," Timothy said, placing a hand on Zachary's shoulder. "You're here; with me; with us. Now gaze at the wonders."

Zachary did just that.

"This is a land of fairy tales," Zachary said. "Why do I feel the urge to swim in that creek and be a fish?"

"I said the same thing!" Timothy clamored.

"Clearly, you didn't say it loud enough, so I'm credited for saying it first," Zachary said.

"No way!" Timothy said, feigning seriousness, as did Zachary when he shoved him.

Timothy shoved back.

The shoving became a frivolous shoving match between the two since they could not contain the excitement seething in them.

Rajur watched queerly. He read the frivolity of their wrestling match but could not understand why two friends would do such a thing for fun.

A distant memory surfaced in his mind—too blurry to envision it. He was a child like them. He, too, interacted in the same way with friends.

If only he could remember having friends as a boy.

If only he could remember *being* a boy.

The boys continued to grapple with each other. For the smallest of seconds, Rajur cracked a smile.

Feeling the smile and not liking it, he obliterated it from his face.

"Quit it! The both of you. This is no time to fool about. In fact, they'll never be time to fool around again."

The boys turned to him somberly.

"Welcome to Eythreal."

What he said sank deep inside the boys. The gravity of his words was far graver than what he had said a short second ago.

"Yes," Timothy said, staring at his surroundings. "But what does that mean?"

"It means we chose well. Our location is a place I'm very familiar with."

"Near that witch's town?" Zachary asked.

"Aye. But I'd refrain from ever referring to her as a witch, unless you want to be turned into a toad."

Zachary gulped down a breath.

"But it's pretty awesome to say you know a witch," Timothy said.

Zachary nodded. "Yeah. How awesome to say you're off to see a witch!"

Zachary's foolishness continued. "Is she ugly?"

"Like real ugly?" Timothy said.

"With a wart on her pointy and crooked nose?"

"And is her skin complexion green?"

"Putrid green," Zachary said.

Rajur shook his head at the immaturity of the two boys.

"Does she ride a broom?"

"With a cat at her side?"

"Maybe she'll let us ride on her broomstick."

"That would be—"

"Stop," Rajur said. "I know you two jest—or maybe you don't. Maybe this is a way for you two to cope with what has happened. Many could not blame you for doing so. Regardless! It is not the time. It is time for you two to be brave—and serious. This is . . . To say this is a matter of life or death would be immeasurably far from an overstatement."

Both boys grew ashamed.

"I don't know," Rajur said. "I wonder if it was wrong. If it *chose* wrong."

"If what chose wrong?" Zachary said while Timothy's face grew more ashamed.

"Did it choose wrong?" Rajur asked Timothy.

Timothy hardened himself. He raised his head and faced Rajur. "It did not."

"Then look around you. Yes, this is beautiful. I will not deny you that. But if you think for one second that most Eythreal resembles this, turn away and give up. Once, maybe. And hopefully, in time, it may return to its past glory. But now, Eythreal is in chaos. And Eythreal's nature imitates this chaos. We are heading to Cyrcle—Sarah's Town. Aye, Sarah is considered a witch, in the bigotry of others. But she is no witch. She is a mage. She went to study to become a mage for two main reasons.

First and foremost, she and her sister were born with an uncanny ability to assimilate mana. Second, her foster parents, the family that found the two and took them in and raised them, were a family of mages, each of them descendants of Thrandor. So it was basically in her cards to become a mage. She had a choice when going to the guild. What to study? Her sister chose black magic. Sarah chose white magic. She chose white because her philosophy follows that of white mages. They believe the best solution to the opposition is defending oneself, only to give time to heal *both* parties by finding the root of the conflict, whereas the ones who choose black magic chose because they feel the best solution to the opposition is the destruction of their opponent and the inevitable eradication of the root of the problem. Neither of the two is wrong. It's just a matter of your perception. I'm telling you this because for not one second do I want you to confuse her with an actual witch you'll more than likely hear about and possibly encounter. The study of black magic is nowhere near the same as studying the Dark.

"This is Sarah's Forest. It is her forest, for she is the one that gave back the forest's true nature and has protected it since. This forest is the truest testament of not only her benevolence but also how powerful she is."

"She made this forest?" Zachary asked.

"No, not *made*. As I said, she brought life to it again and has protected it from harmful trespassers."

"How?"

"A mage can do much. A powerful mage can do much more. To me, Sarah is beyond a powerful mage. She'd easily be an archmage of a guild if she chose that route. That said, to this day and the next, I'll never know exactly what she did or how she did it, for she is no enchantress—she's only a novice in that art, but yes, she placed a very powerful enchantment on this forest long ago, even before her first lesson in enchanting. This enchantment protects the forest and her town from anything malevolent to come through. Of course, some enemies of Iria's Light are powerful enough to enter this forest and town unscathed. But they are few. And those few would never waste their time on such a lonely, reclusive town run by a white mage who abandoned her guild and practice long ago. And even if they did approach these surroundings, Sarah would be alerted of their presence before they could lift a finger against anything and all things."

The boys looked highly impressed.

"Now, let us see the book," Rajur said.

"The book! Yes," Timothy said with enthusiasm, having forgotten about the book.

He pulled the book out for them to see. He turned the page to chapter 3, "Rajur's Awakening." Recalling blank pages to follow, Timothy anxiously turned the page.

Writing, along with sketches.

The sketches were many: Rajur by the creek, Timothy locked up, Zachary overhearing his father's conversation with Tom Sickle.

And more writing.

The sketches continued.

Spiders devouring the entire town—one sketch showed the Youngblood Ranch being a single giant ball of web.

At that moment, Rajur learned how strong and fearless Zachary would prove to be. He glanced toward the boy and saw only determination upon his face. Conviction. Conviction in righting the wrong by whatever it took. Rajur now realized why the book chose him. He was to be Timothy's eternal iron grip when the big heart of Timothy showed weakness, since Rajur had already felt Timothy being the one with the big heart, thus open to more pain, vulnerable to the weakness of the heart. At the same time, Zachary kept a tighter, smaller heart, nowise making him apathetic, only more able to shed off emotions, even if it meant hurting an individual he cared for if they stood in the way of accomplishing the mission.

The two boys would then play off each other and become a powerful tandem.

So he thought . . .

More writing followed.

As before, Rajur could barely translate the writing. He tried, though. He tried to match some of the ancient text with the sketches.

But he failed, as would anyone else on Eythreal.

Finally, the book reached the drawing of the storm coursing over them. The following sketch showed them being swallowed up.

Rajur stopped Timothy's hand from turning the page.

"What is it?" a startled Timothy asked.

"I fear."

"What?"

"I fear what comes next. The book—it acts omniscient if you haven't noticed. Not only does it mark your progress, but it also marks others, all of whom have an intrinsic involvement in the book's story. The book tells the way it wants to. Even though you are the scribe, the book decides what is to be shown and what is not shown. Our chapter is done. We reached the site and passed through the storm. What comes next resides only in the will of the book. It could lead us right to a new chapter, or what I forebode, it could lead us to another integral character. I don't know which one would be better, for I fear what it could show us, although going right to a new chapter tells us very little about what else is happening since we're already aware of Gawul making his way to Migra. If only . . . If only it could just show Gawul and not what I fear."

"And what do you fear?" Timothy asked.

"I fear what ultimately stands in our way and must be reckoned with."

"So I should . . ."

"If you want to finish this book and hope that your world will return once again, then yes, I'd say turn the page."

Timothy nodded and took a deep breath before taking the plunge. Exhaling, he turned the page.

Before the boys could breathe again, Rajur muttered, "Camus."

He said this because the following page depicted a frail, feeble-looking elf, nearly bare of all clothing, manacled to a bench inside a gloomy, rotten dungeon.

Minor writing could be found under the sketch, with a page full of writing beside it.

"Turn the page," Rajur said.

Timothy turned the page.

The following pages showed much writing, along with various sketches. These sketches proved important—and understandable.

"He lies there on the bench since my allies and I duped him into entering Lord Edward's Castle. It is a doomed and abandoned castle at the farthest end of the Desolate Sands of Kiji. We enticed him by luring him with a gem, the same gem he now possesses. See the gem sticking out of that pouch on the ground? That is Misha, the youngest. Near that pouch lies an even bigger pouch. That hilt you see sticking out of that bigger pouch? That is the hilt of Bane Singer. The snakes that twirl about it consist of the venom called Malefaction—an incurable death sentence for all mortal beings. Over there, that pillar—that is where I stood. Yes, I stood with the pouch containing Misha inside, with Bane Singer on the ground.

"Only me. Then I saw the blackness, and I kneeled . . ."

"But he's strapped to the bench? Why fear?"

"Yes, by elvish chains, unbreakable by nearly all Eythreal-made objects. Bane Singer is not Eythreal-made. And see this next sketch?"

Rajur pointed to a sketch of wavy lines over Camus's settled head.

"The book is showing you Camus's mind in action—showing you that he has enough power, though very weak, to conjure a spell."

"What kind of spell?"

"Necromancy." Rajur turned to another sketch. "There. See how those horrible, wretched corpses are trying to shake with life? Camus's chant is passing through the Caverns of the Whispering Dead, searching for a soul that once belonged to a body residing in the dungeon. Not all dead belong to the Caverns of the Whispering Dead, although many do. Much of the dead also belong to the Strays: those trapped in their own deception and roaming about Eythreal as if they are alive. And a good many and counting belong to the Harrowing, a place of eternal suffering governed by the Wardens of Iria's Dark. Some, not many, find themselves in Nervania, a place of eternal restfulness and tranquility. Anyway, finding these souls doesn't help him much if their bodies are too mangled to recover. Again, this is Lord Edward's Castle. One must know its doom, being Lord Edward's Bane, to understand that not one corpse inside the dungeon, castle, and on the outside, including Brickingham, the port town adjacent to it, could come close to resembling life. These corpses have been poisoned from the inside out. They are rotten. Torn apart. Grotesque in all manners. Not one could stand on two feet, let alone crawl; thus, why the next sketch shows you that." Rajur said that as he pointed to a sketch evincing an endless desert. And crouched near a pile of rocks at the base of a towering dune, a recent corpse rattled with life.

Rajur moved back a page and pointed at a medallion over Camus's bare chest.

"The Eye of Xchrysillabis," Rajur said, "otherwise known as Cat's Eye because of its striking resemblance to a feline's green eyes. My allies and I were very ignorant of it when setting our plan. We believed we could just take it off. But no, it was forged upon his body. It is a medallion he received from Got, one of the guardians of the Caverns of the Whispering Dead. It only enhances Camus's power, even though he has lost the ability to assimilate mana because of being bereft of the gems. This eye allows him to search far from his presence for the dead. Seeing that no viable corpse could be found among the countless ones about Lord Edward's Castle, Camus searched beyond, into the near-endless Desolate Sands of Kiji. To our great misfortune, he miraculously found a recent dead. Looks to be a Runner thinking of finding the same fortune Lord Edward found, only to turn into Lord Edward's Bane without nearing the castle long enough to suffer the same doom.

"Let us see more."

Turning the pages again, Rajur summarized more. "He dual cast! How surprising! He was able to control the dead while also conjuring a sand typhoon to bring the dead to the steps of the castle."

"Why does this surprise you?" Zachary asked.

"Much of that answer I will explain later. Just know this: Camus suffers from a similar plight to Goddess Abbigatha. Not as detrimental, though.

"What we learned about Camus's possession of the gems we learned after our successful invasion. We learned that Camus's godlike ability to assimilate mana was stolen from him by the gems. Thus, he must rely solely on them to be anything but an ordinary elf. Aye, still powerful. Still a god's blood in his veins. And more importantly, having not fallen into a catatonic state as Abbigatha has. Well, that we learned, and we also learned that it is Bane Singer and only Bane Singer that gives him a chance to reabsorb his innate ability, for there are three sockets below the orb upon the apex of the scepter that he places the gems into. I did not think he could do so much without one of the gems, even with the residue of power inside him. We starved him—my allies and me. Those chains are enchanted and drain one's entire vitality. And though god he is, he is not all god. Thus, he needs nourishment. And nourishment for him is only one kind. And it is not found in the castle.

"Anyways, he dual cast and brought the dead to the castle, seeing that the dead would find it very hard to reach the castle on its own.

"And there," Rajur said, showing a new sketch. "The dead has arrived in the dungeon and now handles the bag protecting all who touch Bane Singer. And now . . ."

More writing.

"Yes," Rajur said, seeing the following sketch. "He has used Bane Singer to break off the chains. He now goes for the gem that was in my possession the moment the blackness came. And here," he said, showing another sketch, "he has placed the gem into Bane Singer—but look how he stands. He is nowhere near replenished. The gem gave him only a scant power to assimilate mana—not a cure. He is still very weak. It will still be difficult for him to leave. But these next sketches . . ."

Rajur then explained to the boys how Camus left the castle with the dead, arrived at Brickingham Port, scoured the port for a usable vessel, found none, and then searched the poisonous sea.

Not only did he locate a usable vessel, but he also found the dead inside the vessel accessible. Camus had his crew and ship.

"He will use this ship and crew and make his way not back to Daardannea, for even he loathes it there since the curse befell it.

"No. He will make what should have been a long and arduous voyage to Deghrad seem much simpler."

And with that said, Rajur turned away from the book.

Making sure Rajur had finished speaking, Timothy asked, "The book shows this because . . ."

"Camus stands in our way. As I've already repeated, the book wants to be finished as much as you want to finish it. What it shows is more like a cryptic guideline—and cryptic, I say, for it will only grow more difficult to comprehend how best—and *best* is key here—to finish the book. Again, not the only route! The paths to finishing this book are infinite. It shows Camus for it is hinting or recommending to you that you must deal with him before marching to the beat of your own drum, which could prove to be your eternal fallacy, which would possibly mean the same to the book."

"Deal with him?" Zachary said.

"To end his existence on Eythreal's living surface."

"But what about you saying he's like half a god and immortal?"

"All that is true. To kill him will only resurrect him at Heart Stone, a place of mystery in Daardannea. Not sure if he'd be reborn or returned to his former self, for no one has ever ended his life. This resurrection is all due to his sire's blood flowing in him. But he also has his mother's blood flowing in him. And it is his mother's blood that can be used against him. It weakens him. It makes him vulnerable, for no half god could simply erase the mortal essence in him. We can somehow use his mother's blood against him and strike him down by draining his sire's blood, which would leave him mortal. It is something that we learned from Zorlof's thinking, along with the how. We are ahead of the game regarding this how and the planning of it, for my allies and I have invested much time in it. I already started the journey. But now, with the addition of you two, we must strengthen ourselves for what we will face. For lo, you, Timothy, you must be more involved in it than I am now. The *book* must be involved.

And you are the book. We must, therefore, go against my original instinct and planning and bring more to the party.

"Please turn the page," Rajur said nonchalantly.

"Why do I have a feeling you know what's coming next?" Timothy asked.

"None of this would make sense if what I believe will appear doesn't."

Timothy nodded and turned the page.

"And I am right," Rajur said complacently.

The boys looked down at the new chapter title.

Chapter 4
Reflections of a Lonely Wizard

The chapter title did very little to pique the curiosity of the boys. But one look at Rajur and they thought differently. The title meant something important.

But what?

What was so dangerous and important about the reflections of a lonely wizard?

With a nod from Rajur, Timothy turned the page.

The sketch that followed seemed as simple and innocent as the chapter title. The sketch evinced a perfectly symmetrical mountain—nearly too perfect to be real. But it was real. Yes, very real. Besides the mountain's perfect form and shape, the outside of it reflected various colors; thus, the sketch used more than gray, black, or white.

No sketch to this point showed as much color, excluding the depiction of the gem and daughter inside.

Studying the mountain more closely, the boy concluded that it was made up of diamond-shaped shards of glass or crystal, each reflecting various colors. Not one piece of snow could be found on this mountain, although the shards blended in with the intense and prevalent snow that blanketed everything outside this mountain. For this mountain was not alone. No, this mountain towered above a landscape of mountains, and this mountainous range was under fire from an endless winter storm.

"Glass Castle," Rajur said.

"Castle?" Zachary said. "Not a mountain?"

"Mountain. Yes. Castle? Also, yes."

"You're confusing us."

"As it should be. What you see is one of the more mysterious features of Eythreal. Nobody knows the origin of this mountain range and the winter that forever blankets it, hence why we have come to call it the Mountains of Winter."

"What makes this mountain, I mean, castle so important?"

"The book shows us Glass Castle because of what resides inside it."

"And?"

"It is where one hoards a weapon we direly need to defeat Camus."

"And this individual?"

"Zorlof," Rajur said.

Both boys' eyes grew big.

"The wizard you've spoken of?"

"Aye, the one we failed to listen to. The one *I* failed. He pleaded for me to believe him, and I didn't. And it only drove him madder. Madness finally overwhelmed him and . . .

"What more do I need to say? Shortly after leaving Lady Gwynn and me, he exiled himself from all of us and ended up later at the Mountains of the Winter, came to Glass Castle, where his madness went too far, and has never left it since. Nor will he ever be able to leave."

Rajur placed his hand upon Timothy's, hinting for the boy to close the book.

"It will show no more. The path is now in your hands—your choices. The consequences of those choices will soon fill the pages."

Timothy nodded and closed the book. He looked profoundly at Rajur. "So the book wants—"

"Not *wants*," Rajur said. "Recommends—or just gives *its* path to succeed."

"To venture into this Glass Castle, found in the Mountains of Winter?"

"Aye."

"And do what?"

"Slay Zorlof."

"Kill him?"

"It is the only way." Rajur sadly shook his head. "He'll never give up what we need from him. We can try. But no, it'll be in vain. It is only by his death will it be released to us."

"It?"

"The item we so badly need."

Eythreal

"Well, that doesn't sound so bad," Zachary said. "I'm sure wizards are very powerful. But there's one of him and—"

"That is where you err so grossly."

"There's more than one wizard?" Timothy asked.

"There is only him," Rajur said. "But there are countless of him."

"You're not making sense again," Zachary said.

"First off, before explaining what I meant, know that even one wizard is a threat unlike you'd face on Eythreal."

Rajur shuffled in his position, which remained by the campsite since the party had started preparing for breakfast.

Rajur continued, "A wizard is not of Eythreal. Thus, a wizard does not rely solely on the Seven Moons of Iria, the essential objects that give mana its life on Eythreal. They are here already on their own powers while also sharing the capabilities with us on assimilating mana. This empowers them so much more than any of us. Even Camus hesitates to face one like Zorlof in battle, especially Zorlof, seeing that he is one of the prime wizards of the Circle of Ester. Ester is something even I am ignorant of. The only knowledge I can come away with is that it is some source of their power. Or even their dimension. I don't know. Neither does anyone. The wizards do speak of Ester as their source of insight into all things. Regardless, wizards are far too mysterious for one to master their lore."

"Why did they come here?" Zachary asked.

"They came long, long ago, mostly at Iria's bidding. Hers and a few others' requests. But that is not important. What is important—"

"Is why there are so many of him," Timothy said.

"Yes. It is because of reflections."

"Reflections?"

"Aye. When one enters Glass Castle, one walks into a domain of shards of mirrors. These mirrors reflect—"

"Zorlof?" Zachary interrupted.

Rajur gave him a hard stare. "No," Rajur said. "And yes."

"Again with the confusion."

"Aye. The mirrors are the reflection of you, except no . . . It is the very essence of Zorlof that lives in those reflections."

"What do you mean? They show you, but really . . ." Zachary said.

"They are Zorlof?" Timothy asked.

"Aye. And they come alive."

"Alive?"

"The reflection of you will come alive and charge toward you. It charges toward you with the madness of Zorlof's mind, a mind that wants to kill all who trespass against him."

"So we'll have to fight our own reflection? That's not bad," Zachary said.

"If there were only a few mirrors," Rajur said. "There are thousands of them—thousands! Each of them vulnerable to your presence. Do you expect to stay in one place and not manifest more than one reflection at a time? Do you expect me to do the same? You will be fighting countless reflections of you, which are invested in the same skill, weapons, and armor. And that is the easy task! You will also find yourself fighting reflections of everyone *else* in your party, my fighting skills, weapons, and armor."

"You're joking?" Zachary said, looking starkly ill, matching Timothy's looks.

"I do not jest. And it is exactly why I had planned to go alone. But not anymore. The book must be involved. Timothy must be involved. I am no longer the instrument of Eythreal that I once was. Nor is Camus so much Eythreal's harbinger of doom. Eythreal belongs inside that book now. The book belongs to Timothy. Therefore, in a complicated network of fabrics, Timothy *is* Eythreal. And because of that, I fear a dire consequence from the book if we attempt to leave Timothy behind, meaning, leaving the book behind when, clearly, the book wants to be involved with Glass Castle."

"Kind of like the consequence of me letting my pa go into the black house and not me?"

"Do not dwell on that. But aye, kind of like that."

"And me?" Zachary said.

"I'm sure that you could—"

"I'm going!"

"Good," Rajur said, "because as much as I think you could stay out of this, I believe it is very wise that you stay by Timothy. Your existence here, I must believe, is for Timothy's sake."

"So we go to this castle to fight reflections?" Timothy said.

Rajur nodded.

"But you never said how we can kill him."

"That is where it is a bit complicated and, well, dubious. The scholars and historians that gave us what information we have about Zorlof and his final conjuration could not give us much more. No. It was a sorcerer that had befriended another wizard of that same sect that gave us what little we could understand. What we could understand is that once you defeat a reflection, Zorlof's control will be released. He will appear fully dressed and *somewhat* vulnerable. Somewhat vulnerable, because his existence is very short-lived.

"Supposedly, the more reflections, the stronger he is, and the stronger he is, the less vulnerable. Another reason I planned on doing this alone."

"I guess that's better than nothing," Zachary said. "One good strike and—"

"No," Rajur said, "it is not Zorlof's true form that appears. Zorlof no longer belongs to this physical plane of Eythreal's existence. He lost himself. He lost himself inside a spell, which is bound to the castle and mirrors and nothing else on Eythreal. Maybe after the spell is defeated, will he be released from the level of existence we are all blind to and appear in his physical form. But like everything else, it is sheer conjecture. What we believe is that each strike on him weakens the spell—weakens him—only so much. The magnitude of the spell being so gigantic I can only imagine numerous successful strikes to weaken the spell to the point of breaking, which would—well, we better pray—leave behind what it is we seek."

"Numerous strikes?" Timothy said.

"It makes sense."

"But it takes only one decisive blow to end our lives," Timothy said.

"Aye."

The boys sighed in defeat.

"And this is what the book is asking of us?" Timothy asked.

"It sounds like a death trap," Zachary said.

"This item that may be left behind—what's it got to do with Camus?"

"Crystal's Edge," Rajur answered. "If we want to vanquish Camus by the only means we know of, we must have this blade."

"It's a sword?"

"Aye."

"And we use it to kill Camus?"

"Yes," Rajur said, with a hesitant shake of his head. "And no."

"Why do you make things so complicated?" Zachary asked.

"It is not complicated. Zorlof alone forged this blade. He had started long before coming to Lady Gwynn and me to warn us of Camus. Wizards have an uncanny sense of clairvoyance. They are not soothsayers. Nor are they the loom that weaves the patterns of the world. But yes, they have the capacity to study the weaving. They cannot exactly discover the end results—the final pattern. But they have enough in them to work out multiple reliable results. Zorlof sensed the pattern Lady Gwynn put into action when she conceived. He saw the many end results. By his estimation, he didn't like them. Thus, he decided to forge a blade that would end Camus's life. To do so, he must first forge a blade that would be later forged again into a new blade.

"That first blade is Crystal's Edge. And he'd have forged Crystal's Edge to form the essential blade if it weren't for certain obstacles and roadblocks."

"Him going mad?"

"Not exactly, for he was already considered mad. Madness did set in a bit more, and it impeded his course of action. But the main reason fell to the forging of this second blade to be relied upon by others. These important others were already wary of him and his madness. He could not convince them to help. And even if they did agree, which I think in time they would have, the most important item used to forge this second blade would still be in want, for he did try to receive that item. Yes, he tried. He confronted her, and she gave him no chance of coming close to explaining his plan, for I have already told you about this confrontation. To this day, I believe he'd make a second attempt, except . . . It is too late. She no longer exists."

A sad look came over Rajur's face.

"If only I knew. If I'd been more aware of his plotting, I'd have broken my oath and revealed our secret to him."

"Secret?"

Rajur answered by shaking his head.

"The blade's name after this Crystal Edge blade is forged a second time?" Timothy asked, seeing that Rajur was not about to tell his secret.

"Vampyric."

"Vamp-what?" Zachary said.

"Vampyric."

"Like a vampire?" Timothy said.

"Aye. Vampire. Yes. Because it is a blade that must be forged by blood, blood to be chosen wisely. One must choose the right blood for the proper purpose of the blade. The more illustrious the source of blood, the greater the blade's impact. You see, one may use this sword as any other sword. But it would be futile to do so, for it would spoil its reason for being forged. It would also pale in comparison to most other swords. It is to be used for its true intention, its true purpose: to drain the blood of its intended victim. Doing so, the blood will be used as a weapon to that intended target, along with blood that had been used to forge the blade. The combination of both blood types makes the blade far more powerful than you can imagine.

"Unfortunately, you only have one attempt with Vampyric when it is filled with the victim's blood. So one must choose wisely on how to use it."

"I'm guessing we're using it on Camus?"

"Aye, we must drain him of his blood with Vampyric, and with the addition of the blood from what forged Vampyric, we will use them both against him."

"And the blood used to forge this Vampyric?"

"You should not worry yourself about that for now. What I do worry about is the hammer."

"Hammer?"

"Just because Zorlof devised this recipe to forge such a blade did not mean he could just simply use whatever tools he chose to use. To create such a magnificent and godlike weapon meant the same when it came to the tools used to build it. One of these tools is the mandatory use of a certain hammer that most believe doesn't even exist. Most believe this hammer used to forge the blade is only a delusion in his mind. But the few that believe in such a hammer are far more important than the disbelievers, for they are the only ones that possess the two anvils that could handle the power of this enigmatic hammer."

"And I'm guessing you believe?"

"I must."

"And the few anvils?"

"Far more convenient, for I *know* they exist and where to find them."

"So," Zachary continued, "we must procure this Crystal's Edge by defeating a near-invincible wizard, locate a hammer that most don't even think to exist, retrieve one of the only two anvils that do exist, forge the blade Crystal's Edge with the blood of someone you have yet to disclose to us and you *say* is something we shouldn't worry about, create Vampyric out of this creation of anvil, hammer, blood, and Crystal Edge, and then, find a way to meet this Camus through battle, stab him with the blade, drain his blood, and then use the now blood-filled Vampyric and what? Cut off his head?"

"Cut off his head would be appropriate," Rajur said with a nod.

"Well, that sounds easy," Zachary said sarcastically. "What do you think, Timothy?"

Timothy kept his eyes on Rajur. "What about Camus?"

"What about him?"

"Why hasn't Camus found a way to retrieve Crystal's Edge and destroy it, ending any chance of his destruction?"

"A wise question. First, I don't think Camus even knows about the doings of Zorlof. Again, wizards decide how much or how little they want *you* to learn about them. I'm sure the same went with how much Zorlof wanted anyone to know about Crystal's Edge. Second, it would be very imprudent and risky if Camus ever wanted to step foot in Glass Castle. Very imprudent and risky. He'd be facing himself. I can't imagine a battle of Camus against possibly hundreds of Camus, all of whom are possibly equipped with Bane Singer and able to deliver ungodly power against their opponent."

"And if he brought an army inside the castle?"

"That army would face an army of near-infinite numbers, for one single mirror, I'm sure, would reflect a cluster of that army."

Timothy absorbed all of this and turned his eyes to the closed book. "Glass Castle," he said.

Rajur nodded.   "Of course, the choice falls to you."

Choices.

"Yes," Timothy said. "My choices." With a nod of his head, Timothy spoke again. "Then I choose for us to go to Glass Castle and face this wizard. But I'd like some guidance along the way. Isn't that why you're here, besides your fighting skill?"

"I can do that."

Timothy and Zachary waited.

"And?" Timothy said.

"And?"

"What next?"

"Nothing should change from what I mentioned earlier."

"Sarah's Town?"

"Aye. Cyrcle. We go to Cyrcle. It's not far from here. We'll probably want to camp for at least one night before arriving there. Once there, I'll want you boys to strip off these outlandish clothes and dress appropriately. You must look as if you belong here. This way, you won't stick out like a sore thumb, which will only draw even more suspicion to an already suspicious companionship. This you must understand: there are very few, but still enough of them that have felt the shift in our world. They may not come close to understanding the truth of what happened. But they felt a change. You draw suspicion from someone like this, and it will spell disaster.

"You both need weapons and armor too. We could always wait until we reach Ghalia to purchase both since they're abundant there. But what we can find at Sarah's Town would be cheaper, possibly better, since there is a blacksmith in her town that owes me some favors. And Sarah's goods are always preserved exceptionally well. As for price, I may not be poor, but I'm definitely not inexhaustible when it comes to coins and rubies. In Ghalia, even a soul ruby could possibly be spotted, telling one that trading isn't as cheap as it can be."

"Soul ruby?" Zachary asked.

"The highest form of currency found on Eythreal. A small handful of soul rubies could easily buy you a warship or even a sky craft."

"Do you have a soul ruby?" Zachary asked, with inquisitive eyes.

"No. But I have a few empty soul rubies, some of which are cut into quarters and halves, which place them at a far more diminutive price. But with the right enchantment, one can easily complete them into a whole, empty soul ruby. You don't want to possess a filled soul ruby since they only bring you trouble. No. In Sarah's Town, we'll only need a few coins, some rubies, and maybe a quarter or two of an empty soul ruby, although I doubt Sarah would even take a quarter, let alone the smallest chip of an empty soul ruby. The last thing she'd want is a soul ruby running through her currency. Soul rubies are still mysterious to all Eythreal on what they are filled with."

"Not souls?" Zachary asked.

"Oh, no. They are souls. They are surely filled with souls. But the souls of whom?" Rajur said, leaning toward the boys. "And here we are, all this time, passing them around as if they're innocent bargaining chips without a chance of coming back to haunt us, without a single clue of whose soul filled this ruby and if there ever is a chance for that soul to seep through. Hah. Time will tell on soul rubies. And I have an ominous feeling that it will come at our expense and with grave consequences.

"But we speak of matters irrelevant to what is really important at this early juncture of our journey. Sarah's Town—that is the importance here. There, we'll find rest. There, we'll find what I like to call Ranger Field. It is a field where her occasional visitors like to test their might, mostly mage apprentices who have come to Cyrcle to purchase a scroll or two from her magic shop. There, on that field, I'll teach you simple yet very effective combat techniques, especially when it comes to defensive and counteractive moves since I'll be asking very little of you two when it comes to offensive strikes. You two must understand how to wield a weapon successfully and properly before I teach you broader offensive tactics.

"We'll stock up on provisions too. We've got a long haul to Ghalia."

"We're going to Ghalia?" Timothy asked.

"It would be wise of us. We must recruit. We'll find nobody to our liking at Cyrcle. In Ghalia, I have a friend in mind. And I'm almost certain we must confront this friend. Of course, it'll come down to you, Timothy, to make that choice. It would also be wise to stock up on more provisions in Ghalia before heading toward Glass Castle. To reach Glass Castle means a most arduous journey, one that will force us to make more than a few stops to replenish provisions, but Ghalia would help immensely. To reach Ghalia from Cyrcle will not prove so troublesome. The journey should take three or so moons and a good portion of this through her forest. Of course, there is always an exception, for there is one small roadblock to pass."

"And that is?"

"It is nothing. Now about Ghalia—"

"We're there to recruit? But didn't you say the fewer people, the better for the reflections?"

"Aye, if it was just me going there. But now, with you two at my side, I will need others to help deflect the reflections from coming at you while also delivering blows to Zorlof when he appears after a vanquished reflection. The strategy I had in place to fight off the reflections is now obsolete. A new strategy must be implemented, and it has a lot to do with encircling one another while most of us defend and one or two are on the attack. We'll need help for this to work. Not much, but a good five or six strong warriors. And I can aid you in this—in this choosing of recruits. But again, the—"

"The decision falls on me."

"Aye."

"I just don't want to be wrong."

"I wouldn't worry about that. You have done quite well so far."

"You think so?" a dubious Timothy said.

"Look at us now. We are safe. And look who's beside you? Your most loyal and trustworthy friend."

"And you," Zachary said.

"Aye, and me. And know this, Timothy, who knows if and when I'd come to your aid if you had made different choices from the start."

Timothy nodded optimistically.

"It's just," Timothy said after a long pause. "Our families."

"Finish the book," Rajur said.

"But even you said you're not certain they will return."

"Only one way to find out."

"Yes," Timothy nodded.

"Come now. It is time to leave for Cyrcle."

Chapter 2

SARAH OF CYRCLE

Cyrcle.

As mentioned by Rajur, only Sarah knew why Sarah named her town Cycle. The fact of Cyrcle meaning "circle" in the common tongue of Eythreal only confused the matter even more since the town was rectangular shaped, with a picket fence and various shrubs being the enclosure, thus showing no signs of a circle. And it was because of that reason many people called the town Sarah's Town instead of its rightful name of Cyrcle.

Speaking of these residents, there were only about two dozen or so. This was due to the small size of the town. Only a handful of shops resided in the town. This included two magic shops, one selling scrolls that produce white magic, while another produced black magic, for Sarah, held no discrimination over another's philosophy. Many of her friends studied black magic. In town was also a forge run by a blacksmith named Berg. The town also consisted of an armor and weaponry store and a potion shop that sold various goods, including herbs, medicines, tonics, and even elixirs.

Her potion shop had long been considered the pride of her town, besides the enchantment surrounding the town and forest.

Sarah's inn was also considered a popular destination, for weary travelers found much rest there, most of these travelers coming and going from Ghalia. But one must step off the main road leading to Ghalia to reach her town, which would cost them much precious time.

Of course, they also gambled whether they could withstand the repelling effects of her enchantment.

Regarding this enchantment, the spell did not cause death to any creature; nor did it cause permanent harm, no matter how wicked they proved. It manifested more as a deterrent—but a powerful one. The spell repelled the mind of one being wicked. It acted as if an allergic reaction coursed through this individual's mind when nearing the forest. They would find the land pungent and distasteful. They would want nothing else but to further themselves from the repellent feeling, making them think it would cause permanent harm or death in time, which, again, would not happen.

Returning to the permanent residents, Sarah considered them her kin, even though not one came from her mysterious ancestry. These residents had grown far too tired of the machinations of Eythreal, whether it be for the good of Iria's Light or the Dark. These were the ones that had grown troubled by whom to trust, to the point of madness. They wanted peace and tranquility for their wonderful hearts, which Sarah gave them.

Regarding Sarah's age, anyone's guess proved no better or worse. Again, her history could not be traced. Her looks made it harder also, for she was a white mage, and because of that, the residue of the more-healing and less-harmful properties of her philosophy rendered her fresher and younger in looks, showing nearly no sign of aging, especially with her being a very powerful white mage, whereas ones that conjured black magic or studied that philosophy lost one's brightness and freshness because of the inherited nature of the destructive spells. Luckily, being mages, they had ways of slowing down the scarring. Thus, because of her looks, no one could come close to placing an age on her.

They did believe her to be not long in the world. How wrong they were to think that! Sarah was nothing else but long in the world.

As for her beauty, calling her beautiful would be a significant understatement.

Radiant!

She always had a brilliant sheen to her skin and presence, an aura some even felt and tried to see. Even her dresses, whether mage cloaks or casual attire, were pristine and unblemished. She never showed the slightest wear on her clothes or physical complexion. And this radiance of hers was nearly impossible to believe.

Unlike most, and to their great surprise, she did not place any spell on her looks and age. Nor was her lack of aging and change in beauty simply due to her life's philosophy.

Again, a very mysterious ancestry surrounded her and her sister.

Sarah never left her land. Of course, before her arrival and decision to build and enchant the town and forest, she traveled much of Eythreal. But never since.

She had become home to only Cyrcle and her forest. That did not mean many would see her. No. Very seldom could she be spotted in town. Most of her time was spent in the forest.

But on the morning following the storm, she made a rare appearance in town, when everyone around could catch sight of her.

She did that because she was one of those few personages Rajur spoke of who possibly felt a shift in the world. And it scared her.

Strolling casually into town, she showed no sign of this apprehension. She simply made her way to the center portion of the town, where a magnificent fountain resided.

Seeing the fountain, her fear dissipated, and a look of astonishment betrayed her face. This astonishment consisted of curiosity, excitement, and the slightest tinge of fear—fear not from being scared, only from the uncertainty. And this change of demeanor came about when seeing that the fountain's water was anything but murky, ashen gray, or dark. Nor was the water turbulent and erratic. No. The water continued to flow with its usual vibrant colors, now fuller and brighter than ever before, along with a robust and vigorous flow, as if something beyond good came her way, something she had never faced in her life. As if some god, or goddess, improbably came her way.

Thus, Sarah abandoned all ideas of wandering through her forest on this day. Instead, she made her way to the entrance of the town and waited—waited for the impossible to appear.

~

The boys woke up the following morning of their awakening on Eythreal to the two moons from that day before. They recalled the mystery of the vague one from yesterday, only growing to its full strength by the time Rajur had them pitch camp. And now, besides the two full moons and the Star of Nod, edging closer to take over the morning, they saw a third moon vaguely appearing in the sky. They concluded that each new moon started off vague, and the longer the day, the fuller the moon became. Of course, they had no idea what all that meant and what anything about the moons meant.

Thus, during their short morning travel to Sarah's Town, they kept their eyes on this vague moon and tried to notice the moon grow in strength.

It intrigued them.

And because of that, they never noticed Rajur, leading them to this point, stop in his tracks. They would have collided into him if it weren't for him saying, "Should have known."

What Rajur said broke their concentration on the moons' mystery.

They looked ahead at Rajur and noticed the first steps leading up a verdant green hill.

"Should've known what?" Timothy asked.

"She waits for us."

"She?" Zachary said.

"Sarah. She waits for us on the hilltop."

The boys tried to spy the top of the hill but could not.

"You two will soon become accustomed to my heightened senses and vision," Rajur said. "Don't expect to meet many others with a keener vision and hearing than I have."

The boys nodded.

"Is it good she's waiting for us?" Zachary asked.

"I don't know. Not bad. But it may not be the best for us either. I'm sure she waits because she felt the shift. Or possibly, *it* showed her."

"Showed her?" Zachary asked.

"Remember what I said about some having the natural talent and gift to feel the rift in the world when blackness took me, but also the storm came for us? Sarah could easily be one of those few. She also has something in town that is far greater and more susceptible. And this mystery of hers allows her to sense what only mana sense and feel."

A few steps later, Rajur continued, "Like few others, she can sense us. You, Zachary, and me—all three of us reek with mana. As for the book, nothing on Eythreal suffuses as much mana as it does. Fortunately, very few in the world could feel mana like this, even if they were staring at it in plain sight. This is because the mana that exudes from the book isn't necessarily Eythreal's mana. Eythreal's mana is locked inside the book while projecting outward to us."

"So she knows about the book?"

"No, not the book, although she probably feels its strength. But no, too distant of a guess. But the strength of it will evoke suspicion."

"Should we turn back?"

"No. In a way, I suspected this—relied on it. I just didn't want it to occur in a confrontational manner. She may not even allow us our entrance. She may not want such powerful and foreign mana to be suffused in her town, even though no other guest or resident would sense it. She's very protective, like a mother."

"So this book," Zachary said. "You say it carries mana but not Eythreal's mana?"

"Aye. The book is essentially mana in its purest form, a mana unlike what the Seven Moons of Iria produce upon Eythreal. It is a kind of mana that is shared with all worlds that live in the same domain, resting in what Timothy called the Pillars of Worlds. But with Timothy having opened the book, only the mana of Eythreal could be found. All of this, everything around us, we ourselves are inside the book. Thus, the mana of Eythreal that the book gives off does not betray the book since it is felt around us, seen, and tasted—no difference if the physicality of the book is open or closed. It is always open as long as Eythreal is here."

"Do we have mana?" Zachary asked. "I mean, our Earth?"

Rajur nodded.

"Your world resides in that same domain. All those worlds carry the mana the book is made up of, for mana in its truest form is Creation itself. Life on a world cannot be without it."

"Well," Zachary said, "it is unheard of in our world."

"Your world has long abandoned it; forgotten its true creation. And don't think of *mana* being the true term. Some worlds have another name for it."

"So mana is not like magic?" Timothy asked.

"No, not even close. However, one must have mana to have magic. It is mana that helps one produce magic."

"No belief in mana, no magic?" Zachary said.

"In a simple answer, yes."

"What is mana besides the Creation?"

Here, Rajur smiled. "You're asking me something that cannot be answered, for there is no answer. This I can only expound upon. Besides mana, like the book being Creation, many individuals believe the mana we assimilate, meaning the mana produced for us by the Seven Moons of Iria and the same mana found on your world and the rest of the worlds, to be the spirit of gods. But how can this be some question, for mana came before the gods and goddesses? Therefore, there are a few outlandish others, very troublesome in their own beliefs and philosophy of life, which has caused them to be exiled or scorned by many others, who believe that the mana we assimilate gives us our life, is actually the *blood* of gods. At some point, the blood will run dry. If that were to happen, well, the Realm of Cosmos, which many gods and goddesses call home, would fall, perish for eternity. Everything we feed off will be obliterated. We will then become a faithless world. Chaos will reign. Total extinction would soon follow. It is why most *want* to believe in mana being the spirit of gods, for it gives them comfort from what else it could be. It comforts them that their way of life isn't sealing their doom."

A long moment of stillness passed.

"What do you believe?" Timothy asked.

Rajur looked down and then up.

"I believe in the latter. I believe in the mana being the blood of gods. But I don't believe in our self-destruction. I believe in hope, for there must be a compromise. It's just that we haven't discovered it yet; hidden from all eyes. Because why have we been created only to destroy ourselves and our world? What is the point of our evolution? We are not cancer—a plague to all that lives and breathes. Nor are we an insatiable leech feeding off what gives us our life. But yes, we are doing something wrong. And we must soon fix it. We must soon learn our true purpose of life here on Eythreal, for I believe Iria knows this, and it could be why she has been so absent. Someone has chosen to hinder her from executing our true purpose to live upon Eythreal, stopping us from continuing to live the way of life we do now, thus, becoming our own extinction. That is what I believe."

A few steps later, they reached a part of the hill that gave the boys their first sight of the town and its wooden fence enclosure.

The fence looked to be for looks only since the smallest animals could easily leap over it, along with the biggest of animals able to barge through it.

More importantly about this sight, they glanced at Sarah, standing at the front gate, waiting for them, as she had done since the morning *before*.

The higher they climbed the hill, the more beautiful and radiant this mage seemed to them.

~

Regarding height, Sarah stood on the tall end of the stick rather than short. Many freckles riddled her face, shoulders, and even arms. The freckles were of an amber hue, matching her reddish-golden hair while accentuating her chocolate complexion. She possessed a rotund body, although far from being obese. She indulged, one could say—but moderately for her standards. She never scowled, even when angry. She never cringed, even when afraid. She nearly had a permanent smile on her face, a smile that represented everything happy and peaceful. And this peacefulness and happiness exuded from her very pores—like an aura for some to see and feel.

She wore a white-and-yellow lace dress while waiting for the companions. The dress was puffy and exquisite and fit elegantly on her, ending at her calves, revealing a portion of her arms, shoulders, and of course, both hands. She had worn this dress numerous times, and it never looked anything but new. Never did it betray a tinge of use, whether a wrinkle or slight damage to the lace; never did it show a blot or stain of the smallest accident or wear, even after long days in the forest. This was due to the inner sanction of her philosophy and the aura some feel and even see suffuse from her.

She had this innocent intimidating effect on all—mostly due to her stature and beauty. Nearing her, the boys became daunted by her presence. But closing in on her, they felt their minds pacifying. They felt only tranquility seep into their minds. Rajur, familiar with Sarah's presence and natural aura formed by her being a master in white magic, did not feel the change as much as the boys.

"I believe we're going to be fine," Rajur said.

The boys nodded.

~

"Welcome," Sarah said with a wave of her hand and a bright smile.

Seeing the dog, Sarah lowered her body, and Butch had no choice but to accept her embrace. Sarah did not stint in giving the dog love. Butch rolled over multiple times, and the pleasure the dog felt had never been matched before. The dog showed so much pleasure that Timothy became envious, seeing that never had he made Butch so happy. Of course, this envy dissipated, and Timothy felt nothing but joy for the dog being so affectionately caressed on his belly and sides.

"I've never seen him behave like this before *and* with a stranger!"

Sarah looked up at Timothy. "That is because I am no stranger to anyone who walks through this forest. And this also pertains to a dog that does not belong *here*," she said with a slight shake of her head and a not-so-subtle look Rajur's way. "He's a good dog, though," she said, focusing on Butch again, "which tells me a lot. Tells me its master must possess a benevolent heart," she said, looking toward Timothy. "You will find that there are few other dogs in town. I'm sure this dog will appreciate the company, as they will too."

Continuing to love the dog, her eyes landed on Rajur.

"It has been a long time, friend," she said.

"Yes," Rajur said, with a shamed look on his face, "too long. But you understand."

"I do," Sarah said with a forgiving look. "Your absences are always warranted. But that does not absolve the foolishness of hiding the reasons for your latest absence. I would have gone with you if only you had asked for my help."

"There is too much at stake here," Rajur said.

"Blah!" Sarah said, waving that statement off. "It is nothing." Her eyes turned to the boys. "I see you've met new friends. I only wonder . . . how and where did you meet them?"

"You know," Rajur said, "the intricacies of Eythreal."

"Is that so? That's your answer to the mystery of why these two strapping young men look beyond Eythreal? And why that taller one hides something that is not . . . Hmm . . .

"I wonder. Yes," Sarah said, "I wonder . . . I wonder deeply what that boy hides."

Rajur tried to look at her with a deadpan face. He failed. He smiled instead, feeling only praise for Sarah's discernment.

As for the boys, they trembled.

"Come," Sarah said. "Spill it out. What is it? What great importance does the boy try to hide? You insult me by thinking of me as deficient in my innate abilities. This tall boy exudes an amount of mana on his own, which has me terrified. And I believe wholly it is not from him. But, well, yes, he too, along with the other boy, exudes much mana. But it is a mana I feel to be different . . . from us. But I also sense our mana—as if they are now absorbing our mana for the very first time. And they are doing so at a prodigious rate. Am I right so far? What is the object that explodes with mana?"

Rajur's smile widened even more.

"I speak correctly," Sarah said. "Their mana is not of this world. It is from a world that has the smallest of traces of mana. But surprisingly, or not so surprisingly, they are assimilating our mana at an unprecedented rate. Even this second, I sense the boy's mana growing stronger, as if he's some vessel I've never heard of. The growth of mana will, at some point, exceed what is healthy for any individual. It will become a mortal blow to him if not taken care of. He must learn how to absorb the mana properly. He must learn to adapt to Eythreal. But he's got time. Yes. He's got time. And that object he thinks to hide from me . . .

"Boy," Sarah said severely, "tell me. What have you brought us?"

Timothy turned to Rajur.

Rajur felt the boy's stare while staring only at Sarah. "I will not object to any decision of yours, Timothy," Rajur said.

"Timothy!" Sarah said. "Yes. A not-so-unordinary name for anyone of Azaarath. Tell me, Timothy, which of the kingdoms are you a loyal subject to on Azaarath? Or are you just another exiled misfit? Or do you not know what I'm talking about?"

Timothy closed his eyes.

Choices.

He reopened them.

"Tell her," Timothy said to Rajur.

"He comes with a *change*," Rajur said.

"Change?"

"A possession that belongs to him and him only. This possession is nothing else but the change itself."

Sarah squinted her eyes and knitted her eyebrows. "I . . . I don't follow."

Rajur looked grave. "Think about it. Think about . . ." he said, hinting for her to focus on him by making a facial gesture.

Sarah read this. She combined Rajur's mystery with this boy's mystery. She came to one conclusion. "No."

Rajur nodded.

"The shift I felt," Sarah said. "That was . . . Oh my."

"Yes. *Oh my.*"

Sarah let everything sink in. When she did, a certain incident popped up in her mind. "Then is it coincidence or fate?" she said, mostly to herself.

"What are you talking about?" Rajur asked.

"No time to explain," she said. "First, we need to dress these boys in proper clothing. Even in my town, we cannot afford to draw suspicion."

Sarah turned to leave and stopped. She looked at Timothy. "Do I have to tell you not to say a word—"

"You would be foolish to think he needs to be told that," Rajur said. "The boy is wise. Both of them. I do not doubt that each has been chosen wisely."

"And I will never doubt that again," Sarah said. "I am only extra careful because of what's happening of late. Turmoil on Eythreal has reached catastrophic levels. And it's starting to show here. As of late, many of my former visitors have been forbidden from entering my forest and town. Their minds have grown malevolent and want nothing but the destruction of what is good. They have become twisted—twisted by the baleful workings of Eythreal. I cannot see exactly what they harbor in their mind, but I can easily feel the enmity for Iria's Light. But fear not. We are still protected here. You will find rest and be made fresh again. See Hersh at my inn. He'll be the one to give you freshness and beds. I'll personally see to the care of your pets."

"Thank you," Rajur said.

Too nervous about speaking, both boys nodded their thanks.

Sarah stepped aside and gave them room to enter through the gate.

~

The quarter-of-a-mile walk from the gate's entrance to the immediate grounds of the town proved pleasant for the boys. During this time, their minds were at ease while ruminating over endless scenarios of what they will find in town.

Would it be a town of grandeur? Or would it be old and ruinous, dull, and full of boredom? Could it be the size of the smallest lot in their former town? Or would it be grand in size? Would there be elves like the ones they'd read about in fairy tales? Maybe even dwarves. Knights, sprites, fairies, and many more magical creatures from their childhood memories and now placed in this fascinating town. And why not? This town could not be ordinary, right? It must be grand. No way could it be dull and boring. There must be magical creatures from their childhood, and the magic must waft through the air to be felt. Flying witches, they would see. Tiny trolls pestering little old ladies. Lazy and chivalrous knights waiting for the next princess to be kidnapped and in need of rescue. There must be that and much more.

And yet, receiving their first glimpse of the town, both boys looked highly disappointed.

"I thought we'd see elves and dwarves," Zachary said.

Timothy nodded. "It looks more like a quaint village from our world."

And most certainly, it did.

But what gave the boys hope was the attire the visitors and residents wore. Each of them was classified as menfolk or womenfolk or human by some, although the word *human* had never been originated on Eythreal. Their clothes suggested to the boys that they each came from a different part of Eythreal. Because of that, the boys were confident that soon much would be different in this town. This was important to them, for it was the magic of Eythreal—the chance to discover magical creatures and so forth—that kept the sorrow at bay. Of course, the loss of their families and world could never completely be extracted from their minds. But shelved away it had been, and hopefully would continue to be.

The two boys followed Sarah and Rajur into town, and much of the disappointment vanished from their minds and demeanor. The town might not be home to mythical creatures of their world, but it did resemble a town not to be imagined on their Earth; it proved too quaint and odd to be considered quaint and odd. Most of that was due to the buildings being perfectly square-shaped, with an also perfectly shaped triangle for a gable or attic, and everything so oddly colored (not dull and yet not exceedingly vibrant), neat in form, and lawn and garden and so forth, far too healthy and clean to ever be trod on.

Even the artistic and yet plain bridge arched over the finely flowing creek could not be imagined in their former world.

And none of that spoke of the whimsical and extraordinary peaceful characters strolling through the town.

Sarah led them to the largest building in town. It stood at three levels, the bottom level wider than the upper two—Sarah's Inn.

Adjacent to the inn stood the only saloon in town. For that reason, this saloon was habitually busy, mostly from weary, peaceful travelers coming and going while mingling with the permanent residents. Inside the saloon, one would find melodious music coming from a piano that played on its own. Sometimes a live band would form on stage, and this was done by traveling musicians and thespians that came to town. Some of the best tastes of food came from this saloon, along with mead, beer, wine, and other softer drinks for children, although the latter were very scarce in making an appearance.

As Sarah mentioned, Hersh the innkeeper also tended the saloon.

~

"I will see you shortly," Sarah said to Timothy and his few companions while leading them inside the saloon. She turned back and walked out.

Timothy and Zachary first spotted a fiddler playing on the stage. Seeing the newcomers, the fiddler changed tunes while the rest of the patrons glanced their way. On nearly every occasion, not one patron, whether a resident or visitor, cared for anyone walking into the establishment, even on the few times Sarah casually walked inside. But the likes of Rajur and the boys were far too much for the wonderstruck bar patrons.

Unaware of this change in the atmosphere, a grizzly bearded man nearly the size of a bear, looking more like a ruffian than anything else, came rushing out of the kitchen partition of the saloon, carrying a tray of food and mugs of mead, and stopped suddenly when he sensed the thunderstruck patrons.

"Well? What's this all about? Get on with your music, you fiddler. You've been begging me mercilessly to play—so play! And the rest of you, swallow your drink. You know how rare and difficult this mead comes by. Some say the mead has fairy dust sprinkled in it. Who knows? Just guzzle it down 'cause here comes more."

The saloon patrons took the grizzly bearded man seriously, for they pounded down the last of their mead.

Hersh then turned to the source of the disturbance. He spotted Timothy and Zachary and then the tray of food and precious mead rattled.

"My eyes must be deceiving me, because that can't be who I think it to be."

"Your eyes aren't against you," Rajur said with a smile, "old friend."

"Agh!" Hersh said. "Old friend or no friend, it doesn't matter how long it has been. How are you?" Hersh said as he placed a hand on Rajur's shoulder.

Rajur returned the same gesture. "Better times ahead," Rajur said.

"Let us hope."

"All we can do is hope."

"Yes."

"And you?"

Hersh patted his paunchy stomach. "Not losing my appetite . . . yet."

Rajur nodded.

"And who did you bring with you?"

"Friends."

"Friends? You say *friends*, so I must believe you. Don't need an explanation, not from you, certainly not from you. You are here. They are here. Sarah is aware of it. That is all that is needed to know. And now, my friend, they are friends of mine. Come. A hand on the shoulder is how strangers call themselves friends. A hug is what our friendship deserves—one big, hearty bear hug."

Reluctantly, Rajur gave in to Hersh's demand.

"That ain't no hug," Hersh said as Rajur hugged him. "This is a hug." Hersh hugged Rajur as a mama bear would hug its long-lost and found cub.

But Rajur was no cub.

Hersh had a wide girth to his body, much thicker around the belly, but Rajur stood taller, muscular, and with broader shoulders.

The boys watched the two hug it out and it looked as if they formed one giant mass of muscle and brawn. They almost laughed—the boys.

"The young gents smirk," Hersh said. "Never seen a big man hug a bigger man? Come. Get used to it. And go get yourself a table. Juice for them and wine for you?"

Rajur nodded and led the boys to a table. Butch followed since the dog chose not to mingle with the other dogs in town.

"They got juice and wine?" Timothy asked.

"Aye," Rajur said, "and more. Don't be alarmed by the similarities, for there'll be many! Our worlds don't stand too far apart."

Rajur found a table, and they each settled down. Feeling at ease, the fiddler returned to his earlier music. Hersh soon arrived again with a tray of three drinks, one being a goblet of red wine, the other two juices poured into pint glasses. Hersh also placed a water bowl beside the dog. Hersh went to turn away but stopped.

"Is it true?" he asked in a whisper.

"It depends," Rajur said. "What are you referring to?"

In the softest of tones, Hersh said, "Camus."

Rajur stayed stoic.

"And how you and your reclusive friends tricked him. Had him in your grasp, they say."

Rajur softened his stoic look and nodded. "And how did you hear about this?"

"Oh," Hersh said, drawing out the answer, "you know how it is. Odd fellows of the best of nature come into this town at times. Tales they tell. The mead I sometimes produce has an extraordinary effect. Recently, I heard a tale I could not believe. But now, I guess it's not a drunken tale after all. My only question, if you don't mind me asking, is where he is now if you're here."

"He walks," Rajur said. "For now."

"Well, I'm sure he'll face his reckoning soon enough.

"Aye, he shall. But in the end, so shall we all."

Hersh nodded and turned away.

"Everyone really does fear Camus," Timothy said.

"As they should."

The boys fell victim to their exhausted minds and bodies and became silent. The travel to Sarah's Town had been short; the arduous battle mentally and physically since the moment of their awakening became too much of a strain. As much as they wanted to ask more questions, they felt it prudent to rest their weary minds and relax. Rajur would tell them what they needed, they both agreed subconsciously. Thus, they became mindful of themselves sipping on the juice. They tasted pleasure from the juice, unlike any juice they had tasted before. They attributed this fact to the fruits and shrubs of Eythreal, so much more bounteous than any they had seen in their lives. With the addition of the pleasure of the juice, the resting of their minds, and the tranquility of their ambiance, the boys found shelter for their suffering like never before.

Chapter 3

TOLAN'S WISDOM

A half hour later, Sarah made an appearance from Hersh's leave of Timothy's table.

"I have more news to give regarding what I mentioned earlier. I do believe it is the work of fate—and in our favor."

"Tell us," Rajur said.

"A traveler came into town last night. One could not look more lonesome than this person. He asked for a few days of seclusion. I gave him this, and I did so curiously, for something about him puzzled my mind. And it had everything to do with him being an instrument of good for Eythreal. I gave him my personal office to work in since he mentioned he had much work to do and needed complete seclusion. After granting him this, I never thought about him again. Not until you arrived.

"While you were here in the inn, I did some snooping around and deep thinking. You are familiar with the Scholar of Vickensburg?"

"Why do you ask that when you know my answer?"

Sarah shrugged.

"Just being theatrical?" Rajur asked.

"One could never be too dramatic." Sarah said.

Rajur nearly laughed.

"I highly beg to differ. He goes by the name of Tolan. And I've been searching for him high and low for the longest time."

After a second's worth of a pause, Rajur asked, "And you're sure it's him?"

"All signs point to him being that reclusive and highly renowned scholar."

Rajur nodded his head.

"I had just left his office space. I spied many devices that correlated with him being a field scholar—tools and objects that could brave the roughest terrain. And more! I even insidiously discovered what he might be working on. Though I feel like I betrayed him and his desire for secrecy, I cannot stop thinking how impossible this task would be for him to accomplish. But let us forget my injustice to him and pretend that I saw nothing about the possible quest. Outside of that, what I added up means too much. It must be him, and with your mysterious appearance, there must be something far greater going on. Because, imagine, yes, imagine what insight he could give Timothy and what he possesses?"

Rajur stayed silent and thoughtful.

"Why have you been searching for him?" Timothy asked.

"Tolan is much more than a scholar or historian. Much more. He's more of a world traveler. He knows nearly every inch of Eythreal, including its facts, lore, and more. Talk about a lore master? He writes the rules of being a lore master. There is still much I need to know about my quest, which now mostly falls on you, Timothy. Much more. Sarah is right. He's a source of knowledge that we cannot pass up. We must take advantage of this luck."

"We can trust him?"

"Aye."

"Then we go together," Timothy said.

"Aye," Rajur nodded and smiled.

Sarah also nodded.

~

The personal office space belonging to Sarah seemed more along the lines of an attic while it rested above the third floor of her inn. It consisted of a bed, the one Sarah scarcely used if staying up late reading and studying in her office and too tired to find her cozy spots in the forest. A wood-furnished desk also stood inside the room. The craftsmanship of this desk mirrored that of dwarven work. This desk stood in the furthest corner, after a short hallway when entering. It was adjacent to a large gable window shaded with thick drapes, giving all who entered the attic a view of the town and more, along with allowing the Star of Nod to provide light to the room. At night, stars illuminated the room.

At present, what looked to be an older man sat behind the desk. His age could not be defined. If so, his age would prove to be younger than his looks. But this was due to his unsurpassed toil upon Eythreal, especially for a menfolk descendant. This was someone who knew no stop when traveling, regardless of the danger and burden it placed upon him. And outside his aged looks, one would find an eternal fiery spirit. This spirit would surpass almost all others' limitations when it came to explorations and expeditions on Eythreal, each of them for the greater good of Eythreal.

In more concise words, one would look at him and wonder if he could even manage a steep hill. But seeing him in action, they'd imagine not a mountain on Eythreal could stand in his way.

His attire matched his worn-out and old looks, yet the clothes exuded no stench to permeate the air. The boots he wore stuck out the most—elvish made. Much wear and tear could be seen on them from a distance, but on a closer look, they were still finely made, matchless when it came to sturdiness, and more than just comfortable when one put them on. Many would marvel at him and wonder what an old man like him did to possess such boots. Did he steal them? Or did he simply find them during his travels? Of course, both were wrong, for long ago, a band of elves hand-stitched the boots just for him, seeing that they cared much about his future endeavors.

Upon the desk, chaos reigned. The chaos consisted of maps, scrolls, notes and papers, and many other materials pertaining to his work, none of them organized. This did not exclude the disarray of writing and drawing utensils.

A single utility belt sat lazily upon the disheveled desktop. Various tools could be found attached to it.

The old man did not mind this chaotic disorganization one bit. It coincided with his mind. His mind had no limits to its imagination; thus, if he could not draw a fence around knowledge and information, how could he do the same with objects and tools of that same knowledge and information? And because his mind proved far more powerful and maniacal than most, he could easily sift through his chaotic mess and invariably find what he needed as if, in his mind, his mess was simply organized.

On the floor by him sat two backpacks. Each could be found unorganized also, mostly made up of living supplies and cooking utensils.

Essentials for harsh living conditions.

When the door to this office space opened, the old man did not budge, seeing how immersed he had become in his work.

~

Timothy and his companions took their first step inside the attic, and the old man still did not budge.

He did speak, though.

"Have I erred, Sarah of Cyrcle, in thinking I could find seclusion under your sanctuary?"

Sarah took the lead. "No. I mean . . . Sorry. I just thought you might—"

"Sarah of Cyrcle, your reputation for secluded sanctuary withers away before my very own eyes."

"For that, you do her a great injustice," Rajur said, pushing ahead of Sarah.

"That voice," the old man said, putting down his writing utensil and still not taking his eyes off his work. "I have heard that voice before, but only once. I'm sure he doesn't remember when I heard his voice. Or do you, *Rajur*?"

"I do not," Rajur said.

"Which does not surprise me. I was in the crowd. I was mixed up with many other spectators. You were given your first task."

"My ordainment."

"Yes. Daardannea was to be your home away from home."

"You were there?"

"I was. For I was involved in paving the path for you to take. Did you expect another engineer of your quests? Who do you think provided much of the specifics?"

Rajur nodded.

"And now you're here, so long after."

"Aye, here with grave matters. You will be apologizing to Sarah when we're through."

"I am already sorry to offend her. She did right," he said, turning away from his work, and his eyes landed on Sarah. "Forgive my rash insolence."

Sarah nodded.

The old man's eyes studied the rest of the party. His eyes couldn't have grown bigger while scrutinizing the boys.

"What strange friends you have."

"Strange, yes," Rajur said, "and very much worth your time, *Tolan*."

"Well, well, the dragon is unchained. My name has finally resurfaced after so long. You know, I've been far too bored for so long with hearing 'Scholar of Vickensburg'! Ha. I'm hardly the scholar, and I detest the College of Vickensburg, with all their pedantic fools that have cost Eythreal already so much. Tell me, Rajur, did you come here to gloat over discovering my real name?"

"No."

"And how did you discover it?"

"You should know."

"Yes. Those sneaky Elves of Nererrenda, always discovering what I swear I left undiscoverable."

Rajur smiled at the compliment.

"But the question begs to be asked. Why? Why have you and your allies been so keen on finding me?"

"If you had much to do with my ordainment, then that is a foolish question by a wise old man."

"Yes," Tolan said with a nod of his head. "Bow and Arrow."

Rajur nodded.

"But I know nothing about its meaning."

"In time, you may," Rajur said. "But I am not here for that . . . for now. It has been suspended. Something else has come up."

"Oh? Do tell," Tolan said, grabbing his spectacles from the desk. Putting them on, he gave the boys a keener study. "I see you have dressed them in Sarah of Cyrcle's finest attire. Just threw whatever clothes you had nearby on them, did you? Hm . . . what were you hiding? Regardless, they are outlandish, like me. They seem to be ancestry to Azaarath and, with their complexion, more likely Ontairo Kingdom. But no, they are not from Azaarath or any of the other realms. No, they feel . . . I may not have as extransensory perception as you, Sarah, but they do feel like they absorb much mana. It speaks to me as if they are in a direct bloodline of Thrandor, except we all know that is impossible. And yet, there is something else about them. I don't know. But something about them tries to hide from me, afraid of me discovering it. And will not be allowed to be discovered.

"But it's there. That I can feel, for I have experienced too much not to sense the most enigmatic of objects."

"You sensing it shows how right you are—how strong you are mindfully," Rajur said. "We've walked through this village without a whisper of this mystery."

Tolan nodded his head. "I guess I've grown to perceive mana more than most."

"Don't be foolish," Rajur said. "You know as well as I do that you could discern the absorption and assimilation of mana along with the best of them."

"I cannot fool you."

"Now, what is it you feel?"

"The tall boy—he exudes much more mana than the other. And he's the one that holds something . . . something not Eythreal. But it is Eythreal."

Timothy turned to Rajur. Rajur nodded.

"I possess a book," Timothy said.

"A book. What kind of—" Tolan stopped. He placed his spectacles on the table and rubbed his eyes with a handkerchief.

"So that's what I felt the morning before this moon."

"I figured you'd be one of the few," Rajur said.

Tolan nodded his head. "Few. And let us hope that few confuse it with the workings of Eythreal below and not from far away."

"We can only hope."

"Yes. Hope. And where are you from?" Tolan asked Timothy.

"Earth," Timothy said.

"Oh. Earth? Yes. Never heard of it, but the name makes sense—so close, but also too *dull*. And your friend?"

"Same," Zachary said.

"As I assumed, for your mana growth is also frightening." Tolan's eyes switched to Timothy's. "But your mana's growth is far more aggressive. Far *too* aggressive," he said, with eyes on Timothy. "And it's not solely because of the book, although most of it is. You're absorbing Eythreal's mana like no other, except you are not of Eythreal. Not yet. Of course, much of this is because of your bond with the book, and though the book is Eythreal and much more, making you almost the same, you are not right now. You are too much of a human from Earth, and that needs to be rectified. You need to find a way to adapt to the mana you're absorbing, for if you don't, in time, the consequences will be dire."

"Sarah mentioned something similar to that," Timothy said.

Tolan nodded his head.

"Sarah is a great asset to Eythreal," Tolan said. "Her discernment cannot be valued as less than priceless. Now, let me see the book, young man."

Timothy looked to Rajur, and the latter nodded. He pulled the book from behind and revealed its front to Tolan. Tolan retrieved his spectacles and put them back on. He studied the front, back, and sides of the book. He showed no change in his look when doing so.

"You may open it up and turn to the first page."

Timothy did that, and not long after, Tolan asked for the page to be turned and did so to the last page.

Tolan sank back a bit in his chair with a nod.

"I assume you cannot read the writing?" Timothy asked.

"No. And unless we've all been duped, no one else on Eythreal can read this writing."

Timothy didn't look surprised.

"Now, what is your intention?"

"I intend to finish this book and bring my world back to normal."

"A tall order. One that is not sure to happen. Let me see your hands."

"My hands?" Timothy said quizzically.

"Yes, your hands."

Timothy put away the book and extended his hands.

Tolan grabbed both hands and massaged them.

"What are you doing?" Sarah asked, slightly alarmed and confused.

"I need to know," Tolan said. "One can easily judge another's strength by his hands and feet alone. I'm not asking him to take those boots off, so I must be content with the hands alone. These hands must be durable. They must be strong and able, for if they are, I believe he may have what it takes, and this better be true. The fate of Eythreal rests on what I believe this book wants to be accomplished. And a much greater fate rests on the events that will follow this accomplishment," Tolan said, with his eyes glaring at Rajur, though nobody did notice but the two.

A second later, Tolan released Timothy's hands.

"*Gem and Spider*," Tolan said. "I'm sure they've given you counsel on what the title possibly means?"

"Bits and pieces," Timothy said.

"Yes. For that is all we know—bits and pieces. Even I! You've been cast into a vortex of what could be Eythreal's darkest time."

"So I've also been told."

"Yet we don't even have the Dark to battle with."

"Then you will help?" Timothy asked.

"I already have," Tolan said.

"How?"

Tolan smiled.

"Your hands are strong and resilient. You will do well. Your hands will handle the worst yet, for blood will spill. And I speak not only of your enemies. Some of your closest allies, ones that may be standing by you at this second or others you will meet in time, will spill their blood right upon your grieving lap. And you must swallow that fact and move on."

Timothy choked down a gulp of fear.

"And about those future allies . . ." Tolan said.

"Rajur said we are going to recruit more," Timothy said.

"Where?"

"Ghalia," Rajur said.

"Of course. Stupid me. You'd be wise to recruit her."

"Her?" Zachary said.

"Who else?"

"A few others," Rajur said.

"Good. But while you're at it, do an old man a favor."

"You're not that old, Tolan."

"Maybe. Nonetheless, while in Ghalia Trade Center, stop by the Muddled Turtle. Are you familiar with the fine establishment?"

"No. And why do I have the feeling it is not as fine as you say?"

"Because it's not. Ha ha. But then again, you'll be in Ghalia Trade Center: you won't find any place of rectitude in that cesspool. Stop by. Stop by the place and pay a musician a courteous visit. You'll find him behind the piano. He spits out the most pathetic, tragic, and ridiculous dirges you can imagine. A sad man he is. Say hello to him. Make him happy, Timothy."

"You think that's smart? What if he . . ." Timothy said and stopped.

"You asked for help? Well, here's some more. Say hello to this dementedly sad man."

Timothy looked to Rajur. Rajur shrugged his shoulders.

"Now, if there isn't any other pressing matter, I'd like to be left alone, now more than ever!"

Timothy and Zachary hung back.

"What?" Tolan said, sensing their hesitation.

"Will our world come back?" Zachary asked.

"I thought we went over this. I don't know."

Zachary looked downcast. "It's just, we're—"

"Tired of uncertainties," Timothy said.

"Yes," Tolan said. "Uncertainties. But get used to it. It'll only grow more uncertain."

"But can you tell us something?"

Tolan shrugged one of his shoulders. "If I had to guess, by my deduction alone, I'd say no. Your world will not return. And if it does, not how you remember it. And why? Because whether our world and your world have been taken from us—our world being locked inside this book, while your world floats in a place of Void—what happens to the two worlds happens, for we are still consequential to our actions. Kill a man here, and he stays dead, regardless of you finishing the book. The same must be said about your Earth. Thus, with Earth entirely out of your control, unlike Eythreal, how can you imagine its return, if so, without the effects of what happened, only to lead you to this very moment?

"See what I'm saying? If Earth does return to you, how can it return to you without the effects that led you here on Eythreal?

"Your presence wouldn't exist on Eythreal if Earth returned to you as it was before you opened the book. If it did, everything you accomplished on Eythreal would not exist.

"We'd be right back where we were before you arrived here."

"So our world is dead?" Timothy said.

"That, or what could be worse, ravaged by the Void and the consequences of your actions that led you here."

"Don't listen to him," Sarah said. "He's only assuming. Isn't that right, *Tolan*?"

Tolan shrugged his shoulders.

"And you, Rajur?" Timothy asked. "Is that what you've been afraid to tell me? That no matter what, nothing will be normal again *if* my world returns?"

Rajur looked gravely at Timothy. "Whether I agree with him or not, it matters not, for he must agree with me on one very important matter."

"Which is?"

"Finish the book, and you shall see."

"Yes," Tolan said. "It is the only true deduction we have. The book must be finished, and it has chosen you to finish it; never think that *you* chose it. It has always chosen you, and well . . . *others*."

"My choices," Timothy muttered.

"Yes. And so far, I believe you've chosen well."

Timothy nodded.

"At your side, you have one of the greatest warriors that have ever walked upon Eythreal as a mortal being. I wouldn't substitute him with a single other, even one that is *supposedly* dead."

"Supposedly dead? What do you mean by that?"

Tolan smiled. "Visit the Muddled Turtle. Send a hello from me to what could be your new friend."

And with that said, Tolan turned away from them and returned to his work.

Rajur took Timothy by his shoulders and escorted him out.

Chapter 4

ONE LAST STOP

"He's a bit odd," Zachary said while leaving the upstairs portion of Sarah's Inn.

"And not much help either," Timothy said.

"It is far too early to judge that," Sarah said. "I'm sure the eccentric old man has his own ways of conveying the help we need."

"But you'd think a person of that much knowledge could say more than just 'I've already helped you.'"

"You'd be committing a grave mistake if you think it wise to ask many others for words of advice or guidance on the matter," Rajur said.

"Why is that?" Timothy asked.

"It is simple. The best advice is your own advice. Advice given by anyone else is impossibly not impartial. Where does one's advice come from? From one's own experience, instinct, and *heart*, being nonetheless one's own path through life, along with the bumps and roadblocks on one's way and what one felt while going along that path. No magical tool could extract that from one's advice when trying to guide you on what to do. It comes only from them. Remember that. And that given advice must not be, for it is you, and you only, that matters when it comes to decision-making. Try hard to remember that when you do ask advice from the few people you choose to be at your side."

"So the advice you give me . . . it is smeared with your own wants and wishes?"

Rajur half nodded, half shook his head. "But in time, you'll understand that my experience and your experience are wrapped up a bit tighter than anyone else's. And what advice and guidance I have suggested so far has been anything but narrow and tight. Open and broad, the suggestions have been deliberately done to give you room to navigate and find your *own* answers and guidance.

"In my humble *opinion*," Rajur said. "Tolan proved his worth by giving you very little to no advice."

"Don't forget about the musician," Zachary chimed in.

"Aye," Rajur said, "a gamble. But let us see when we get to Ghalia."

"You think it's worth the risk?"

"I see a greater reward than not ignoring it since it came from Tolan."
Timothy nodded.

A few steps later, they reached the bottom floor of the establishment.
Sarah opened the door, and a sunny day came streaking through.

"You're free to gather more clothing for the road ahead. What you wear
now is only temporary. As for everything else, well, I passed the word to
every shopkeeper to give you a discount on what you choose. I'd charge
you no coin or ruby, but that would draw suspicion. And I'd waste little
time, Rajur. The sooner you equip them, the sooner you can take them out
to Ranger Field and train them for the rest of the day. You may not think
it's much training, boys, but a simple hour with Rajur is a moon cycle or
more of excessive training with a master swordsman of a Swords Guild.
Afterward, when it's dark, see Hersh again. He'll serve you supper, and
rooms will be ready."

"Thank you," Rajur said.

Sarah did not answer. Instead, she shrugged her shoulders and went
back inside.

"She's a bit odd too," Zachary said.

"Is anyone not odd to you?" Rajur asked.

"You're definitely not one of them, for you are odder than those two
combined."

~

The training field known as Ranger Field was outside the fence
enclosing the northeast portion of the town. Visitors and residents rarely
visited this field since most came to Cyrcle to be away from such doings,
hence why the field wasn't exactly inside town boundaries, allowing peace
and tranquility to be solemnly enclosed from the training field. Ones
that did visit this field usually belonged to a guild, whether it be a mage
or weaponry guild, and wanted time to study their arts, especially since
Sarah's magic shops consisted of quality spells, which needed more practice
than others.

Some just went to the field to try out their new sword or armor, never
anything with violent intentions toward the good of Eythreal. Because of
that, Ranger Field would be found empty on most occasions, just as it was
when Rajur led the boys there.

As planned, Rajur trained the boys mostly on defensive tactics.

The training also dealt with the vital parts of the oppressor—or worse, oppressors. Vital parts Rajur wanted the boys to strike after a successful dodge, parry, or block. He also instructed them on how to disable their attacker before going in for the kill shot since Rajur urged them not to go for a kill shot at the first opportunity because of their more-than-likely inferiority. He explained to them that their lack of strength, agility, and of course, fighting experience, hindered them from successfully delivering a first mortal blow to their enemy.

Most importantly, Rajur drilled the boys on defending themselves after a failed strike.

For weapons, Rajur purchased each of them a well-made steel dagger. Their primary weapon was an iron middle sword.

Not long into the training, Rajur found himself recanting his earlier presumption of the boys' fighting skills. Not only did the boys wield the weapons with little to no awkwardness, but they also learned on the fly and showed more progress in such a short matter of time that it left Rajur astounded. No longer did he doubt the book's choice of Zachary. Seeing Zachary maneuver with the weapons and armor, Rajur pictured the makings of a great warrior, not saying Timothy wasn't skillful. It was only that Zachary surpassed him and would surpass any other boy Rajur had met. What he saw in Zachary that stood out the most was his quickness and his agile movement, along with his hands being precise and razor-sharp, far surpassing any boy his age—surpassing even veteran fighters on this single training day.

Timothy's strength was his perception. He saw the opponent's move sooner than Zachary, although the latter also excelled in perception. Outside of that, Zachary dominated Ranger Field.

Rajur also learned another helpful attribute of the boys: their stamina.

They seemed indefatigable.

Their near-inexhaustible energy could easily be attributed to their endless toil on their family's land—day after day, night after night.

Rajur ended the training not long after the final descent of the Star of Nod. He would have continued longer, seeing that the boys showed no signs of stopping, but he wanted their minds calm and less aggressive when returning to the inn. He also wanted to reach the blacksmith's forge before it grew too late. He hoped the blacksmith would sharpen and improve their weapons and armor a bit before their morning departure.

On leaving the Ranger Field, both boys noticed the change in the moons.

The third moon, the one that had been vague and growing stronger all day long, came to its near zenith, matching the brilliance of the other two moons.

Seeing the moon raised a question.

"What's the deal with the moons?" Zachary asked. "It's like every morning we wake up, there is a faint moon, only to grow stronger as the day wanes."

"Aye," Rajur said. "Your observation does not deceive you. You woke up this morning to the third moon of Atris's Calling—third moon because it is the newest one that appeared at the very peak of last night's full brilliance of the second moon of Atris's Calling, for yesterday, when you woke up, the day belonged to exactly that: the second moon of Atris's Calling. The morning before our awakening of the storm, when we had not been transferred here, the moon day belonged to the first moon of Atris's Calling since there was only one very vague moon to start the morning."

"You're joking, right?" Zachary said.

"Joking about what?"

"The moons! Please tell me you're not expecting us to learn all this, like, your days, weeks, months, and years."

"It will be imperative for you to learn it. But aye, not now. This I will say. We don't use weeks and months as you do. We don't even use days, except, well . . . over time, the foreign word became a norm for our language when depicting a moon. On Eythreal, days are called moons, whereas weeks are considered moon cycles. And a month to you is a full moon cycle to Eythreal. Years are also used sparingly, although the term is growing. But what we call the end of seven full moon cycles is a greater moon cycle, which means, for you two, a year being three hundred and forty-three moons. And I'm not worried about you two calling it by days and so forth. You'll find it has grown rampant. But you'll need to know the cycles, the names of the cycles, the terms we give to the moons, and how it all works."

"And the powers of the moons?" Timothy asked.

"What about them?"

"You mentioned how they give life to Eythreal."

"They do."

208

"And how they give you your mana—the spirit of gods or the blood of gods."

"I did not say that."

"But you—"

"I said the Seven Moons of Iria produce the mana we assimilate on Eythreal. We are still alive without the moons. The moons give life to the mana on Eythreal for us to absorb. Think about it as a plant. You can have a seed and so forth, meaning the right soil. But you need the right light. The power invested in those moons is exactly that, mana being the seed and Eythreal its soil. Star of Nod is *not* what the mana needs, although, I believe, on your former planet, your sun is what the plants and so forth need, just like ours too. But we're talking about mana here, not actual plant life."

"What about when the moons are not around? Does Eythreal—the mana—grow weak?"

"Wise question, and one you both need to know. The easy answer is no. Eythreal's mana does not need the Seven Moons of Iria to be in the sky to continue its production, for the moons truly never leave. They do diminish. But they diminish in our sight alone. They're still producing power. The mana does not decline. Now, yes, if the moons were taken away from us for a long period, our lives would eventually grow dimmer and dimmer. Without mana to absorb, we will only become shadows of what we once were, and this, yes, this is something we must fear, for I have a terrible intuition that Iria's disappearance and the capture of her daughters have something to do with one wanting this to happen. And I truly believe that the Daughters of Iria have much to say about this and would have said it if given a chance before the abduction. It is their freedom that will give us so much—not only about Abbigatha, but so much more."

"So freeing the daughters is pretty darn important?" Zachary said.

"Aye."

"Are you in love with one of them?" Timothy asked.

"What makes you ask that?"

"When we first met," Timothy said, "in the jail cell, you rambled on and on about the gems and Abbigatha's eyes. And you were . . ."

"What?"

"Holding on dearly to that locket you hide under your clothes. You were holding it ever dearly when discussing the Daughters of Iria."

"And I've even caught you twice doing it," Zachary said.

"Is it a picture of one?"

Rajur looked ahead. He looked for a distraction from the question. He received one.

Not far ahead sat a dark silhouette of a tall, skinny figure by the blacksmith forge.

"There," Rajur said. "Berg."

"Who's Berg?"

"Besides being a cousin of Hersh, Berg is the town's only blacksmith, and it looks to me like he's been expecting us."

Staring through the darkness, the boys caught sight of the blacksmith. The blacksmith sat upon a rocking chair, smoking a pipe, and if he was standing, the boys would discover him taller than his cousin while being gaunt and starved from life's essentials compared to Hersh's bearlike physique. As they approached, they noticed Berg's convulsive right eye. The blinking of his eye caused his right face to twitch noticeably.

Puffing out a loud ring of smoke, Berg spoke. "Have you made men out of these boys?" Berg said, with his face twitching far worse when speaking and his eye fluttering even faster. "Or did they put you to shame?"

"It was Rajur who put us to shame," Timothy said. "Sir."

"Sir? I love it. Never been called sir in my life. Step closer, boys. Let me see you with my good eye."

The boys stepped closer, and that was when they realized that his good eye was the rapidly fluttering eye since the other eye was opaque—blind to any *light*.

"Yes. You both are nowise frail. You will do."

"Do for what?" Zachary asked.

"To save our arses."

"What?" Timothy said.

"Save the world. Isn't that why you two are here?"

Both boys stepped back confoundedly and in trepidation of what he might know.

Berg laughed. "Just stirring the pot. Should have seen your faces."

"Don't mind him," Rajur said. "Clearly, he has too much time for himself."

"And you're one to talk?" Berg said with a hearty laugh.

Rajur nearly followed with the same laugh. "It's been long," Rajur said.

"Aye, so it has," Berg said. "How are those precious items of yours?" Berg said, with his flickering eye staring at the Moon Beams.

Rajur unsheathed one of the Moon Beams. Berg's admiration of the objects settled calmly upon him.

"Maybe the finest treasure one could imagine," Berg said. "How they shine! And yet, how they don't shine as a light or a beacon. Never to betray you."

The calmness took a turn as he looked at the hilt of Storm Breaker.

"Storm Breaker. The Sword of Wonder. The Sword of Mystery. I tire not of seeing it. Please. It has been a long time."

Rajur nodded, and not afraid of Berg's admiration of the blade turning into desire, he unsheathed Storm Breaker.

"Yes. The blade and the hands that possessed it when vanquishing Satay-Ri, the last of the dragons under Eythreal. Yes. The songs they will write about this blade and you when it is all over, for no bard can imagine a single script until the time comes and the end dissipates before our eyes. But I can say this. I can say where it started. And they must say that it started very near here. Now let us study the boys more . . ."

Berg ran his good eye over both the boys. "You two are dressed properly. Good iron and steel. If only we had iron from the Iron Dwarves. What a pity! But this iron will suffice. And with a little improvement, it will only become better, for I have a bit of fabric and material to aid in strengthening them. Aye, it will turn all right. The time has come. Yes. There's some stuff I have. Not anymore. It will belong to you. The time has come. The moons. I've been watching them," Berg said, staring into the night sky and zeroing in on the moons.

"Now is the time." Berg readjusted his pipe and continued—but did so solemnly. "Leave your weapons and armor and any other trinkets you want enhancing. I'll have them ready the moment you leave."

"We'll be off very early in the morning," Rajur said. "Maybe you should—"

"Rajur," Berg said, "you of all people know that sleep has long eluded me."

Rajur nodded. He turned to the boys. "Do as he says."

Beside Berg and his rocking chair, the boys unloaded their dagger, sword, and armor, along with a few trinkets Rajur purchased for them.

"Thank you," Timothy said, turning to leave.

Zachary did the same by nodding.

Berg responded by returning to his pipe and rocking back and forth.

Out of earshot, Zachary questioned Rajur. "How come the hilt of your sword didn't come alive?"

"Desire is a far greater risk and sin than to admire."

"I desired it that much?"

"That is what the sword read through your mind and heart."

"It can do that?"

Rajur looked at Zachary and smiled. "It can do a lot."

"What happened to Berg?" Timothy asked.

"You mean his eye and facial twitches?"

"Yes."

"Nerve damage. Berg was once a master swordsman. In fact, he was close to being ordained as a headmaster of a guild before . . ."

"Before?"

"A battle-ax was driven into his spine. His survival was a miracle, let alone being able to surpass paralysis. To feel any nerve is a miracle."

"A battle-ax? And he never saw it coming?"

"No, for he was betrayed."

"By whom?"

"His own father.

Both boys looked alarmed.

"It is not an anecdote I'd like to share with you right now, nor do I wish to share it with you boys unless I have to. We need to rest our minds. We're leaving early."

"Ghalia?"

"Yes."

"How long till we get there?"

"As I mentioned before, it should take us three moons, most of it through Sarah's Forest, although, again, there are exceptions to take account of."

"Which are?"

"A burdensome roadblock is one of them."

"And?"

"Gladson," Rajur said.

"Gladson?"

"It's a very old name for a very old one. But never mind that for now. I plan on us not encountering him and his others."

"Others?"

"His kind."

"Are they . . . dangerous?"

"Hardly. Pesky? Irritable? Troublesome? Deceiving little buggers? Yes to all of that."

"Great. Can't wait to meet them," Zachary said.

"What don't you understand about me saying we're not planning on encountering them? Now rest your minds. We sup and then sleep. Tomorrow, our adventure takes its first step toward finishing the book."

Chapter 5

THE PARTY GROWS STRONGER

"Go now," came the voice of the Wood Dweller. *"Go and follow his guidance. Soon, you shall lead, and you'll want to absorb everything you learned from him."*

"And he's the right choice to lead me?" Timothy asked.

"Right or wrong, he is already your choice. It is too late. You must follow him or risk a far more difficult road. Whether he ends up being your unsung hero or leads you to your demise and the demise of all Eythreal, only time will tell."

"Will we be alone?"

"More will follow."

"And this Scholar of Vickensburg? He said my world would not return. I thought you said—"

"How could a mortal like him, regardless of being a lore master, give his opinion on a matter that is infinitely beyond his scope and reality? And why worry? It is now out of your hands. Do not call me with questions like that. I have already given you too much. Go. Go and follow his lead. And this time, yes, this time, I mean it when I say I'm done giving you help. I cannot keep doing this."

~

Timothy woke up to that same sensation of having dreamed and, not only that, conversing with another person inside this dream.

But no memory of it could be found, not a single clue, only the feeling.

He also woke up to Rajur shaking his shoulder.

"Did I dream?" Timothy asked Rajur.

"How am I supposed to know that? I am no DreamWalker."

"I just feel like I did, yet I don't remember anything. I must sound—"

"Normal," Rajur said and nodded. "Dreams can be like that." Rajur then moved over to Zachary and woke him up.

"It's still pitch-black outside," Zachary protested.

"Aye. Now hush—both of you. We must depart without being noticed."

"Not even Sarah?"

"Especially not Sarah."

The boys wanted to question Rajur but found it wise not to. Instead, they kept silent and dressed. When dressed, they left through the hallway of the room. Not a single sound could be heard by them upon reaching the lobby room of the inn. The entrance and exit of the inn stood cracked open across from the lobby room desk. Continuing to be silent, they opened the door a bit more and slipped through. The pitch-black night surrounded them. But they quickly learned how not-so-dark it turned out to be. Three strong moons illuminated the sky, while many of the leftover stars from the night still survived. But like Rajur's Moon Beams, these moons did not empower brightness upon the surface of Eythreal, only the stars.

Zachary looked closer into the sky. He noticed the smallest, vaguest outline of a fourth moon.

Timothy also saw it and nodded.

Rajur had no time for this. He headed toward the stable, with the boys in tow and Butch being just as silent.

Retrieving Abigail and Breeze, the companions made their way to the forge.

"You don't think he's up still?" Zachary asked.

"He said sleep eludes him," Timothy said.

"Yes, but isn't that a figure of speech?"

"It's no figure of speech, boy," came the voice of Berg.

The boys tried to spot him through the darkness of the early morning. Only by the flick of a match did Berg reveal himself. He sat on the same rocking chair and smoked his pipe as he did not long ago. "Nor would the two of you find sleep as you know it if what binds you to this life is of darkness."

The boys attempted to understand what he meant. Of course, they could not.

Rajur stepped up to Berg, signaling the boys to do the same.

"I know what road you are to follow," Berg said, "for why would you choose Cambridge Road from here with the traffic you'd find? And why go even farther to reach Road to Ghalia, although fast it would prove but at what cost, for it is even busier? No, you will take the side road to Cambridge Road, and what I mean by that . . . Oh, how I don't envy you! I don't envy anyone who travels close to those menacing little runts. Damn buggers. They think life is but a single playground. Give me Shirkel's Rope, and I'll have them all strung up by their hairy bottoms."

"Is he talking about that Gladson person?" Zachary asked.

"Aye."

"Person. Thing. Deformed creature. Unholy forest rat."

"What's he talking about?" Timothy asked.

Seeing that he couldn't keep the secret longer, Rajur nodded. "Gladson is the father of a clan of mischievous gnomes."

"Gnomes!" Zachary shouted.

"Yes," Rajur said, "a clan of gnomes that inhabit—"

"Gnomes," Zachary said again, with Timothy's eyes just as bright with glee.

"Yes, I said that. There are gnomes on Eythreal, many of them, many different clans and kinds. Now can I finish?"

Both boys nodded.

"Gladson and these gnomes inhabit a sacred forest on the outskirts of a glade we must pass through. The gnomes tend to use this glade and other parts outside their forest for their own playground, meaning mischief, hence why most don't try this way, besides it being longer, and decide to travel upon Cambridge Road or make their way to Road to Ghalia, even though, as Berg said, both ways are suffocating to a traveler. Of course, at some point, we must find our way onto Cambridge Road—but not yet! We must go the side path, and that means nearing this glade where, yes, the gnomes could catch us if we don't choose wisely when nearing it. The gnomes like to get drunk from their special mead. But they are creatures of all hours, so the timing of their drunkenness is tricky. Plus, I never really sensed much of a stupor from their intoxication. It will be a gamble we must take."

"And then there is the Lady of the Forest," Berg said.

"Lady of the Forest?" Zachary said. "And gnomes? Sounds—"

"It does not matter how it sounds. This is not a sightseeing trip. We are to reach Ghalia, and that's it."

A disappointed Zachary nodded.

"About the gear?" Rajur said.

Berg tilted his twitching face toward the fence where a blanket shrouded protruding objects.

Rajur made his way to the blanket and pulled it off the gear. As soon as he did, both boys gasped in astonishment. Even Rajur showed a bit of surprise.

Each weapon and armor, including their miscellaneous trinkets, gave off a slight glow—very faint but noticeable in the darkness.

"Sarah's doing," Berg said.

"She's grown fast in her enchantment," Rajur said.

"Aye. She's had some help. A frequent visitor has given her much enlightenment."

"May I ask who?"

"You may, but you'll receive no answer, for not even I know the true identity of this frequent visitor."

Rajur nodded.

"Anyway, yes, she's improved greatly. She's turning into something far more than a mage. I tremble—no! I can only imagine her enemies tremble before what she could end up being."

"But this isn't just her work," Rajur said. "She needed the right blacksmith to forge the spells into these common weapons and armors. And I see only you here."

"Again," Berg said. "You've been gone a while, for I too have become a bit more *enlightened.*"

Rajur nodded. "But no help with the . . ." Rajur said and stopped.

Berg slowly shook his head.

Rajur again nodded.

"Come," Berg said to the boys. "Let me enlighten you on what you have. First off, your middle swords are enhanced with stamina and accuracy. Both will be absorbed into you when putting the sword into action. But the stamina attribute will actually come into play when just equipping the blade since your mana growth will bind to the mana of the blade, lessening the weight of the blade. And I already see rapid growth of mana in both of you, so this should not be a problem. But we won't speak of that strange and unusual mana and its growth, will we?" Berg said, with a wink of an eye. "As for the armor, they're also enhanced with stamina, making them less burdensome when just casually walking and in battle, while improving their durability. But Sarah did not stop there. She placed an enhancement of both dodge and block when wearing the armor and handling the shield. Again, it comes to you by binding the enchantment and your assimilation of mana. You will find yourself dodging and blocking at a higher rate. This was not easy for her, especially when given just one night to accomplish. Only skilled enchanters, enchantresses, and sorcerers could do such a thing. Powerful mages like her are not accustomed to the power of enchanting. But as I've said, Sarah has had some help."

Berg leaned off his chair, seeing no break in the boys' wonder at the weapons and armor.

"Well? Don't just stand there agape. Pick 'em up. Give 'em a thrust or two. You won't be disappointed."

The boys broke their trance and grabbed the weapons and armor.

Berg smiled. "I am sorry we couldn't do more. You will find that enchanting common weapons and armor like these requires much more than being skilled."

"You've far surpassed what I ever imagined Sarah and you could do," Rajur said. After a pause, he added, "And we thank you."

"I have a feeling one day we'll be thanking each and every one of you. If you haven't noticed, Rajur, I've dimmed the enchantment's natural glow. Of course, I couldn't get rid of the glow completely. In the end, it would only dull the enchantment. But the dimness now does not affect the enchantment, while also making it not so noticeable when traveling under stealth at night. Or the darkness of a vast cave. And many other bleak places on Eythreal."

"Do others not carry around enchanted weapons?" Timothy asked.

"Seldom," Berg said. "It is not so easy to acquire enchanted weapons. And to buy 'em, well, one must have much in the pocket. The practice of enchanting falls under one being an enchanter or enchantress. It is a learning and ability only a few have. Study as much as you want in alchemy. You must be born with the innate ability to consume a wealth of mana and know how to put it to use. And then there is the intelligence of one's mind—the calmness of one's mind, the ability to exert godly energy to bring life into an inanimate object, and of course, again, the expertise in alchemy, which gives them the instructions on how to solve the equation of exerting the godly energy. No. To enchant weapons, armor, items, and so forth is a skill that far surpasses a mage or even a sorcerer. However, a sorcerer or sorceress has the innate ability to enchant to a certain degree. And to make things harder for Sarah, she was forced to enchant weapons of crude birth, for many enchanted weapons, armor, or various other items are wrought originally to be enhanced by enchantment. You'll discover that by noticing rune stones or empty cavities for rune stones, called rune marks, forged into the object. The task of enchanting comes much more easily, for you'll need no obscure blacksmith to forge the rune stone and so forth. And the application of mana used by the enchanter is much less than without."

"Berg speaks accurately," Rajur said. "When in Ghalia, you may see *some* enchanted objects for sale. What you'll see mostly are weapons and items ready for enchantment. Thus, rune marks or actual rune stones inserted into the rune marks but no enchantment. And what you'll very seldom see is one owning or equipped with an enchanted weapon or armor roaming around the port city. They are not cheap, as Berg mentioned. And they draw much attention to one—that could spell trouble in a place like Ghalia Trade Center. The thieves of Ghalia are bountiful and highly skilled since their Thieves' Guild is noted to be one of the more fortified of any Thieves' Guild found on Eythreal. Again, we owe Sarah and Berg much more than ever since they dimmed the natural glow to lessen our trouble."

Berg nodded.

Rajur turned to the boys. "Ready?"

"Ready," they said.

Rajur nodded and led them away.

Berg returned to his pipe and the rocking of his chair.

~

Rajur wanted to escape Cyrcle by climbing over the fence and using the shrubs as a screen to protect them from being noticed—mainly by Sarah.

But something caught his eye: the fountain.

With his keen eyesight, Rajur sensed something different about the flowing water. He noticed the vibrant colors and healthy flowing water to be immensely more vibrant and healthier. This change in the fountain lured him closer.

And for the first time, the boys placed their eyes on the fountain, seeing how captivated Rajur had become.

"This is it?" Timothy said. "This is what gives the town and forest its protection," the boy said as if there was no refuting it.

Rajur nodded. "In the simplest of forms to understand her spell, yes. But," he said, eyes staring profoundly at the fountain, "something is different."

"What?" Zachary asked.

"It's too bright, too strong. I've never seen . . . It's as if . . . Is it the book?" Rajur turned to Timothy. The next voice speaking turned him back around to the fountain.

"It is not *just* the book," the voice of Sarah said.

Both boys and Rajur looked past the fountain and saw Sarah standing on the other side. Yesterday's attire had been changed to a more close-fitting dress, one of satin material, more in the line of a white mage attire, except puffy at the lower skirt bottom. The dress was blue, although a very light bluish color, with a hint of pinkish hue around the edges. And even more faintly seen were glittering symbols of stars and cursive writing upon the dress, each of them of various colors. She wore a sash full of pocketed objects, mostly potions and so forth, over her waist; a second sash, the given mage apothecary sack, rested across her back and shoulder, giving her much wiggle room to move around. She held a staff in one hand, this staff that is far more grand and intimidating than the one she carried around the day before. Eldorian's Verge, many called it. Those same many say it was given to Sarah by her foster parents when she decided to leave and enter the Mage Guild. And a few of those many say the staff was born in the land of giants.

In her other hand, she held a small pouch with room enough to fit a book and more. This pouch she tossed toward Timothy.

Timothy caught the pouch.

"It is for you," Sarah said, "for your book. I worked on it all night as Berg handled the forging of the rune stones onto your gear. This is no ordinary pouch. It should bind with the book's essence and—well, I do hope the book receives it well. Because if it does, the book will then make it into what it needs to be. The pouch will also help dim the exuberant presence of mana, regardless of it being already difficult to sense, but since you'll be encountering ones like me and even greater than me, this will prove immeasurable when it comes to not betraying you and the book."

"Thank you," Timothy said.

Sarah nodded and stepped closer. She reached the fountain's vicinity and waved her hand through the water. The water splashed from her hand, and yet when she pulled her hand out, no signs of the hand entering the water could be seen.

"My villagers have always insisted this water must be the source of my enchantment. Never have I hinted at that to them. And yet they still obey. They still find peace and tranquility, along with everything else, and not once do they judge me. Not once do they ridicule my ways. They trust me."

"As they should," Rajur said.

"Yes, I guess so. Trust. To never betray them."

After a long, ruminating pause, waving her hand in and out of the water, she placed her hand back to her side and spoke again. "I have given the last of what this fountain needs. It will not be in want for a very, very long time, just in case, well . . ."

"Things may not go so well, and I may never return here."

"You're leaving?" Timothy said.

Sarah smiled bleakly compared to Rajur's dismay.

Timothy noticed both looks.

"You don't have to do this," Timothy said. "I understand what risk you take if abandoning your town and forest."

"He speaks wisely," Rajur said. "You shouldn't do this."

"But," Sarah said, "it is not your decision. The choice falls to Timothy."

Timothy stared into Sarah's eyes. He sensed her importance if coming along.

"But your town and forest?"

"In good hands. As I mentioned, there won't be a decrease in the strength of the enchantment for many, many greater moon cycles. You know how long a—"

"A year to us," Zachary said.

"Very good. A long way away, far long enough to give me time to return. And if return I do not, it won't matter. No spell or enchantment could save this town or forest from the triumph of our enemies. The book fails, and all is over.

"But if I don't make it and yet the book does not fail, meaning you succeed, then my town and forest won't need the enchantment."

After a shake of her head, she said, "No. My help is needed now with you—not here. With me at your side, your burden will be less heavy. You'll be stocked with potions, draughts, tonics, and so forth without having to bounce frequently from town to town to resupply. My knowledge of plants and herbal medicine is far greater than most people you'll ever meet. When low, there is not much I do not know about what is given to us by Eythreal's nature. And none of that includes what I could do when it comes to casting healing spells. So much more can I assist you and your future companions. This is Eythreal. And if Rajur hasn't told you, my knowledge of Eythreal is near that of a lore master. So what do you say, Timothy? Would you like a former mage of a mage guild at your side?"

Timothy attempted to question this request seriously. But that he could not, for he couldn't contain the excitement of her joining them.

"I'd be honored," Timothy said.

"Then I am at your command."
The two turned to Rajur.
Rajur still looked grieved.
"Shall we go now?" Sarah asked.
Rajur, resigned to fate, nodded.

Chapter 6

DOWN BY THE RIVER

On the early morning of the sixth moon of Atris's Calling, the companions came to their first break in Sarah's Forest. This break in the forest saddened the boys. For two full days, the boys found her forest peaceful and delightful. They wanted nothing more than to live on the nourishment of the forest forever and ever. The snacks they chewed on— nuts, berries, seeds, and so forth—they found to be similar and yet far more nourishing than those of their former world. The mushrooms, potatoes, and other edible roots Rajur helped discover and cook felt the same to the boys—and all this while traveling from one beautiful meadow to another, one pond after another. Fish of many kinds were found in these ponds, and surprisingly, Sarah allowed them to catch and cook these fish, for she said the fish was a part of the cycle of rebirth inside her forest. As for land creatures and ones of wings, the boys found them harmless and friendly.

The weather also helped the boys grieve over the imminent loss of this forest, for never did it prove too cold or too warm. No. The boys did not want to think about life outside Sarah's Forest.

Sadly, Rajur crushed their wishes.

"We're coming to the end of Sarah's Forest." Rajur stopped in his tracks and turned to Sarah. "Are you sure? It is not too late to turn around?"

"You keep asking me that question, and I'll have my sister turn you into a foul-smelling, hideous frog."

Rajur nearly smiled.

"That's right," Zachary said. "Rajur earlier mentioned you had a sister. What's she like?"

Sarah stepped faster along the path, hoping to leave Zachary's question behind.

But the boys kept up with her, demanding an answer.

"She's not like me," Sarah said.

"Oh. Well, where is she?" Timothy asked.

Sarah shook her head and answered. "In a place of shadows," she said dismally and angrily, "where I hope to Iria she never finds her way out."

The tone of her voice convinced the boys to drop the subject, possibly for the remainder of their friendship with Sarah.

Sarah sensed the change in the boys' dropping the subject and grew lighthearted again. "To expound on what Rajur said about leaving my forest . . . Yes, we are leaving the comforts of my forest. But worry not, boys. They'll be plenty of beauty ahead of us. After Old Wicker's Forest—"

"Wait!" Timothy said while Zachary's eyes also grew big. "You call the forest Old Wicker's Forest?"

"Yes. Why?"

"We call the forest that surrounds a portion of our town by the same name."

Sarah looked startled and stared at Rajur. Rajur looked blank.

"Too much to be a coincidence."

"It is as I've said before," Rajur said. "The similarities are very tangible. Just the smallest leak from this world to the next can cause these similarities."

"But who does the leaking?" Zachary asked.

"A question I'm sure none of us will ever be able to answer," Rajur said. They each nodded.

Sarah returned to her subject. "But yes, after my forest, we enter Old Wicker's Forest, and then afterward, we'll find ourselves in a dell, and this dell will lead us into another forest, and this forest—"

"One you should not be excited about," Rajur said.

"And why is that?" Zachary asked.

"There is this—" Rajur tried to say.

Sarah interrupted him by making a scratching sound in her throat. "It's not the forest he speaks of," Sarah said.

"What is it, then?"

"It's . . ." Rajur said, but he looked to Sarah.

"It's what resides after."

"After?"

Rajur and Sarah continued to eye one another as if trading secrets. They both nodded.

"Gladson's Glade," Rajur said.

"The pesky gnome you spoke of earlier?"

Rajur nodded tentatively, not divulging the whole truth.

"You must really dislike him," Zachary said.

"He's a trickster and may easily prove to be a nuisance."

"OK. He plays tricks."

"Yes, tricks. It is why we'll be pitching camp at the halfway spot of the forest that follows the dell that comes after this forest. So strap in, boys, for it's going to be a long haul before we camp."

~

Rajur very seldom jests, for it was not in his nature to do so. And he certainly did not jest when warning the boys about the long haul that awaited them.

Early afternoon came and went, and when it was behind them, they broke through the last of Old Wicker's Forest and reached the dell. Nothing changed when it came to beauty. This dell consisted of a wholesome verdant green land, with many bushes, copses along with bigger trees scattered about, gentle flowing streams, each of them leading into a small lake, and a plethora of living creatures, especially friendly winged insects going from flower bed to the next.

"You weren't kidding," Zachary said about the beauty of the dell.

"You won't think that about the forest we'll soon approach," Rajur said.

"Don't listen to him," Sarah said. "The forest that nears us may not be as salubrious and enchanting as mine, but that is not to say it's not beautiful. It is not a forest where we may encounter an irksome elf, a stubborn dwarf, or trolls of dangerous intentions, along with many other creatures it is unwise of us to face. It is a feral forest, maybe too feral, for parts of it are hard to cross because of the wildness of the trees and branches and foliage surrounding your every step. Outside that, the forest is but a hop and skip through. Many travelers of my town take the forest path to reach Cambridge Road. Only a few have reported anything out of the ordinary."

"And those few?" Rajur said with a sly look on his face.

Sarah's pleasantness dropped.

"Go on, Sarah. What is out of the ordinary?"

"I'd rather not," she said, grinning at Rajur. "If we don't speak of it, the less chance it occurs."

The boys did not know what to think of this conversation between the two. They did feel it had something to do with the earlier strange behavior of the two, the conversation that Rajur ended by saying 'Gladson's Glade.'

No longer could the boys imbibe the beauty of the dell. They had to know.

"What is this 'out-of-the-ordinary'?" Timothy asked.

"It's not important," Sarah said as Rajur smiled. "Really, nothing to be concerned with. You'll do fine. I promise."

"Why do you do that?" Zachary asked.

"Do what?" Sarah said.

"You say things pleasantly, only to follow it up with something foreboding. You don't stop there. You end the ominous talk with pleasantry again."

"How about them wits?" Rajur said, finding it difficult not to enjoy this.

"Yes," Sarah said, "so they have sense. But I don't know what you mean by all that."

The boys were about to give her numerous examples.

Rajur stopped them. "You'd be wasting your breath. She would never understand this part of her."

"Part of me?"

"Your motherly instincts. She'll tell you one thing while coating it with another, only to throw a whole new batch of coating, keeping you safe from what could prove to be harmful, even if you and I think it is relevant that it remains harmful to the mind. And throw in her being a master in white magic. Well, it further fortifies her benevolence. You'll get used to it as I have. And when you get used to it, you'll fall deeply in love with her, as we all have."

Blushing, Sarah barely said, "I don't act like that. I only want to encourage and keep them aware of the dangers ahead."

"How is that any different from what I just said?"

"Oh, bugger off!" Sarah said.

Both boys and Rajur chuckled.

The banter accomplished the mission. The boys forgot about the out-of-the-ordinary subject.

~

The day slowly ended, and no sign of the forest appeared before them.

"This dell is endless," Zachary said.

"I thought we'd see the forest by now," Timothy said.

"Soon," Rajur said.

"And we're still not stopping upon reaching this forest?" Zachary asked.

"Not till we reach the halfway spot."

"And is there a certain landmark for this halfway spot?" Timothy asked.

Rajur and Sarah looked at each other. The same strange behavior between the two appeared again.

Rajur nodded his head but did so with a sign of caution. He wanted Sarah to explain but to do so on the cautious side.

Sarah nodded back. "At the crossing," she said.

"Crossing?"

"The Annieby River."

"The what?"

"A river too wide and deep for us to ford without a ferry," Rajur said.

"There'll be a ferry?"

"Aye, that and . . ." Rajur stopped.

"And?"

Rajur smiled and turned to Sarah.

"OK," Timothy said. "You two have been going back and forth with something all day. What is this? Is it the out-of-the-ordinary thing?"

"We have to tell him," Rajur said.

"But you don't even believe in it," Sarah said.

"Doesn't matter what I believe. And I never said I didn't believe it. I just think it could be something else. Not a . . ."

"Not a what?" Timothy asked.

Sarah answered. "A ghost."

"What?" Zachary said. "Did you say 'a ghost'?"

"So they say," Rajur said.

"From many accounts."

"But you've never met one of these so-called *witnesses*."

"That's because I don't leave my forest."

"So why are you so sure of this myth?"

Sarah shrugged her shoulders.

"Why don't you two tell us what you do know?" Timothy said.

Sarah did the honors of explaining first. "At the crossing, well, one who waits to cross the river will be visited by another person who has gone missing for a long period, too long to be . . ."

"Alive?" Zachary said.

Sarah looked displeased. "Sure. Whatever. Anyways, this missing individual will be found inside the boat when the traveler is ready to cross the river. Thus, the traveler is accompanied by the missing person from start to finish. When the traveler reaches the other end and climbs out of the ferry, they go their way, while the missing person rows back to the other side and is never seen again, for not one traveler has mentioned they've encountered the same missing individual."

"Where do these missing people come from?" Timothy asked.

Rajur answered, "From the crossing."

"Huh?"

"They are the individuals that *never* reach the other side."

"What do you mean they never reach the other side?"

"They—" Sarah said and stopped.

"Go ahead," Rajur said. "Give them your perspective of the mystery."

"They go missing."

"No. Don't hide your opinion. Say to them what others declare to you."

"They are taken, stolen away by the ghost that resides on the boat."

"Taken where?" Timothy asked.

"I'm afraid that's all we know," Sarah said.

"And your thoughts?" Timothy asked Rajur.

"I believe they do go missing, but as far as—"

"So you're saying we're crossing a river using a haunted boat?" Zachary said, not letting Rajur finish.

"It isn't haunted," Sarah said.

"But the river could be," Rajur said.

Sarah looked to Rajur and back to the boys. "Not to worry," she said. "There's four of us. And that does not count the dog and two steeds."

"What's that mean?" Zachary said.

"Quite simple. Nobody has ever come forward after witnessing one of these takings. Thus, if you do your calculations correctly, it only happens when one is alone. We are four. We are safe."

"And if you're wrong?" Zachary said. "What if there has never been a witness because *everyone* on board was taken?"

Sarah looked displeased at Zachary. She found no evidence to overturn his statement.

The companions kept moving.

The long and tiring and beautiful journey through the dell continued in silence. For the most part, the boys ended all thoughts about the crossing. Just being around Rajur and Sarah, and understanding their powerful natures, allowed them to ease their minds about some haunted river or ferryboat. They were able to enjoy the last of the dell's surroundings before the final stray light from the Star of Nod ended. And as it grew darker, the six moons, five of which were at full capacity, shone brightly in the sky and shared none of their glow with Eythreal's surface. The countless stars in the cloudless night did.

Thus, the brightness of the stars led the companions through the last of the dell, where a near-impenetrable wall of forestry stood starkly at the end.

"We're going in there?" Zachary said with a tinge of fear in his voice.

"It's not that bad," Sarah said.

"It certainly looks bad."

"I'm with Zachary on this," Timothy said. "How long in the forest till the crossing?"

"Not too long," Rajur said. "Three hours."

"Three hours in that forest till we rest and camp?"

"Aye," Rajur said, "unless you want to cross the *haunted* river in the darkness of the night."

"Not funny," Zachary said. "Not funny whatsoever."

Surprisingly, Zachary stepped into the foreboding forest before the others. He did so intrepidly. Timothy followed, with Butch at his heels. Rajur and Sarah entered last, bringing with them Abigail and Breeze, while Sarah gave off a faint glowing light from her staff. The two watched the boys march into the unknown without a scruple of fear. This impressed them, seeing how well the boys steeled themselves when entering a dark and suspicious forest and, consequently, a dark and suspicious forest found in a world far beyond theirs, a world full of magic and a world with danger lurking at every corner.

~

As mentioned before, the forest they entered consisted of not one harmful creature to the companions. The forest was mostly home to birds or creatures skilled in traveling from tree to tree, although most were not seen during the dark. But the companions did catch sight of some land creatures, including critters that hopped along the ground, only to climb upon the tree as the companions grew closer, thus stretching their limbs until they became wings, which they used to glide from one tree to the next.

The forest's biggest fault came from its rough terrain. This was primarily due to horrendously disorganized root placement of its trees. To make matters worse, this forest, unlike Sarah's, Old Wicker's Forest, and of course, the Forest Beyond, could not hide its age, although in truth, it was far younger than those other forests. The steeds made matters worse, for Sarah and Rajur took great pains to find a way through the forest at times because of the size of the creatures. All through the forest, they had to be very careful about tripping over fallen trees and such. And never did they find a clean path to tread upon.

Luckily, Rajur was not an amateur when it came to tracking or paving his way through the most difficult of lands.

When it came to the sound of the forest, chirping could be heard, but this chirping did not come from birds singing.

"Tekers," Rajur said.

"The squirrel-like animals that also look like monkeys that have been running up and down the land and flying on trees?" Zachary said.

"Sure," Rajur said, nodding his head.

The chirping from the creatures became louder and more ubiquitous.

"The forest is now full of them."

"Aye," Rajur said, "and not only that."

"What?" both boys said. They each sighted a creature similar to a lizard, but much bigger and colorful even in the darkness of the forest.

"Lizards!" Zachary said. "They're harmless?"

"To us, yes."

"What about snakes?" Timothy asked.

Rajur nearly came to a halt.

"Pray to Iria that no snake of any kind rests in this forest, for the snakes of Eythreal are not like the ones you're used to."

The boys looked daunted.

"Unfortunately, the two of you will more than likely have an encounter with one or more."

"I'm already looking forward to that encounter," Zachary said.

Deep inside Rajur, he did not feel as if Zachary spoke sarcastically.

~

They pressed on through the forest. As they did, the forest became quieter. No longer could they hear the tekers. Nor could they spot them scurrying on the ground and up the tree, only to fly away. The lizards did stick around. In fact, their numbers grew.

Along with the silence came darker surroundings. The forest trees and foliage became swallowed up by the darkness, for the stars from before could no longer penetrate through the canopy and give the companions natural light to use upon their travel, including the faint glow from Eldorian's Verge.

But as the darkness fell upon them, the companions were saved by the emergence of bright, shining circular light.

Eyes!

Timothy first surmised Sarah had cast an illumination spell of some kind.

No. The light came from bulbous eyes nearly surrounding every inch of this portion of the forest.

The eyes were no bigger than their own eyes. Some blinked. Some did not. Not one of the eyes came an inch closer to the companions.

"Those are eyes, right?" Zachary said, seeing the strange luminosity of the eyes.

"They are," Sarah said.

"Are they dangerous?"

"By Iria, no!" Sarah said. "They are as harmless to us as everything else in this forest."

"But what are they?"

"Hannies," Rajur said.

"I'm sorry?"

"Trolls," Rajur said. "Hannies are a rare genus of trolls, one of the few classes of trolls that do not inhabit mountains, caverns, or other chasms upon Eythreal."

"Tree trolls," Sarah said jubilantly.

"Aren't trolls bad?"

"Bad?" came a squeaky voice.

Before the boys could discover who made that voice, they felt the legs of their pants being pulled down. They looked down.

A single hannie stood before them with one hand on each of their pant legs.

The troll was far from being ugly and disfigured as the boys assumed them to be from the fairy tales told to them.

But that did not mean they were pleasant to look at either.

What struck the boys most was the fuzzy and hairy bodies resembling small boys or girls.

"Bad?" the troll said again. "Me no bad."

The troll proceeded to climb upon Timothy while the latter stood flabbergasted.

Zachary was not exempt from this. He, too, had his own troll to deal with.

Sarah smiled as she watched the two hannies climb upon the boys. She lifted her staff. When it was raised, she muttered a few words none could understand, and a second later, Eldorian's Verge conjured a bright orb to appear not far above them in the air. Once hovering steady, the orb brightened more, becoming a friendly beacon of light for the surroundings to be seen. The eyes were revealed as the countless hannies; the boys stared at the numerous naked trolls, each similar in shape and with a thick coat of fuzzy hair.

"You must be Gumpy," Sarah said, directing her eyes at the troll that climbed upon Timothy and now sat chest level in the boy's arms. "Visitors have told me that you speak our language."

"Yes. Gumpy. That's me. You Sarah. We thank you. Thank you, Sarah."

"I'm the one that should be thanking you for making it easy for my visitors to travel."

Gumpy nodded, and as he did, many other hannies climbed down the trees and made their way to the companions.

Only Rajur attempted to resist their lovable greeting.

"Off!" he said, trying to untangle three trolls from climbing upon him, with that same amount climbing up his legs.

"Why?" Sarah said, standing calmly with trolls all over her. "The visitors tell me they are good luck."

The boys no longer felt flabbergasted. They found much enjoyment in the playful character of the hannies.

Again, the hannies stood short, the average height about two feet, the tallest of them standing at three feet, and the smallest ranging around six inches. Each hannie had a yellow skin complexion under their short and fuzzy hair. Males and females were separated by males looking softer and less calloused, while the females were sturdier, stronger- and tougher-looking. This was because the female gender of the hannies dominated over the males while leading the hunt and left the gentler tasks to the males. Hannies had four fingers on each hand, while a thumb could be found on the lower and central portions of the hand. As for the feet, only three toes could be found, each toe capable of doing much for them.

Like most trolls upon Eythreal, hannies had stubby ears and yet a bit pointy like elves'. As for their noses, they were smashed a bit, unlike most trolls with long and sharp noses or rotund and flat.

Even with indented noses, their sense of smell was as keen as any troll upon Eythreal.

Sarah received most of the attention from the hannies, each expressing their gratitude to her.

"Why?" Timothy asked. "Why do they thank you so much?"

"They thank me because of my spell."

"But I thought it ended?"

"Not exactly, for no iron wall could stop the residue of my spell from seeping beyond its boundary. Not until it reaches the river does it—"

"The crossing? Of course, it must end there," Zachary said.

Sarah nodded.   "These woods we travel through share enough of my spell to block some of the bad from entering. And not all trolls are bad, either! To be honest, not one single troll should be considered wicked, for they are not of Iria's Dark, although the seeds of their creation fell through the cracks and crannies of Eythreal, too close to the surface of Iria's Dark to give them Light, thus the strength needed to change what they are. Can they be mean and ill-tempered? Ugly and grotesque? A slob? Filthy and sickening? Yes. And can they be insanely territorial? Of course. And their appetite! Their appetite is far more than just being ravenous. It is their hunger that gives them the worst of names. Trolls find everything irresistible, especially succulent, fleshy human meat.

"But not our hannies here! They are a peculiar set of trolls. They eat only plants—no meat, never meat."

"Speaking of food," Zachary said. "Shouldn't we—"

"Get moving?" Rajur said impatiently. "Yes!"

"Can we take a few of these trolls with us?" Zachary asked.

"I don't think we have a choice in that matter," Sarah said. "Seems to me they'll follow us to the very end."

"The end as in the river?"

Sarah nodded.

"Because the residue of your spell goes no farther than the river?"

"Yes and no," Rajur said.

"Why yes and no?"

"Gladson," Rajur said.

Each troll shrank in size and cowered in silence upon hearing that said.

Rajur continued, "The forest on the other side of the river leads directly to Gladson's Glade. From what we've heard, the gnomes have a bit of an appetite for hannies. Luckily, they don't often pass the river."

"Sarah's spell?"

"No," Sarah said. "The residue of my spell found in this forest is far too little and minor to impede such powerful beings."

"Lizards," Rajur said.

"What?" both boys said.

"The lizards are very protective of the hannies. And being voracious and sneaky creatures, they, in turn, could easily make a meal out of a gnome."

"You think that link between the hannies and lizards is due to—"

"My enchantment?" Sarah said. "Yes. I do."

Once the talk centered on the lizards and enchantment, each troll released the tension from being dreadfully scared and continued their journey with the companions.

Two hours later, they reached the halfway spot.

Rajur stopped them about one hundred yards from the river. He hoped the distance was too long for the boys to view the river and ferry. He would have had them stop earlier, but the clearing of the forest had been nonexistent, and this was the closest best stop. Because of the clearing, the boys found a clear view of the river and the ferry anchored beside it.

"It's dark," Zachary said. "But my guess is that it's empty."

Timothy looked to Rajur. Rajur nodded and started to unpack. The hannies gave him and the others a hand in setting up camp.

"Shouldn't we think about crossing now?" Timothy asked.

Rajur looked to Sarah and signaled for her to answer.

She looked back, hesitant.

"It's your theory, not mine," Rajur said.

"Theory?" Timothy said.

Sarah surrendered. "Supposedly, well, the river, or whatever that haunts the river, knows your consciousness. It reads through you. You come to cross the river—it will know. You come simply to set up camp, and it'll know that too. We simply came here to set up camp. We change our minds, and the river will read this. Maybe a ghost appears, maybe not. But

I know this: it is safer to pitch camp on this side of the river than over there, for I, too, am not in favor of placing ourselves at the mercy of gnomes."

"Then I guess we cross in the morning," Timothy said.

"Aye," Rajur said. "And don't think you're squeezing out of training tonight."

"What? At this late hour and—"

"You do want to survive, right?"

Chapter 7

HURON'S CRYPT

"There's somebody in the boat!"

Unlike the mornings before, Timothy woke up last and did so to Zachary's shout. He ripped off the blanket and bolted upright. He stared ahead. Zachary's back blocked his view of the ferry. The early morning hour also impeded him from receiving a view, for the Star of Nod had barely made its presence known to the former darkness of the night.

"Get up and look at this!" Zachary shouted. "I think it's a ghost."

Standing up and already dressed, Timothy walked toward Zachary. Behind the boys, Sarah and Rajur tended the fire they built, nowise surprised or concerned about the supposed ghost.

"He doesn't look like a ghost," Timothy said. "Looks too real."

"None of them ever do," Sarah said. "So I've been told."

"Do you find yourself afraid?" Rajur asked.

Both boys shook their heads.

"Nor do I think anyone should be afraid when seeing the missing person," Timothy said.

"And why is that?"

"Maybe we have it all wrong. Maybe a ghost in the boat means you'll cross safely over, as if they are your guardian, whereas being alone, you're vulnerable."

"A solid theory of yours," Rajur said. "Doesn't explain the eyewitnesses, but that could be coincidental."

"But how certain are we of this person being a ghost—a missing person?" Zachary asked.

"Leave that to me," Sarah said. "Travelers that cross this portion of the river often come through my forest and town."

Sarah left the fire and stopped beside the two boys. Rajur joined her and gave her a spyglass from his girdle.

"This will help."

"Are you saying my eyes—"

"I'm saying you'll receive a better view."

Sarah squinted her eyes at Rajur and procured the spyglass from his hand.

She placed the spyglass over her eye and gazed upon the person sitting in the ferryboat. Without a change of looks, she gave back the spyglass.

"And?" Zachary said.

"His name is Hanns Tamnerick."

"And?"

"He's been missing for far too long to be alive—and more importantly, he's wearing the same outfit he wore last time I saw him in our village."

"A ghost," Zachary exhaled. "But we're in good hands. Timothy tells us that we have a friend to help us across the river. But if you're wrong . . ."

Sarah stared irksomely at Zachary.

"Only fooling about. I'm actually excited! My first encounter with a ghost."

With that budding excitement, Zachary turned away and made himself busy by putting away the last of the campsite. He also helped prepare breakfast. And before he and the rest knew it, they were packed, satisfied from breakfast, and ready to make their way to the river.

They did so slowly. Their eyes never left Hanns, as the latter never budged an inch. He sat in the boat, oblivious to anyone's presence.

No scruple of fear could be found invested in the boys. But consternation did swirl through their minds.

We're about to sit next to a ghost inside a boat, and not only that, but a boat known to steal people away.

Why? How? How are they taken? Is it the boat? Or is it the river? Maybe it is the ghost.

And when taken, where? Where does one go?

Less than twenty yards from the river's edge and ferry, Timothy turned to Rajur.

"Why is it you've never crossed the river? You say you've been to Ghalia more than a few times. And you don't like Cambridge Road or that other road. How do you get there by not crossing the river?"

"First off, I hardly go to Ghalia. There's nothing but trouble for me there. And the few times I've traveled there from Cyrcle, I've gone by another route. This other route is longer, yet it still curves alongside Gladson's Glade, flirting too closely for my liking. But it does bypass this river. And I do this not because of some ghost they say, but for other reasons. There is a certain stop I like to make along that long route."

"And we didn't go that way because . . ."

"Because that route, along with the stop I make, is not suitable for everyone. And the distance is much longer."

"What about you?" Zachary asked Sarah. "You've never crossed it either, right?"

"Never."

"So this is the first for all of us?" Timothy said.

"Correct," Rajur said.

"Now it has become exciting," Zachary said.

The companions reached the bottom of the hill that led to the river's edge. They stopped right beside the boat. They looked at Hanns.

He still sat motionless and oblivious to their presence.

"Who's climbing in first?" Zachary said.

Rajur smiled, finding this very amusing.

"This is absurd," Sarah said and climbed into the boat. She sat one open spot away from Hanns. Sitting upright, she folded both hands on her lap. She kept her staff at her side and stared at the rest. "Well?"

The companions nodded.

Rajur and the boys led the horses into the boat first and tied them down. Butch found his way to Sarah and sat questioningly near Hanns Tamnerick. The boys settled across Hanns and Sarah. Rajur did the same but sat farthest from the companions, wanting to be close to the rope that needed to be pulled. He also ordered the boys to grab the rope and give strength.

Sarah watched—watched their struggle.

"This ferry is not made for the likes of all of us, along with two steeds and a dog. Why not let me assist?"

"No," Rajur shouted while the boys were about to say yes.

"Stubborn man."

A few minutes later, the boys noticed that only ten feet had been traversed along the river, with about hundred and fifty or more feet left. They weren't winded, or sore in the arms and shoulders and back. But they did feel that exhaustion would set in not much longer if it took this much to surpass ten feet, along with the strain of so many muscles being used to pull along.

"Why not let her help us?" Zachary asked.

"We don't need it," Rajur said. "And we don't want it. We let her help now, and we'll be asking her for help far too many times. It is too easy to fall dependent on her."

"But didn't we choose her to join us for times like this?" Timothy asked.

"This does not compare to the times we *will* need her."

"But we may never reach those moments if we don't get across this river," Timothy said.

"It is your choice," Rajur said. "You decide."

"I don't see the big deal," Zachary said. "What all can she do in this situation of ours?"

Sarah smiled as Rajur turned to her sternly.

"Is this what you want?" Rajur asked Timothy.

"It is."

He nodded back. "Keep it—" Rajur said.

Sarah interrupted him with "At a low potency."

"Potency?" Zachary said.

Sarah shrugged her shoulders. She then asked each of the boys to place their hands on her staff. She looked to Rajur. He shook his head and continued to pull the rope on his own strength. The boys wavered between the two and finally succumbed to the curiosity and intrigue of what Sarah could do by placing their hands on the staff. Once they did so, they felt a tingling run up their spines. The tingling ended, but they now felt different, as if their physical exterior separated from their insides. Seeing Sarah close her eyes and hearing the foreign words emitted by her made this feeling grow stronger. They stared at their hands, for they felt their hands being the center of this change. Their hands glowed. The glowing eased the feeling of separation. In fact, it brought back their physical exterior to the interior of their bodies. The glow slowly permeated along their entire body while doing the same: healing them of the disembodiment they felt.

And as their entire bodies were suffused with this glow, the glow darkened, and their skin complexion returned to normal. But *normal* could not be said about how they felt.

"Holy heck!" Zachary cried out. "I feel . . . so damn strong!" he said as he pulled his hands off the staff while clenching his fists.

"Stronger than my pa," Timothy said.

"Ten times my pa," Zachary said.

Rajur shook his head. Sarah smiled.

"What did you do to us?"

"Just a small boost of vigor and endurance. Go on. Pull us across the river."

The boys grabbed the rope and pulled with their new strength. They doubled the distance they had already covered in under thirty seconds. And no sign of exhaustion kicked in.

"How long does this last?"

"Very short," Sarah said. "So hurry it up."

And they did.

"This is amazing!"

"Awesome!"

"Can this not be permanent?"

"Never to go away."

"Magic."

"Magic!"

Rajur stared at Sarah vexedly. "See what you did?"

"I gave it to them at a low potency."

"I believe that. I also sensed that they'd absorb it far stronger than most. Their mana assimilation is far—"

Rajur stopped, along with the rest, upon feeling a great quake from underneath them, which rocked the ferryboat. Something seemingly alive trembled not far below them.

By now, they had reached the halfway portion of the river.

"What do you think that was?" Timothy asked.

Rajur and Sarah shook their heads dubiously. A little sign of worry could be read on their faces.

Zachary looked at Hanns. "Hey! He moved. He's now staring at us instead of his feet."

The companions looked at Hanns and noticed his glare at them.

"He's watching us," Timothy said.

Hanns's eyes scanned from one companion to the next, and upon returning his eyes to Timothy, the eyes stopped. Each of their eyes locked onto one another.

"Do you feel that?" Timothy asked the others, sensing something uncanny about Hanns's eyes.

"Feel what?" Sarah said. "What do you feel, Timothy?"

"I feel—" Timothy said and stopped. "A burning . . ."

"A burning what?" Sarah asked.

"A burning sensation from his eyes. Burning my eyes!"

"Move out of the way!" Rajur shouted. "I'm going to cut down this guy." He said that as he unsheathed Storm Breaker.

"Wait!" Sarah shouted back.

"Wait for what?'

"What if it hurts him?"

"Who bloody cares?"

"No, not Hanns. Timothy. What if a connection between the two could end up hurting Timothy?"

Rajur perceived her point and ceased his action. He stared at both Hanns and Timothy. He felt a bond between the two, as Sarah surmised.

"Why aren't you helping him?" Zachary said, seeing a painful grimace growing upon Timothy's face. "He's in pain!"

"Sarah is right," Rajur said. "There's a bond, and I feel that cutting off this bond so abruptly may lead to a grave consequence for Timothy."

"So that's that? We're just going to sit back and let this happen to him? You heard him. His eyes are burning!"

"We have to hurry to the other side," Sarah said.

Rajur nodded, and he and Sarah jumped over to the rope and started pulling.

"Help us, Zachary!" Sarah shouted.

Zachary sat motionlessly, staring at Hanns and Timothy.

"Zachary!" Rajur shouted.

"But how is this going to help him? What about your magic?"

"He's already under some sort of spell. And until I know what it is, I cannot just banish it with dispel. The spell could be anything."

"And what does crossing the river do?"

"Gives us hope."

Reluctantly, Zachary left his spot by Timothy and grabbed the rope. The boat moved at a greater pace.

"We're almost there," Sarah said.

Zachary's eyes went to Timothy and Hanns as he sensed the vigor and endurance slipping away.

Hanns's face turned malevolent.

"He's going to do something!" Zachary shouted. "Something bad."

Sarah and Rajur both stopped. Rajur read this malevolent look upon Hanns's face and leaped toward the two while unsheathing Storm Breaker again.

But Hanns reacted faster.

Hanns jumped from his side of the boat and landed on Timothy. The two tumbled to the ground, and Hanns climbed upon the boy, grabbing Timothy by the sides of his face.

"Cut him down!" Zachary screamed, having unsheathed his sword.

Rajur towered over the two and found the strike difficult.

"Please. Now. He's hurting him."

Rajur nodded. He sheathed Storm Breaker and unsheathed one of the Moon Beams. He readied the Moon Beam under Hanns's throat.

"Wait!" Sarah said. "Look. He's loosening his grip on Timothy. And his face. He looks . . ."

Sarah spoke correctly. Hanns loosened his grip on Timothy, and his malevolent look turned to sadness.

Timothy also showed this sadness on his face. Or was it compassion?

"I think he's speaking to him," Zachary said, noticing Hanns's lips trembling as if muttering silent words toward Timothy.

The moving lips stopped. As they stopped, Timothy's and Hanns's eyes closed—and stayed closed.

"He's showing him something," Sarah said.

A long minute later, Hanns's eyes opened. Staring into Timothy's closed eyes, Hanns released his hands from the boy.

Timothy cried out in pain as his eyes opened.

Before anyone could move, Hanns returned to his position on the boat, looking down at his feet, oblivious to all living things.

For Timothy, the pain passed as his whole body shuddered. Sarah and Zachary quickly came to his side and lifted him off the ground.

Rajur had eyes only for Hanns.

"What happened?" Zachary asked, seeing Timothy regain some life. "Sarah thinks he showed you something."

"He did," Timothy said. "And it was horrible."

Timothy no longer shuddered, nor did he feel any more ramifications from what Hanns did to him. He stood up on the boat and stared at Hanns.

"I know where they all are. I know what happens. And I know who and what takes them."

"Who, Timothy?" Sarah said.

Without a single problem in pronouncing the unfamiliar word, Timothy uttered, "Jalzeer."

~

"What did you say?" a startled Rajur said while placing an aggressive hand on Timothy's shoulder.

Timothy could not respond so easily. Rajur baffled him by gripping his shoulder aggressively.

"I said," Timothy said, discomposed by the aggressiveness Rajur showed, "Jalzeer."

Rajur relaxed his grip on Timothy. He returned to his stoic look. "That is a name I have not heard for some time."

"Jalzeer?" Sarah questioned.

Rajur turned to Sarah. "A soul wraith, or what others like me call Eater of Souls. What I've read about Jalzeer's time on Eythreal tells me he's mighty. None of what I read placed him at this location. No, he must have escaped one haunting and found a nice little nest around here."

"Under the river," Timothy said. "Not too far a swim from here."

"Aye," Rajur said. "It would make sense. He must have found a hidden burrow under this river. Wraiths hardly ever create their own burrow. They occupy others' burrows. Death and treasure entice them. This river is old—very old. Someone long ago may have found a chasm or something under the river and turned it into a cave, one made for a particular burial ground or something that hid important artifacts or such. Wraiths do not care for the living world on the outside. They care about the treasures that belong to the dead and the dead themselves—all the while fattening themselves up with *living* souls. The concept of exploring more of Eythreal and growing in power over the world has long vanished from their minds. More than likely, Jalzeer placed a powerful spell on this river to lure its prey. Most wraiths are capable of some degree of magic—but not like this. No. Only the powerful ones like Jalzeer. Somehow, someway, he has triggered a spell to fall upon his victims by getting them to dive into his chamber without drowning, for their souls would be already released if drowned. Most wraiths use music, some sort of sound. I think Jalzeer uses props like Hanns as a way to transfer the spell. Hanns may be dead, but his embodiment could easily be used as a vessel, especially when belonging to a powerful wraith."

"I think you're right," Timothy said. "There are so many of the dead."

"Yes. That is because soul wraiths live off the souls. They grow stronger because of these souls."

"Are their souls lost forever?" Timothy asked.

"No. By absorbing their souls, Jalzeer keeps the souls from being eradicated. In torment, they suffer until released."

"Released how?"

"Released by destroying the wraith."

"Then we must destroy the wraith," Timothy said.

"It is not possible," Rajur said, shaking his head, "not now, and not just the four of us. We must be stronger."

"But Hanns said we're strong enough. He said we're the strongest to have come this way."

"Hanns doesn't know."

"He does know. There are hundreds upon hundreds of souls down wherever this domain may be, crying for help. They feel us. They know of our presence. We can't just abandon them."

"We can and we will."

"No," Timothy said adamantly. "Hanns came to us to show us that we can save them. And Jalzeer knows this too. Jalzeer is afraid. He spoke to me. Warned me not to come. Why would he do that if he's as all-powerful as you say he is?"

"He's not all-powerful. I never said that. Jalzeer is a soul wraith. Wraiths are powerful spiritual entities of the dead. They lack a corporeal body, and because of that, they are limited."

"Then we can defeat him. I heard it in his voice. He's scared—scared of what we might be able to do and . . ."

"And what?" Sarah said.

"Awaken. Something about our presence awakening someone. I assume—"

"The one this burrow belongs to," Sarah said.

"It doesn't matter. Too risky."

"I don't care," Timothy said. "We're not abandoning them. Their suffering is intolerable. We must do this."

"Not now. It's not wise to do so now."

"Don't you want to see what we're capable of?" Zachary asked.

"Aye. But not like this—too much, too soon. You don't understand the burden falling on us if we faced Jalzeer."

"You can't defeat this Jalzeer alone?" Zachary asked.

"That's the problem. He won't be alone."

"It doesn't matter. I'm not letting them suffer more, plus the many more that will also suffer because of our cowardice."

The word *cowardice* stoked a fire inside Rajur. But the imprudence of facing such a danger made the fire simmer down a bit.

He turned to Sarah. "Are you not going to help me change this foolish boy's mind?"

"You know as much as I do that I cannot just walk away from the suffering of others—especially many of these being my visitors. I have a responsibility not to look the other way, although," she said, staring at her surroundings, "I'll be staying in the boat."

"You're what?" Zachary said.

Sarah looked at the water. "I . . . I love bodies of water, especially ones flowing through my forest. But I'm not much of a swimmer. Call it a phobia of mine. But this I will guarantee...

"I will find a way to help even from here."

"I trust you will," Timothy said.

Sarah looked relieved.

"I can't believe my ears," Rajur said. "This is insanity! Your decision could not be any more unwise."

"But it must be done."

"At a later time!"

"You know there's no later time," Sarah said.

Rajur glowered her way. "This is all your fault," he said, sharing his scorn for Sarah with Hanns.

Surprisingly, Hanns responded by muttering, "Save us."

Rajur grinned upon hearing that. "Fine," he said a second later. "Fine, fine, fine! But you two will be following my every command! Not a single rebuttal from either of you. You understand me?"

The boys nodded.

"Now strip off your armor."

"What?" both boys exclaimed.

"Enhancement or not, I need you faster than you've been through training. Don't even worry about the shields, either. You won't be facing many weapons. And the ones you face will be old, rusty, and dull. More than likely, not even a fighter's weapons, more for simple self-defense. Speed is the essence because of that. Your survival will mostly depend on your speed. And because of all that, well . . . pretty much shelve the defensive tactics you've been training on so much more than offensive tactics. You'll be on the offensive this battle, going from one body to the next."

"What about getting there?" Timothy said. "What I discovered is that the burrow is deep below the water's surface. Unless we know the exact spot, as if fallen to the spell, we'll likely drown finding it."

"Leave that to me," Sarah said.

The boys nodded and stripped off their heavier pieces of armor, keeping only the lighter clothes on. They also put away their shields but kept their dagger and sword. They did this fearlessly. Rajur perceived this fearlessness about them to be propitious, even if a part of him felt uneasy at their eagerness, as if the boys showed much ignorance of what danger they were soon to face. But no. That part of him was very small and had been defeated by his conscious and subconscious in seeing the boys fully aware of the danger and not taking anything for granted, thus the reason for their staunch nature. He seriously believed these two boys to be the most fearless of any boys he could imagine on Eythreal, which was why it made perfect sense for them to be here.

Once ready, the boys stepped toward Sarah at the side of the boat.

"Take this first," she said, handing Timothy a wrist bracelet with an amulet attached to it. "I'll want it back. But take it for now."

"What is it?"

"Eldorian's Reach," Sarah said, "an amulet that goes alongside my staff given to me by my foster family. Wear it over your wrist, and with Eldorian's Verge's far reach, I should be able to locate your party and help deliver some . . . I'll just have to discern well what you three may need. Other than that, take this too," she said, holding a vial filled with liquid in her other hand. "Because of my phobia of swimming, I have yet to test this formula out since I created it long ago."

"What's it for?"

"For your presence underwater."

"But you don't know it'll work?" Rajur said.

"Have I ever failed you?"

Rajur didn't have to answer.

"Then, by Iria, stop complaining, take the smallest of sips, and pass it around."

Timothy grabbed the wrist amulet from Sarah while Rajur procured the vial. As Timothy strapped the bracelet over his wrist, Rajur squeezed a small drop of the formula into his mouth.

He passed it over to the boys.

"Now be warned," Sarah said to the boys. "You are not so inoculated to our mana as we are. This may not go down easy."

Both boys nodded and squeezed a drop into their mouths.

Zachary shrugged his shoulders.

"I feel nothing."

"Same here," Timothy said.

"I guess we should stop comparing these boys' mana growth to other boys," Sarah said.

Rajur nodded. "Or your formula did not work."

"Test your hands in the water," Sarah said.

Timothy placed his hand over the side of the boat and plunged it through the water. An orange glow appeared as the hand crossed the surface, surrounding his entire hand and everything else that crossed through the water barrier. Moving his hand and arm in the water, Timothy felt only air.

"What is it?"

"A shield. And this shield will give you five hours of breathing air. And if five hours isn't enough—"

"It's enough," Rajur said.

Sarah leered at him. "If five hours isn't enough, take another sip. Just not too much."

The boys nodded.

Zachary placed his hand in the river.

"Pretty neat, I must say."

Both boys pulled out their dry hands from the water while leaving behind the orange glow.

They looked to Rajur.

"We're ready."

~

The three wasted no time. They dove into the water. Upon doing so, their entire body, possessions, and so forth emitted the orange-colored shield. The shield allowed air to be breathed, as it allowed seven inches of space from the shield to the surface of their skin, and it acted as goggles, allowing them to see the beautiful plant and fish life. Some fish swam toward them—curious and wanting to inspect the orange glow. These fish weren't as odd and beautifully drawn up as the fish they witnessed throughout most of Sarah's Forest, but they still had some unique patterns and were a bit similar and not so similar to their world. Along with the fish, many other creatures of this river, including eels, came stealing away from their hiding spots, in awe of this charge of mana entering their domain. Because of this unexpected panorama, the boys found it difficult to pass through since they wanted to linger about and study the river's life.

Rajur pushed them on.

Timothy led them west through the river, and they noticed a stark difference in the scenery as soon as he did.

The aquatic life became scarce—terribly scarce! And worse: deteriorated. Morbid fish swam by, looking for a place to end their misery, yet too sick to find a place to die, thus deciding to die right then and there. Unlike the fish before, none of these fish showed interest in the companions. And the botanic life of the river looked just as bad—dead, decomposed. All this was seen through the murkiest of waters, even with the shield's enhanced vision. The murkiness became so bad that the companions kept one hand on another's foot as Timothy tried his best to follow the directions strangely given to his mind.

Timothy found success in leading them on the right way. They found themselves in the deepest and remotest part of the river, and when there, he noticed a slight clearness through the murky water. He stared through it, along with Rajur's eyes, and they each noticed an opening at the bottommost portion of the wall alongside the river. Rajur, the first to notice it, yanked Timothy's foot. Timothy nodded and led them toward this crevice. The opening of the crevice was sufficient for each of them to pass through. And not long through it, they reached an end.

They looked up.

The surface of the water could be seen.

They swam directly up and broke the surface. They found themselves in a grotto. They descended upon the surface of the grotto and looked around. Behind the decay and stench that made up the grotto, they sensed something beautiful and marvelous, something even Rajur could not have imagined.

Above them, drips of water fell from the ceiling, telling them that they were still underneath the actual surface of the river.

"I imagine the victims dive into the water directly above us, reach the crevice opening we passed through, and then find themselves in this grotto."

"That's some lung power," Zachary said.

"It is doable. You'll find this river isn't as deep as you think."

The boys nodded.

"There," Rajur said, pointing to what looked like a door. "Come. No time to spare."

The boys followed Rajur, and passing along the grotto, they reached the door.

"This has to be the entrance."

"But there is no handle," Zachary said.

"It's more of a gateway. It opens by sliding up and closes by sliding down."

"OK. Then how do we do that?"

"Most of the time, there is a lever or chain you need to pull."

Rajur looked around for one. He did not find one. "What else do you remember?" he asked Timothy.

"I remember that this is the way."

"Nothing else on how to get through?"

Timothy closed his eyes. "I see this as the passage we must cross through. But how it opens, I don't see."

Before anyone else could say a word, a deep, resonant voice spoke from behind them. "That is because it is not meant to be opened from the outside."

The companions grew alert upon hearing the voice and readied themselves for battle, only to turn around and discover what they believed to be a *real* ghost; the figure standing before them did resemble a ghost since it emitted a translucent blue glow.

The ghostly figure stood as tall as Rajur and just as formidable. It betrayed no race, being no man, elf, and definitely not a dwarf or qharthylion. If anything, it had more of a menfolk look with the stature and elegance of an elf. The attire the figure wore resembled that of a splendid knight or an illustrious warrior while handling a deadly morning star that also produced a translucent bluish glow.

Seeing the powerful figure before them, the companions, even Rajur, stood hesitant.

The figure spoke calmly and peacefully with his deep, resonant voice. "Huron is my name. And this here is the entrance to my crypt. It is where I placed a shard of my Everlasting Peace."

"But not anymore," Timothy said.

"No," Huron said. "It has been disturbed. Jalzeer found a way in and polluted my crypt. No longer do I rest in Everlasting Peace."

"Will you let us through?" Timothy asked.

"Do you wish to vanquish Jalzeer and put to rest my Everlasting Peace?"

"Will it save the others?"

"It will free each soul that has been taken from him."

"Then we will free the others, and you'll have your Everlasting Peace again."

"Very brave of you, and yet . . . you are not of Eythreal."

Uncertain of why, Timothy felt secure about the truth being known to Huron.

"It matters not," Huron said before Timothy could respond. "I will open the crypt. Beware. Death comes to you in great numbers."

Timothy nodded, as did Huron while stepping around the companions and passing through the closed gateway.

A second later, the companions felt the ground below them rumble. Looking ahead, they noticed the gateway tremble too.

Huron passed through again and faced the companions.

"I have opened the gate to my crypt. Defeat Jalzeer and save the others. Do that, and I will reward you with a shard of my Everlasting Peace."

With that said, the gate lifted upward.

"Go now and be with Iria in life and in death." Huron stepped aside.

Rajur looked at him one last time and passed through the opening. The boys followed. The gate closed.

"I guess there's no going back," Timothy said, seeing they came to a long, dark corridor. "And where does this meager light come from?"

The companions looked directly through the corridor where they presumed the meager source of light emitted from.

"So, through there, right?" Zachary said.

Rajur nodded.

"I hope this is worth it," Zachary said sarcastically. "I wonder what he means by his shard of Everlasting Peace?" Zachary asked.

Both boys turned to Rajur for the answer.

"Huron I know very little of, and less than that do I know of this shard of Everlasting Peace, for Huron is far beyond my time. But one who studies lore must come across him somehow."

"And? This little you know of?"

"Not much again. But what little I know is that he came to King Thaddus I of Thrandor as a spiritual warrior. King Thaddus was the first monarch to rule over menfolk and womenfolk. This was before the establishment of the Four Kingdoms. This was in a time far before Abbigatha's presence. It was a time when the battle of Iria's Light and Dark seemingly ended. Of course, some of the Dark lingered upon the surface of Eythreal, and Huron gave himself to the king for assistance until peace reigned. Thus, with his help and other prominent figures never to be seen since, Thrandor and the rest of Eythreal pushed back the last of the Dark, forcing them to return to the Harrowing. When all was completed, most went their way. Huron also went his way—but not away from Eythreal. No. He promised King Thaddus I that he'd be at Thrandor's side until Thrandor was ready to move on. In time, Thrandor helped build the Four Kingdoms, and seeing that nothing else remained, Huron vanished for his Everlasting Peace. A theory has it that there supposedly remain on Eythreal fragments of what Huron was before the Everlasting Peace. My guess is maybe this shard is one of them. And he left these artifacts for future kings of Thrandor to call upon him, but we forgot where they rested, and because of that, Huron was not there when catastrophe struck Thrandor."

"So Huron is then very powerful?"

"Who he is, nobody has truly defined. He isn't exactly mortal! And legend has it that he's a devil with that morning star."

"Then let us hope this shard comes in handy," Timothy said.

"Aye. We need to prove our worthiness to possess it first."

The boys nodded and turned to face the dark corridor again. The full extent of what they walked into manifested before them. This included the air. The stench of the grotto proved breathable. The stench inside this corridor proved far more pungent and rancid. It smelled as if the air itself had become rotten. Even Rajur found it difficult to breathe without grimacing, for he had traveled through some of the filthiest places above and under Eythreal.

"Jalzeer has long burrowed himself here," Rajur said. "It is a stench of possibly hundreds of greater moon cycles."

"Hundreds of years? That many?"

"Aye. Again, wraiths, especially powerful ones like Jalzeer, sense some of the most hidden burrows because of the immense treasure inside. My guess is that Jalzeer felt threatened long, long ago, moved from his burrow, and sensed this treasure found in Huron's crypt."

"The shard?"

"I can only imagine so."

"What *is* a wraith?" Timothy said.

"Simply put, a wraith is a ghost—a spirit of the dead that never went where it was supposed to go, not always by their own will. You'll find cultists or simply wicked people summoning ones about to die so that they can cast a spirit into a designed object and hope to control them. Most of the time, it is the work of very powerful summoners, ones able to capture the spirit *after* their death, although very shortly after their death, and place them in a similar vessel. There are other ways to become a wraith. Anyways, wraiths are called wraiths and not ghosts, mostly because they have a bit of life inside them, the smallest of remnants. This life needs to be filled. Treasures, jewelry, weapons, and so forth fulfill this life—this desire. But wraiths also need substance to continue this new life. Souls, for example. And this is because all wraiths come from the spirit of one that should have gone to the Harrowing instead of the other realms of the dead. Thus, before all else, wraiths are creatures of evil. Nothing good is found in them. And never shall there be a sliver of Iria's Light to penetrate them."

"And we destroy it by?"

"We don't kill it," Rajur said. "For how can one kill what is already dead? We are but mortals. The power you speak of rests with the immortal only. Or one ordained by gods, which we are not."

"You were ordained, right? That's what that Tolan guy said."

"Ordained by Eythreal. Not by a god or goddess. Ordained because of a prophecy among infinite others."

"Then what do we do?"

"We must weaken it to its original state, being the single soul of the damned individual, capture it, and in time, release it to the Harrowing by various means, each of them not exactly wise to do."

"That's . . ."

"Why do you think I said *later*?" Rajur said.

"But the souls?"

"They won't need to wait long. Once we weaken Jalzeer, the souls will be disconnected from his spirit and find their way to one of the realms of the dead."

"And where do we put this spirit of Jalzeer until we dispose of it?" Zachary said.

"Let us hope there is a sufficient vessel found inside the crypt. Almost all wraiths cannot be far from the vessel that possessed them."

"But you're not sure of this?"

"Some wraiths are powerful enough to separate themselves from that single vessel. Some."

"So our plan is to strip away the souls and hope to find a specific object to place his soul into?"

"Quite right."

"Now I understand the *later*."

Rajur cracked a smile.

A few seconds later, while turning a corner…

Crunch.

The boys stopped upon hearing the crunching sound and felt it under their boots. Too dark to see, they turned to Rajur.

"Do you want to know?" Rajur asked.

"Bones?" Zachary said.

Rajur pulled from his girdle a small trinket. He shook the trinket full of yellow liquid, and as the liquid shook, it glowed brightly.

The boys looked down.

Skulls and bones.

The illumination also gave the boys a better view of their surroundings. The boys discovered the surroundings to be full of not only bones, but also the recently perished bodies of the dead. And the dead piled upon the dead along the walls and floor of the corridor.

"Jalzeer has been at it for much longer than even I had guessed," Rajur said, "which isn't good."

"Are we supposed to be afraid of these bodies of the dead?" Zachary asked. "They're dead."

"As I said, you have no idea what you two have involved yourselves in. Alas! It is too late. There is no turning back."

A minute later, they came to another corner. Turning the corner, they found themselves staring into a spacious room: Huron's crypt.

In better times, this capacious chamber would be attractive to the eyes. It had all the makings of a peaceful and restful place for the dead. Many archaic tapestries would be seen decorating the walls. The mosaic flooring would be a sight to see. And the candle lights strewn about would be the envy of any candlemaker. But now? The discolored tapestries upon the wall had turned into rags. The mosaic floor had crumbled and become hard to see for many reasons, from spider webs to inches-thick of dust and, most prevalently, the dead. The candle lights had been smashed and fallen into decay. The foul stench matched that of the corridors taken to reach here. As for those bodies of the dead, the skeletons continued to pile up one after another, even though the numbers were much less than in the corridors.

The boys did not focus on the dead. They focused mainly on a coffin set in the center of the chamber but more toward the rear. The coffin resided on an elevated sanctuary, with four lit torches at each corner. The torches alone gave the crypt light, and surprisingly, the torches were in decent shape.

As for the coffin, it had seen much better times.

"Is that . . ." Timothy said and let go.

"I can only imagine so. Huron's resting place. And now Jalzeer sleeps there."

Rajur said that and took his first steps toward the great coffin.

The boys followed.

"No," Rajur said. "You boys stay farther from the coffin than me. Be ready."

The boys obeyed Rajur as he cautiously made his way to the coffin. Once there, Rajur studied the coffin better, and in doing so, he realized that it would prove heavier than he first thought. He wanted to call back the boys to give him a hand. But he feared doing that, for the uncertainty of what resided in the coffin proved too risky. He also didn't want to use both hands to open the lid since that would disarm him and leave him vulnerable to that same unknown.

In the end, Rajur sided with risking himself by using both hands. Thus, he placed one hand on the coffin. He went to put his second hand on the coffin.

The coffin rattled.

Quickly did he release his hand.

Seeing nothing come from this rattling except a warning at the most, Rajur placed his hand back on the coffin.

The rattling grew stronger. So strong the rattling became, Rajur took a step back, seeing that the lid could very well explode off the ample-sized coffin.

But it never came to that. Instead, a dense stream of grayish smoke seeped out of the sides of the coffin and condensed into a heavier stream of smoke. The smoke turned mostly into a fog and proceeded to spread through every inch of the crypt's surface.

Rajur looked down at his feet and watched this fog stream beyond him. He turned to the boys. The boys stood disconcerted.

The fog of smoke neared them.

"What is this stuff?"

"Don't fear it," Rajur said, seeing the vapor of smoke pass them by, covering every inch of the crypt while entering the corridors. "It is not for us."

"Not for us? For whom is it for?"

"For them," Rajur said.

The boys stared at him quizzically. What did he mean by *them*?

The answer came to them through the sounds of rattling. This rattling came not from the lid of the coffin. Instead, the rattling came from the farthest portions of the crypt's corridors.

The sound of scratching and clawing joined in with the sound of rattling.

"We should never have come here," Rajur said.

As much as Rajur wanted to rip off the coffin's lid and pray to Iria he could end this with one swing of Storm Breaker, he knew it to be too risky. He might not find what he needed to find in the coffin. And the boys needed him. Only seconds were left until they would be surrounded—by the dead. Therefore, Rajur backpedaled toward the boys and stood by them.

"Remember your training," Rajur said. "They'll come at once and will do so chaotically. They'll have no rhyme or reason in their attack strategy. These are common folks, like farmers, merchants, drifters, and so forth—none of them with the training you boys have had even in such a limited time. But there could be a few fighters in the mix. And I can't imagine their cadaverous bodies being much of a threat if singled out. But in great numbers . . ."

"What about Jalzeer?" Timothy asked.

Rajur looked back at the incessant rattling of the coffin lid. "We shall see. For now—" He stopped because of footsteps.

"They're coming."

The footsteps turned the corner and entered the crypt.

Seven of them—seven of the more recently perished bodies entered the crypt. Not one of them carried a weapon.

"We're going to kill them?" Zachary asked, seeing that the seven dead were no different from Timothy and him.

"They're long dead, so you're not going to kill them."

"Then what do we do?"

"Immobilize them. Sever their limbs from their bodies. Leave only their torso, and don't forget to crush their head. They bite!"

Hearing that, the boys, for a short second, felt squeamishness in their stomachs while also feeling an unprecedented exhilaration for battle. They could hardly contain this thirst for battle, especially Zachary. Zachary nearly drooled from his mouth. And as if instincts taught them well, they prepared for this battle, which they believed to be the first of many more, by giving reverence to their most treasured possessions. Timothy pulled out the necklace from under his light armor and kissed the stone he once shared with his sister while Zachary placed his hand into a pocket and grasped the mysterious arrowhead.

Besides these devotions, they asked for the strength and courage from their lost families.

The battle commenced.

~

The lone female of the seven dead initiated the battle. Most recent in death, she made a sprightly leap (for a rotting corpse) toward the three. But with a single swipe from Storm Breaker, her head detached itself from the neck. Rajur's fluid and smooth motion did not stop there. By the time he put the sword to rest, the dead's torso fell to the ground without arms and legs. All the dead could do was watch and hope to find a way to bite their assailants.

That came to a *crunching* halt when Rajur crushed her jaw with his boot.

The six other dead followed right behind her.

Rajur deliberately stayed put when the six arrived. He watched Timothy decapitate one of them in a single fluid strike while Zachary severed two heads in one effortless stroke. The boys did not stop there. Headless, the dead lost arms, legs, and so forth from the boys' strikes and fell to the ground, unable to move again. Rajur returned to the fray and cut down the rest of the dead with Storm Breaker and one of the Moon Beams.

The battle lasted less than a minute. But the three found little time to gloat.

A horde of fifteen dead turned the corner.

As the dead approached, the companions were reminded about the coffin...

By a voice.

"You dare to enter?"

Holding their ground, the companions found a way to capture the sight of Jalzeer.

"To enter is to lose one's soul, for death is upon you."

Remarkably, Rajur stood diminutive compared to Jalzeer's size. His entire being seemed impossible to the boys. He had to be a giant, but he wasn't.

The boys could not believe that behind that ginormous body, under its black hooded cape encompassing nearly every inch of its amorphous entity, no trace of flesh remained. Not a single bone, tissue, muscle, and so forth, unless one considered the physical embodiment of the souls that gave structure to his form. Each of these souls of the dead formed into what looked to be ashen-gray, thick, tubular worms squirming underneath the cape. Each of these many souls had the vague impression of the deceased's face outlined at the end, eyes glowering at the boys and Rajur, mouth screaming wildly, their ravenous teeth wanting nothing more than to devour the living and feed their wraith its soul.

Two giant double-edged battle-axes, each nearly the size of the boys, were held effortlessly in the amorphous hands of Jalzeer.

Rajur stared at the axes.

"Those are no mundane battle-axes," he muttered. "Those axes are the possession of the Dark, given to man for wicked use."

The boys looked at Rajur with their first panic on their faces.

"I must leave you," Rajur said.

"You're leaving us?" Timothy said.

"Those axes are made to withstand my Moon Beams and Iria's light. We must split this battle in two. You boys have zero chance against Jalzeer. Focus on the dead while I try to get rid of Jalzeer before the dead mount up too high and prove to be our demise."

Rajur took a step toward Jalzeer.

"Good luck. And Iria bless you."

The fifteen dead continued their charge toward the boys. Most of the dead had perished recently; thus, they were nimble and not yet decrepit. The few others were skeletons with some flesh and tissue. Six of the fifteen carried shoddy swords, rusty daggers, and a dull but penetrable halberd. The boys noticed the weapons and assessed them.

They were ready. They stood taller and more courageous than ever before.

"Ready, my friend?" Timothy said.

"Ready to crush their skulls to pieces."

"Then let's do this!"

Two of the fifteen leaped toward the boys. The boys anticipated this and veered to the side while swinging their swords toward the throats of the dead.

One head, two arms, and even a leg flew in the air. The one with the missing arm but his head intact came close to biting Timothy. Timothy dodged in time, squared his shoulders, and succeeded where he failed: he decapitated the dead.

The boys proceeded to crush the skulls with their boots.

"Against the wall," Zachary shouted, thinking of using the wall to hinder the dead from surrounding them.

Timothy shook his head. "Not safe."

He said that because many more corpses along the wall were stirring back to life.

The former fifteen became more. The boys stared around and noticed the fifteen soon-to-be fifty or more dead, not including the many more still taking their time, from inside the corridors.

~

Rajur had no time to notice the mass number of dead soon to encircle the boys, although he never denied it would happen. He had to dodge one attack after another from Jalzeer and the battle-axes. He also had to deal with the wormlike entities trying to deliver death to him with their cursed mouths full of teeth. Rajur avoided a blow from a battle-ax by rolling to his side. Continuing the roll, he reached the back of the wraith and struck with Storm Breaker. Jalzeer proved insanely agile and quick for his massive frame and slapped away the sword with the other battle-ax. Most weapons on Eythreal could not do such a thing when clashing against the likes of Storm Breaker or his Moon Beams.

But as Rajur discovered before the fight, these battle-axes were not ordinary. Rajur observed this deftness of the wraith and realized he had underestimated what he had already underestimated.

This battle would prove to be a mighty challenge. With that in mind, he turned to discover the boys' plight.

Seeing what advanced upon the boys, he felt a seldom-felt emotion: fear.

Rajur dodged another battle-ax blow and rolled to the ground again. As he did, he unsheathed a Moon Beam and hurled it toward the horde of dead coming for the boys. The Moon Beam soared through the air and did not stop till it cut through a vast number of the dead and, thus, returned to the gauntlets belonging only to Rajur. At least fifteen heads and many more body parts fell to the ground because of this one fling of the Moon Beam. After receiving the Moon Beam and seeing the damage it affected, Rajur decided that he would fight Jalzeer in an evasive manner, thus giving much help to the boys instead of fully committing himself to battle Jalzeer. He felt comfortable with this decision. Even though Jalzeer proved far swifter and more agile than Rajur had imagined, along with the wraith's battle-axes impervious to the Moon Beams' mysterious effect, he felt the wraith to be laborious at times and predictable. He firmly believed he could keep up with Jalzeer while engaging the dead coming for the boys. By doing that, he hoped to cleanse the crypt of all the dead and then place his undivided attention on Jalzeer.

Of course, this plan was formulated by conjecture alone. He knew not the exact body count of the dead that would soon encircle the boys. And what if Jalzeer shrugged off Rajur and went for the boys? Regardless, he felt it to be the best plan available.

Not surprisingly, this plan evinced its imminent doom seconds into it.

Jalzeer continued to surprise Rajur with his prowess, hindering Rajur from aiding the boys.

~

The boys fought valiantly. But exhaustion slowly made its way into their lungs and movements. The relentless dead finally took its toll on them.

They just kept coming and coming.

Unable to decapitate them and crush their skulls, the boys found the dead a real nuisance to them, as they crawled, jumped, and did whatever they could to bite them.

Worse, the floor was submerged still by the fog, so the boys barely could see when a head crawled their way. Not only that, but the boys also fought in every direction.

Zachary's plan now made perfect sense. The two acted on that. They slipped toward the wall and cleared the space of any dead. Placing their backs against the wall, they waited for the rest of the dead.

And they came.

"Not looking so good," Zachary said while dodging one blow after another.

"We've seen worse," Timothy said.

"We have?"

"Sure. The farm."

"The farm. What the heck are you talking about?"

"The drought, the one that led to the fires, which led to the flooding after that storm some five years ago."

"You're comparing that to this?"

"Well, why not? Our backs are against the wall, and a deluge of death comes before us."

'Oh, OK, Mr. Poet."

"Hey, it's something."

"Something to motivate us?"

"Sure."

"Nah," Zachary said. "You know what motivates me?"

"What's that?"

"Seeing my sisters again, even if that means them being bossy and butt-headed and all."

Timothy said. "Yes. I miss Katelyn."

"I miss them all."

"So why don't we stop acting tired and afraid and really kick some ass." Zachary nodded.

And as both boys allowed themselves to imbibe that, a fresh wave of energy swept through them.

But this jolt of energy didn't last so long.

~

The battle did not look any better for Rajur. He believed he could defeat Jalzeer, but he didn't think he had the time. He kept glancing the boys' way and questioned his decision to leave them alone. After receiving a few more glimpses of their plight and deliberating over his predicament, he decided that his first plan failed and he must return to the boys and engage in the slaughter of the dead while praying to Iria that Jalzeer would not leave his spot.

As Rajur took his first step in executing this new plan, a thunderous explosion erupted *above* the crypt.

This explosion alarmed Jalzeer. All the dead stopped. Above them, a shimmering white light flooded the ceiling of the crypt. The white shimmer turned to blue, to red, and then to purple. And as it turned purple, the light disintegrated, leaving behind flakes of its old self to fall upon the dead. As some of these flakes fell on the boys, they felt no effect.

"What do you think it is?" Timothy asked.

"Am I supposed to know that?" Zachary said. "But if there is a time for us to take back what ground we lost, well . . . no better time than now."

Zachary said that when seeing the discombobulated dead. He rushed headfirst and attacked.

The dead regained composure and returned to the fight. But something different came about them.

"You notice something different about them?" Zachary asked, seeing Timothy join in the fight. "They're uh . . . slow."

"Very slow," Timothy said.

"And we're not."

"No," Timothy said with a smile. "We're not."

Surmising what happened was due to Sarah and her spell-casting, the boys raised their weapons and shouted, "For our families!"

From then on, the boys showed no letting up while smiling in appreciation of what Sarah must have done.

But the dead kept on coming.

~

Rajur smiled in appreciation upon seeing what transpired. He knew Sarah must have cast a potent and complicated slow-target neutral spell.

But he also saw no end to the dead, no matter how slow they became.

He thus continued his decision to fall back and stand by the boys, hoping again that Jalzeer did not follow.

But this decision never came to fruition.

~

While the boys engaged with the listless dead, a harsh voice echoed throughout the entire crypt. The voice reminded the boys of Huron. The words of this voice proved more powerful than any attack on the dead so far. There was no doubt in these words. No second guesses. No chance of failing. The words were indomitable and would happen even if the world ended.

Those words belonged to Huron: "I will have vengeance!"

Again, the voice came from everywhere inside the crypt. But the second the voice ended, the morning star's bluish translucent glow appeared beside the boys. And upon appearing, it crushed all the dead in its path—crushing their bodies to pieces. Following the morning star came the entire silhouette of Huron, shimmering with the same bluish and translucent glow, holding on to the morning star in one hand and the other with his fist clenched tightly, angrily.

"Vengeance," Huron muttered toward the boys. "Join me, and we will cleanse this crypt of Jalzeer's foul stench."

As if the boys needed him to say that!

The boys joined Huron and quickly realized that for each of the dead they decapitated and crushed, Huron had done the same to ten others, or more.

The onslaught on the boys became now a massacre upon the dead.

~

Before Huron's voice echoed throughout the crypt, Rajur still faced his decision to retreat and join the boys. He attempted to wheel around, but this gave Jalzeer ample opportunity to counter, for to wheel away from the wraith caused hesitation in Rajur, a hesitation Jalzeer seized upon. The Eater of Souls captured Rajur by the throat, pinning him to the ground. It was then that Jalzeer committed his own blunder. He raised his battle-ax but did so flauntingly, thus giving Rajur room to counter, which he did by finding a firm enough grip on a Moon Beam, unsheathing it, and then scorching through a thick mat of souls. This weakened Jalzeer, allowing Rajur to use his other hand, holding on to Storm Breaker, which he used to cut down a dozen or more souls.

This single action proved to be an immensely decisive blow to Jalzeer. Jalzeer shouted in agony while also releasing Rajur's throat.

The consequences of the blow did not stop there. Jalzeer shrank. He shrank because of the blows of so many souls and their eventual release from bondage.

Fortune continued to favor Rajur, for at that moment, Huron's voice came alive and blasted through the crypt. Rajur never even looked ahead to the boys.

He knew.

He believed the rest of the way it would be Jalzeer and him alone in the battle. No longer did he have to attend to the boys.

They had Huron.

Focusing entirely on the squirming souls, Rajur attacked. And with every blow to a soul, which came in numbers, Jalzeer shrank and weakened, to the point of being unable to hold on to the great battle-axes.

The battle-axes fell from Jalzeer's grip.

Rajur's attacks continued, to the point of him having to rip off the cloak to reach the last of the wormlike creatures. And while ripping the cloak off, he stared only at the squirming souls, each of them still trying to attack him. Thus, he cut away at the very core of this evil creature.

And by freeing the souls, Rajur helped the boys and Huron out, although they needed no help. Once a soul became free of Jalzeer, no longer could the latter possess it. The dead belonging to that soul would stay dead.

But again, the boys and Huron did not need help. By the time Rajur cut away to the very core of the wraith, the boys and Huron had finished the last of the dead.

They turned away and joined Rajur on the elevated sanctuary—joined Rajur in the massacre of what remained of Jalzeer. And what remained could only be defined as an unshaped *thing*—in other words, the corporeal embodiment of Jalzeer's soul.

Even without eyes and mouth, the entity belonging to Jalzeer's soul stared at the companions.

"You foolish mortals!" the entity said, showing what almost looked like a mouth. The voice of the entity sounded much different from before. It sounded now as if it choked on its own vomit. "Foolish, foolish mortals, do you not know what I am?"

"A disease—an abominable plague upon Eythreal," Rajur said.

Jalzeer laughed, his laugh being grotesquely worse than his spoken words. "Maybe I am. Maybe I'm not. But this shall ring true. Not one of your pitiful weapons will be able to end me. I will find another place to burrow. I will not end here."

"No," said the voice of Huron. "You will end here, for I am no mortal. And the weapon I wield is no mortal's weapon."

Jalzeer's unseen eyes looked past the companions and stared at Huron.

"It cannot be! I released you, crypt keeper."

"I have been called back. Someone . . . something has called me back."

Before Jalzeer could say another word, Huron swung his morning star and crushed the amorphous thing, sending Jalzeer's soul where it belonged: the Harrowing.

An explosion of bright light where Jalzeer's soul last resided illuminated the entire crypt. As the light slowly dimmed, each decrepit torch burned with a translucent bluish flame. Along with that, the four candles that had already been burning turned from a yellow-and-amber glow to the same translucent bluish glow. As for the rest of the crypt, every single corpse of the dead turned to ashes, and these ashes, scorched by the radiance of the explosive light, vanished along with the thick fog that layered the surface. And as this explosive light completely faded away, the companions found themselves surrounded by countless ghosts.

"We thank you," came a single, powerful voice—the voice of all the dead infused into one. "We are now free—free to claim our last home."

The ghostly silhouettes of the dead vanished. Huron turned to the companions. "My gratitude to every one of you. What you have done cannot be measured by anyone. Thank you. And you, Timothy—"

"You know my name?"

"How can I not? It was you and especially what you carry that brought me back. And this I can tell you. I know many things, for I am not just old—I am ancient."

Hearing that said, Rajur's eyes grew large.

Huron continued. "I came here, Timothy, not long after this old river possessed this land. I came here to rest my Everlasting Peace. This wraith must have been driven out from somewhere else, for he was strong when he came here—strong to come here and interrupt my Everlasting Peace. Given up on my rest, I had no one to call for help. No shout of mine could be heard by any mortal being. And for others that are not mortal, they have long been deaf to each of our cries for help. I was forced to surrender my Everlasting Peace to his wicked demise and be imprisoned for a time I could not imagine.

"But you, Timothy, I felt. I sensed you near me. The closer you came, the more life you gave back to me. What seeps from you is a strength for some that could prove detrimental to all Eythreal, for good . . . and bad. And as for the rest, I also felt you. There is much in each of you, including the one waiting for you not far from here, above the surface of this river, Sarah of Cyrcle. You, Rajur, need no introduction. And Zachary, yes, Zachary, I know of you also. Do not go in the ways of anger. As your journey proceeds, so will you understand why it is you are here."

"You know all this about us?" Timothy said.

"If Iria knows it, then so do I."

Rajur's already large eyes loomed larger.

Huron stared deeply into those eyes.

"You reflect too much," Huron said. "Do not overthink. Stay on course, and all will be revealed to you. As for you, Timothy, you're owed a reward. This reward I give you is a shard of my Everlasting Peace. You will always want to be in possession of the item. I suggest wearing it as a necklace, which best suits it. It will prove to be devastating to the enemies you may face. But I cannot always promise its presence. And I certainly cannot promise its presence even when you call for it. And call for it whenever you need it. Use it then when encircled by the worst of your enemies and the troubling fears of what awaits. Call for its presence and pray that the light of the item glows. But most importantly, my Everlasting Peace will invariably want its rest."

Huron nodded after saying that. He took a step back.

"I must leave now. For too long has my rest been disturbed. For too long has that ill creature kept me from my Everlasting Peace."

Huron took another step back again and vanished.

"But not anymore," came the last of his fading words. "Thanks to all of you."

~

The last words faded away, and Zachary turned to the coffin a few feet away.

"I imagine we'll find this shard in there," Zachary said, pointing to the coffin.

Rajur nodded his head. "But it won't be easy."

"Why is that?"

"Because the lid closed upon it. Good luck trying to—"

Zachary didn't give Rajur a chance to finish his sentence before placing both hands upon the lid and, with much ease, sliding the lid over.

"You were about to say?" Zachary said. "Weakling. Maybe he needs a few days at our farm. What do you think?"

Timothy smiled and nodded.

The three stepped up to the open coffin. They looked in.

No corpse resided inside the coffin. But a thick necklace with a single *cracked* amulet rested neatly upon a cushion of fabric inside the coffin. The amulet had a dull bluish surface to it. The crack looked to be in thirds. Rajur lowered his hands into the coffin and grasped the necklace. He extended the necklace to Timothy.

"This is what I'm supposed to wear?"

"It is what he wanted," Rajur said.

"Then I will wear it," Timothy said, taking the necklace from Rajur's hand and placing it over his neck. "It will rest alongside the stone I share with my sister. It will become *almost* as important to me."

"What do you think it is?" Zachary said. "And all that talk about its presence and glowing?"

"I don't know much about that," Rajur said. "I do know by touching it that it's not made of Eythreal. No elf, dwarf, or sorcerer could have wrought it."

"Who, then?"

"If I knew, I'd tell you."

"OK," Zachary said. "But if you had one guess . . ."

"One guess?" Rajur said.

"Yes, only one. What would it be?"

"Fine," Rajur said. "I'll play along."

After a silent second went by, Rajur continued, "Did you catch him saying he's not old, instead . . . *ancient*?"

Both boys nodded.

"Well, that is my guess."

"What does that mean?" Zachary said.

"It means I don't expect you to understand."

"Why?"

"Why? Because I've never spoken about it before."

"We're listening now."

"I see that. But there isn't much to say."

"Say what you know."

Rajur smiled at the boy's tenacity. He nodded his head. "Huron makes me wonder about old lore—something unfathomable for most to believe in. This old lore has everything to do with Iria and her Seven Moons. And if true, it makes much sense to Eythreal while confusing what we thought had already made sense."

"Like what you just did to us," Zachary said.

Rajur almost smiled. "Yes. Confusing. But this I must say! It will prove to be a great folly of yours if you share the presence of this amulet with anyone outside your closest companions. I may not know what it is, but that does not mean others may not. And even if they don't know what it is, curiosity alone could spark an interest we don't want. It will drive ones close to our business. And as for the glow, I'm sure we'll learn about it at some point. For now, that is not the time. It is only time for us to leave Huron to his Everlasting Peace."

"Thank Iria!" Zachary said. "It's starting to get a bit stuffy in here."

Zachary noticed the two staring at him.

"What?"

Rajur smiled. "Yes. Thank Iria."

~

The companions departed the crypt and arrived inside the grotto. They did not hesitate while stepping into the water and swimming down. Once through the cavern, they swam up and reached the surface of the Annieby. The morning had fully made its appearance when their heads popped up. The Star of Nod could be seen in its complete circular shape. They looked to the east and spotted the ferry anchored on the side of the river that they aimed to reach. They even spotted Sarah sitting upon the peaceful river's edge, petting Butch while the steeds chewed on grass.

Seeing the three, Sarah waved.

The three swam toward her, enjoying the last of the water before heading on land.

When stepping out of the water, the boys again marveled at the dryness of their clothes and bodies. They bowed their heads in gratitude toward Sarah.

"Thank you," Rajur said.

"Yes," Timothy said. "That was—"

"Perfect timing!" Zachary said.

"I wish I could have done more," Sarah said. "But to penetrate whatever walls surrounded you proved very, very trying—nearly too difficult. It was like trying to break down a castle wall with your fist alone. Jalzeer must have placed a fortified charm on his surroundings, something very powerful to empower the walls. But it is strange, for even a strong wraith does not have power like that. Something else must have resided in that place. Something . . . I don't know. Regardless, it took much of my strength to break through. But I succeeded. Yes. And then I saw the souls rise from the surface of the water, and I felt better. I felt a wave of strength flow through me. I felt fully recovered. They then smiled. They thanked us. Hanns was most appreciative. And when they vanished, I swear I felt something else enter and pass through me. Was it Jalzeer? I don't think so. It felt anything but evil. I think it was whatever empowered the place you three went to. Maybe you can help fill in the blanks."

"Crypt," Rajur first said. "A very spacious and once magnificent-looking crypt."

"Yes. I am right, for I felt it was a tomb or something like that, not Jalzeer's."

"No. Not Jalzeer's tomb. Jalzeer did prove to be one of the more powerful wraiths I've encountered. But you are right to think there was a much greater power inside that crypt. And now, it once again rests." Rajur turned to Timothy and nodded.

Timothy responded to the nod by pulling off the necklace and showing Sarah the cracked amulet.

Sarah's eyes came together. "How?" she said, examining the amulet with the faintest touch. "This isn't Eythreal. This isn't even Gailala."

"Gailala?" Zachary asked.

"Godstone," Rajur said.

"Again," Zachary said. "What? Or do I have to remind you we're not from around here?"

"Yes," Rajur said. "I see. Gailala, otherwise known as Godstone, is a nonmetallic mineral found upon Eythreal, except it did not originate on Eythreal. Nor does it ever belong to Eythreal."

"And where does this Godstone come from?"

"We do not know. Somewhere beyond the Realm of Cosmos, I believe."

"The realm of what?"

"Humph," Sarah said. "Aren't you forgetting that that is your conjecture? That most do not believe in it?"

"It is what I believe. And I'm sure you believe the same—at least the belief that it does not originate from Eythreal."

Sarah nodded.

"Anyway," Rajur said. "This stone can be found scarcely upon Eythreal, whether under its surface or in the mountains and so forth—very scarce. But nowadays, they've found a way to materialize it into a synthetic metal form, which we call Orculite."

"Which isn't good," Sarah added.

"No," Rajur said. "It could fast become our doom."

"Why?"

"Because if you believe what I believe in, you know that Gailala is made by the gods and goddess worlds far from here. And to create a replica of what belongs to them only can be our downfall, for we are not meant to trivialize what we are meant to never understand."

Sarah slightly shrugged her shoulders upon hearing that.

"You disagree?" Rajur said.

"I only disagree that we shouldn't be so sure of its origin."

"But not its consequence?"

"The synthetic alloy of Godstone? Orculite? No. I agree. But back to this amulet. How did it come to you?"

Timothy explained to her how it came into his possession.

"Huron?" Sarah said. "As in the spiritual warrior of King Thaddus I of Thrandor?"

"That one," Rajur said.

"Hmm. His lore certainly runs far deeper than most others. Of course, he is no mortal being; but he also isn't an immortal. I do know that he stood by King Thaddus the First until Thrandor paved the way for man and woman on Eythreal. Anything more about him is enshrouded by mystery."

"And the plot of this mystery only thickens," Rajur said.

"What do you mean?"

Rajur described to Sarah the innuendos given to him by Huron.

"Ancient Ones?" Sarah said.

"What are Ancient Ones?" Timothy asked.

"It is the lore I mentioned—what may make sense, only to confuse what already made sense."

"Oh. Yes. That one," Zachary said.

"If he is an Ancient One, then I guess that validates the mythical rumor of there being Ancient Ones," Sarah said.

"Then what those few esoteric scholars and historians said about Ancient Ones must ring true."

"Possibly."

"More than possibly," Rajur said.

"Um," Zachary said. "Mind filling us in?"

Rajur turned to Sarah. Sarah turned to the boys.

"You must understand this very, very important statement. Goddess Iria's arrival here is far beyond anyone's knowledge."

"And that is not only Iria but also her seven moons."

"Am I doing the talking or you?"

Rajur bowed his head.

"But yes, he's right. No one knows anything about the moons. Only they give life to the seeds of mana, which we know very little about too! There are, of course . . . rumors. Some of these rumors speak about the Harvesters of Eythreal when pertaining to the so-called seeds of mana. Some rumors speak of the Ancient Ones regarding the seven moons. Seven Ancient Ones—seven moons. But only a few of these historians and scholars *attempt* to stand by these rumors—very few!"

"What is it about the Ancient Ones they believe?" Timothy asked.

Rajur answered, "It is believed by the very few that Iria brought with her seven guardians, each one of them devoted to the safekeeping of a moon—the safety for all Eythreal. When they came here, Iria had them live on Eythreal and do so in disguise, to blend in with all of Eythreal, for they are not only immortal—they are gods and goddesses. They are not to be known, for they are in a way the embodiment of the Seven Moons of Iria, thus the protectors and guardians of her moons. If they are revealed, it could prove disastrous."

"And you don't believe in this?" Timothy asked Sarah.

"It is hard to believe," Sarah said. "Because I ask myself: Where are they? How come they are not conscious of Eythreal's possible doom?"

"Aye," Rajur said. "What she said is precisely why most scholars, historians, and El-Dahn—El-Dahn being chosen ones that have sanction over particular scrolls and learnings of Eythreal—do not believe in this rumor. Very few believe but they don't go as far as believing the Ancient Ones to be gods and goddesses. They only see them as an Old Power long decayed and forgotten. But seeing Huron so strong after so long being dormant—so long. I'm talking hundreds and thousands of years dormant. It is hard to question this. And why? Why did he show up now? It is not because of us. No. As he said, he felt not only you, Timothy, but what you possessed. He felt the book. The book—a power far greater than any god or goddess—woke him up. Nothing else, not even Iria and her daughters, could wake him up. Only the power invested in you, given to you by that book."

"You make a compelling argument, Rajur," Sarah said. "It's hard to doubt you. But it troubles me if you are right."

"Why?" Zachary asked.

"Where are they? Why haven't they come to fulfill their duty?"

Chapter 8

GLADSON'S GLADE

Following the discussion about the possibility of the Ancient Ones, Rajur led Timothy and the rest upon a path not far from where the ferry resided. This path led them into the second half of the forest they had been traveling through from the other side of the Annieby. And as soon as they stepped foot into this portion of the forest, both boys noticed the difference, so much so that Zachary voiced his observation.

"Just want to point out that this is my least favorite forest. I mean, look at it! It's so dreary, nothing imaginative about it."

"Your imagination is quite young," Sarah said.

"Are you saying it's not dreary?"

"I'm saying—"

"It's definitely dreary," Timothy said.

"See," Zachary said. "Argument over. The question is, why? Why is this forest bleak of life?"

"Gnomes," Rajur said.

"Oh yeah, that again," Zachary said. "But you said we wouldn't encounter them until the glade?"

"That is right. But remember that they sometimes leave their glade and come as far as the river."

"Yes. To hunt down the poor hannies and eat them."

"We don't know that for sure," Sarah said.

"Sounds to me you're in denial."

"Anyways, you're right," Rajur said.

"They do eat hannies?" Zachary said.

"No," Rajur said. "I mean you're right about the gnomes infrequently traveling this far. But that does not mean their possible presence doesn't unnerve creatures from wanting to flourish in this half of the forest."

"Like how their possible presence unnerves you?" Zachary said.

"They don't unnerve me!"

"Oh," Zachary said, with a laugh. "That's a big fat lie. They've been nothing short of a cause of anxiety for you the second I met you. Am I not right?"

Timothy smiled and nodded.

"He does have a point," Sarah said. "You've always fretted about them."

"Rightfully so!" Rajur said, shaking his head. "And you'll see. You'll see firsthand why I wanted us to cross the glade during the earliest hours."

"I'm sure it'll be fine," Sarah said.

"What do you know?"

"Enough," Sarah said. "I've heard much from my town."

"Aye. That's because your visitors fawn over the chance of seeing Lady Nesia—a chance that never comes to them."

"Lady who?" Zachary said.

"The Lady of the Forest," Sarah said.

"The lady Berg spoke about?"

"Aye," Rajur said. "She goes by many names. Most prominent are the Lady of the Forest, Lady Nesia, and Lady Mother of the Tree Horn Forest Fairies. It is said that it was she who brought the life that is now found in what is called Tree Horn Forest. Gladson may be considered the Father of the Gnomes of Tree Horn Forest, but he, along with all his gnomes, belongs to her, just as the fairies do—fairies that cause just as much trouble as the gnomes. But the fairies rarely leave the forest, whereas as you know, the gnomes spread out a bit. But not one gnome or fairy belonging to the forest *ever* leaves Lady Nesia's surroundings. And I mean never."

"Fairies," Zachary said, with a mischievous glee on his face.

"Pesky gnats I like to refer to them," Rajur said.

"Don't call them that," Sarah said. "Although a few wicked fairies are roaming about Eythreal, for the most part, fairies are benevolent, and the Fairies of Tree Horn Forest, I have heard are as benevolent as any fairy. And not to mention, they're reported to be beautiful."

"There is nothing beautiful about them," Rajur said.

"So we may encounter fairies, with the addition of gnomes?" Zachary asked.

"No!" Rajur said. "Our plan is to see neither one of them. Most surely not the fairies! Not the fairies. To see the fairies means . . . I don't want to even speak of that scenario. Skirting around the gnomes will prove to be a difficult task since we are going to be crossing through Gladson's Glade. But may fortune smile upon us. Maybe we'll get lucky and not encounter them."

"Well, that stinks," Zachary said. "And no fun."

"This isn't about fun."

"Got to have fun sometimes."

"Never."

"Wow. I bet where you came from, you had no friends."

"Who needs friends?" Rajur said somberly.

"Exactly."

~

Besides the dreariness of the forest, the companions at least found this path much easier to travel upon. This pleased Rajur, for he didn't have to spur them on as he planned on doing because of losing valuable time under the river. He also didn't have to face many obstacles, namely, the tekers and, of course, what took even more time: the introduction of the hannies. No. Like the boys discerned, very little life could be found in this forest; thus, allowing a smoother journey.

"We've made good time," Rajur said. "We should be reaching Gladson's Glade very shortly. It's still not an ideal time, but it gives us a small window to squeak by without being disturbed. I reckon this could be nearing their nap time, for gnomes love naps besides their ceaseless play—love naps. Let us hope that I am right and they are napping the early afternoon away. Because once they're up, I don't see them not running about and playing, possibly playing in the glade."

"Have you ever thought perhaps they are a nuisance to you only? As if they don't like you?" Zachary asked.

"I doubt that's the reason."

Zachary shrugged his shoulders. "How do we know? They don't sound bad to me."

"Me neither," Timothy said.

"I'd watch what you both say," Rajur said. "You'll regret it—especially if you ever meet Gladson."

"What about Lady Nesia?" Sarah said. "You can't say the same about her. I'm with the boys. I wouldn't mind encountering the gnomes and fairies."

"Then you've changed your tune," Rajur said.

"So I have."

"Foolish—for you say this because of the slimmest of slim chances of meeting Lady Nesia."

"Maybe."

"Get that out of your mind. You'll never meet her. Nobody does."

"Not even you?" Timothy asked.

"Never."

"It all makes sense, then," Zachary said. "You despise these gnomes and fairies because of a grudge you have over them for never meeting this Lady of the Forest."

"A grudge?" Rajur said.

"Or is it jealousy?" Zachary said.

Timothy laughed.

"You two are incorrigible," Rajur said, pressing forth toward the glade. "Let us hurry. We pass along the outskirts of Tree Horn Forest, and we'll soon arrive on Cambridge Road."

"I thought you said we're not taking that road?" Timothy said.

"For the most part, no. But at some point, yes. Once we leave the edges of Tree Horn Forest, we'll cut through and land on an auxiliary path of Cambridge Road, which very few use for many reasons, one of them being the tediousness of finding this path. We'll be on this path for most of our way while also passing through a small village, and because of that, we'll have to camp out for a few nights, possibly three or even four. The path will come to an end, which will be Cambridge Road. Luckily, we won't be on the massively populated Cambridge Road for long because of this auxiliary path."

"So we have some moons ahead of us," Zachary said, deliberately using *moons* over *days*.

"Yes. Sure. *Moons.*"

~

Gladson's Glade finally came into view from their dull side of the forest. From this distance, they noticed no gnome. Even when stepping out of the forest and into the glade, surrounded by a different forest, with a far greater forest ahead, they did not catch sight of a gnome. But they did notice a significant shift when leaving the forest and entering the glade. Life. An abundant amount of energy was found in this glade and the surrounding forest. The boys noticed all sorts of insects, most, if not all of them pretty and delightful to look at, instead of the insects they'd been used to all their life. They noticed many other little winged and land creatures about this glade. They were full of color and vivacity, flying from one garden bush to the next. They also watched bunnies scamper about, not one of them afraid of the companions.

Seeing the rabbits, Timothy felt a chill run up his spine.

This all started with a rabbit. *One. Stupid. Rabbit.*

The chill ran its course, and Timothy kept going. No turning back now.

Outside the animal life, many flowers, plants, vegetables, verdant lawns, and even small green rolling hills spread about the glade.

This was no average glade.

This was Gladson's Glade.

In the center of the glade, a watering well caught the boys' attention.

"A well by its lonesome in the center of this fantastical glade. I wonder . . ." Zachary said.

"Don't wonder too much," Rajur said.

"You know what I wonder?" Zachary said.

"I have a grave feeling what you do."

"What do you wonder?" Timothy asked.

"Well," Zachary said. "What if it isn't a watering well? What if it is disguised as one? This is a magical world. Couldn't it be a—"

"No!" Rajur shouted. "It can't. And you're not in a magical world. You're walking on a world that has the source to—"

"Yes, yes," Zachary said, "whatever you say. But I think my guess is right, by the harsh tone of your voice. You betray yourself, Rajur."

"It was not a harsh tone."

"So says you," Sarah said. "The boy is right. You grew angry at his supposition."

Zachary smiled. "Let's go find out if I'm right!" he said.

Before Zachary could move another step, Rajur took him by the shoulder.

"OK. Fine. How you guessed it so easily amazes me. But yes, it is not exactly a watering well. It is a wishing well. And I recommend you not trifling with it."

"Why?"

"Because it does the wishing for you."

"You mean . . ."

"It means you have no choice in the matter. The wishing well decides what wish yours is to be."

"Huh," Zachary said, "interesting, far more interesting than before. Thanks!"

"I wouldn't be so interested in it," Rajur said. "The wishing well measures the importance of what you give. Give something it doesn't agree with . . . Do you see where I'm going with this? A wish you may not want in a million years may come true at the worst time."

"Then I guess I'll have to be smart about it."

"No. It's not that easy. You don't know what value that item has on Eythreal or yourself. Drop an average coin in the well, and you'll receive a coin's worth of a drop. Drop a thousand coins, and you'll receive the same. But drop the very last coin in your wallet, one that you worked hard for, one that will determine whether you starve or not, you may receive something equivalent to a thousand coins or more. It is the measure of what the gift means to you and, of course, what it means to Eythreal—and these measures are very hard for one to comprehend. For example, I know someone who came to this well and dropped a rusty, old, dull dagger. This dagger was worth zero currency in Ghalia or any other market town. But this dagger, mind you, was the very last possession this good man had to defend against any robbers, bandits, highwaymen, and so forth, although he never expected to encounter one of these villains. Inside the wishing well it went. And off he traveled to Ghalia to sell what he could, thus placing him in dangerous places unprotected.

"Well, believe it or not, camping one night, he was assailed by three thieves, thieves thinking he had much merchandise on him. Forgetting he gave away his only weapon to defend himself, he searched for his dagger and found a shiny and sharp sword, polished shield, and chain mail situated not far from him, each of them, I'm sure, an item once dropped in this well. Before the assailants jumped him, he was afforded the time to dress and give battle. He defeated each of them and not only that, but he also found a surplus of food in his knapsack, a knapsack that had only a crumb of bread left. And lastly, a small case of jewelry to be sold was placed near where he found the weapon and armor. All items coming from the well.

"Now, if that dagger meant more to Eythreal, well . . . who knows what he'd have found. But then again, his survival probably meant *much* to Eythreal, for he was no ordinary man."

Sarah looked at Rajur. "You do know by telling them that story, they now want to see this well more than ever."

Rajur perceived his mistake. "I wish you wouldn't throw anything in," Rajur said. "It could turn into a big blunder."

"Don't worry," Timothy said, taking Abigail by the reins. "We're only curious."

Zachary took Breeze by the reins, and the two hurried over to the watering well. Reaching it, they heard water swirling far below.

But upon looking down, they saw no water.

"It's mana," Sarah said. "And a lot of it too."

"Like your fountain?" Zachary asked.

"In a sense, but this mana is purer. It is why you don't see water as you do when it comes to my fountain. I'm the one that did that. I augmented the mana with my own enchantment. Of course, my fountain had been a source of mana long before I did that. I only took advantage of finding the spot and strengthened it. This mana you sense has never been diluted, strengthened, or altered. Its pristine form naturally makes it stronger."

"Your fountain was made by you but had already been a great source of mana? Like one drilling for water, only to end up with a pool of mana?"

"Yes," Sarah said. "It is why I made the fountain the center of my town."

"What about this well?" Zachary said.

Sarah looked to Rajur. Rajur shook his head.

"Some say the gnomes made the wishing well—which I highly doubt."

"Can anyone steal or drain this mana from here?" Zachary asked.

"No. One can only assimilate mana—like what we're doing this very second."

"But you can enhance objects, namely weapons and armor that absorb the mana, right?" Timothy asked. "Isn't your fountain like that?"

"Absolutely," Sarah said. "My fountain is one large, beautifully made device that absorbs mana, just like your weapons and armor. But never, ever do your weapons or armor, or my fountain, come close to draining or stealing mana. They are only enchanted devices, enchanted items that rely on the source of the owner's ability to assimilate mana. The fountain relies on what I placed into it, thus the strength of my enchantment, while the weapons and armor rely on you boys' mana strength. Thus, one with very little strength in absorbing mana may not come close to using the true value of the enchantment of the weapons or armor. They'll receive only what comes from the weapons or armor, but nothing else. You boys, well, you boys, I've got a feeling, are only going to augment the enchantment of those items."

"Are there any weapons or devices that drain or steal mana?"

Both Rajur and Sarah turned to each other.

"Let us hope not."

"For now," Rajur said.

"What do you mean by that?"

"Well," Sarah said. "'Not yet' is what Rajur means. Not even Camus has a weapon that drains or steals away mana. But some say—"

"Tales," Rajur said. "But possibly tales that will come true. About powerful individuals attempting to find a way to steal the presence of mana from Eythreal."

"But doesn't Camus do that already?" Zachary said. "You said that he is only strong with the gems?"

"Because he's absorbing his own power taken from him."

"But right there," Zachary said. "Somebody took his powers away. The gems stole—"

"Yes," Rajur said. "I see your point. The gems are a device. The gems . . . I can only say that the gems stole his ability to assimilate mana by absorbing it."

"What about Abbigatha?" Timothy said. "You say she's in a catatonic state due to being bereft of the gems."

"Yes. Yes, to that too. But she placed her entire essence into the gems. Willing or not, it wasn't stolen."

"Or was it?" Sarah asked.

Rajur did not argue back.

"It sounds like you two cannot guarantee that there are not already objects—devices—on Eythreal that can steal or drain one's mana."

"Zachary has a point," Sarah said.

"Yes," Rajur said. "A grave point. The machinations of these three gems are beyond all of Eythreal's scope together. What I can say is that . . ."

Rajur could only shrug his shoulders.

"The gems are a mystery to us all," Rajur said, "just like why Camus lost only his ability to absorb mana when possessing the gems and he did not fall into a catatonic state like Abbigatha. Why? Why to so many questions regarding the gems."

"Yes," Sarah said, "so much of Eythreal is a mystery for even the greatest lore masters."

"Like this wishing well," Zachary said.

"Like this wishing well," Sarah said.

"The very reason why we shouldn't trifle with it, for it must be older than the gnomes."

"Older than Gladson?"

"Gladson? Old One? Maybe, maybe not. Gladson's origin is as inscrutable as giants'."

"Did you say *giants*?" Zachary said.

"Extinct," Rajur said, "long before our time."

"But not forever," Sarah chimed in.

"What about extinct is not forever?" Rajur said sharply at Sarah.

"The part when *extinct* is used incorrectly."

"And what word would you have me use?"

"*Asleep*," Sarah said.

Rajur smiled and shook his head.

"Something tells me they've had this argument before," Zachary said. Timothy nodded.

"Well, here we are," Rajur said, staring at the wishing well. "You came. You saw. Let us go."

"Go?" came a deep, venerable old voice. "Go?" the voice said again. "But you just got here. How could you possibly go so soon?'

Sarah and the boys tracked the voice from within the well. They stepped closer to the well and looked down through the hole while a perturbed Rajur stayed put. While looking down, the three saw nothing but air, with what looked to be floating flakes far below and the sound of swirling mana. The floating flakes were far too deep to touch with their hands. They pulled their heads out of the well and looked confounded at one another.

"I swear the voice came from there," Zachary said.

The three shrugged their shoulders and stepped back.

"It had to have come from there," Timothy said.

Looking at the perturbed Rajur, they heard the voice again, coming from inside the well. "Why go when you haven't even made a single wish?"

This time, the three hurried faster and looked down the well. Rajur continued to stay put, seeming more perturbed than before.

"I don't see him," Zachary said.

"Me neither," Timothy said.

"He must be—" Sarah said, but she was interrupted.

"It's because I'm not down there, silly," the old, venerable voice said. "Up here!"

Rajur shook his head peevishly while the three others looked above at the awning of the well.

Nothing.

"He's not there," Zachary said.

"Say something again," Timothy said.

"Something again," the voice said from behind them.

The three turned around and saw only the glade.

"He's playing you for fools," Rajur said.

"Who?" Zachary said.

Rajur shook his head. "And to think even you fell for this," he said with eyes on Sarah.

"Gladson," Timothy said.

"Gladson?" came the voice. "But that's my name."

The companions now tracked the voice to the bucket above the well's opening and hanging down from the awning.

Not a minute ago, the bucket had been empty. But now, after they heard the voice, Gladson, father of the gnomes of Tree Horn Forest, popped out of the bucket. Eyes wide and big, the gnome stared at the four. He looked hoary and old to the boys and far more diminutive than any man. Gnomes were small, smaller than a dwarf. Gladson sported a silvery-white beard, the beard showing more youth than any part of him. A green pointy hat, tilted downwards as if bent, rested upon his head. He wore a forest-green vest and a long-sleeved shirt, and each sleeve rolled up to the elbows. Over the vest was a sleeveless red coat, unbuttoned and not afraid to expose his vast and paunchy little belly. As for pants, he wore what looked to be pajamas, and these pants were a vibrant red hue. The boots he wore were pointed and straight as an arrow. The boots' color matched that of the vest.

Gladson smiled while staring at the companions. His smile could not be anything but genuine, especially with eyes being azure, a pinkish skin tone, and bright rosy-red cheeks that intensified his white and silvery beard.

"He looks like a miniature elf," Zachary said. "Where are the rest of your elves, elf?"

"Elf?" Gladson said, startled. "I'm not an elf. I'm a forest gnome, and a very old one."

"Looks like an elf to me."

"Not an elf, not an elf. Gladson. That's me. *Me*! Father of the gnomes of Tree Horn Forest."

"So we've heard," Zachary said. "We've also been told you're a bit of a nuisance."

"What? No, not a nuisance, not a nuisance," Gladson said, with eyes on Rajur. "Did he tell you that? I think he did. Only he could. But don't listen to everything he says. He can be very moody and sad. Sad, Rajur. So, so very sad. Never wants to play, always in a hurry. Hurry, hurry, hurry. Hurry has no time for happiness. Playing with gnomes invariably brings happiness. Yes. Yes. I'm Gladson. Me! Father of the—"

"Yes," Timothy said. "You've told us already.

"So I have. Good. Great. *Wonderful!* Now let's play!"

"No," Rajur said sternly. "We're not playing."

"See?" Gladson said. "Moody and mean and sad," Gladson said, mimicking a sad clown's face. "Ruining fun for everyone. But they want to play! We all want to play."

"No, we don't," Rajur said. "What we do want is a safe passage through your glade and along the outskirts of the forest—without being hassled. Can you do that for us? I'm asking nicely, Gladson. I've never asked this nicely before. Please. This journey—" Rajur said and stopped. "This journey is of much importance. And time is crucial for us all."

"Hassle?" a downcast Gladson said. "When have we been a hassle to you?"

"Fine," Rajur said, lying through his teeth. "You've never been a hassle. But I'd feel better if you and your gnomes let us be on our way."

"Off to Ghalia Trade Center?"

"Is it any of your business to know?"

Gladson smiled. "Long trip from here."

"There's been worse."

"And traveling only on your feet?" Gladson asked.

"We're not on our feet the whole time. We have our—"

Rajur stopped. He knew even without turning around to discover the veracity of what Gladson said. With a scowl on his face, Rajur asked, "Where are the steeds, Gladson?"

Gladson responded in bewilderment. "Me? You're asking me? Me about your steeds? Gladson, father of the gnomes of Tree Horn Forest? But I've been here with you the whole time."

"What are you talking about?" Timothy asked Rajur.

"Turn around," Rajur said.

The boys and Sarah turned around to find only Butch—not the horses. But Butch wasn't exactly alone. Three playful gnomes, dressed in the same attire as Gladson, shared their playful zealousness with Butch as they tickled, caressed, and scratched the dog's belly, while Butch loved it so much that he could not stop himself from rolling around the grass.

No horses could be found in the rest of the surroundings.

"Abigail?" Timothy shouted.

"Breeze?" Zachary shouted.

"Don't waste your voices," Rajur said to the boys. He turned to Gladson sharply—and angrily. "Now you listen to me, Gladson. I want those steeds back here now! Not later. Now."

Gladson put up both hands in a show of peace. "Be nice. Be kind. Be p-l-e-a-s-a-n-t," he said, with the last word spoken in a drawn-out fashion. "Your steeds are in good hands. Nothing has happened to them. They're being cared for as we speak since they have been conveyed to the village, where food and rest await them. They're awfully famished and weary. Did you know? Those are some beautiful creatures. Need to be a bit more careful with them, especially when they don't belong here," Gladson said with a wink of an eye. "But don't worry. Gladson looks out for you. I look out for everyone. I have done you a good deed—one friend to another. I've taken the steeds and given them what they need because we are friends, such excellent friends. Now, if you don't mind, why don't you, your two special friends there, along with their special pet, and that even more majestically beautiful special guest we've imagined for so very long to meet finally," Gladson said, with his eyes on Sarah, "follow me to the village. I'll show you firsthand what I've done to your steeds and, more importantly, how pleased they are. You can unburden yourselves there and stay with us for supper."

"No," Rajur said.

"What do you mean no?"

"I mean no. You just call those gnomes back that took away our steeds."

Gladson shrugged his shoulders. "Sorry. No can do. I know no gnome that took away your pets. And whoever did take them has gone too far to be heard. Guess we'll be going to the village after all."

Rajur turned to the three companions. "You see? This is why I make it a priority to time it right when crossing through this Iria-forsaken glade."

Gladson giggled. His concentration fell upon Sarah. "I spoke nothing but the truth about you and how wonderful it is to meet you finally," Gladson said to Sarah.

"Likewise," Sarah said, flaunting an elegant bow.

Gladson's rosy-red cheeks flamed brighter as he blushed. His blushing led to taking his cap off and trying to hide his face inside it. This excitement over Sarah's beauty and elegant bow proved more than just a blush, for he proceeded to jump and skip in the air many times, each time landing back in the bucket, and even finding a way to dance inside the bucket while crying out, "She likes me. She likes me. She really, really, really, really, really, *really* likes me."

Gladson's sprightliness impressed both the boys and Sarah. Sarah could only giggle in response to Gladson's smitten feelings for her.

"I'll say this," Zachary said. "The old man clearly knows how to dance."

"Dance?" Gladson said, lively. "I love to dance."

"It's not whether they can dance," Rajur said. "It's whether they know how to stop dancing. It's all they do—sing and dance and drink."

"Exactly," Gladson said. "We're forest gnomes. We're supposed to be a bunch of merrymaking, silly fools."

"Too merry," Rajur said, "and far too silly."

"Say what you want, but how can there ever be too much merriness and silliness in this world we live in?"

"When it is time to be serious and take action," Rajur said.

"As I said," Zachary said. "No friends where he came from."

Rajur grinned at Zachary.

"I like how the boy thinks," Gladson said. "What's your name?"

"Zachary."

"Zachary what?"

Zachary looked quizzically at the gnome. "Youngblood?" Zachary said.

"Family name. But what about a signal? What is your position? Where are you from? Azaarath? If so, what kingdom? What town? What province? Where are you actually from, Zachary?"

"Where he's from is not your business to know," Rajur said. "Give us our steeds back, and we'll be on our way."

"You can have them once you join us at Tree Horn Village for festivities."

"There'll be no festivities for us," Rajur said.

Gladson ignored him and turned to Timothy. "And who might you be?"

"Timothy," Rajur said on behalf of Timothy.

"Does the grumpy Rajur speak for you?"

"No," Timothy said.

"What is your name?"

"Timothy."

"And?"

"Huntsinger," Timothy said. "And yes, he's Zachary Youngblood. We don't have a signal name, nor do we have a rank."

"Nor do we have a town or province we hail from," Zachary said, setting aside the joviality.

Gladson grinned mischievously. "So I'm right. Even though I never did doubt myself. But now it's confirmed. You two are not from around here. Now that begs the question where. Where must you be from?"

Before anyone answered, Rajur answered by leaving behind his angry and irksome look and replacing it with a sterner and more serious one. One could find no trivial matter in this look. One could find death and despair if ever crossing this look. He also answered by slipping his left hand into the custom-made gauntlet, which he took off as they strode peacefully along the path, and with this gauntlet on, his hand braced the sheath of one of his Moon Beams, creeping closer to unsheathe the weapon. Again, he did not stare at Gladson with any sort of anger. He didn't even stare threateningly at the gnome. The action of readying his weapon alone spoke volumes far more daunting than anything else. Rajur cared not for the consequences of ridding himself of what could prove to be a problem, although he hoped to Iria it would not come to that.

Gladson read this look entirely well.

A second or two after a stare-off between gnome and warrior, the latter said, "They're with me."

"And me," Sarah said, also having ditched her earlier benevolent and enlivened mood. She now elevated her staff from off the ground.

Gladson never changed his merry looks. But if one stared closely, they'd have seen a change.

"Yes," Gladson said apathetically. "So they are. Very good."

Gladson looked down into the bucket and back up at the companions. He continued to smile merrily, but his looks now obviously changed—a bit wounded. The following words he spoke were furthest from the merry tone from before. No sign of impassiveness could be found in it either. Instead, his tone and demeanor nearly matched the razor-sharp sternness of Rajur's while also matching the sincerity of Sarah's. When he spoke next, his words came out in a powerful voice, although much lighter—more like a whisper, but a whisper that carried a force to be reckoned with.

"I am not your enemy, Rajur."

"I never said you were. But one confuses the other by being an obstacle in their path."

"Yes," Gladson said. "Well, I don't mean to be an obstacle, either. I only wonder. Where and why. And how am I not supposed to think that after what we felt some moons ago?"

"Aye. I'm sure you did feel it. But if you did feel it, then I'm also sure you may know what it was, and if that is true, then you should know it is something not to be discussed with any of us."

Seeing that Rajur spoke the truth, Gladson felt defeated, and in doing so, his smile returned to the jovial and merrymaking one.

This smile gave relief to the companions.

"You're right," Gladson said. "And when you're right, you're right!"

Falling back into his frolicsome ways, Gladson skipped and danced in the bucket for a few seconds, only to end up jumping out of the bucket and landing beside the companions.

The gnome stood a little over three feet tall.

Rajur shelved his determined look as he also slipped off the gauntlets. Sarah also dissolved her conviction, and her staff lazily fell to the ground.

"Then I must say it is good to meet you both," Gladson said, extending his surprisingly large hand to the boys.

Before Rajur could stop them, Zachary returned the favor and shook Gladson's hand.

Gladson smiled in triumph. "Yes. A handshake. Something we do so *little* on *Eythreal*," the gnome said. "Wouldn't you say?" he asked Rajur with a wink of an eye.

Defying reality, Rajur smiled, seeing the gnome best him this time.

"And you," Gladson said to Timothy. "Do you share the same courteous greeting?"

Timothy lowered his body and extended his hand. When he did so, both the stone and amulet showed themselves to the gnome.

Gladson gently pulled Timothy down by tugging on his sleeves. The gnome went to grab one of the necklaces.

"What are these?" he asked.

Timothy quickly pulled back in time, fearing which one, and Gladson failed to grasp a necklace.

"This one?" Timothy said, showing off the amulet received from Huron. "Oh. It's nothing, just a gift."

"No, silly," Gladson said. "The other one! The one with a rope that is not made from here. But shh . . . We won't tell anyone. It'll be our little secret. What a beautiful stone it is. And the stone, like the fibrous string used for a necklace, not from around, only, well . . . it does have a little of Eythreal, maybe a little of everything."

Timothy felt relieved that the gnome had no clue about the amulet given to him by Huron. But he also sensed a threat to his most prized possession.

"What about it?" Timothy said defensively.

"It is not complete," Gladson said. "It is missing another . . . *half.*"

Trying to be indifferent, Timothy shrugged and said, "So?"

"So? It's not complete. It needs the other. Without it—"

"I gave it to someone else."

"Someone very important?"

"The dearest person to me."

"Uh. And who—"

"My sister."

Saying the word *sister* brought back some stored-away emotions. Timothy's eyes became glossy.

"Yes. Your sister, a very dear person to you. And where is—" Gladson stopped himself upon seeing how wrecked the boy became. "I'm sorry. I truly am."

Timothy nodded. "It's OK. I'll get her back. I'll get them all back. But until then, well, this is the most important item of mine. It's the last thing I have of family."

"Yes," Gladson said. "I sense that. But the stone . . . The importance is . . . very important."

"To me, right?" Timothy said, continuing to grip the stone.

Gladson shrugged his shoulders. His eyes turned to Zachary. "You too possess something you don't know how vital it is. But you'll need it. Yes. You'll need it at the very right moment. But as far as"—his eyes returned to Timothy—"that stone . . ."

"What about it?"

"Hmm," Gladson said, acting as if he pondered deeply when, in fact, he knew the answer far before reaching this point. He looked gleefully at Timothy. "Make a wish!"

"What?" Timothy said.

"What, what? I said make a wish."

"I know what you said."

"Good. Now make a wish."

"Inside this well?"

"You see any other well?"

"It's just," Timothy said, "Rajur told us about this well."

"Great. Make a wish."

Timothy's grip on the stone became more protective than ever before. "No," he said.

"No?" Gladson looked puzzled. "But, Timothy, if you know how this well works, then you must know how great a wish this could prove to be. Make a wish. Throw the stone and necklace down the well, and the wish will be made."

Hearing that atrocity angered Timothy. "Did I not tell you how important this stone is to me?"

"Yes, you did. And I thank you very much for that. It was wise of you, for it strengthens my belief even more on how wise it would be of you to make a wish."

"No," Timothy said, shaking his head. "No. And never will it be anything but no."

"But why?" Gladson said.

"Because of exactly what I said. It is the last remnant of my family, the promise I gave to my sister, my . . . my entire life. It is all I have left," Timothy said, with the return of the glossy eyes.

Gladson stared profoundly at the boy. He wanted to continue to gnaw away at the boy, but he also saw more steel in the boy than he first thought. Regardless of the wish's importance, Gladson felt he could do no more.

"OK. Suit yourself," he said frivolously as if his earnest pleading was only a whim. "It is not me on the path you're traveling upon. I can only do so much."

Gladson sauntered past the companions and joined the three gnomes petting Butch. "Such a good dog," Gladson said, petting Butch, "even if he doesn't come from this world. Oh well."

Seeing Gladson at peace, Timothy walked over to him. "I'm sorry. I know you were trying to help. But it is a request I cannot grant you. Or ever will," Timothy said.

Gladson again shrugged his shoulders frivolously. "How about this—at the very least?" Gladson said. "Be a good sport and indulge us in spending the rest of the Star of Nod and the early part of the evening at our village. I promise you'll receive the best of rest from your weary travel. By Iria, we've already prepared a festival for your coming, for we've known of this moment for about six moons to this very day. You do understand that? You do feel a sort of mystique about these surroundings? I thought so. Good. The festival will be merry and the food a delight. So come. Come all. Let us show you how our Lady of the Forest takes care of the most honorable guests to step foot in her forest. And can I imagine that these boys have never laid eyes on a fairy or gnome until this moment?"

"Only in books and puzzles," Zachary said.

"Only in books and puzzles! Ha! Well, we are a sort of puzzle. So you'll come."

"No," Rajur said flatly.

Gladson loosened his shoulders and stared at Rajur. "Your stern and determined nature far exceeds you, great Rajur. And I most highly respect you for it. But in this, you must take a step back. You," Gladson said, staring at Timothy. "You are the one to decide. Yes. This I feel. What you possess must be led by your choices and decisions. Yes. Clear as day to me—and not too clear to many others, so don't get all fearful. But this I know. The decision falls on you, Timothy. So I ask, is it wonders you want to see? If it is . . ."

Gladson waved his hand in the air. And as his hand waved through the air, specks of fairy dust fell sparkling from his hand, and yet, not one of these glistening particles touched the ground. The fairy dust continued to pour from his waving hand, more in slow motion than in real time, and afterward, as the particles thickened and came together, they formed a blurry image for the companions to behold.

The blurriness of this image became clear. It depicted what would be Tree Horn Village. Thus, the boys stared in wonder at a single tree, far greater than any tree possible to be imagined, and a tree the size of hundreds or more trees coming together to form one. This included branches that stretched out to be a mile or longer. And upon these branches, built into the fabric of the tree, were doors, which led to homes the gnomes and fairies lived in.

The doors, especially the branches, were also used as paths and bridges for all to wander about. Porches, verandas, and other common places could also be seen, neatly arrayed and wrought by the gnomes, along with the addition of firepits and chairs to sit upon around the fire. The fires of these pits had no consequences for the forest, for they were a part of Lady Nesia's magic. Even inside the dwellings, one could discover fireplaces and hearths.

Upon the tree's highest point, hundreds of feet above the forest floor, a grand gazebo resided, the largest gazebo of the many others shared by the gnomes and fairies. Young, old, male, and female gnomes danced, sang, and played upon this gazebo, along with a live musical band. Many more gnomes were scampering about the tree, working on their daily duties. Whether the work looked tedious to the boys or not, the gnomes made fun out of everything they did, for there was no gnome to be found anywhere on the tree without their merrymaking demeanor.

This manifestation lasted for a long minute, and when the fairy dust dispersed, so did the image. Gladson's hand returned to his side.

But the image proved indelible to the boys' minds. And it only grew in wonder. They witnessed the greatest of feasts, enjoyed upon a single table stretching far enough for every gnome to take a seat. At this table, only joy and happiness could be found. And there, yes, there at the head of the table, the boys saw themselves, along with Rajur and Sarah and countless fairies buzzing about, each fairy picking from a gnome's plate of food, and not a gnome thinking to stop them.

They also watched goblets of wine and mugs of mead being passed around. The boys didn't even know what mead tasted of, yet they felt the powerful sensation of the fermented honey concoction.

"So what do you say?" Gladson said. "Want to join us for the day and an evening full of fun?"

Timothy pondered over the pros and cons of going. And as he did, he heard giggling. The giggling sounded like animated mice laughing in his ears. "Fairies," Timothy said, understanding what the giggling came from.

"What?" Sarah asked.

"I hear fairies. There's going to be fairies? Just like what I saw and heard?"

"Well, of course, silly. Who do you think carried away your pets?"

Timothy nodded.

Fairies.

~

Gladson led Timothy and the companions the rest of the way by gamboling through the glade. The three other gnomes also hopped and skipped alongside everyone. Butch kept close to the gnomes, for their jubilant demeanor was contagious and highly addictive. Also, the gnomes ceaselessly gave him attention; thus, Butch became insatiable, unstoppable when it came to wagging his tail as he shifted from one gnome to the next, allowing much love under and behind his ears, and rubbing his tummy the few times Butch just *had to* roll upon the smooth grassy ground. Timothy and the others did nothing like skipping or dancing while passing through the glade. Instead, their attention rested upon the wonders that must be inside the grand forest approaching them.

Except for Rajur. Rajur brooded and sulked his way through the glade.

To his dismay, Timothy chose this. Timothy chose to take a large bite out of their precious and valuable time and use it frivolously. Even though Timothy agreed to spend the day with the gnomes and fairies, along with an early evening supper and nothing more—Rajur knew the evening would turn into much more. Once partaking in the merrymaking of the fairies and gnomes while taking in the entire surroundings of the beauty and magic of the forest, the boys would find it impossible not to stay the night.

For that was Gladson's aim the entire time, Rajur surmised. And it was Gladson's *reason* for the boys to stay the night that worried Rajur.

What does Gladson have in store for us? For Timothy?

On the other hand, Sarah worried much less than Rajur while also feeling no sulkiness over Timothy's decision, even though she sided with Rajur. The boy chose wrong.

But Sarah found herself too enthralled by the chance of meeting Lady Nesia to criticize Timothy's decision. She also didn't worry as much because of her ignorance of how mischievous Gladson could be. However, she understood Rajur's worry after what happened with Gladson coercing Timothy into making a wish with the boy's most prized possession. Also, she wasn't exactly a fan of how Gladson swooped up the steeds without them knowing.

Zachary wanted this more than any one of them—including Timothy. He wanted Timothy to make this decision so much that if Timothy chose otherwise, he had thought—a very weak and transient thought—of going into the forest alone.   Of course, he would never have done such a thing if it came to that.

The boys needed this. The two had made it very far without the sorrow and anger for their lost family and the world eroding their inner spirit. It was their inner spirit that kept them strong—steeled. But it had to be restored. It had to be filled up with happiness at times. It could not be drained of its happiness, or they'd both fall into an empty tank. They'd have nothing left to stop them from succumbing to despair and wretchedness, which would become their inner spirit. And they had made it this far because of the magic of this new world: a magical kingdom to them. It had softened the pain and suffering one invariably feels when losing one's family—not to mention one's entire world.

It had replenished what was lost from their reservoir of inner spirit. But it runs dry. The inner spirit is drained of its essence by each moment. It needs more—and more.

They needed this.

Timothy felt this too. He felt guilty for making what he knew to be the wrong decision. But he just had to.

Choices, another voice, a familiar one, spoke in his mind.

Did I choose right? Are we wasting much time? Time we'll never receive again? And Gladson? Can I fully trust him and his gnomes? Or . . .

Should *I trust them?*

Chapter 9

A MERRY WELCOMING

Only a quarter of a mile remained till the companions reached the start of the forest. And as they neared it, Timothy and Zachary set eyes on what was by far the grandest of forests. Sarah could almost say the same, except for the trip she made long ago to a land where giants once roamed—a land of much importance to her. As for Rajur, he had already seen this forest and even entered it, along with other archaic forests that were far bigger than this forest. But that did not stop him from staring in wonder at the approaching forest.

Along with this sight came an inscrutable sound. Soon, the sound became more conclusive.

Humming. Or buzzing?

"Hummingbirds?" Zachary asked. "Is that what I hear? If it is, there must be millions of them."

"Hummingbirds?" Gladson said. "Sure. We have hummingbirds in our forest. But unless you have hearing like our friend here," Gladson said, winking Rajur's way, "you're not going to hear our hummingbirds so easily, for most of them live very deep in the forest. However, you'll see and hear some in the village, which isn't far from here. What you hear is singing."

"Singing?"

"Yes," Gladson said. "What you hear is the forest singing. The forest knows you're coming. It hums to you. And then there is the gnomes' endless singing. They too know you're coming."

"I hope they know we're coming hungry," Zachary said.

"Hehehe," Gladson said. "I love where this boy has his head at all times. Hungry? Well, well, not to worry."

"Good," Zachary said. "And let us hope hannies are not on the menu tonight."

Rajur found this well said and chuckled. Sarah looked astonished—and amused. Timothy could not hold back his laughter.

Gladson, though, felt like he had been victimized. "Who told you that? Lies! Such scandalous lies they are! We do no such thing. Horrible, just horrible. And just to think if it was true. They hardly have any meat on them."

"Then why is that even I hear those same tales?" Sarah asked. "Are you saying it is one big lie about you sneaking away with hannies?"

"Big lie? Sneaking away adorable and innocent hannies? Misinformed, I'd call it. One giant piece of misinformation."

"But *do you* capture them and sneak them into your forest?" Timothy asked.

Puzzled, Gladson shook his head while also nodding. "It's complicated."

"How complicated can it be? Do you, or do you not?" Zachary asked.

"Humph," Gladson said, seeing all eyes on him. "If we do harmlessly *capture* them—as you so maliciously stated—and bring them to our forest, well, that is for Lady Nesia to give the answer on why. We are at her command. And so are many other creatures that stretch beyond Tree Horn Forest. But I assure you! Oh yes, I 100, and another 100 on top of that, percent assure you that no harm comes to them. I cannot give you a greater promise than that. With all my heart and not a scruple of falsehood, I profess that no harm comes to them whatsoever. What little I can say is that it is for their own good. At some point, yes, you're going to thank us. And not just you folks. The whole of Eythreal may one day thank Lady Nesia."

Gladson stepped up his pace toward the forest, hoping to leave behind the controversial discussion over the hannies' fate. As for the others, they slowed down a bit, pondering over what he said and wondering whom to believe. Except for Rajur—he just didn't care.

Soon enough, though, the subject of the hannies' fate dissolved in their minds as they closed in on the forest while the humming grew louder.

But the humming sound, which Gladson told them was singing, was not alone. Something else, far more prevalent and yet far too difficult to track, could be heard inside the forest as they inched closer. Something that sounded like—

"Is that a horn blasting?" Zachary asked. "Or am I hearing things that aren't there?"

"You're not hearing things that aren't there. That is a horn sound," Rajur said.

"What is it about?" Timothy said.

"What do you mean about?" Gladson said. "It's a horn. We don't call this Tree Horn Forest for no reason. Like some square-shaped town being named Cyrcle."

"Hey!" Sarah said.

Gladson winked at her and gave an irresistible smile, for an old, hoary gnome—a smile that could melt anyone's anger against him.

"But why a horn?" Zachary asked.

This question brought confusion to Gladson's eyes. But upon understanding the meat of the question, Gladson changed his demeanor.

He became impatient and sullen. This change in him became far more obvious than any behavioral change he'd shown so far.

"It is the forest, and nothing else," Gladson said after a long minute. "Now, you just forget about it!" Gladson's pace quickened again toward the forest.

The others watched him, a bit alarmed by his words and change in demeanor. But this alarm of theirs did not last long. They noticed Gladson having returned to his frolicsome ways. Therefore, they attributed his transient petulant mood to the discourse on the hannies and *not* the strange horn sounding through the forest.

~

The companions finally reached the wall of trees of Tree Horn Forest and seeing signs of sparkling flakes floating about the air inside the forest, the boys took their first steps into the forest. Upon doing so, they each felt a faint tingling sensation along their skin.

The boys stopped.

"It is mana," Sarah said. "The forest exudes such a powerful and excessive amount of mana it is palpable to us. I don't think I've ever felt such a surge of mana before. Maybe. Maybe in the earliest times of my life, when I . . ."

The boys waited for her to finish. But seeing she continued to move on in silence, the boys did the same. And as they did, the first of the countless flakes drifting through the air landed on them. Each glistening flake resembled a snowflake, excluding the fact this flake sparkled and could not be dissipated no matter what you did to it. The flakes only continued their endless drift throughout the whole forest.

"Mana?" Zachary asked.

Rajur nodded his head.

"But I thought you said mana has no true physical form?"

"And you're right to say that, my boy," Gladson said.

"Then why are we seeing these flakes?" Zachary asked, opening his hands and allowing one to land.

"These flakes are like my fountain," Sarah said, "an artificial embodiment of mana. But, well, this is—"

"A true essence of mana Lady Nesia manifested into playful, wonderful, sparkling flakes," Gladson said.

"Like how you made water as your embodiment of mana the fountain produced?"

"In the simplest of terms, yes," Sarah said. "But as Gladson said, my fountain is only a *source* of mana, whereas these flakes are mana themselves. And what Lady Nesia did to conjure the mana into flakes makes what I did to my town and forest and fountain child's play—much less than child's play!"

"Oh no," Gladson said. "Don't be thinking or saying that, Sarah of Cyrcle. The enchantment of your forest, town, and so forth is very powerful. I know only a handful of sorcerers or sorceresses who could come close to your conjuration—very few. The difference between the two is that your forest is old, yes, very old, and it borders a much *older* forest. But your forest is not as old as this forest. No. This forest is *old* too. Not to mention, Lady Nesia is *old*, so very old. Some would say she's past being old. So, of course, her assimilation of mana is far, very, very, very far more powerful than yours. I don't know another person on Eythreal that could match her potency when it comes to assimilating mana. But then again, my travels have been scarce."

As if the boys weren't already enthralled, they looked at the forest with greater reverence. In doing so, they endeavored to catch the flakes with their hands and failed each time, as if the flakes had their own mind and never wanted to be captured. They even tried to smash the flakes. Not for violent reasons, only for the same reason any boy or girl would: to play, of course. Thus, they learned that the flakes did not want to be smashed.

"You'll be at it forever," Rajur said, seeing the futility the boys exhibited. "As said before, mana cannot be taken so simply."

The boys nodded and continued their way into the forest. The more they traveled, the more they believed they had crossed into another world, one brimming with magic and wonders, as if they had not already crossed into a new world brimming with magic and wonders. The trees they passed by seemed to belong to giants. And yet, not one of these trees came close to the one shown to them by Gladson. The boys often stopped and examined a tree and its wonder, only for Rajur to spur them on.

Sarah also marveled at this scenery. But she also noticed something else. "The breeze," she said, waving her hand through the air. "It is always so—"

"Calm and soothing," Gladson said.

"Yes. For the nerves. Much more than mine."

Gladson nodded.

"What about rain and other changes in weather?"

"Rain? Sure. We receive what Eythreal also receives. The Star of Nod and the clouds above us are no different from anywhere else. As for the breeze, well, what can I say? Lady Nesia likes to have it calming and soothing at each hour of the day."

"How strange," Sarah said. "How ridiculously powerful this forest is."

~

A mile had passed since Sarah alerted everyone to the soft mystic breeze. The horn continued to wail throughout the forest, never growing louder or weaker, never coming close to exposing where its source resided. As for the humming sound, much had changed. The more the travelers neared their destination, the more the humming sound revealed its true identity.

As Gladson said, the companions heard singing, vague but audible enough to listen to the words being sung.

Up and up, we go.
To the left, to the right, we go.
Down, down, we sometimes may go.
For we are the gnomes of Tree Horn Forest.
And that we are.

For we are the gnomes of Tree Horn Forest.
And that we certainly are.

The last words of the cheerful tune ended. A loud blasting horn sounded off, one not to be confused with the mysterious other that echoed through the entire forest. The companions now passed a portion of the forest that held the thickest and most dense trees, and while doing so, they found themselves nearing a clearing, only for this clearing to give a view of Tree Horn Village. In this view, the boys spied the exact replica of what they saw in Gladson's manifestation. But no imagery of any kind, whether by magic or something else, could come close to matching the true majesty of this single tree. The boys, along with Sarah and Rajur, for this view could never get old, even to Rajur, stood motionless and watched the countless gnomes travel from one spot to the next, all of them in a caper, thus never ceasing to smile, laugh, and sing, never showing the slightest touch of exhaustion, all the while working on one duty after another. Of course, the gnomes were not alone.

Fairies the size of a gnome's hand (which isn't that small since gnomes have great big hands, for their short stature) could be seen everywhere. They too could be found only capering about. They too could be found helping the gnomes prepare for the visitors. They helped mostly by pouring fairy dust everywhere to lighten the gnomes' load when it came to setting up the grand table with chairs and so forth, along with preparing food for the tour through the gnomes' dwellings and helping set up the many gazebos where gnomes and fairies would make merry. The fairies also came and went with drinks and snacks for all the workers while indulging in the wine and drinks and snacks themselves.

And like the gnomes, each fairy sang.

They have come, they have come,
Lady Nesia promised they'd come.
They have come, they have come,
They have come to taste our roasted meat.

They have come, they have come,
They have come to drink our fairy mead.
They have come, they have come,
For Lady Nesia promised they'd come.

Welcome, welcome, all you travelers
Welcome to Tree Horn Forest.
Welcome, welcome, travelers not of Eythreal
Welcome, you have made us so very happy.

Welcome, welcome, O fabled warrior,

Welcome, your presence delights us all.
Welcome, welcome, good-natured witch,
Won't you sing us a few bedtime songs?

For we are the fairies and gnomes of Tree Horn Forest,
And that we are.

The boys continued to goggle at the gnomes and fairies bringing life to the festival. This also included the final setup of the near-endless dinner table: the polishing of a single chair, far bigger than the rest, and one befitting only a queen, with ornaments and decorations blazoned upon it. The boys assumed this grand chair set at the very end of the table belonged to Lady Nesia. This time, they assumed correctly.

The first of many fairies made their way to the companions. The one in the lead landed on Timothy's shoulder.

"Hel-lo," the tiny and exquisitely cute fairy said.

On impulse, Timothy stepped back. He stepped back in fear of harming the fragile little creature, thus showing his ignorance of a fairy's sprightliness and adept nature, plus his ignorance of how tough they could prove to be.

"He must be the one called Timothy," a second fairy said as she landed upon Timothy's other shoulder, this fairy no less exquisite and cute.

"Yes," the first fairy said. "He must be. I sense him all too much," she said while sniffing Timothy as if she could discover his entire life inside a few smells. "Yes. Timothy. For he reeks of Eythreal. How wonderful it is to smell our world. But how horribly tragic it is too."

"Tragic indeed," the second fairy said. "To be so young and handsome, and yet, his burden is the size of a world."

"Our world," the first fairy said.

"Indeed so. Our world exudes from his every pore, like dust pouring from our wings," the second fairy said as she flapped her wings.

Fairy dust of a significant amount poured from her flapping wings.

The other fairy joined in the flapping of the wings while both giggled.

Some of the fairy dust landed on both boys' shoulders. Unlike the flakes of mana found gliding throughout the entire forest, the fairy dust dissolved the second it hit the surface.

The boys watched the dust dissolve upon their skin; afterward, they felt a loss of gravity as if their feet were about to lift off the ground.

"Well?" the first fairy said. "Are you not going to introduce yourself to us formally? Or will we be presuming you to be Timothy the whole time?"

"I'm Timothy," Timothy said bashfully.

"Oh. He's a shy guy," the second fairy said.

"The tallest shy guy I've ever seen, and sturdy-looking," the first fairy said. "I'm Yana," Yana said as she flew off Timothy's shoulder and dropped into his open hand. She twirled about.

"I may be the size of an apple in your hand, but am I not beautiful?" She giggled.

"Yes," Timothy said, continuing to blush.

"How about my jewelry? You like my rings, my necklaces, my wrist bracelets, my earrings, my—"

"Yes," Timothy said. "But isn't it too much?"

"Too much?" Yana shrieked.

"Yeah," Zachary said. "You look like a traveling gypsy we've been told about."

"But far more beautiful, right?"

"Very," Zachary said.

Yana again giggled and swirled in a circle, ending with an extension of her tiny, five-finger hand, each finger home to a shiny ring—possibly to some, a gaudy set of rings.

"Handshake?" Yana asked.

"Um," Timothy said, unsure of what to do.

"Just use your pinky," the second fairy said, flying off Timothy's shoulder and landing upon Zachary's open hand.

Timothy stretched out his pinky finger and touched it against her open hand. A spurt of fairy dust exploded from behind her wings.

"And what another handsome and very muscularly built boy!" the second fairy said. "And you are?"

"Zachary. I'm Timothy's best friend."

"Uh, don't sell yourself short. You're more than that, I *promise*. But it is nice to meet you, Zachary. I'm Magnelia the Fair," she said, extending her hand to Zachary.

Zachary returned the favor with his pinky landing in her hand, only for an explosion of fairy dust to burst from behind her wings.

"You'll meet other fairies named Magnelia. But remember, only *I* am called Magnelia *the Fair*, for I am more beautiful than them."

Zachary nodded his head.

"Now, let's go and meet the rest," Yana said.

A swarm of fairies, far too many to count, came flying toward the boys. Both boys and Butch gaped at the sight of the fairies. One by one, a fairy landed on their shoulders, hands, elbows, chest, anywhere they could find access on the three and introduced themselves. Just as impossible as it was for them to count the number of fairies, the boys found the same difficulty when trying to memorize their names, excluding Magnelia the Fair and Yana, for they both never left the boys' presence.

The endless swarm continued. And believe it or not, it would have lasted much longer if it weren't for Gladson.

"Stop! Enough! You crazy nymphs!" he bellowed.

"Nymphs?" they each shouted in angry protest, hating it when being confused with the much bigger nymphs.

Gladson smiled and shrugged his shoulders, fully aware of how badly the insult pained them.

"They'll never stop," Gladson said to the boys. "And it is high time for you to meet the gnomes of Tree Horn Forest."

The boys' eyes grew large while staring at the tree and the hundreds and hundreds of gnomes making their way toward them.

"You're joking?" Zachary said.

"Joking?" Gladson said. "I love to joke."

"Then you're joking about us meeting them all?" Timothy said.

Gladson kept quiet. The gnomes kept coming.

To their dismay, the boys found it far more exhausting to meet the gnomes, although gathering their names was a bit less challenging. The names of the gnomes were odd and foreign to the boys, as were the fairies', but far less extravagant, superficial, tedious, and at times, confusing, excluding a few of them, like Yana. The gnomes' names were also a bit more interesting to the boys. Some of these names: Sven, Tiptop, Murdok, Laffy, Grr. Yes, a Grrr. And he looked like a Grr.

The boys did take more notice of one gnome over the rest. This gnome went by the name of Petru.

Petru showed no excitement while having to meet the boys. Petru had been coerced into this meeting, by the look on his face.

Gladson even had to shove Petru before the boys and speak for him. "This here, boys, is Petru. Don't mind his silence. He speaks only . . . Well, let us leave it at that. Petru? Say hello to Timothy and Zachary. And their dog, Butch."

Petru's disgruntled look turned shy as he managed a nod.

Timothy smiled back humbly. "Nice to meet you, Petru," Timothy said.

Petru nodded a second time and quickly turned away afterward.

"Don't mind him," Gladson said as they watched the gnome hurry away. "He's an odd one. Even his beard is odd, for it is short like the young male gnomes'—but he is not young! It's almost as if he's only now learning to be a gnome."

"I'm sure it's difficult," Timothy said.

"Bet your bottoms it's difficult. It's an odd job being a gnome, more so when being an odd gnome." Gladson turned away.

The boys looked ahead and discovered no gnome coming their way.

"That's it? We're done?" Zachary said with rising relief.

"Done? Done meeting the gnomes. But now—"

"Now what?"

Gladson smiled.

Zachary did not like that smile.

Chapter 10

THE SEVEN MOONS OF IRIA

The rest of the day seemed to have no end, for Gladson took them on a village tour.

This tour first consisted of the boys visiting gnome dwellings. Inside these dwellings, the companions met with at least one member of the household, that member being a gnome with a tray of their own fairy water and fairy bread waiting to be drunk and munched on by the visitors. The gnomes would each act as if the water and bread came from their own special recipe; thus, they would have the companions judge whether their water and bread were any better than the former dwelling. Of course, there was no difference, for the bread and water only required one substance to change everything about their recipe: fairy dust. And with no difference in the fairies' fairy dust except for potency, the bread and water always tasted the same.

These same members of the abode shoved out platters full of nuts, berries, grapes, and other small assortments of snacks found in the forest. This came with various dried and smoked mushrooms, along with many sorts of roots. The home dwellers would watch the boys eat along with Sarah, Rajur, and even Butch, who would once again try to judge how it tasted.

And again, everything tasted the same from one home to another.

Gladson, fully aware of this vain boast and judging, put an end to it halfway through the tour. "They'll be far too stuffed for the main feast!"

"But it's so good," Zachary said, finding it difficult to stop eating. "Let me at least finish the bread."

"There'll be bread in the next home," Gladson said.

"But you'll let us eat the bread?" Timothy remarked.

"Go to town on all the bread you want," Gladson said. "Just stay away from the nuts and berries and foraged mushrooms and roots."

"Why not the bread?"

"You've had bread on every stop," Gladson said. "Ask yourself, Do you feel stuffed from the bread?"

The answer the boys found surprised them. "No."

"Exactly! Onward! The day wanes."

Onward they went.

~

The companions went from one dwelling to the next, each time munching on fairy bread, only to slug down a glass full of fairy water afterward.

Sometimes, the boys, and even Sarah, snuck in a berry or two, including a nut, with the help of the dweller.

Gladson deliberately showed ignorance, but he knew. He knew anything and everything that went on with the gnomes.

The food and greetings by the household members were not alone.

Singing. Besides the constant singing among the entire village, the visitation came with singing on each visit to a home. The songs were melodic and dealt with the nature of Eythreal. The singing also mentioned gnomes and fairies, including Lady Nesia. Some of the singing disclosed a portion of Lady Nesia's history, along with the background of the forest. But those songs came as riddles, too incomprehensible for the boys and even Rajur and Sarah to solve.

Gladson shrugged his shoulders on the few times the boys asked him for help in understanding the songs.

Yana and Magnelia the Fair did help the boys out with a few whispering truths, but never so consequential.

What came as a surprise to the companions was Rajur not being sulky over this enduring tour of the dwellings. But that could not be said at first.

On the first visitation, the gnome of that dwelling handed a mug of mead to a sulky Rajur. Rajur hesitated. Many times had he been offered a mug of their special mead, and on every time he said no, for never had he visited the center of Tree Horn Village. He only passed alongside it when free of the mischievous and playful gnomes. His reluctance didn't last this time. He saw a long, tedious day against his control and was resigned to the fates.

He took the mead from the gnome's hand and sipped it. His world nearly changed.

"So this is the mead you've been using as bait for me to enter your village?" he asked Gladson.

"It is."

"The same mead that legends tell about?"

"Legends? How wonderful! But yes, it is a mead only we can ferment."

"Is it because of the fairy water? Is that what makes it so special? The magic of Lady Nesia's forest?"

A disgruntled Gladson lowered his head. "I'm afraid so."

"Why so perturbed?" Rajur asked. "The legends speak true. I've never tasted anything so good."

"Yes. Excellent taste. But it doesn't have to be an excess of fairy dust. We gnomes could do it ourselves. But *no*, fairies always have to have their way."

"Fairy dust is poured into it?" Zachary asked, wanting to try it.

"I'm afraid so. I've lamented before Lady Nesia, pleaded for her to tell her fairies to calm down on the fairy dust. But no, they keep adding it to the water we brew our beer and mead with when the water is already an essence of fairy dust since it comes from this forest! I don't know how many times I've told them to take it easy on adding more to our brewing tanks. It's just too much! Too much! But you know fairies. As I said, they do only what they want, and what they want is as whimsical as a traveling caravan full of theatrical jesters. I have even posted sentries by the fermenting tanks, and still, they get through and ruin the flavor we seek, probably by seduction or getting that sentry drunk from their liquor and wine. Crafty little fairies. Damn them *sometimes*," he said, with his renowned wink of an eye.

"Well," Rajur said, gulping down more mead, "did I not say it's delicious?"

A stunned Zachary and Timothy stared at Rajur.

"Did you just say delicious?" Zachary said.

"What?" Rajur said.

"You said delicious."

"I did not."

"Did too."

"Didn't even know that's in your vocabulary," Sarah said.

Rajur eyed them each. "The mead," he said, staring at the delicious-looking brew. Rajur shrugged and took another big gulp. "So be it. Delicious it is."

From then on, Rajur couldn't wait to reach the next house and taste their not-so-*own* mead.

~

The endless day came to its inevitable end, and as it did, the Star of Nod left behind the slimmest of light. The boys could capture a better view of the seven moons in the darkening sky, their first time witnessing the moon cycle's soon passing.

"I forgot how beautiful they are when at such a higher elevation," Sarah said since they had followed Gladson to the highest point of the tree one could reach.

"Seven moons," Zachary said. "So today would be like an end of a week, which you call . . ."

"Moon cycle," Rajur said.

"Yes," Zachary said. "If you'd let me finish, I was going to say that. How I am supposed to learn about your days, weeks, months, and years?"

"You seemed to let it linger," Rajur said. "I only wanted to help."

"Well, I was waiting for a dramatic entrance to the words *moon cycle*."

Rajur smiled and nodded.

"And what happens when all seven moons disappear again?" Timothy asked.

"A new moon will vaguely appear in the sky after the shortest second of Twilight."

"Twilight? But isn't Twilight when the sun—"

"Twilight may mean different from somewhere else," Rajur said. "Here, Twilight happens when our seven moons fade away simultaneously."

"For the shortest of seconds?"

"Shorter than a second, but aye."

"And the next moon?"

"The moon to vaguely appear after this Twilight will be Legolas. Next week, we'll call it Legolas's Calling."

"And again, the end of a week is what you call moon cycle?"

"Yes," Rajur said.

"Twilight to follow?"

"Yes."

"And a full moon cycle, more like a month?"

"Very good."

"Twilight after that?"

"No, something greater. Passing of Twilight."

"The what?" both boys said.

Rajur shook his head.

The boys saw no further information from Rajur.

"And an end of seven full moon cycles is a year, right?" Timothy said.

"Correct. A greater moon cycle."

"What about *that* Twilight?" Zachary asked.

"The Passage of Twilight."

"You've got Twilight, Passing of Twilight, and Passage of Twilight?"

"Correct."

"This is nuts," Zachary said. "It's even more confusing now."

"Soon," Rajur said.

The boys wanted to argue back and protest that being ignorant of the calendar only made things worse. But they were too enthralled by the view of seven moons together in the sky to ask for harsh lessons in the working of Eythreal's calendar. Seeing the moons did evoke one very important thought.

"Lady Nesia," Timothy said. "Will we see her?"

Gladson turned to Timothy apologetically as if he already knew the answer. "Maybe."

Timothy's shoulders slumped upon hearing that.

"Come," Gladson said, trying to cheer him up. "Think positive. Be positive. And let us eat!"

The thought of food besides the snacks they'd been given gave new excitement to the boys.

"Like real food? Food that will fill us up, unlike bread, nuts, berries, and so forth?" Zachary asked.

"Our grand feast consisting of nuts, berries, and so forth stuff?" Gladson said that while slapping his paunchy stomach. "No, no, no. How do you think we gnomes grow such healthy fat tummies? A lot of work goes into making a gnome's tummy-tummy. And it's hardly just beer, wine, and mead."

The gnome fell to singing.

There'll be meat, there'll be meat,
And there'll be potatoes.
There'll be meat, there'll be meat,
And even more potatoes.
There'll be meat, there'll be meat,
Did I say potatoes?

"Just potatoes and meat?" Zachary said.

Gladson placed a hand on Zachary's shoulder. "Did I not promise you a feast for all feasts?"

"You did. Or I would have eaten more nuts and berries."

Gladson chuckled. "Come," he said. "It is time. Time to get your swell on."

"Wait!" Sarah said, seeing the companions following Gladson. "The seventh moon isn't in full display yet."

"As you wish," Gladson said, retracing his steps to the ledge over the platform.

A few minutes passed, and as it did, the very last amber glow from the Star of Nod vanished.

"So beautiful," Sarah said.

The boys looked at the moons in a new light. The complete darkness of the night sky gave the moons a brilliance not seen a moment ago.

"What are the names of the moons?" Timothy asked.

The eyes belonging to Gladson and Rajur looked skeptically at Timothy, while Sarah looked amused.

"This is, uh, well, a very, uh, well . . . difficult question to answer," Gladson said.

"I've heard one of them being called Atris, and now a minute ago, Legolas—but that is just the name of the moon day and not the moon itself, right?"

Gladson gave him a tentative nod of his head. "Very difficult to answer," the gnome said.

"What about the Star of Nod?" Zachary asked.

"The Star of Nod is the Star of Nod," Gladson said. "Although I understand, the term *sun* is being forged into Eythreal's language."

"But why is it called the Star of Nod?"

"It speaks of the Council of Nod, for it was the Council of Nod that approved Iria's use of the seven moons. And they gave her the Star of Nod to further her development of Eythreal."

"But what is this Council of Nod?"

"That, my friend, is a wallop of a question. The best I could do is to have you imagine a place full of gods and goddesses sitting around and doing zilch, except for the occasional meddling in the affairs of mortal beings, since these same gods and goddesses think they are the ones that rule the Realm of Cosmos, when nobody, not even a god or goddess, has almighty power over the cosmos. This same place is where our Goddess Iria came from."

"Why did she leave?"

"To create and rule over Eythreal," Gladson said.

"Yes," Zachary said, turning to Sarah and Rajur. "They've told us that, but not much. Is it true that Eythreal would be a lifeless planet without the Seven Moons of Iria?"

"Lifeless? No. But it wouldn't be a life as we know it today. Without the moons, mana's seeds would never have sprouted."

"Yes," Timothy said. "Rajur somehow explained that mana is like seeds."

"Something like that—easier for them to relate to," Rajur said.

"A good explanation," Gladson said. "Without the Seven Moons of Iria, no seeds to be sprouted, no mana to give life to all things you see now."

"And the smell," Zachary said. "Because I think I smell food."

"And you do!" Gladson said.

"Good," Zachary said, sniffing the air more. "Never thought hannies smelled so delightful when cooked."

"Hey!" Gladson said.   Gladson fell into a mirthful state, going along with this joke more easily than last time.

"Come," the gnomes said. "Food."

Gladson turned away, and the companions followed. They arrived at the spiral staircase they used when climbing up, which was built into the wood of the tree. They didn't have to go far down to reach the branch where the evening festival table resided, where the gnomes of the forest had already gathered, including the fairies flying about. Six empty chairs sat near one another. Five of those six chairs were identical to every other chair a gnome sat upon.

The sixth chair waited for someone else.

Timothy looked at this majestic chair and became sad again. "She's not coming," he said.

"I'm afraid not," Gladson said. "But not to worry. Nothing else will disappoint."

Timothy nodded and sat on the chair closest to Lady Nesia's chair.

Chapter 11

FIREWORKS

Timothy forgot his sadness about Lady Nesia not making an appearance the second he sat down and stared at the incredible amount of food platters. Many of these platters of food were meats and potatoes, sung by Gladson and ridiculed by Zachary.

But there was so much more, so much more!

There were dishes of fish, each of a various kind, and each fish caught in the many streams that flowed through the forest. There were dishes full of mushrooms, roots, and other foraged vegetation, along with seeds and berries found only in Tree Horn Forest, similar to what the companions munched on during their tour.

There were dishes of gravy: white gravy, brown gravy, red gravy, green gravy, and even multicolored gravy.

The gravies were not alone. Sauces—hot, cold, spicy, mild. Sauces that changed temperatures during each second in the mouth. Dressings of even more sorts.

And much more than that!

What amazed Timothy the most was the amount of food, for he saw only the smallest portions since he could not describe every plate of food that the table consisted of because the table was far too elongated to study each spot. Once again, this table befitted every gnome that lived on Tree Horn Forest, along with fairies, but each had their own seat and, in a way, their own table directly above. The table belonging to the fairies was narrow and consisted of tiny little seats where each fairy could fly down to the main table, steal what food or drink they wanted, fly right back to their tiny little table, and sit properly.

But the fairies seldom followed such a custom. The fairies plagued the main table by eating and drinking whatever they wanted, never with a utensil and never flying back to their seats and table, consequently leaving behind spilled crumbs and a massive mess on the table. Never during this time did their unruly behavior upset the gnomes. The gnomes couldn't care less—well, except for a few. A few gnomes did try to swipe the fairies away but did so in a friendly fashion.

Seeing this behavior, Timothy realized this wasn't going to be easy. A second later, he noticed a bombardment of food coming his way.

Unsure what to do, Timothy would have a dish in one hand, just given to him a second before, only for another dish to be extended toward him. He'd grab the second dish, thus unable to plate food from the first dish, and then a file of three more dishes came his way. Worse, two other hands reaching out to him from each side of him would be asking for the plates in his hands. Therefore, he'd give one away, only to be forced to handle one of the three new dishes. He'd try to use his other hand, but a plate occupied it. He'd give that plate away, only to capture another plate. He'd be back in the same pickle he found himself in a second ago.

The cycle confounded him. He had no way of serving his food before it was taken away and his hands occupied by three more.

He slowly turned crazy. He just couldn't handle the situation. He looked around and studied the others.

What he learned by studying the fairies and gnomes threw the rules of civil dining he grew up with out the window. Like the fairies, most gnomes ignored the sparkling silverware that took them hours to polish and chose to use their hands instead. Yes, they used their hands like fast-paced shovels to serve food onto their plate and pass it to the next gnome. Sometimes, Timothy caught sight of the gnomes going even further: cupping *both* hands, scooping out a very generous portion of food, and plopping it onto their plate. Sometimes, a gnome or two would ignore their plate and instead shove their face into the sharing plate and eat from it while passing the plate to the next gnome.

Solely because of this eating style, the train of food was never hindered.

Timothy looked to Zachary. Zachary had a big smile on his face. He also found no trouble or qualm about shoveling food onto his plate. He even had help. Magnelia the Fair sat beside him, and they worked as a team. He did the shoveling while she did the passing. Sometimes they swapped jobs. Regardless, they shared the same plate.

Timothy looked at Yana at his side.

Yana twinkled with a smile. "Are you ready?" she asked expectantly.

Timothy nodded vigorously.

"And you want to try everything?"

"Everything."

Yana smiled again. "OK. Let's begin!"

Yana flew from her position, which was on the main table, and perched upon Timothy's shoulder. She became Timothy's third and fourth hand—third and fourth eye. She demonstrated the best way to grab as much food as possible before being skipped. And they operated this way through eating, for the fairies never liked to sit and be settled when it came to a grand feast, which was a nightly routine in Tree Horn Forest. As mentioned before, the fairies simply flew where they wanted to, took what food they wanted, and drank what drink they wanted, with little resistance from the gnomes.

The fairies even had their own beer and mead, a much sweeter mead and a much less hoppy beer. As for wine, the varietals were too many to describe.

Yana proved to be an excellent expeditor. She chose wisely what Timothy should eat first and how much, even when Timothy wanted it all. In a short time, Timothy's plate became full of various foods without the struggle to keep up, all the while picking at the plate of food.

But what came next dilated his eyes even more.

The spoken-about mead and wine came his way.

Rajur and Sarah watched the mugs full of smooth honey-amber mead come toward the boys with questionable thoughts in their minds. The boys stared at these mugs of mead, ignoring the wine with a sense of hesitance, fully aware they were made with alcohol. For a short second, they felt what their parents would think if they drank this illicit drink. That thought did not last long, although it incited them to look Sarah and Rajur's way since they had become like parent figures. Seeing Rajur and Sarah not decline but also not giving them a thumbs-up, *go ahead, try if you want,* the boys took hold of a mug of mead and set it down before them.

They looked around.

No adults to tell them no.

They again looked at Rajur and Sarah.

What they saw eased their tension. Rajur and Sarah smiled and even lifted their goblet of wine and mug of mead.

The boys smiled back and lifted their mugs in the air. They took a sip. Quickly after, they both burped *loudly*!

The entire table fell into a roar of laughter, from the closest gnome to the farthest one down the table. Sarah and Rajur also laughed.

"He's really laughing," Zachary said, wiping the foamy mead from his mouth and taking a second sip.

"I've laughed before," Rajur said.

"You may call it a laugh. We've been calling it a smirk."

"It's something," Rajur said.

"You know," Sarah said. "I think the boy is right. I've seen you chuckle but never full-blown laughter."

"Maybe it is the company I wisely choose to laugh around," Rajur said.

"You mean the company of me, myself, and I?" Zachary said.

"As I said," Rajur said, "I choose wisely."

"You tell them, Rajur!" Gladson said, pumping his fist in the air.

"Great. Now I have Gladson defending me. You know, I don't need you to defend me."

"Of course, you don't," Gladson said. "You don't ever need *anyone* to defend you, Rajur."

"You know what I mean."

"I do. But wait! It's time for a toast or two."

Gladson stood. The gnomes surprisingly stopped chewing and drinking their wine and mead. As for the fairies, it took a bit longer for their feeding frenzy to settle down.

"Let us first give a toast to everyone here," Gladson said. "Without you gnomes and fairies, I don't see Tree Horn Forest as even a sketch on Eythreal's map. You've made it what it is now, and everyone on Eythreal thanks you. Cheers."

"Cheers!" the crowd of gnomes, fairies, and companions said, followed by a sip of their chosen drink.

"Another toast, of course," Gladson said, "for our guests—gracious visitors that deserve much more than a toast."

Gladson raised his wine along with everyone else. His focus fell on Sarah.

"I said earlier that Sarah's visit here has been our long and enduring wish. It is true. Finally, finally, we've been afforded the encounter with this goddess of a mortal being. To us, there is no rival, of course excluding Lady Nesia. Sarah of Cyrcle, White Mage of Hederdolm, welcome. Welcome to Tree Horn Forest. We are so, so, so, so, so, so very glad you are here. And when I say *we*, I mean Lady Nesia also. Do not think otherwise, even if she does not make an appearance tonight. She admires you. Oh Iria, how much she admires you.

"To Sarah!" Gladson said that, lifting his goblet of wine a bit more into the air, as the rest did, and brought it down for a sip.

"To Sarah!" the rest said, also sipping their drinks.

Sarah responded kindly by smiling Gladson's way and then toward everyone else. "Thank you," she said after sipping her wine.

"Thank you," Gladson said.

A short pause followed. Not a single gnome, fairy, or companion took a bite of food.

"Another toast!" Gladson shouted. "We must. Right? Ha ha. He must have his own toast. It would not be fair."

Gladson looked at Rajur. "O Fabled Warrior, the Prophecy, the Myth, the Legend, and everything else that comes to mind to describe your ethereal presence here on Eythreal.

"And is he a myth? Is he just a fabled rumor? What about the prophecy? Does Iria's sake revolve around his prophecy? Who knows? But I do know one thing. He has become, and will always be, our favorite wanderer among these lands. He may think we're up to no good. He may think we eat tree trolls—ew, yuck!" Gladson said, imitating one vomiting. "He may conclude that we are more trouble than good. But we know where his heart is. We know deep down inside, he loves us. We know how vital you are to this forest, Rajur, even Lady Nesia. She knows this. Don't change. Don't ever lose that edge you've sharpened up since the dawn of your arrival on Eythreal. And if that means you scowl at us, so be it. We'll live. We'll continue to live, knowing that Rajur is here for our protection. And then, we'll sleep better at night.

"Thank you," Gladson said, lifting his wine again.

The crowd of gnomes and fairies and companions did the same.

As for Rajur, he bowed his head as everyone else shouted "Thank you!" and took a sip of their drink. Rajur followed with a sip of his mead.

"And lastly, a few words about our *true* visitors. Of course, their pets too," Gladson said, with his eyes resting on Butch.

Butch emitted a friendly bark.

Gladson turned his eyes to Zachary. He nodded. Zachary nodded back. And then Gladson's eyes rested firmly on Timothy.

"Some may whisper that your arrival here is a tragedy upon Eythreal, a telltale sign that the worst has befallen us. And why? Because it tells us nobody on Eythreal could have saved it, for why are you here, then? For now, it is only you that the fates have chosen to save Eythreal. It is true. Whether you like it or not, we're all pawns in this tragedy to play out from what you must hide from everyone on Eythreal. Well! If that is the case, then we must stand loyal to you. Surround yourself with the best. Equip yourself with the best. Do the best you can. I believe you and what you hide from us will not fail us.

"No. Do not doubt yourself. Do not doubt what choices you must make. Never. Never do such a thing."

Gladson somberly lowered his wine, took a sip, and fell into an also somber song.

> To the ends of the land
> You must make your way,
> Even if trapped under the sand,
> You must never be led astray.
>
> It is the moon's darkness you may think,
> But it will be light if you know how to see
> On the very edge of the brink
> Of what you must believe to be.
>
> In the hollow dungeons of Migra
> One must always know:
> When it crawls, it must go
> To its accursed and perpetual woe.
>
> And there, breathing in the end,
> You will see no more,
> Nor will you ever be a friend
> To that bitter defeat of nevermore.

A solemn gasp of air punctured the once-lively mood of the dining table as Timothy discerned a pale gloom sweeping over each gnome and fairy.

Gladson, especially, felt affected by this pale gloom. He even seemed to shiver.

The shivering ended, as did the pale gloom, with Gladson breaking into a smile and a caper upon the dining table.

"Wait!" Gladson cried out, abruptly ending his dance. "One last toast. Yes, one last toast, to our very own Lady Mother of Tree Horn Forest. For we all know, she is watching us," Gladson said with his eyes upon Timothy. "And we all know that she cares—cares so very much. We wouldn't be here if she didn't care. Nor would we be here if she didn't know what is in store for *you*."

Gladson solemnly lifted his wine. "Hear! Hear!" he said.

"Hear! Hear!" the rest said, each of them sipping their drink, as did Gladson, with eyes on Timothy still.

Timothy could only stare back and sip his mead.

The rest of the gnomes and fairies returned to their jolly ways while continuing their feast.

As for Timothy, with eyes no longer on Gladson and having sipped his last drop of mead, he immediately felt an emptiness swallow him up. The emptiness came neither from his stomach nor from consuming the last drop of mead. It came from his entire body. He fought against this emptiness, this feeling of being swallowed up, carving into him; he blamed it on the mead and food. But as he did, he also felt something else rise within him. This feeling came about like a sickness, a nausea to permeate his entire insides, causing these same insides to become soft and droopy as if one ate something of the worst quality.

Timothy tried his best to hide this cringing feeling. He felt embarrassed, weak—as if only he got sick because he was not strong like the rest, like Zachary.

While Yana slowed down on passing the food, he acted the best he could and concentrated on what they had already gathered.

He looked around. Nobody else noticed his cringing.

Thus, he fought and fought—fought off this horrible destruction of his insides.

Finally, the feeling of his insides being flaccid and the nausea that pervaded his entire insides passed away. Unfortunately, they left behind excruciating pain. He held back a scream, although he felt he didn't need to scream. No. He felt his conscious and subconscious minds were being torn away from his physical body. He could even feel the tearing of strings, joints, and inner flesh that kept them together. Thus, both his mind and body formed a separate entity when fully severed from each other.

Luckily for him, when the two were tearing apart from each other, it tore away from the inner essence of him, not the physical, hence no scream—not yet.

But that did not mean his body did not react to the pain. Again, he cringed even more so than before because of this pain. He shook and shivered.

Someone had to have noticed.

Timothy strained to look around. Nobody *seemed* to have noticed.

Timothy felt relieved by this, and with that relief came the relief of the pain.

The shivering of his body ended.

It's the mead, he told himself. *That, and all the food.*

~

The feast ended, and a relieved Timothy sat back in awe of how much he ate. His left hand moved to his stomach and rested upon what he believed to be the most bloated stomach he'd ever had, a stomach ten times what it was, for how could it not be after all the food and mead he indulged in? But resting his hand on the supposed bloated tummy, he felt no such thing, not a single consequence of overindulging. His stomach felt fine, better than fine.

He looked toward Zachary.

Zachary smiled in astonishment, discovering the same feeling.

Timothy smiled back.

The male gnomes also rested back in their chairs while most female gnomes got up and took away the platters of food. They headed toward their dwelling, where they would clean and rinse the plates and put them back in their designated spot. Most of the fairies assisted in this cleanup, making it far easier for the gnomes, for the fairies weren't shy when it came to pouring fairy dust over the gnomes, allowing them to travel and clean at a much greater speed.

With most of the female gnomes at work, especially the older ones, for it was they who demanded the others to stay put at the table, the male gnomes fell into their jubilant ways. They danced. They sang. And they never bothered about the remaining plates and glasses on the table, for they used the table as a dance floor.

Live music also returned to the village since many gnomes carried with them their flutes and fiddles, harmonicas and harps, banjos and guitars, and many other musical instruments, and again played upon the table while some fairies that stuck around helped with fairy dust, giving the older gnomes a boost where they lacked. The fairy dust also spread upon the dancing gnomes, invigorating them even more; not one mug of mead, pint of beer, goblet of wine, or jar of fairy milk for the younger gnomes was safe from the exuberant and precarious dancing.

But once the female gnomes returned from cleaning the dishes, with dessert in their hands, the carousing gnomes came to a stop.

"Dancing and skipping and playing raucous tunes before dessert?" many female gnomes protested while scolding the male gnomes. "How dare you! What reckless rogues you are!"

With their heads tucked down, the male gnomes cowered back to the nearest seat. The boys and Sarah laughed at this exchange.

Dessert had arrived.

Nothing changed when it came to the dessert. The boys stared at an endless storm of plates filled with sweets, tarts, cakes, pies, donuts, and other assorted pastries coming their way. The boys' first instinct told them it would be impossible to consume a single morsel of dessert. This instinct proved to be premature and a lie since their stomach growled for food, as if they had not consumed the greatest amount of food ever imagined!

The boys utilized the fairies again when it came to devouring as much dessert as possible.

Finally, after nearly hundreds of bites, the desserts stopped, and the gnomes, fairies, and each of the companions sat back and smiled. Their appetite had been surfeited.

Gladson stood up.

He stood up with a mug of mead in hand since he had already drunk all the wine he wanted. The entire crowd of fairies, gnomes, and companions looked at him.

"And now, my frenzy friends, prepare the evening festivities!"

The fairies flew from their position and landed on their narrow table. They poured down a deluge of fairy dust from above, ensuring it fell onto everyone and everything. Because of the excessive amount of fairy dust being poured down, the gnomes, platters of food, mugs of mead, tankards of beer, goblets of wine, and everything else loosely set on the table, floated into the air.

The massive dose of fairy dust quickened the cleaning more than last time. Within minutes, the elegant dining table turned into an exquisite dance floor, where every gnome danced and skipped while drinking and playing an instrument.

Not a single residue from the evening supper could be traced on the table.

The festivities were not centered on the table only. The congregation spread to every branch of Tree Horn Forest. The gazebos turned into stages full of dancing and live bands, each stationed on a higher platform. Most gnomes refrained from dancing with their feet on the floor. Instead, they took full advantage of the potent and excessive fairy dust and hovered over the dance floor. Some gnomes went further than just hovering or floating over the dance floor. Some gnomes zoomed about the entire village, shouting in glee the whole way as if it were their first time flying, which, of course, it wasn't.

From the start, Timothy and Zachary joined in the festivities. Sarah only waited a minute longer.   Butch had joined in before the start.

Sarah delighted in the many dances with the gnomes. Most of the gnomes hovered in the air when dancing with her. And a long line of suitors started from one end of the table to the other, consisting of females, males, young, and old. And not a single gnome was envious of another. Even the fairies waited in line to dance with Sarah.

Rajur took part in the festivity by never leaving his spot on the now-turned dancing and musical stage. He found comfort in his mead and never sulked. He could be spotted smiling a few times while watching the boys and Sarah find much pleasure and happiness in the festivities. Rajur wanted them to have a good time. Of course, he never wanted to be here, but he couldn't change that anymore. He now felt it best for them to soak in as much fun as possible, seeing that fun of any kind was soon to elude them for a long time.

The festivities lasted a good two hours and then some. Gladson, in the end, disappeared for a bit and returned with the loudest shout of the evening.

"Fireworks!"

Gladson conveyed with him a sack three or four times his size. He proceeded to climb back to the highest portion of the tree where earlier, the companions stood and gaped at the Seven Moons of Iria. The boys watched him climb to this spot. In less than a few minutes, they watched him climb back down.

"You have to see this!" an energetic Yana said, pulling Timothy over to an empty seat by Rajur while Sarah made her way back.

"These fireworks will never, ever in a trillion greater moon cycles, disappoint!" Magnelia the Fair said, pulling Zachary over to a seat also.

Once the boys sat on their chairs, the two fairies settled on their shoulders and clapped in anticipation of the fireworks.

The rest of the gnomes and fairies also settled down and clapped in a prelude to the final and main event.

And the fireworks did not disappoint.

Timothy and Zachary sat back in awe. The first two waves of fireworks proved more explosive and dynamic than any fireworks they'd witnessed around their town's lake during celebratory times. They watched the fireworks become multidimensional bursts; thus, each explosive burst turned into another explosive burst, only for that new round of explosion to emit its own explosive burst, and so on and so on. Some of these explosions seemed to last forever, leaving behind traces from all spectrums in the night sky. Some explosions dissipated without a trace, darkening the sky to the point of no light, excluding the stars and solitaire glow of the Seven Moons of Iria. Most, if not all, these fireworks proved to have a mind of their own, as they swirled about in all directions, not sporadically but more in an aimed direction, wanting to survey the surrounding. When the fireworks left the vicinity and traveled into the forest, they lit up the forest with vibrant colors while being chased around the forest by other explosive bursts of fireworks, as if they were playing tag.

Everything about the fireworks proved to be magical to the boys.

And the magic continued.

The third wave of fireworks burst on the scene. These explosions were unlike the first two waves. These explosions manifested drawings, all of which looked too real to be true. These drawings proved to be various items, including swords, shields, and many other pieces of equipment one carried along on an adventurous adventure. Then came drawings of mountains, forests, deserts, rivers, and different notable landscapes found on Eythreal. Manifestations of familiar kinds also appeared, including tekers, hannies, and even villagers from Cyrcle and the thankful ones whose souls had been rescued from Huron's crypt.

The third wave of fireworks ended, and a fourth came bursting on the scene. This wave of fireworks was much like the third since they again manifested drawings but did so by showing drawings of more intimate relation to the companions, along with some having a deep and hidden meaning.

The first of these manifestations proved to be Abigail and Breeze. Butch followed, and then came Timothy, Zachary, Sarah, and Rajur.

Gladson and many other gnomes and fairies also appeared in the sky.

A single raindrop appeared in the sky, following the vivid drawings of Gladson, the gnomes, and the fairies. Inside the raindrop were various colors. The colors formed a scintillating rainbow that appeared *inside* the raindrop. This rainbow grew and soon filled every space of the raindrop and continued to grow. The swelling of the rainbow stretched the raindrop further, causing it to be nearly half the size of the entire sky. But the raindrop could not stretch any farther, and the rainbow wanted to grow even more. The raindrop looked ready to explode. But it did not explode. Instead, the rainbow exploded, causing the raindrop to shrink a tiny bit in size, nowise too small for any to see every detail inside of it since the exploded rainbow caused streaks of various colors to soar through the inside of the raindrop, like comets flying through the sky.

These comet-like light streaks crashed into the raindrop walls and formed a land.

More explosions from the comets.

Mountains formed around this land.

More explosions.

A verdant green valley cut through the mountains.

More explosions.

A lake formed on the outskirts of this valley and a large tributary near it.

More explosions.

Forest and other natural landscapes surrounded the mountains, valley, lake, and river.

More explosions.

A quaint and colorful village came about alongside the lake and inside the valley. Shops and markets formed inside this village. At the same time, homes were found high in the mountains surrounding the village.

And lastly, a final explosion erupted, and a single grand rainbow appeared in the sky of this mountainous village setting.

Nothing on Eythreal seemed to come close to the beauty and tranquility of this setting.

The jaws belonging to the boys fell to the ground.

"Um . . ." Zachary tried to say. "Where on Iria's Eythreal is that?"

Gladson chuckled. "Oh where, or where indeed?" he said. Gladson looked in all directions as if somebody could answer.

"No?" he asked. Gladson shrugged his shoulders. "Not even I and not even Lady Nesia know where. It is hidden from all eyes, excluding our Goddess Iria and her daughters, although they'd hesitate to tell even if free and awake."

"OK," Zachary said. "Fine. You don't know where it's at. But that means it's real?"

"Very real," Sarah said. "It's Yorah's Village."

"And Yorah is?"

"Some say the mightiest of wizards that came to Eythreal."

"And where is he now?" Timothy said.

"Well, silly, that's easy," Gladson said. "He's in his village. And why not? The wizards that stayed behind long went rogue on us."

"Or went mad," Rajur said.

"Yes," Gladson said. "There's that too. There are so many screws attached to an incomprehensible mind that surely a few will grow loose in time. These loose screws will eventually fall from their places, and a great eruption will occur in an already mind-blowing mind!"

Everyone's focus returned to Yorah's Village, except for Timothy.

His eyes fell on Gladson. "These fireworks," Timothy said.

"Yes?"

"What are they telling us?"

"Hmm," Gladson said while shrugging his shoulders. "I don't know. Maybe nothing, maybe everything."

Sensing Gladson holding back on much, Timothy shook his head and returned to Yorah's Village, only for the image to dissolve into tiny specks and another firework rocket into the sky. The firework exploded, and this time, the explosion manifested into a silvery silhouette of a man, or one everyone presumed to be a man because of his physique. This silvery depiction kept growing. The silver hue of the figure prevailed in every part, including his silvery eyes. The silver also shone bright, so bright that most had to adjust their eyes until they acclimated to the glow. Once acclimated, they noticed the silvery figure carrying a silvery bow and arrow with him. And nocked in the bow could be seen one silvery arrow, except this arrow's back end burned with fire. The fire that burned the back end of the arrow could only be described as glistening specks of matter dissolved in the air.

This image captivated the boys and everyone else just as much as the other explosions. But for Rajur, this image proved more important to him than any other, including Yorah's Village; he betrayed this importance by letting slip a gasping sigh for others to hear.

"What is it?" Sarah asked as the rest turned to Rajur, with Rajur staring only at the silvery figure with a single burning arrow nocked in the bow.

"Bow and Arrow," Rajur said.

Rajur turned his attention to Gladson. "What do you know about this?" he asked sternly.

Gladson responded with his own stern look, which looked flimsy compared to Rajur's. "I only know it is a mystery you'll need to unravel at some point. Other than that, I'm sorry . . . I am of no help."

"But it's your fireworks!"

"They are not my fireworks," Gladson said urgently. "And you know this. These fireworks belong to the forest and have their own agenda, whims, and caprices, although I dare say that what they show is intended for all of you."

Rajur lost his stern look, and disappointment filled in the void.

"What is it?" Timothy asked. "Bow and Arrow? Wait! Didn't you mention something like that to Tolan?"

"Aye," Rajur said. "Bow and Arrow. And yet, it still matters not, for we know nothing."

"Is there anything you can tell us?" Timothy asked. "It seems to be very important to you. Shouldn't that mean it's important to us too?"

Rajur nodded his head. He looked to the companions and spoke. "What I speak of is very confidential. But aye, it is for the best of us for each of you to know. It was a time not too long before this. My allies and I were searching for certain riddles and clues that dealt with more than just our assignment: Camus. It dealt with Iria herself. During this search, we employed a scholar, one renowned in her profession, along with the risk of an El-Dahn. Yes, an El-Dahn. We could not afford to find what we sought only for it to be unreadable except by an El-Dahn. As you know, there are many scrolls even the elders of the elves of Nererrenda and the most renowned scholars cannot interpret, along with libraries found on Eythreal only the El-Dahn are aware of and accepted inside. Therefore, we found an El-Dahn we trusted—that *I* trusted.

"To hasten my point, this El-Dahn quickly proved his worth. He led us to a very secretive, hidden library, one that consisted of ancient scrolls. This very library was located in *Migra*."

The table shook as if an ill breeze passed through every listener, causing them to shiver.

"Yes," Rajur said, feeling the coldness to inspire every gnome and fairy. "Migra, a sizable realm far too lost to the Dark to recover, and now but a worshipping ground for the evilness that walks upon Eythreal, not to mention the homeland of Abbigatha and her origin on Eythreal, something many people believe are connected, for the coincidences are just too much to deny. But as you also know, life still breathes in Migra—not all too twisted and foul and evil.

"Nevertheless, Migra we traveled to, following the tracks of the El-Dahn we hired. We found this hidden library, but we were too late.

"On entering, we stepped into a single blaze of fire, and this fire was white fire as it engulfed the entire library. There was nothing we could do.

"But when matters looked irreparable, in came rushing our hired El-Dahn, or what we assumed to be since the white fire was on him.

"Miraculously, he clung to life. And with this life, he found a way to fall before our feet with a burning scroll in his hand. Gayleerk, a powerful mage belonging to the elves of Nererrenda, along with his proven apprentice Barbossa, exhausted all they had in trying to mend the lives of the El-Dahn and the scroll. Unfortunately, the white fire spread too much, and the El-Dahn could not be saved. As for the scroll, the mages were able to extinguish the fire, which seemed improbable, but their miracle work could go no further when it came to the impossible task of reversing the effects of white fire, thus the substantial difference between most fires and white fire—along with a few more differences.

"What remained to us was the tiniest portion of the scroll. We learned little from it while also learning much. Meekila, a reader of scrolls for the elves of Nererrenda, and Gabby, the renowned female scholar we brought from Rhinehart, combined their minds' intellect and deciphered what they could on what we believed to be an ancient scroll. But even the writing they barely deciphered proved difficult to bring together. Most of the text they deciphered made no sense.

"But some did. Yes, some did. Bow and Arrow had been mentioned a few times. What could be understood from the words that came before and after that term is that it denotes a god. So we think. It talks of a single god ordained to end Abbigatha's existence forever."

"But that's impossible," Sarah said. "Abbigatha is no half god. Even in her filthy, hideous Aarachè form, she is a goddess of full might. Not a god or goddess can simply—"

"Not kill her"—this came from Gladson—"but cause her to cease to exist."

Rajur looked to Gladson and nodded. "He speaks right," Rajur said. "To say gods and goddesses are not to be accountable for their ways is simply foolish. Death they may not know. But nonexistence of their presence whether here or anywhere else, including the Realm of Cosmos, can be."

"But how?"

"The how is all about what you believe—or want to believe," Rajur said. "If you want to believe what most don't, it is possible."

"And what is that?" Timothy asked.

"It is told that every god and goddess has one nemesis—one enemy for their destruction. This enemy they are ignorant of, this enemy chosen before their awakening, before the cosmos created such beings, and this enemy was ordained by the Realm of Cosmos to be that god or goddess's only complete destruction. But they are ignorant of this. They are unaware of one single entity that could cease their existence. Not a single god or goddess reigns in the Realm of Cosmos or even sits in the Council of Nod that knows their true nemesis, their true executioner. But there are scrolls that do tell. These scrolls are some of the hardest scrolls to find on any world, for they exist not just here. They exist where any god or goddess can exist—everywhere."

Rajur continued after a beat. "The coming of Abbigatha had been foreseen. I'm sure of it. For this scroll, I do not doubt, had been found by us and now ruined. But it gave enough. Yes. I believe her destruction rests in the hand of this Bow and Arrow, whoever he or she might be—a god or goddess it must be! And this Bow and Arrow and the one that wields it is the sole weapon to end Abbigatha's complete existence. But no easy task. No, no easy task. What little more we learned of this lost and forever-forgotten scroll, something I had not wanted to divulge to you so soon, is that Abbigatha must be fully awake for her destruction to happen. She must be in possession of all three gems, thus empowered by her own powers and the powers of the Daughters of Iria. Only then can this Bow and Arrow destroy her without destruction to the captured Daughters of Iria, for Abbigatha's entire essence would no longer be absorbed by the gems. She'd be free—free for the taking. The gems—well, the gems, we hope, would release the Daughters of Iria. And it is that hope we must tend to."

"Yes," Gladson said with a tinge of dejection. "Hope."

"You have doubts," Rajur said.

Gladson shrugged his shoulders.

"Tell me," Rajur said.

Gladson nodded. "It just seems very overly fortunate for all of us that the one entity, the one god or goddess that can end the life of Abbigatha, resides here—here! Eythreal, a world where Abbigatha should never have ended up. And to say that this Bow and Arrow has always been ordained to end her life—well, it's fishy, just too fishy. Why is this god you speak of and the Bow and Arrow here when Abbigatha does not belong here? How remarkable the one scroll—so you supposed—that speaks of this Bow and Arrow and Abbigatha's destruction is to be found here, on Eythreal, of all places! Especially miraculous since you say this scroll pertaining to this Bow and Arrow could be found on the other infinite number of worlds that coincide with ours. Fishy."

Rajur nodded. "Aye. I understand your misgiving, for I have them too. It is too . . . fishy, you call it."

"Yes," Gladson said.

"But what if it is some kind of plan?" Sarah said.

"Plan?"

"Yes. What if Abbigatha's reason to be here falls under the same reason why the scroll is here and this Bow and Arrow?"

"Why do such a thing when it means her end?" Rajur said. "Why even orchestrate Abbigatha's arrival here, only to give us a way to kill her?"

"The mysteries behind Abbigatha are infinite," Gladson said.

"Aye."

"And then there is the fact that you think this Bow and Arrow is a god," Sarah said. "Another god or goddess on Eythreal without us feeling its presence?"

"It has happened before," Rajur said.

"And I'm sure it'll continue to happen," Gladson interjected.

"And as I said, this Bow and Arrow have long been here. Long enough to be—"

"Ancient?" Timothy said out of nowhere.

Each one of them turned grave upon hearing that said.

Timothy pushed ahead. "Didn't you say these Ancient Ones are a god or goddess?"

"If what I believe in is true, aye. That they would be."

"If it is true," Sarah said, showing no sign of believing it.

"What about you, Gladson?" Timothy said. "Do you believe in this notion of there being Ancient Ones?"

A confounded look appeared on Gladson when he turned to Timothy and the rest. The question baffled him. He squirmed in his chair. Shortly after, he regained composure; this composure was far from his jovial demeanor. He looked ill. He looked as one does when eating something unexpectedly raw and squishy when it was supposed to be cooked and dense. When he spoke, his tone surprised them all since it sounded perfunctory, as if he had been programmed like a machine to speak, along with a sense of one plagiarizing another's written speech, using the original's exact words, never his own words.

"You mean the notion of Iria coming here with seven guardians before giving power to Eythreal? And the seven guardians being symbols of the Seven Moons of Iria?"

With eyebrows knitted, Timothy nodded. "Yes. That one."

Gladson's ill look ended. A look of grave seriousness took over. "No," he said sternly.

His serious look now became full of petulant anger—again, something not to be seen from a forest gnome. "No, no, no! I absolutely, one hundred times, 100 percent do not believe in that foolish notion. There are no Ancient Ones. No gods and goddesses are hiding among us on Eythreal."

Seeing the confounded looks on the companions, Gladson's petulant anger faded away. He looked ashamed.

"I am sorry. I have insulted all of you. I just feel the talk of Ancient Ones is banal and has been for so long. There are no Ancient Ones."

"Maybe a change of topic will do us good," Sarah said. "I'd love to hear more about this scroll you found."

Rajur nodded. "So would I. But that's all we gathered from it. It took so much already from Meekila and Gabby. And to be honest, they said what they deciphered may not even be true, for again, the text could not make absolute truth of anything."

"You never said that," Zachary said.

"It is because I believe in their work."

"But that's you," Zachary said. "What you just said may not even be true."

A disgruntled Rajur conceded with a nod.

"But why the sign?" Rajur pointed to the sky, mainly at the depiction of the silvery figure with a bow and arrow. "How coincidental is that?" Rajur said.

"You think Iria is showing us these fireworks?" Sarah said. "I think that's—"

"I didn't say Iria," Rajur said. "But Gladson did say the forest. Is the forest not Eythreal? And is Eythreal not—"

Timothy answered for him. "My book."

Rajur nodded. "It wants to be finished," Rajur said. "Never, ever forget that."

Chapter 12

THE PROMISE

The drawing of the silvery figure came to an end. Before anyone could blink, another firework scorched the sky and exploded.

On this explosion, Sarah gasped excitedly. "Mygor!" she said, seeing the manifestation of a burly giant crouched on one knee.

The excitement wore off. The reality of his existence struck her.

"The last of them," she said. "And now . . . gone."

"You have a great fondness for him," Gladson remarked.

"And you're surprised?" Sarah said. "You introduced me as White Mage of Hederdolm. I kept quiet at that time. Not now. How did you know? I can count on one of my hands the number of people who know where my foster family hailed from."

"Lady Nesia knows," Gladson said. "Yes. Hederdolm, the last nesting ground for giants."

Sarah nodded. "Yes. I believe so."

Mygor left the scene a minute or two after appearing. The following firework proved even mightier. Its explosion nearly took up the entire night sky.

When the sketch appeared, the entire village of gnomes, fairies, and a few companions stared with more amazement than they did at Yorah's village.

Even the boys felt the power of this manifestation to be different.

And Timothy quickly recognized one of them—the one wearing the blue midnight dress. "The Daughters of Iria?" he said.

"The Daughters of Iria," Sarah confirmed.

"It's Yvonne in the blue dress, right?" he asked.

"Aye," Rajur said. "The oldest of three. And the one—"

"I lost," Timothy said.

"Do not think of it like that," Rajur said.

"The one in the middle," Zachary said, "in the yellow dress. Is that the one—"

"Misha—the youngest. And the one that escaped me too," Rajur said.

"And it's Hildadore on the far right? The tallest in the red dress."

"Yes. Hildadore. The middle child."

"Missing, right?" Timothy asked.

"Not missing," Rajur said. "No. It would be a mistake to say so."

"Where is she, then?"

"Right where she belongs—where the book wants her to be."

"But her whereabouts are unknown to everyone but the book?" Zachary said.

"Correct."

"That sounds like missing to me," Zachary said.

"Whatever you want to call it. I call it not missing."

"And how do we find it?"

"That . . . That remains a mystery. I believe, in time, you'll have to stumble upon it."

"Unless someone else stumbles upon it first," Timothy said.

"Aye," Rajur said gravely.

The idea of having to stumble upon this missing gem to discover it weighed heavy in each of their minds as they tried to regain the excitement captured by staring at the Daughters of Iria. Turning their focus back on them, they noticed the daughters giggling and whispering to one another as if they were not imprisoned or cursed inside gems, gems belonging to a malevolent, bestial goddess, but instead, alive and well, standing in the celestial sky and looking down at the companions, gnomes, and fairies, while blowing kisses their way. And their eyes made each gnome, fairy, and companion feel this. They each felt as if the daughters stared only into their eyes, as if the eyes of the Daughters of Iria were made for them personally only.

This stare to single out each and every person in the village could be felt as one sentiment and only one sentiment: an urge to save them at any cost.

The giggling, whispering, and blowing of kisses continued. Each gnome, fairy, and companion felt the physical presence of a soft kiss upon their cheek.

The urge to save them could not be any more powerful.

The grand image of the daughters dissolved.

A troubled *and* frightened Rajur turned to Gladson. "Are you sure you're ignorant of these fireworks?"

Gladson read the pain on Rajur's face. "I am sorry. Even our Lady of the Forest does not know these fireworks' doings."

Rajur nodded as a new firework came on the scene. Before its explosion, Rajur closed his eyes and muttered for only him to hear, "Please don't let it be her." He muttered that while also clutching the locket now over his attire.

To his dismay, Sarah gasped out, "Iria."

She said that when Goddess Iria's immaculate and undefinable image manifested as the drawing.

Rajur opened his eyes.

Iria stood radiantly upon a platform floating inside a celestial body of stars. The stars glistened before the spectators, and among them could be seen shooting stars. Some of the shooting stars acted like the fireworks from before, thus shooting in any direction they wanted, around the table and even inside the forest, lighting up the dark green forest along the way. Iria held a long gilded staff. On her head, she wore a tiara exhibiting her seven moons floating slightly above it.

To describe Iria's color, namely, her skin complexion, dress, and so forth, excluding her gilded staff, would be impossible, for they changed colors randomly. Her dress, skin complexion, and eyes never stayed put on one color. And never did they match. Never did her eyes show a green color, only for her dress and skin complexion to be green.

No. The colors scintillated differently every time. There was no pattern, rhyme, or reason for the changing colors. This was because it was how Iria wanted them to see her, for there were infinite ways to see a god or goddess. The latter usually chose what the other could best interpret.

Iria was a goddess, not confined to a single particle belonging to matter.

Goddess Iria did not wave at anyone. She did not giggle. She blew no kisses in anyone's direction. She simply smiled.

But her smile seemed to single out one person—the same person in everyone's view.

Timothy looked at this person, envious and bitter that it was not him. Rajur.

The bitterness and envy ended upon seeing how pale Rajur's dark skin had turned. He also noticed Rajur holding tight to the locket, staring with saturated eyes at Iria.

Timothy sensed more about Rajur. He sensed an inner turmoil inside Rajur, as if half of him wanted to wallow in sorrow while another half fermented with wrath.

Timothy was not blind to what this meant. He tried to say something but found no words to use.

It wasn't until Rajur turned to Timothy that the latter person could speak.

"I was wrong," Timothy said in a whisper for only Rajur to hear. "It is not one of the Daughters of Iria you're in love with. You're in love with—"

"Iria."

"And your love for her—it isn't like any other's love for their goddess. You're actually madly in love with her as if she's no goddess but a common person like you and me."

Rajur nodded.

"This love," Timothy said. "It's all that matters to you, isn't it?"

"It is why I'm here," Rajur said.

"But how?" Timothy asked. "How could someone like you, me, or any other mortal creature think it's possible?"

"I . . . I don't know. But that does not mean I can stop."

"This isn't good," Timothy said with a shake of his head. "You're in pain. I see it now. I've watched you battle a monster that eats one's soul. No pain. But staring at this goddess, all I can see is pain and sorrow. And anger. There is anger inside you I would never have thought possible. This anger, sorrow, and pain don't add up too well."

Rajur nodded. "No. They don't," Rajur said.

"Again, this isn't good," Timothy said. "Not for our present situation, not for my situation, along with the book. Your mind—it is vulnerable. It can lead us astray. I can't have that. We can't have that. *You* can't have that."

An even more sad and subdued Rajur nodded. "I know this," Rajur said. "But it is too late. The burden has long been given to me without freedom from it. To be free of this burden is to be in her arms—as impossible as that is. So it is my destination."

"Your prophecy they speak of?"

"My prophecy can only *lead* me to her arms, never destined. There is a wide gap between the two."

"Whatever it is, I can't have it," Timothy said. "In time, you can become our enemy. You can easily lead me to harm."

"That," Rajur said, far more determined than before, "will never happen."

"What guarantee can you give me?"

"The guarantee of my word, for what you say has never been ignored in my mind. I have already discovered what my love could do. And simply put, I will walk away when I become the slightest of interference."

"Just like that?"

"Aye."

"I can believe you?"

Rajur leaned closely to Timothy. "Search your mind. Would you ever think I'd want anything to rupture what must be done? Because for me to ever think to follow this path I've been chosen to follow, you must succeed. For again and again and again if I must, you and the book are all that matters. I may be alive and breathing before you. But just like everyone else and things on Eythreal, I've become irrelevant compared to you and the book. What I need to be done cannot be done until Eythreal is free from that book.

"But yes. That does not mean I may not be . . . deceived by my love and passion for Iria to lead you away from your goal inadvertently. But I'll know. I will know the very second *before* it happens. In this, you must believe me."

"And I do believe you," Timothy said honestly. "I don't know why. But I do."

"Good," Rajur said with the faintest of smiles, still very pained and beleaguered to discover Iria.

A second or two went by, and Rajur leaned toward Timothy again.

"By the way, what you deduced could not be any wiser and more discerning. And what truth you came away with is no less wise."

"It's strange," Timothy said. "I feel like my senses have become heightened."

"It is your mind that is increasing—increasing because of your rapid growth and assimilation of mana on Eythreal. Too rapid."

"You fear that, don't you?"

"At some point in time, we all will." Rajur relaxed his body near Timothy as Timothy also loosened his posture.

Zachary took notice of the two and nudged Timothy. "What was that all about?" Zachary asked, having been too enthralled by Iria's depiction to eavesdrop on the whispered conversation between Timothy and Rajur.

"Just small talk," Timothy said.

"What kind of small talk? Seemed important."

Timothy looked hard at Zachary. He didn't want to lie. But he also felt it was not for Zachary.

"Not important."

Before Zachary could rebuff this, Gladson sounded a horn, and the festivities came to a standstill.

"The festivities . . . are over," Gladson said.

Instead of hearing shouts of disproval, the gnomes and fairies shouted in glee and applauded the night's entire events.

Timothy and Zachary also joined in the applauding, while Sarah did the same, and Rajur sat back in thought.

"I imagine," Gladson said near Timothy, "that it would be foolish and unwise to set off on your journey this evening."

Rajur's train of thought ended as he glared Gladson's way. Timothy couldn't help but smile. Looking toward the empty chair, his smile lessened.

"If only she had come to meet us," Timothy said. "I thought she would."

"Wishful thinking," Gladson said. "Never anything wrong with a little wishful thinking."

"As long as it's in moderation," Sarah said.

"Yes," Gladson said. "Moderation. Oh well. Just don't forget that she's watching. Yes. She's fully aware of you."

"Then why not visit us?" Zachary said.

"What can I say?" Gladson said. "She's a fairy. And fairies, my friend, will invariably do what fairies want to do."

"And what we want to do is due to our whims and fancies," Yana said.

"Got to keep you on your toes," Magnelia the Fair said.

"Yes. I believe that is so," Gladson said.

Changing his voice entirely to one as if closing a great, big deal, Gladson said, "So you'll stay the night?"

"I will?"

"You think it wise and not foolish to venture out now?"

Timothy looked to Rajur.

"Don't look at me," Rajur said. "I told you this was going to happen."

Again, Timothy couldn't help but smile as he nodded.

"Splendid!" Gladson said. "Now we need to show you to your dwellings for the night."

"Dwellings?" Zachary said. "Are you saying we'll spend the night in those burrows?"

"Burrows, dwellings, what's the difference?" Gladson said.

Zachary smiled in excitement. Even Timothy showed excitement in his look.

"The two of you, along with your pet—I mean Butch," Gladson said, seeing the dog scowl when referred to as a pet, "will share one dwelling, while Sarah and Rajur will share another. Unless you two are against shacking up?" Gladson said, with a bit of wiggle to his body and a wink of an eye.

Zachary found this funny, for he could not help but picture Rajur and Sarah as possibly more than just friends.

Timothy knew better not to. In fact, when Gladson jested about the two being together, Timothy sighed mournfully and muttered to himself. *If only. Maybe then we wouldn't have to say goodbye to him.*

~

Gladson led the way. He led the companions from one branch to the next, one burrow after another. And on each time did the companions hear music playing inside the burrows, the theme being mirthful while also carrying an air of tranquility, thus fusing the two and forming a happy calmness for one's mind to receive, only for that mind to find a night of restful sleep, filled with joyful dreams.

Never had the lives of these gnomes and fairies experienced an ill dream.

"The music that plays inside the homes," Timothy said. "It's always the same."

"And so shall it always be," Gladson said. "For this music you hear in every home is for the fairies and gnomes to fall asleep to. But can you faintly hear the second music?"

"The second music?" Zachary said.

"Listen carefully," Gladson said.

The boys quieted their minds and listened. They heard the constant, perpetual horn, but they also heard something else: more music.

"And it'll only grow louder—but not too loud!" Gladson said.

"The singing from the forest like before?" Timothy said.

"Yes. It is for all to hear and to know when every last gnome and fairy has fallen asleep."

"It stops?" Zachary said.

"It does."

"But how are you to know the music stops if you're asleep?"

"Asleep? Me? Gladson? Father of the gnomes of Tree Horn Forest? Asleep? Hardly. Not to mention Lady Nesia."

"And I'm sure you're also the watchman for enemies since the end of the music gives one the advantage of attacking unawares?"

"Attack us? How delightful a thought. Never."

"And the horn?" Sarah mentioned, forgetting how unsettled Gladson became when the horn had been mentioned not long before. "It never ends, does it?"

"Never," came a bitter response by Gladson, showing his earlier and impatient demeanor.

Gladson pushed forward, leaving behind the talk of the horn. His smile returned to his face as he stopped before a dwelling with two ladders at each side of the entrance, one of the ladders leading up and the other leading downward. The ladder leading up led to another burrow, and this burrow adjacent to a thick contoured branch, another bridge for one to pass on. Instead of leading them up this ladder, Gladson led them into the dwelling with the stairs at its sides.

Inside the dwelling, the boys stared at a wood-burning hearth along with a large multipurpose kettle hanging above it and a small cauldron to the side of the fire, ready to be moved into position at any time. A single table stood in the center of the dwelling. Upon this table rested a large basket full of bread, fruits, nuts, and many more provisions to munch on, including smoked fish. Two beds resided on one side of the dwelling; each burrowed into its nook. Alongside the beds were neatly folded sheets and blankets.

"Your beds for the night and more comfy blankets for Butch to sleep upon," Gladson said.

Timothy and Zachary stepped farther into the dwelling.

"And that?" Zachary pointed to a fancy cage, which looked more like a shrunk duplex home hanging from the ceiling not far from the boys' beds.

This luxurious duplex was embellished with all kinds of decorations and art, far too glamorous for the boys.

"Oh yes," Gladson said. "I forgot," he said as Magnelia the Fair and Yana flew off the boys' shoulders and headed toward the cage. "Dear me. How did I forget to tell you? Dear, dear, dear, dear me. My manners. You see, every gnome's dwelling is also a fairy's dwelling. Ha ha. Yes. And they can get out of control at times. But I'm sure you won't mind this. No. Not at all. Tonight, you four—I mean five—will be bunkmates. Of course, this must be OKed by you."

Timothy smiled. "I don't mind."

"Me neither," Zachary said, although nobody seemed to care what he thought.

Both fairies flapped their wings happily and flew back down to join the companions. Butch surrendered to them and rolled to the ground, giving way for his belly to be caressed. The fairies could not refuse. They tickled, petted, caressed, and smothered the dog with love.

"Now, now, delightful little creatures!" Gladson said. "You'll excite Butch too much. And the boys too! They need to find rest. It's almost sleepy time. I'm sure Rajur wants them up at first signs of the Star of Nod. And it's also high time to show Rajur and Sarah their own dwelling."

Gladson turned to Rajur and Sarah. "I will lead. You will follow."

Sensing the leave of the two adults, the boys' excitement dimmed, and a touch of sadness spread through them. The leave of Rajur and Sarah reminded them of their bereavement of their parents, for the two of them filled in the gap in a strange yet meaningful way. Rajur and Sarah had always sensed this too; thus, they each turned to the boys with a pained look, feeling the separation already. Seeing their pained looks did not help the boys, for much of the truth of their unfortunate situation came back to them.

Sarah read this and came quickly to their side. She opened both arms, and the boys dug into her. She wrapped her arms around them and squeezed.

The boys opened up the floodgates to their emotions for the first time on Eythreal. Tears fell from their eyes.

But never did they sob. Never did they speak a word. They just needed to cry.

The crying upon Sarah's chest helped. They felt their suffering emotions shifting back to the furthest portions of the mind again.

They steeled themselves.

"We're going to be right above you," Sarah said, combing through both boys' hair. "And until you return safely to your world, we'll always be right near you."

Both boys nodded their heads and freed themselves from her embrace.

"And be sharp tomorrow," Rajur said. "We lost a night and day of training. We'll have to make it up on our way to Ghalia."

The boys found Rajur's comment about training comforting.

"Rajur being Rajur," Zachary said.

"Yes," Rajur said. "Rajur being Rajur."

Rajur and Sarah turned away from the boys and followed Gladson out of the dwelling.

The door closed behind them.

"So what now?" Zachary said to Timothy. "I don't know about you, but I'm far from being sleepy."

"Same here," Timothy said, "which is quite odd. All that food and drink . . ."

"And to think all those drunks in town on our Earth are asleep after half a bottle of alcohol."

"Asleep or mad."

"And I don't feel intoxicated at all."

"Fairy dust," Yana said.

"In the mead?" Zachary said. "That makes sense, for I saw Gladson upset about you adding too much fairy dust."

"Yes," Magnelia the Fair said. "We add it in as an additive also."

"When it is naturally inside our mead, no matter what," Yana said.

"Along with everything else that belongs to Tree Horn Forest."

"So no matter what you eat."

"Drink."

"Even breathe."

"It's fairy mana!"

"Is there a difference between the two?" Timothy asked.

"The two?"

"Mana and fairy mana?"

"Oh no," Yana said with a smile.

"But we being fairies—" Magnelia the Fair said.

"And living in a forest governed by a mighty fairy . . ."

"With countless other fairies . . ."

"We like to call it fairy mana."

"But!"

"We emit our own fairy dust that belongs strictly to this forest."

Saying that, the two fairies flapped their wings and emitted a cloud of fairy dust.

"Fair enough," Timothy said.

"So we're not tired because of fairy dust?" Zachary said.

"You're not tired," Yana said.

"But we can change that," Magnelia the Fair said.

"And how's that?"

"Sleepy fairy bread!" both fairies said while pointing with their tiny fingers at the basket full of snacks, including a loaf of bread that the boys now discerned to be different from the bread they had all day long.

"This isn't the same bread as before?"

"This isn't the same bread as before. What you ate earlier is fairy bread."

"The bread there is—"

"*Sleepy* fairy bread."

"Mostly for gnomes. They drink and overeat and are too excited even for the music to calm them down."

"A little of sleepy fairy bread and it's—"

"Night night."

"Sleepy fairy bread?" Zachary said.

"Yep."

"Nighttime use only."

"Hazardous during the day."

"Don't attempt to operate any heavy machinery during use."

The boys walked cautiously toward the basket, afraid of what the bread could do. Upon reaching the basket, they ripped off a piece of bread.

"Don't need much," Yana said, grabbing a small piece and giving it to Butch.

"Butch too?" Timothy asked.

"He probably needs it more than you two combined."

"He's been nothing short of a furry ball of excitement the moment he met us."

"He'll need double the bread!"

Seeing the dog chew and swallow the bread, the boys followed suit.

"Best get comfy," Magnelia the Fair said, seeing the boys finish the few bites of the bread.

"Sometimes, it can knock you out faster than you expected."

"One moment, your eyes are staring at the darkness."

"Only for them to close and wake up to the Star of Nod staring down at you."

"But we're in a dwelling," Timothy said.

"And Rajur is going to have us awake before your sun shines on us," Zachary said.

"You just worry about receiving a restful sleep."

"We'll worry about the Star of Nod shining on you."

"And if sleep goes longer than he expected . . ."

"Rajur's a tough cookie. He'll get over it."

The boys nodded and slipped into their beds. Putting the blankets over their bodies, they could already feel sleepiness.

Not two minutes later, while listening to the music, the boys' eyes shut for good.

The music of the forest ended.

~

An uncanny feeling swept over Timothy while asleep. His subconscious, being aware of this, decided to wake him up. Eyes awake, Timothy felt this strange feeling. The uncanniness had grown stronger, for the boy felt a cold shudder run up his entire body. He attributed this shudder to a sharp, cold breeze swirling inside the dwelling. This awareness baffled him since the door of the dwelling remained closed and the windows, being only slightly opened, were thus far too small an opening to emit such a draft. What confounded him more was that this breeze was anything but calm and soothing, contradicting what Gladson professed about the breeze that swirled through all of Tree Horn Forest.

So what could this breeze mean?

Finding no answer to his thought, Timothy looked around.

The fairies were sound asleep. Butch also slept soundly. And Zachary looked no different.

Timothy grew envious. He recalled everything he had been told about rest in Tree Horn Forest.

"Best sleep ever?" he said mockingly. "Sleepy fairy bread? Well, why am I not still asleep?"

Deciding to try the sleepy fairy bread again, Timothy stepped out of bed and made his way to the basket full of snacks without making a sound. This time, he made sure to pull off an entire slice of the bread.

"It better work," he said, staring at the chunk of bread in his hand.

But he never placed the bread in his mouth. No. Instead, the bread fell out of his hands and landed on the ground.

Why?

Because as he turned around to eat the bread, thus thinking of walking back to his bed while chewing, his eyes landed on—

"What the hell?" Timothy said with a gaping mouth.

His enlarged eyes stared at *himself* sleeping in the bed.

"But—" he said and stopped. *I must be dreaming.*

"Or is this even a dream?" Timothy now questioned while knitting his eyebrows together.

"You *are* the dream," came a soft-toned, ultrafeminine voice heard through the breeze swirling around the dwelling.

Timothy stepped back upon hearing the voice. He sensed the breeze growing stronger, now tracing it to the door.

The door rattled.

"Timothy," the voice said in a slow, drawn-out, lustful, and enticing way.

Timothy stood motionlessly.

"Oh, Timothy," the same voice said in an even more compelling and alluring voice.

To Timothy, no voice could ever be as soft and serene to his ears.

"Come, Timothy. Come out and play. I want to play with you—play with you throughout the *whole* forest."

Timothy believed the voice came from a fairy. It was impossible to confirm this belief because the voice seemed too strong—even as soft as it appeared—to come from any tiny little fairy. What he did imagine was a single giant fairy standing outside the door, and because of that (the wonder in meeting such a fairy), he decided that he must learn firsthand. He must appease his rapidly growing curiosity. Thus, Timothy ignored the bread on the ground and stepped toward the rattling door, and the closer he came to the door, the stronger the rattling.

He did not care to think about how the rattling did not wake up the others.

"Tim-Tim-Timothy," the voice said. "Come-come-come . . . come out and play with me."

As he extended his hand toward the door, the rattling ended. With the end of the rattling came the opening of the door.

Standing on the other side of the opening was no other than a giant fairy, in all her grandeur, illuminating the dark forest night with her brilliant radiance. This radiance caused Timothy to close his eyes, only to slowly reopen them.

His eyes adjusted to her radiance; while doing so, he could only stare.

The struggle to talk lasted a long time. Finally, out came "Are you . . ."

He couldn't manage any more. Her breathtaking beauty and magnificence proved too much.

The giant fairy could only giggle at the boy's difficulties. Seeing that if she did not intervene, the night might grow too long, she spoke. "I am," she said. "Lady Nesia at your service," she said, curtsying before him.

Aroused far too much to stay incoherent, Timothy found the strength to communicate. "So you did make it," he said.

Lady Nesia nodded her head. While nodding, she maneuvered her hand behind her back.

"I believed wholeheartedly you'd find a way to meet me in person," Timothy said.

"Yes. Well. Here I am," Lady Nesia said, with a smile.

"Lady Nesia," Timothy said in awe of her standing before him.

Lady Nesia stood over three times Timothy's height, thus, making her not only taller than Rajur but also taller than Jalzeer; therefore, she was the tallest individual Timothy had ever laid eyes on. She wore a pink dress, and this dress floated outside her perfectly symmetrical figure. Her ears were pointy, and her nose the same, matching every other fairy in her forest. Her unruly hair, which could be said about every other fairy too, fell to the ground, consisting of gold, silver, and pinkish streaks, each color intertwined. The two wings to her side were also full of splendor, decorated with various colors; her feet were bare, unlike her fairies, for the fairies of her forest liked to wear shiny and gaudy slippers.

"Timothy Huntsinger," Lady Nesia said in response.

"You too know my full name?"

"I do. I have eyes and ears that go far beyond one's normal scope. And you, Timothy, you are not so hidden on Eythreal as you think. Not when Eythreal's entire fate rests on your shoulders."

"You mean the book," Timothy said.

"No, silly! I mean *you*."

"Me?" Timothy said with a shake of his head. "No. I'm just the pawn, and the book is—"

"Pawn?" Lady Nesia interrupted Timothy. "You? A pawn? Like on a chessboard? A weak subordinate for something far more powerful? Never," Lady Nesia said convincingly. "If anything, the book is the pawn, and you the knight. Eythreal is your chessboard."

"That's a strange way to put it."

"The key is that you being a pawn is furthest from the truth."

"OK. I just . . . I just don't see it that way."

"It is because you still imagine that you were chosen for mere fun— from the fancy of one's mind."

"Am I not?"

"What? Stop that. Stop that right now."

Here, Lady Nesia leaned into Timothy to whisper a grave secret. "You were chosen because Eythreal chose you."

"What? How?"

Lady Nesia shrugged her shoulders while also nodding. "It is true. You were chosen by the book long before you placed hands upon it. That unworldly creature you call the Wood Dweller acted only as a messenger."

"But that does not make sense," Timothy said.

"And why not?" Lady Nesia asked.

"Because . . ."

"Because what?"

"Because I'm just a boy, an average fifteen-year-old boy, no different from the rest."

"Just a boy? No different from the rest? Yes. And I'm just a fairy," Lady Nesia said with a wink of an eye.

"None of this makes sense," Timothy said again.

"Oh, it does. It really does."

"What about this?" Timothy said in all directions. "Was it your voice that said *I am the dream*?"

"I did say that."

"What does that mean?"

"What does it sound like it means?"

"I don't know. That's why I'm asking."

"You're the dream, Timothy."

Timothy nodded, seeing that nothing further would be learned from Lady Nesia.

"OK. So what now?"

"What now?"

"What now."

"Fly," Lady Nesia said.

"I'm sorry?"

"Fly with me, Timothy."

With a simple wave of her hand and a flutter of her grand wings, an explosion of fairy dust poured from behind her and landed on Timothy. This profusion of fairy dust affected Timothy more strongly than before, as it immediately sent a harsher tingling sensation up his body, while his skin felt as if it had received a small burn. This tingling sensation grew even stronger while Timothy's entire body grew lighter, and as his body grew lighter, he lifted off the floor as the other gnomes hovered along the dance floor; but this being a much more potent and impactful wave of fairy dust, he no longer felt even a pound of his weight, and because of that, he no longer hovered, but instead floated.

And the impactful wave of fairy dust strengthened him even more.

Timothy felt compelled to fly.

Lady Nesia perceived this and took hold of his hand. "Now hang on," Lady Nesia said.

"Hang on?"

Before Timothy could utter another word, Lady Nesia lifted from her position, and the two soared through the air.

"I'm flying!" Timothy shouted.

"You most certainly are," Lady Nesia said, never letting go of his hand.

The two continued to soar through the forest. As they did, Lady Nesia's glowing aura collided with the sparkling flakes of mana, far brighter than they were when the companions first entered the forest and village, only for the two glistening radiances to combine strengths and present a much more luminous trail through the forest. The combination of lights gave Timothy a greater view of the forest. He marveled over the forest like never before, seeing how illuminated everything became, compared to his entrance to the forest when the Star of Nod was its only light.

As for the soaring, well, truth be told, Timothy felt afraid a few times—for Lady Nesia did not shy from her flying abilities.

She performed acrobatic flips in the air and other tricks, not to mention her erratic behavior sometimes: nearing a tree only to veer away from it at the very last second.

She turned this way, so many ways, in such a small amount of space.

And during all this time, the forest lit up wherever they went.

Once he got used to her whimsical flying, Timothy no longer felt afraid. He enjoyed her erratic flying. He trusted her.

Thus, he found this experience to be more marvelous and magical than anything he'd done in his entire life, by a landslide.

Lady Nesia also exuded the same joy and excitement as Timothy. Lady Nesia also matched the wonder and awe Timothy felt. She laughed and cried. The laughing and crying came from the sublime emotions of enjoying this fun for the first time. And to prove that statement to be false would be erroneous, for Lady Nesia was like any other fairy. To know a fairy, one must understand that a fairy could perform the same fun activity over and over and feel the same pleasure and joy the fairy felt the very first time, as if they'd never done it before. This cycle of fun is what constitutes a fairy. And a fairy never stops being a fairy.

~

"This is so amazing!" Timothy shouted in glee. "I never want to stop."

Lady Nesia looked at him upon hearing that as they had soared throughout most of the forest by this time. Her smile grew.

She then winked at him and said, "Now swim through the air!"

Before Timothy could ask what she meant by that, she released her grip on his hand.

At first, Timothy tottered. But he remained calm. And remaining calm, he listened to what she had said and put it to use.

He swam through the air. Meaning, he soared through the air on his very own.

On and on they went, with no end in sight. But finding themselves leaving the forest soon and Gladson's Glade in sight, Timothy noticed Lady Nesia's decrease in velocity. He did the same. Thus, they each slowed down a bit, left the forest's confines, and entered the glade. Timothy quickly realized that the flakes of mana filtered into the glade now, whereas before, no flakes of mana could be seen until they reached inside the forest. Timothy also caught sight of the seven moons on full display. They were as beautiful as they were when he viewed them from high above. Besides flakes of mana and seven moons on full display, nothing else seemed to have changed in the glade since his first appearance.

Timothy wanted to ask about the flakes and why now? Why weren't they wafting through the glade before? But this puzzlement he attributed to this being a dream. He let it drop.

Seeing that they were soaring at a lower speed and no branch or tree stood in his way, Timothy returned to the amusing game of catching a flake of mana. He found it far more entertaining this time because of his flying and the darkness of night allowing the flakes of mana to give off a brighter glow, not including the radiance that came with his and Lady Nesia's flying.

And just as before, the game proved impossible.

Lady Nesia smiled while watching Timothy. She too joined in on the fun.

"First one to catch one wins," she said.

Timothy nodded, and for a long moment and more, the two swirled around the glade, trying to catch a flake of mana while laughing and giggling.

Timothy did most of the laughing while Lady Nesia did the giggling.

Their soaring slowly placed them near the wishing well. When nearing it, Lady Nesia slowed down even more and came to a landing.

Timothy looked on fearfully.

Now, how the heck am I going to land? he thought, dreading the landing.

Lady Nesia read this apprehension of his and extended her hand.

"It's OK," she said. "It's really, really easy. Once you stop flying, you'll still be floating a bit. Let go. Let go of the floating, and you'll feel your weight again. Then you'll be hovering. Do the same. Let go. Let go, and you'll land feet first on the ground."

"Just let go?" Timothy said. "Sure."

Slowing his swimming motion, Timothy came to a stop. His body continued to float. He let go. From head to toe, he let go, mindfully.

He hovered. While hovering, he let go even more.

His eyes were closed when his feet hit the ground.

"I did it!" he shouted.

"Amazing," Lady Nesia said. "Very impressive. You're a fast learner. I see much in you . . ."

Timothy smiled. He looked deliberately away from the well and at the Seven Moons of Iria.

He noticed something he had not seen a minute ago.

"Are they . . ."

"Starting their fading away?" Lady Nesia said.

"Yes."

"Yes, they are."

"And then . . ."

"Twilight," Lady Nesia said. "For the briefest of seconds. The next moon—"

"Legolas?"

"Very good."

"But that's all I know."

"In time, you'll know more."

"But you won't be my teacher?"

"Teacher? Oh no. Not now. Not now. We're here for another reason."

"OK. But could you at least help me with one thing about these moons?"

Lady Nesia gave a tentative nod of her head.

Timothy ignored this hesitancy in her and plowed on. "What are the names of the moons? It seems to be some sort of argument."

"Names? Of the moons?" Lady Nesia said with an inquisitive look on her face. If one could study her face longer, one would see a harbinger of fear.

"Yes. I asked Gladson, and he became a bit confused. Sarah thinks they're average names."

"Names of the moons?" Lady Nesia questioned again.

"Rajur, though, thinks the moons corroborate the theory of there being Ancient Ones. Do you believe in these Ancient Ones?"

"Anci—" Lady Nesta started to say and stopped. Her inquisitive look turned into confusion, which also led to fright.

Lady Nesia cringed with fear.

Timothy noticed this change. "Lady Nesia? Is there something the matter?"

Lady Nesia's cringing face turned to the ground. She sought composure. Not finding it, she looked up in the sky, and upon spying the Seven Moons of Iria, her frightened and bewildered look turned stern and even angry.

"There are no names to the moons. Period. And we're not here to discuss mythical rumors. We're here . . ." Lady Nesia said and again stopped. Her look showed much annoyance.

Wanting to change the subject, Timothy continued for her. "Why are we here?"

It worked. Lady Nesia found composure and returned to her jovial demeanor. "To make a wish!" Lady Nesia said.

Timothy now felt a dreadful presence in his heart and mind.

"Oh," he said, looking at the wishing well and recalling Gladson's adamant plea for him to make a wish. "That."

"That's right, silly. Time to make a wish."

Eyes still on the well, Timothy pulled out the necklace belonging to Huron's Shard of Everlasting Peace and showed it to Lady Nesia.

"I can give you this," he said.

"Oh, Timothy," Lady Nesia said solemnly. "If only you knew what power is invested in that amulet, you'd think twice about getting rid of it.

You'd not even harbor the thought of giving away such a treasure. It is a treasure you should never, ever trifle with. And of course, you shouldn't be revealing it to anyone, excluding the lone companions that stand by you in battle. Use it wisely. I sense something about it that contradicts what you may or may not use it for. Don't abuse it. I believe the less you count on it, the more times you will be able to count on it. That is what I sense . . .

"And no!" she continued. "That is not what I'm talking about. But it is quite a treasure," she said as she tentatively reached out her right hand out to grab the amulet—the shard. Before she could grab it, she sensed a slight power of the shard, and just a little of it caused her entire body to stiffen as if suffering through rigor mortis. For a long moment did Lady Nesia stay motionless. Even her extended right hand did not pull back.

"Lady Nesia?" a concerned Timothy said, now putting the amulet away.

With the amulet put away, Lady Nesia returned to life. "Yes?" she said as if suffering from memory loss. "Oh," she said, recalling some of what had just occurred. "Dear me. What just happened?"

"You went to touch—"

Remembering everything now, Lady Nesia waved him off. "Water under the bridge," she said.

"I believe that pertains only to—"

"Does it matter, Timothy?"

"No. I guess not."

"What does matter is you making a wish."

"I have very little with me to make a wish."

"You have that *other* necklace, and its stone."

"You're speaking of the most precious item I possess."

"Yes," Lady Nesia said. "Very precious to you. A very great sacrifice for Eythreal. I feel the importance of the stone as much as I do with your book. I truly do."

"Then, if you know how important it is to me, why are you asking me to get rid of it?"

"Not get rid of it. Only to make a—"

"Rid of it!" Timothy said harshly. "Whether I throw it in the well or throw it in the sea to be swallowed up, it is the same to me. I'll be without it."

"Yes."

"So why?"

"Because the importance of it to you is far greater to Eythreal. Do you understand that?" Lady Nesia said. "Timothy! You *are* Eythreal."

"I understand the book is Eythreal. But I'm—"

"Attached to the book as if you two share the same body. There is not another soul or entity in this world or the next that could ever be joined to this book but you. How is it any different when I say you're Eythreal because the book is Eythreal, and the book and you are one? No difference. Thus, what is very important and meaningful to you is even more important and meaningful to Eythreal, and it must be shared. You must not keep this to yourself. It must be deposited where all Eythreal can feel this importance."

Timothy ruminated over what she said.

"Why don't I just come back here with the book and drop the *book* into the well?" he said, trying to be serious, although understanding the task to be foolish.

"Oh, Timothy," Lady Nesia said, clapping her hands and laughing heartily as if she heard a wild comic joke. "Do be serious. You'd be a wonderful fairy. Ha ha ha. Throw the book in the well? Ha ha ha. Yes. Risk an outcome that no single entity could predict, except, well . . . except for disassociation of you and the book, which would inevitably lead to Eythreal's final demise. And not only Eythreal's demise, but also the crumbling of your world and its final fall. Both worlds would then lead to oblivion. And, Timothy, nothing ever can be retrieved from oblivion."

"You speak of my world?"

"In a suspension above oblivion. A void."

"So my world is not eternally lost to me?"

"Make a wish, Timothy. That is the best I can do for you regarding that question and many more questions."

Timothy looked at the well again. Could a single wish with the necklace and stone bring his world back when the book came to an end? What about now? Could he not wish for all this to go away? But then . . .

"You don't get to choose the wish," Timothy said. "That's what I've been told."

"And that is no lie."

"So then—"

"It can't help but try."

Timothy again stared at the well. He then pulled away from the well and stared sadly at Lady Nesia.

"I'm sorry," he said with a shake of his head. "I can't. I mean, I won't do it. It's all I have left of what may never be again."

Lady Nesia nodded. "As I thought," she said with a smile on her face, showing anything but disappointment in Timothy's choice.

"You're not upset?"

"No, silly."

"And you understand?"

"Of course, silly. But do I have to remind you?"

"About?"

"This is a dream."

"You mean . . ."

"You're a dream. This is a dream. I'm even a dream."

"Are you saying—"

"I'm saying that aren't you lying down in bed right now? Sound asleep?"

"I . . . Yes. I was."

"Then this is a dream, right? Nothing here matters when awake," Lady Nesia said. Again, she maneuvered one of her hands behind her back.

She continued to speak. "Make a wish by dropping your necklace and stone in the well, and you'll wake up to it right around your neck and over your chest," she said, hand behind her back.

"Still in my possession?" Timothy asked.

Lady Nesia nodded.

"Of course, silly-willy. This is just a dream."

"So if this is just a dream, then we haven't really met? You didn't make an appearance since I'm dreaming you?"

"In this dream, you can say we did meet, for this is me! How could you dream of me if you've never met me?"

"Will I ever *really* meet you?"

"Time will certainly tell, for no one can predict the future like time. And time is running fast. Fulfill this dream's wish and make a wish. Drop the stone and necklace in the well and be at peace during your travel to Ghalia."

Timothy stepped up the well. He looked down. The darkness of the night gave him a better view of the swirling, colorful mana deep below.

It is a dream, he thought to himself, *anything else would be impossible? So what is the harm? She's only trying to help.*

Timothy lifted his head back up. He felt something different. He felt naked. He looked to his right hand. In his open right hand rested the necklace and stone. Scared, he closed his right hand when he saw the necklace and stone and wondered how he took it off his neck and held it in his hand without ever recalling doing so.

Nothing on the how came to him. But the memory of when he gave the other half to Katelyn came back to him.

He recalled the promise.

His eyes became teary. Tears fell from his eyes.

Why do I cry when this is a dream?

Lady Nesia answered in his mind. *Do you not feel emotions such as happiness and fear in your dreams?*

Yes.

Then why cannot one cry in a dream, especially when that person is the dream?

Timothy nodded. He closed his eyes.

"It's only a dream," he said with a sniffle.

"It's only a dream," Lady Nesia said. "Now open your hand."

Eyes remaining closed, thus not wanting to see the necklace and stone of bereavement, Timothy opened his hand and felt the necklace and stone slip out of his possession.

Lady Nesia smiled.

Her smile turned into a consolatory look full of affection. Timothy felt her hands on his shoulders.

And her following three words he'd never forget in his entire life.

"Open your eyes."

~

Timothy's eyes opened to him standing not by Lady Nesia and the wishing well. No. He opened his eyes to find himself lying in bed, the same bed he went to sleep in, only to be awakened by a supposed dream. Making sure what he woke to was real, he rubbed the last of his sleep from his eyes and looked around to find everyone still asleep while he felt replenished and ready for the day's travel. Examining his surroundings more, he realized that he did dream and that never once did he get out of bed to eat more bread, thus being enticed to meet Lady Nesia on the other side of the door. But if his eyes were a bit sharper when they looked toward the ground, he would have seen the piece of bread he dropped before leaving the dwelling. Unaware of that, he understood the harsh reality of it being a dream.

He never did truly meet Lady Nesia.

But recalling what occurred at Gladson's Glade, his disappointment ended. "I never did lose you," he said, smiling while reaching for the stone.

His hand grasped only Huron's cracked amulet.

"But it was only a dream," a tremulous and frightened Timothy said while investigating more.

The investigation lasted a second longer.

He no longer possessed the most precious and, to him, most important item—the last of the promise.

What came next was the loudest shout emitted from Timothy's mouth in all his life.

"No!"

Zachary and the fairies burst out of their sleep and found Timothy ranting and raving.

"She lied! She lied, she lied, she lied! She lied! She told me it was a dream—that I was a dream. She lied! Your stupid, evil fairy mother lied!"

"What? Who? What are you saying?" Zachary cried out.

"She lied!" Timothy shouted again. "Liar! She's a liar! A wicked, wicked, *wicked* liar!"

By this time, the fairies had left their cages and fluttered endlessly around the dwelling, each of them highly perturbed by the anger emitted by Timothy.

"Again," Zachary said, taking Timothy by his shoulders, "who lied?"

"Lady Nesia," Timothy said. "Lady Nesia lied to me, lied to me before my very own face."

Surprisingly, Timothy's anger mitigated a bit while saying her name. The fairies also felt a bit calmer and thus felt sympathy for the poor boy.

No longer were the fairies so ignorant of what happened.

"She lied to me, Zachary. Lady Nesia—she . . . she came to me, I think. She came to me in this dream—a dream like no other. She came to me—"

A rapping at the closed dwelling door interrupted Timothy.

"You must all be awake, for I believe I heard a bit of shouting," came the voice of Gladson on the other side of the door.

"You know damn well we're awake!" Timothy shouted back.

"Then if awake, may I come in?"

Without waiting for a response, Gladson opened the door and took one step inside the dwelling. Behind him stood Rajur and Sarah.

"She lied to me!" Timothy said, directing his renewed anger at

Gladson. "Your marvelous Lady of the Forest downright right lied to me, tricked me."

"I—" Gladson tried to say.

"Don't talk. Listen! Rajur was right—about all of you. You're nothing but a conniving, deceiving bunch of ruthless creatures—the whole lot of you. *Damn* her."

"What happened?" Sarah said, stepping past Rajur and Gladson.

Rajur stayed put, having sensed what the fairies and Gladson sensed. But he did lean toward Sarah and whisper in her ear.

"The stone!" Sarah shouted in disbelief, betraying her emotions.

"Yes," Timothy said. "She tricked me into giving away my necklace and stone."

"Is this true?" Sarah said to Gladson.

Gladson nodded.

"But she did it for the best of—"

"Shut up!" Timothy said. "It wasn't her choice, just like it wasn't your choice yesterday. You each did wrong."

Gladson looked down.

"I'm sorry you feel so angry about it. I really am."

Timothy felt nothing else but honesty from Gladson. The latter's unfeigned apologetic look even soothed the boy's wrath.

"In time," Gladson said, and seeing that Timothy allowed him more words, he continued, "I hope you forgive her—forgive us all!" He finished saying that by extending to Timothy his hand, which held a sealed envelope. "For now, you must have this."

The sealed envelope dripped a profusion of fairy dust while held in Gladson's hand. The stamp sealed on it had the exact markings of Lady Nesia's grand wings.

Timothy stared hesitantly at the envelope.

"Lady Nesia dropped it off at your door," Gladson said.

"I don't care," the seemingly petulant Timothy said.

"Angry or not, you should care," Gladson said. He then looked to Rajur. "Do I speak correctly, Rajur?"

A reluctant Rajur answered. "Unfortunately, yes," Rajur said. "Gladson is right. Never allow your anger and wrath to do your thinking. You're refusing this letter for the wrong reasons."

"Fine," Timothy said. He grabbed the envelope from Gladson's hand,

and even more fairy dust poured from under it. "But nothing she wrote will change my mind on how I think of her and the trick she did to me. Got it?"

Gladson nodded.

Timothy studied the envelope a bit more. He discovered his full name on the front, written in an elegant cursive style.

He opened the envelope. And when he did, a burst of even more fairy dust exploded from inside the envelope as he took out a folded note that diffused its fairy dust. Unfolding the note, he found, to his amazement, the writing style was similar to the writing style found in the book.

This amazement of his also confounded him since he could not decipher what she said.

"What the heck?" he said toward Gladson. He went to show the gnome the folded note inside when suddenly he heard Lady Nesia speak to him, from the letter and into his mind—only for him to hear.

> *Dear Timothy,*
>
> *My sincerest apologies. By now, there is an anger in you that cannot be so easily mitigated by words or even this letter. I understand that. I wholeheartedly do. I deceived you, tricked you, although, to be honest, the few times I did, I had my fingers crossed—but that's not important here. What is important is that I was compelled to trick you. Yes. I found it to be an obligation of mine, for I am not deceived by what surrounds me and the path that I take. Nor must you be! You must be open to what surrounds you and the path that you must take. You must understand that the shadows that are hidden from you now will be revealed to you soon enough. For now, though, understand that your road is nearly endless. And this road is fraught with dangers and horror that even the legendary warrior beside you cannot begin to picture and hope to make you understand.*
>
> *And I am afraid that your travel upon this road must be done alone—not a single companion at your side.*
>
> *You will face what you must face to be a true embodiment of Eythreal.*
>
> *Until then, though, I have convinced you to make a wish. A wish for Eythreal, for I did not lie when I said you are Eythreal.*

The stone and even the necklace—but mostly the stone— will prove to be a foundation that Eythreal will at some point rely upon when it comes to being saved, even if that doesn't mean it happens during your *time.*

And now, Timothy, the unexpected reason to write to you.

Whether you forgive me or not, I must ask a favor from you. Again, this favor I ask is in your best interest. I'd like you to take along Yana and Magnelia the Fair on this adventure of yours. The two will prove to be great assets to you and your companions. But I am not done. I would also ask you to take one last individual. This individual is none other than the gnome they call Petru. Surely you must have met him? He's an anomaly when it comes to gnomes, a bit quirky and quiet and even shy. But there is much there that does not meet the eye. That, I assure you, is the honest truth. He has his own calling, and this calling stretches beyond Tree Horn Forest. His calling follows a path very much the same as yours.

Of course, these choices and decisions to be made fall squarely on you. You don't have to take the fairies if you choose not to. Nor do you have to take Petru along.

You have more of a choice here than you had at the wishing well.

Believe it or not, you alone made that decision.

I wasn't even there.

And now, to say goodbye.

Before saying goodbye, a few essential words.

Trust in your companions, especially that stoic and grumpy Rajur, for his path relies more on you than you rely upon him.

To say Rajur is not as much as Eythreal as you would be a great fallacy.

And it would undoubtedly end in Eythreal's final demise, not to mention your Earth's doom.

And that, my friend, is the truth.

Goodbye, Timothy. And try to forgive me.

Yours truly,
Lady Nesia

P.S. You dreamed a fairy dream last night. In a fairy dream, one truly never leaves their subconscious. It is why fairies dream fantasies for their very own subconscious. Someone conjured a mighty spell upon you and placed you inside this fairy dream, where he or she knew I'd be fully aware of your presence since even in my sleep do I walk through Tree Horn Forest. Hence, you must not be mad at me for taking full advantage of what so gratefully and easily fell into my lap, for I never asked this to be done to you. Someone else. Someone chose this path to be done to you.

Now, who conjured this spell, I'm honestly ignorant of.

Except . . .

Hint, hint—not one of the fairies or gnomes of Tree Horn Forest conjured this spell.

Time will only tell who did this to you.

With the last words spoken, the letter disintegrated into a plethora of fairy dust. This fairy dust wafted through the air and found its way out of the dwelling. It did not stop there. The fairy dust continued beyond Tree Horn Forest Village and into the thickness of the forest, where it could never be summoned again for one to read. Timothy watched this voyage of the fairy dust, even when it vanished from his sight. His mind vividly imagined the fairy dust separated into all corners of the forest, integrating with an infinite amount of mana flakes. When he was done watching this in his mind, he turned to the companions and Gladson without an angry look on his face. Suspicion had now replaced the anger for Lady Nesia's deception. This suspicion led him to investigate each of the companions' faces, hoping one would betray themselves on being last night's culprit.

A second into the investigation, he dropped this suspicion of his. No way could he entertain the thought of Zachary betraying him. Nor did he have it in him to suspect Rajur and Sarah to do the same.

No. Impossible.

Timothy now entertained the thought of Lady Nesia deceiving him again.

But why? Why would she want me to question my companions? What would she be afraid of if telling me the truth?

She already confessed to tricking me once. What's the difference if a second time?

Unsure what to think, believe, or do next, Timothy shrugged his shoulders and muttered in his mind: *Time will tell. And only after finishing this book will time finally tell.*

"Are you all right?" Sarah asked.

Timothy looked at her. In his eyes could be found determination—determination to finish the book.

"Are we all set with provisions?" Timothy said, looking Rajur's way.

Rajur nodded.

"And Lady Nesia replenished much," Gladson said. "Everything is waiting for you on the leave of Tree Horn Village."

"Then we should get going," Timothy said.

Rajur nodded again. "Yes. It is a long journey from here, on foot."

"What about the horses?" Zachary asked.

"They'll be no use to us," Rajur said. "Not for a long time, maybe forever."

"What are you saying?" Zachary said.

"He's saying that it would be wise of us to leave them here," Timothy said. "Am I not right?"

"You are right. They'll be too much of a burden."

"And they're not alone when it comes to us leaving behind burdens, are they?" Timothy asked.

Before anyone could respond, Timothy placed his eyes on Butch. Timothy's eyes became wet with tears.

"Not to fear," Gladson said, placing a hand on the boy's shoulder. "Butch will be in the best of hands. I *so* promise you!"

"I believe you," Timothy said.

Timothy bent down and embraced his dog for what could be the very last time.

"I'm going to miss you. God, I'm going to miss you. But this is best for you—the best. You'll be safe. No harm will come to you. I promise. And I'll see you again. Yes, I will. We'll both go home together."

Timothy stood back up. He wiped the remaining tears from his eyes.

"OK," Timothy said. "I'm ready."

Rajur nodded, and the companions stepped to leave the dwelling.

Timothy stopped. "Wait! I almost forgot," he said.

He turned to Magnelia the Fair and Yana. He opened both hands. Both fairies landed in each of his hands.

"I have an offer for the both of you. You don't have to accept it."

The fairies buzzed with anticipation.

"The offer is for you two to join us."

"Join?" they both said.

"Yes. On our . . . *adventures*. Lady Nesia—she, uh, she asked if I could bring you two along with her. She said it would be wise of me to do so."

The fairies answered Timothy by causing an explosion of fairy dust to cloud the air around them.

"I take that as a yes?"

"It's a yes!" they said.

Rajur stepped in. "Do you know what you're consenting to?" he asked the fairies.

"Dangerous, dangerous waters," Yana said.

"More dangerous than Blackwood's wicked basilisks and their toxic breath!"

"And the spiders that dwell under the marshes found in Nererrenda."

"Along with long-lost dragons that breathe green fire."

"Yes," they both said again. "We know exactly what we're agreeing to."

"Good," Timothy said. "But there is one last task to accomplish."

Timothy turned to Gladson. Not a single word needed to be spoken by the two. Timothy knew that Gladson knew, and the latter nodded.

Gladson thus left the dwelling and returned a minute later. At his side stood a shy Petru.

"Petru?" Gladson said to the gnome. "Timothy has a question for you."

Petru barely nodded back.

"Hello, Petru," Timothy said. "You're here because Lady Nesia— mother of the gnomes and fairies of Tree Horn Forest—has asked me to bring you along with us."

Hearing that, Zachary, Rajur, and Sarah each reacted with surprise. Both Gladson and Petru did not.

"I don't know why," Timothy said. "But she said something about your calling to leading you elsewhere. Anyway, I feel that Lady Nesia would not lead me astray, even after deceiving me. So I ask you, Petru, would you like to join our party?"

Petru looked up and stared back into Timothy's eyes.

Timothy shivered, for he felt something in those eyes. Something . . . Petru nodded.

"Good," Timothy said. He looked at Rajur. "Now we're ready!"

Rajur nodded. He then ushered Timothy and Zachary out of the dwelling, and not long into the travel did they reach the ground floor of Tree Horn Forest Village and noticed hundreds of gnomes and fairies smiling gleefully at them. They did not come to greet them goodbye or send their warmest wishes. They came to see the companions off because the moment had come.

The moment had come for Timothy, the moment for him to move on from his life before and take a significant turn of a page inside the book.

This was his moment. With this leave of Tree Horn Forest, he felt that he had finally put his Earth behind him, even after all he saw.

He now had to learn to be Eythreal.

No more Earth. He must strip away everything about his former world and learn to be Eythreal.

He must.

And maybe, he thought, that was why she wanted him to let go of the necklace.

I must be Eythreal.

I must step beyond Earth and become Eythreal.

Nodding his head, Timothy turned to Rajur. "So, this is Eythreal?"

My Last Words…

Hello again, Reader:

First, thank you for reading this story. Hopefully, you enjoyed it. I understand the end was a bit curt. I want to apologize for that. It was never meant to be. You must understand, many years ago, I came to the idea of a trilogy named Gem and Spider. All I had was a boy losing himself in a forest and finding a book that transports his world to another dimension and replaces it with another world governed by three goddesses locked away inside a gem, each gem guarded by a spider. Anyways, I sat down to write it, which proved to be the first writing of my entire life when it came to writing novels and not screenwriting. After writing two pages, I realized that maybe this shouldn't be the first project to work on, seeing how large and complex it would be, and that I should start small. So I did, and many years passed.

Finally, around eight or seven years ago, I returned to this three-book epic called Gem and Spider and decided, *why put it off longer?*

Like the scripture says, what can be today should not be put off tomorrow.

Thus, I began what was to be book 1: *Camus*.

After some bumps in the road dealing with my mental illness, I finally finished book 1, *Camus*, and saw how impossible it was to be a single book. The book's length was more extensive than all three Lord of the Rings books combined. I did not panic. I only decided to split it up, and while doing that, I decided each of the other books would also be split. Therefore, what was to be a three-book epic turned into a six-book epic.

A year or two passed, and finally, I finished *Eythreal*, book 1 of the Gem and Spider series. I sent it in for evaluation. I was told the book is fabulous, but no literature agent or publishing agent would read a 230,000-word book (750–850 pages) and that I must cut it down, once again.

I was grieved. There was no spot to make a clean ending without hurting the story's integrity. But I did what I had to; thus, you have the abrupt end you just read.

And I'm sorry about that.

But the good news is that book 2, *The Last King* (again, it was to be the second half of book 1) is all set to go. Its ending is so much better too.

The problem lies in that self-publishing isn't cheap. So once I get the funds, I will publish it and allow you to read what was to be the actual ideal ending of book 1.

So with each book purchase, I'm one step closer to publishing the newest book.

Tell everyone you know if you can't wait to read about Timothy's journey and the others that join his companionship.

The best way to tell others is to write a review on Amazon, Goodreads, or both. Good or bad, a review goes a long, long way in this time we live in.